OH, TO BE A DRAGONRIDER

The only thing Keevan wanted in life was to be a dragonrider, just like his father. Surely nothing could ever be as thrilling as soaring through the air while sitting between the two powerful wings of a dragon.

But Keevan was small and there always were more boys who wanted to be dragonriders than there were dragons. So someone surely would be disappointed.

When Impression time came, Keevan couldn't be there. His cracked skull and broken leg would make him the poorest candidate of all, even if he could get to the cave where the dragon eggs hatched.

At least that's what the other boys thought.

But dragons have a different set of standards, especially the bronzes—the most highly prized dragons of all!

Get Off the Unicorn

Anne McCaffrey

A Del Rey Book

BALLANTINE BOOKS • NEW YORK

A Del Rey Book
Published by Ballantine Books

Library of Congress Catalog Card Number: 77-1709

ISBN: 0-345-30577-9

Manufactured in the United States of America

First Edition: June 1977
Ninth Printing: September 1983

Cover art by Paul Alexander

This book goes, with love,
to my other sons and daughters,
to Derval, Anto, Ann, Orla & Lian, Hilary,
Weasel, Mary Pitz, Penny, Kim *and* Eamonn (Gary),
Alan, Rickie, Anders, Geoffrey and David
who keep my house ringing with laughter
and music and who keep me . . . young!

Contents

Introduction   xi

Lady in the Tower   3

A Meeting of Minds   24

Daughter   60

Dull Drums   82

Changeling   99

Weather on Welladay   118

The Thorns of Barevi   155

Horse from a Different Sea   167

Great Canine Chorus   174

Finder's Keeper   192

A Proper Santa Claus   207

The Smallest Dragonboy   217

Apple   233

Honeymoon   266

Introduction

MOST OF YOU KIND PEOPLE WHO ARE BUYING this volume will have done so because of the author's name on the cover. I say this with due modesty because, Gentle Reader, you would certainly not choose to buy a book of short stories unless you liked other work by the author.

The title of this collection, although it *fits* most of the stories if you know the old tale about unicorn-bait, comes from a misprint in the Ballantine roster of unfilled contracts. Someone kept asking my long-suffering editor, Judy-Lynn del Rey, what was this book called *Get Off the Unicorn*. (The working title *had* been *Get Of the Unicorn*, provocative enough originally.) So, Judy-Lynn asked me what I could do about that theme.

As an author I have been extremely fortunate in finding several themes and characters that have been well received: the Dragons of Pern, Helva, my Ship who Sings, the Parapsychic and the Crystal Singer yarns. I tend to write in broad tapestries and get caught up in the lives of my heroines and heroes, not to mention the fantastical creatures, and go on, and on, and on. Sometimes it is extremely difficult for me to write short or concise. That can be a great handicap. But those rather short stories I have managed to write are included in this volume. There are also several coupled yarns of ideas that did not ever generate enough impetus to make a novel. I'll explain as I go along.

"Lady in the Tower" and "A Meeting of Minds" are really logical extensions of the concept found in "To Ride Pegasus," in which parapsychic powers are combined with machines in a gestalt that gives the mind enough power to reach the stars. They both predate Dai op Owen and the Eastern Parapsychic Center.

"Lady" is the story I prefer to acknowledge as my first; it appeared in the *Magazine of Fantasy and Science Fiction* in April 1959, in the distinguished company of Daniel Keyes' "Flowers for Algernon." Algis Budrys was a reader for Bob Mills at the time and he brought the story to Bob's notice. They both felt that it needed some reworking and asked my permission, which, needless to say, I immediately and ecstatically gave. (Someone wanted to *publish* a story of mine? Leap, grab, say YES!) I don't remember all the changes Algis made, and I've made a few myself with the wisdom and expertise of twenty years of writing and publishing. But basically, it's the same story.

Ten years later, "A Meeting of Minds" was published by Ed Ferman, the new editor of *Fantasy and Science Fiction*. I have also done a good deal of rewriting on it, since that story had appeared so long after its parent story.

Both are unashamed love stories. That's what I do best: combining either science fact or fantasy with heterogenous inter-reaction.

These two stories were supposed to be part of a novel I'd tentatively entitled *The Bitter Tower*. But, when I got started on the story "A Womanly Talent," I got involved with Dai op Owen and wrote the four stories which comprise *To Ride Pegasus*. So these two stories never became part of a novel. But the Raven women are good strong characters, and who knows when I'll write about that third generation of Ravens.

Lady in the Tower

WHEN THE ROWAN CAME STORMING TOWARD the station, its personnel mentally and literally ducked. Mentally, because she was apt to forget to shield. Literally, because the Rowan was prone to slamming around desks and filing cabinets when she got upset. Today, however, she was in fair command of herself and merely stamped up the stairs into the tower. A vague rumble of noisy thoughts tossed around the first floor of the station for a few minutes, but the computer and analogue men ignored the depressing effects with the gratitude of those saved from greater disaster.

From the residue of her passage, Brian Ackerman, the stationmaster, caught the impression of intense purple frustration. He was basically only a T-9, but constant association with the Rowan had widened his area of perception. Ackerman appreciated this side effect of his position—when he was anywhere else but at the station.

He had been trying to quit Callisto for more than five years, with no success. Federal Telepathers and Teleporters, Inc., had established a routine regarding his continuous applications for transfer. The first one handed in each quarter was ignored; the second brought an adroitly worded reply on how sensitive and crucial a position he held at Callisto Prime Station; his third—often a violently worded demand—always got him a special shipment of scotch and tobacco; his fourth—a piteous wail—brought the Section Supervisor out for a face-to-face chat and, only then, a few discreet words to the Rowan.

Ackerman was positive she always knew the full story before the Supervisor finally approached her. It pleased her to be difficult, but the one time Ackerman discarded protocol and snarled back at her, she had mended her ways for a whole quarter. It had reluctantly dawned on Ackerman that she must like him and he had since used this knowledge to advantage. He had lasted eight years, as against five stationmasters in three months before his appointment.

Each of the twenty-three station staff members had gone through a similar shuffling until the Rowan had accepted them. It took a very delicate balance of mental talent, personality, and intelligence to achieve the proper *gestalt* needed to move giant liners and tons of freight. Federal Tel and Tel had only five complete Primes—five T-l's—each strategically placed in a station near the five major and most central stars to effect the best possible transmission of commerce and communications throughout the sprawling Nine-Star League. The lesser staff positions at each Prime Station were filled by personnel who could only teleport, or telepath. It was FT & T's dream someday to provide instantaneous transmission of anything, anywhere, anytime. Until that day, FT & T exercised patient diplomacy with its five T-l's, putting up with their vagaries like the doting owners of so many golden geese. If keeping the Rowan happy had meant changing the entire lesser personnel twice daily, it would probably have been done. As it happened, the present staff had been intact for over two years and only minor soothing had been necessary.

Ackerman hoped that only minor soothing would be needed today. The Rowan had been peevish for a week, and he was beginning to smart under the backlash. So far no one knew why the Rowan was upset.

Ready for the liner! Her thought lashed out so piercingly that Ackerman was sure everyone in the ship waiting outside had heard her. But he switched the intercom in to the ship's captain.

"I heard," the captain said wryly. "Give me a five-count and then set us off."

Ackerman didn't bother to relay the message to the Rowan. In her mood, she'd be hearing straight

4

to Capella and back. The generator men were hopping between switches, bringing the booster field up to peak, while she impatiently revved up the launching units to push-off strength. She was well ahead of the standard timing, and the pent-up power seemed to keen through the station. The countdown came fast as the singing power note increased past endurable limits.

ROWAN, NO TRICKS, Ackerman said.

He caught her mental laugh, and barked a warning to the captain. He hoped the man had heard it, because the Rowan was on zero before he could finish and the ship was gone beyond radio transmission distance in seconds.

The keening dynamos lost only a minute edge of sharpness before they sang at peak again. The lots on the launchers snapped out into space as fast as they could be set up. Then the loads rocketed into receiving area from other Prime Stations, and the ground crews hustled rerouting and hold orders. The power note settled to a bearable hum as the Rowan worked out her mood without losing the efficient and accurate thrust that made her FT & T's best Prime.

One of the ground crew signaled a frantic yellow across the board, then red as ten tons of cargo from Earth settled on the Priority Receiving cradle. The waybill said Deneb VIII, which was at the Rowan's limit. But the shipment was marked "Rush/Emergency, priority medicine for a virulent plague on the colony planet." And the waybill specified direct transmission.

Well, where're my coordinates and my placement photo? snapped the Rowan. *I can't thrust blind, you know, and we've always rerouted for Deneb VIII.*

Bill Powers was flipping through the indexed catalogue, but the Rowan reached out and grabbed the photo.

Zowie! Do I have to land all that mass there myself?

No, Lazybones, I'll pick it up at 24.578.82—that nice little convenient black dwarf midway. You won't have to strain a single convolution. The lazy masculine voice drawled in every mind.

5

The silence was deafening.

Well, I'll be . . . came from the Rowan.

Of course, you are, sweetheart—just push that nice little package out my way. Or is it too much for you? The lazy voice was solicitous rather than insulting.

You'll get your package! replied the Rowan, and the dynamos keened piercingly just once as the ten tons disappeared out of the cradle.

Why, you little minx . . . slow it down or I'll burn your ears back!

Come out and catch it! The Rowan's laugh broke off in a gasp of surprise and Ackerman could feel her slamming up her mental shields.

I want that stuff in one piece, not smeared a millimeter thin on the surface, my dear, the voice said sternly. *Okay, I've got it. Thanks! We need this.*

Hey, who the blazes are you? What's your placement?

Deneb Sender, my dear, and a busy little boy right now. Ta ta.

The silence was broken only by the whine of the dynamos dying to an idle burr.

Not a hint of what the Rowan was thinking came through now, but Ackerman could pick up the aura of incredulity, shock, speculation, and satisfaction that pervaded the thoughts of everyone else in the station. The Rowan had met her match. No one except a T-1 could have projected that far. There'd been no mention of another T-1 at FT & T, and, as far as Ackerman knew, FT & T had all of the five known T-1s. However, Deneb was now in its third generation and colonial peculiarities had produced the Rowan in two.

"Hey, people," Ackerman said, "sock up your shields. She's not going to like your drift."

Dutifully the aura was dampened, but the grins did not fade and Powers started to whistle cheerfully.

Another yellow flag came up from a ground man on the Altair hurdle and the waybill designated *Live shipment to Betelgeuse.* The dynamos whined noisily and then the launcher was empty. Whatever might be going through her mind at the moment, the Rowan was doing her work.

All told, it was an odd day, and Ackerman didn't

6

know whether to be thankful or not. He had no precedents to go on and the Rowan wasn't leaking any clues. She spun the day's lot in and out with careless ease. By the time Jupiter's bulk had moved around to blanket out-system traffic, Callisto's day was over, and the Rowan wasn't off-power as much as decibel one. Once the in-Sun traffic was finished with, Ackerman signed off for the day. The computer banks and dynamos were slapped off . . . but the Rowan did not come down.

Ray Loftus and Afra, the Capellan T-4, came over to sit on the edge of Ackerman's desk. They took out cigarettes. As usual, Afra's yellow eyes began to water from the smoke.

"I was going to ask her Highness to give me a lift home," Loftus said, "but I dunno now. Got a date with—"

He disappeared. A moment later, Ackerman could see him near a personnel carrier. Not only had he been set gently down, but various small necessities, among them a shaving kit, floated out of nowhere onto a neat pile in the carrier. Ray was given time to settle himself before the hatch sealed and he was whisked off.

Powers joined Afra and Ackerman.

"She's sure in a funny mood," he said.

When the Rowan got peevish, few of the men at the station asked her to transport them to Earth. She was psychologically held planetbound, and resented the fact that lesser talents could be moved about through space without suffering traumatic shock.

Anyone else?

Adler and Toglia spoke up and promptly disappeared together. Ackerman and Powers exchanged looks which they hastily suppressed as the Rowan appeared before them, smiling. It was the first time that welcome and totally unexpected expression had crossed her face for two weeks.

She smiled but said nothing. She took a drag of Ackerman's cigarette and handed it back with a thank-you. For all her temperament, the Rowan acted with propriety face to face. She had grown up with

7

her skill, carefully taught by the old and original T-1, Siglen, the Altairian. She'd had certain courtesies drilled into her: the less gifted could be alienated by inappropriate use of talent. She was perfectly justified in "reaching" things during business hours, but she employed the usual methods at other times.

"The big boys mention our Denebian friend before?" she asked, all too casually.

Ackerman shook his head. "Those planets are three generations colonized, and you came out of Altair in two."

"That could explain it, but there isn't even an FT & T station. And you know they advertise continuously for anyone with Talent."

"He's a wild talent?" Powers helpfully suggested.

"Too far off the beaten track." She shook her head. "I checked it. All I can get from Center is that they received an urgent call about a virus, were given a rundown on the syndrome and symptoms. Lab came up with a serum, batched and packed it. They were assured that there was someone capable of picking it up and taking it the rest of the way past 24.578.82 if a Prime would get it that far. And that's all anybody knows." Then she added thoughtfully, "Deneb VIII isn't a very big colony."

Oh, we're big enough, sweetheart, interrupted the drawling voice. *Sorry to get you after hours, my dear, but I can't seem to get in to Terra and I heard you coloring the atmosphere.*

What's wrong? the Rowan asked. *Did you smear your serum after all that proud talk?*

Smear it hell! I've been drinking it. We've got some ET visitors. They think they're exterminators. Thirty UFO's are perched four thousand miles above us. That batch of serum you wafted out to me this morning was for the sixth virus we've been socked with in the last two weeks. Soon as our boys whip up something to knock out one, another takes its place. It's always worse than the one before. We've lost 25 percent of our population already and this last virus is a beaut. I want two top germdogs out here on the double and about three patrol squadrons. We're flat on our backs now. I doubt our friends will hover

8

around, dousing us with nasty bugs much longer. They're going to start blowing holes in us any minute now. So sort of push the word along to Earth, will you, sweetheart? And get us some heavy support!

I'll relay, naturally. But why don't you send direct?

To whom? You're the only one I can hear.

Your isolation won't last much longer if I know my bosses.

You may know your bosses, but you don't know me.

That can always be arranged.

This is no time for flirting. Get that message through for me like a good girl.

Which message?

The one I just gave you.

That old one? They say you can have two germdogs in the morning as soon as we clear Jupiter. But Earth says no squadrons. No armed attack.

You can double-talk too, huh? You're talented. But the morning does us no good. Now is when we need them. Can't you sling them . . . no, they might leave a few important atoms or something in Jupiter's mass. But I've got to have some pretty potent help, and if six viruses don't constitute armed attack, what does?

Missiles constitute armed attack, the Rowan said primly.

I'll notify my friends up there. Missiles would be preferable. Them I can see. I need those germdogs now. Can't you turn your sweet little mind to a solution?

As you mentioned, it's after hours.

By the Horsehead, woman! the drawl was replaced by a cutting mental roar. *My friends are dying!*

Look, after hours here means we're behind Jupiter . . . But . . . Wait! How deep is your range?

I don't honestly know. And doubt crept into the bodiless voice in their minds.

"Ackerman." The Rowan turned to her stationmaster.

"I've been listening."

Hang on, Deneb, I've got an idea. I'll deliver your germdogs. Open to me in half an hour.

The Rowan whirled on Ackerman. "I want my

9

shell." Her brilliant eyes were flashing and her face was alight. "Afra!"

The station's T-4, a handsome yellow-eyed Capellan, raised himself from the chair in which he'd been quietly watching her. Afra was second in command of the station.

"Yes, Rowan?"

Abruptly she realized that her mental conversation with the Denebian had been heard by all the others. Her fleeting frown was replaced by the miraculous smile that always disconcerted Ackerman with its hint of suppressed passion. She looked at each of the men, bathing them in that smile.

"I want to be launched, slowly, over Jupiter's curve," she said to Afra. Ackerman switched up the dynamos, Bill Powers punched for her special shell to be deposited on the launching rack. "Real slow, Afra. Then I'll want to draw heavy." She took a deep breath. Like all Primes, she was unable to launch herself through space. Her initial trip from Altair to Callisto had almost driven her mad with agoraphobia. Only by the exercise of severe self-discipline was she able to take her specially opaque shell a short way off Callisto.

She took another deep breath and disappeared from the station. Then she was beside the launcher. She settled daintily into the shock couch of the shell. The moment the lock whistle shut off, she could feel the shell moving gently, gently away from Callisto. She could sense Afra's reassuring mental touch. Only when the shell had swung into position over Jupiter's great curve did she reply to the priority call coming from Earth Central.

Now what the Billy blue blazes are you doing, Rowan? The voice of Reidinger, the FT & T Central Prime, cracked across the void. *Have you lost what's left of your precious mind?*

She's doing me a favor, Deneb said, unexpectedly joining them.

Who'n hell're you? demanded Reidinger. Then, in shocked surprise, *Deneb! How'd you get out there?*

Wishful thinking. Hey, push those germdogs to my pretty friend here, huh?

10

Now, wait a minute! You're going a little too far, Deneb. You can't burn out my best prime with an unbased send like this.

Oh, I'll pick up midway. Like those antibiotics this morning.

Deneb, what's this business with antibiotics and germdogs? What're you cooking up out there in that heathenish hole?

Oh, we're merely fighting a few plagues with one hand and keeping thirty bogey ET's upstairs. Deneb gave them a look with his vision at an enormous hospital, a continuous stream of airborne ambulances coming in: at crowded wards, grim-faced nurses and doctors, and uncomfortable high piles of sheeted still figures.

Well, I didn't realize. All right, you can have anything you want—within reason. But I want a full report, said Reidinger.

And patrol squadrons?

Reidinger's tone changed to impatience. *You've obviously got an exaggerated idea of our capabilities. I can't mobilize patrol squadrons like that!* There was a mental snap of fingers.

Would you perhaps drop a little word in the C.O.C's ear? Those ET's may gobble Deneb tonight and go after Terra tomorrow.

I'll do what I can, of course, but you colonists agreed to the risks when you signed up. The ET's were probably hoping for a soft touch. You're showing them different. They'll give up and get—

You're all heart, said Deneb.

Reidinger was silent for a moment. Then he said, *Germdogs sealed, Rowan; Pick 'em up and throw 'em out,* and signed off.

Rowan—that's a pretty name, said Deneb.

Thanks, she said absently. She had followed along Reidinger's initial push, and picked up the two personnel carriers as they materialized beside her shell. She pressed into the station dynamos and gathered strength. The generators whined and she pushed out. The carriers disappeared.

They're coming in, Rowan. Thanks a lot.

A passionate and tender kiss was blown to her

across eighteen light-years of space. She tried to follow after the carriers and pick up his touch again, but he was no longer receiving.

She sank back in her couch. Deneb's sudden appearance had disconcerted her completely. All of the Primes were isolated in their high talents, but the Rowan was more alone than any of the others.

Siglen, the Altairian Prime who had discovered the Rowan as a child and carefully nursed her talent into its tremendous potential, was the oldest Prime of all. The Rowan, a scant twenty-three now, had never gotten anything from Siglen to comfort her except old-fashioned platitudes. Betelgeuse Prime David was madly in love with his T-2 wife and occupied with raising a brood of high-potential brats. Although Reidinger was always open to the Rowan, he also had to keep open every single minute to all the vast problems of the FT & T system. Capella was available but so mixed up herself that her touch aggravated the Rowan to the point of fury.

Reidinger had tried to ease her devastating loneliness by sending up T-3's and T-4's like Afra, but she had never taken to any of them. The only male T-2 ever discovered in the Nine-Star League had been a confirmed homosexual. Ackerman was a nice, barely talented guy, devoted to his wife. And now, on Deneb, a T-1 had emerged, out of nowhere—and so very, very far away.

Afra, take me home now, she said, very tired.

Afra brought the shell down with infinite care.

After the others had left the station, the Rowan lay for a long while on her couch in the personnel carrier. In her unsleeping consciousness, she was aware that the station was closing down, that Ackerman and the others had left for their homes until Callisto once more came out from behind Jupiter's titan bulk. Everyone had some place to go, except the Rowan who made it all possible. The bitter, screaming loneliness that overcame her during her off hours welled up—the frustration of being unable to go off-planet past Afra's sharply limited range—alone, alone with her two-edged talent. Murky green and black swamped her mind until she

12

remembered the blown kiss. Suddenly, completely, she fell into her first restful sleep in two weeks.

Rowan. It was Deneb's touch that roused her. *Rowan, please wake up.*

Hmmmm? Her sleepy response was reluctant.

Our guests are getting rougher . . . since the germdogs . . . whipped up a broad spectrum antibiotic . . . that phase . . . of their attack failed . . . so now they're . . . pounding us . . . with missiles . . . give my regards to your space-lawyer friend . . . Reidinger.

You're playing pitch with missiles? The Rowan came awake hurriedly. She could feel Deneb's contact cutting in and out as he interrupted himself to catch incoming missiles and fling them back.

I need backup help, sweetheart, like you and . . . any twin sisters . . . you happen . . . to have . . . handy. Buzz over . . . here, will you?

Buzz? What? I can't go there!

Why not?

I can't! I can't! The Rowan moaned, twisting against the web of the couch.

But I've got . . . to . . . have . . . help, he said and faded away.

Reidinger! The Rowan's call was a scream.

Rowan, I don't care if you are a T-1. There are certain limits to my patience and you've stretched every blasted one of them, you little white-haired ape!

His answer scorched her. She blocked automatically but clung to his touch. *Someone has got to help Deneb!* she cried, transmitting the Mayday.

What? He's joking!

How could he, about a thing like that!

Did you see the missiles? Did he show you what he was actually doing?

No, but I felt him thrusting. And since when does one of us distrust another when he asks for help.

Since when? Reidinger's reply crackled across space. *Since Eve handed Adam a rosy round fruit and said "eat." And exactly since Deneb's never been integrated into the prime network. We can't be sure who or what he is—or exactly where he is. I don't like this taking*

13

everything at his word. Try and get him back for me to hear.

I can't reach him! He's too busy lobbing missiles spaceward.

That's a hot one! Look, he can tap any other potentials on his own planet. That's all the help he needs.

But . . .

But me no buts and leave me alone. I'll play cupid only so far. Meanwhile I've got a company—a league— to hold together. Reidinger signed off with a backlash that stung. The Rowan lay in her couch, bewildered by Reidinger's response. He was always busy, always gruff. But he had never been stupidly unreasonable. While out there, Deneb was growing weaker . . .

Callisto was clear of Jupiter and the station was operating again. Incoming cargoes were piling up on the launchers. But there was no outgoing traffic. Tension and worry hung over the station.

"There must be something we can do for him . . . something," the Rowan said, choked with tears.

Afra looked down at her sadly and compassionately, and patted her frail shoulder.

"What? Not even you can reach all the way out to him. Patrol Squadrons are needed by what you've said, but *we* can't send them. Did you ask him if he's tried to find help on his own planet?"

"He needs Prime help and—"

"You're all tied to your little worlds with the umbilical cord of space-fear," Afra finished for her, a blunt summation of the problem that made her wince for her devastating inability.

Kerrist! The radar warning! Ackerman's mental shout startled both of them.

Instantly the Rowan linked her mind to his as Ackerman plunged toward the little-used radar screen. As she probed into space, she found the intruder, a highly powered projectile, arrowing in from behind Uranus. Guiltily she flushed, for she ought to have detected it away beyond the radar's range.

There was no time to run up the idling dynamos. The projectile was coming in too fast.

I want a wide-open mind from everyone on this moon! The Rowan's broadcast was inescapable. She felt the surge of power as forty-eight talents on Callisto, including Ackerman's ten-year-old son, lowered their shields. She picked up their power—from the least 12 to Afra's sturdy 4—sent her touch racing out beyond Jupiter, and reached the alien bomb. She had to wrestle for a moment with the totally unfamiliar molecular structure of its constituents. Then, with her augmented energy, it was easy enough to deactivate the trigger and then scatter the fissionables from the warhead into Jupiter's seething mass.

She released the others who had joined her and fell back into the couch.

"How in hell did that thing find us?" Afra asked from the chair in which he had slumped.

She shook her head wearily. Without the dynamos, there had been no surge of power to act as the initial carrier wave for her touch. Even with the help of the others—and all of them put together didn't add up to one-third the strength of another Prime—it had been a wearying exercise. She thought of Deneb—alone, without an FT & T Station to assist him—doing this again, and again, and again—and her heart twisted.

Warm up the dynamos, Brian—there'll be more of those missiles.

Afra looked up, startled.

Prime Rowan of Callisto Station alerting Earth Prime Reidinger and all other primes! Prepare for possible attack by fissionable projectiles of alien origin. Alert all radar watch stations and patrol forces. She lost her official calm and added angrily, *We've got to help Deneb now—we've got to! It's no longer an isolated aggression against an outlying colony. It's a concerted attack on our heart world. It's an attack on every prime in the nine-star league.*

Rowan! Before Reidinger got more than her name into her mind, she opened to him and showed the five new projectiles driving toward Callisto. *For the love of little apples!* Reidinger's mind radiated incredulity. *What has our little man been stirring up?*

Shall we find out? Rowan asked with deadly sweetness.

Reidinger transmitted impatience, fury, misery and then shock as he gathered her intention.

15

Your plan won't work. It's impossible. We can't merge minds to fight. All of us are too egocentric. Too unstable. We'd burn out, fighting each other.

You, me, Altair, Betelgeuse and Capella. We can do it. If I can deactivate one of those hell missiles with only forty-eight minor talents and no power for help, five primes plus full power ought to be able to turn the trick. We can knock the missiles off. Then we can merge with Deneb to help him, that'll make six of us. Show me the ET who could stand up to such a counter-assault!

Look girl, Reidinger replied, almost pleading, *We don't have his measure. We can't just merge—He could split us apart, or we could burn him up. We don't know him. We can't gauge a telepath of unknown ability.*

You'd better catch that missile coming at you, she said calmly. *I can't handle more than ten at a time and keep up a sensible conversation.*

She felt Reidinger's resistance to her plan weakening. She pushed the advantage. *If Deneb's been handling a planet-wide barrage, that's a pretty good indication of his strength. I'll handle the ego-merge because I damned well want to. Besides, there isn't any other course open to us now, is there?*

We could launch patrol squadrons.

We should have done that the first time he asked. It's too late now.

Their conversation was taking the briefest possible time and yet more missiles were coming in. All the Prime stations were under bombardment.

All right, Reidinger said in angry resignation, and contacted the other Primes.

No, no, no! You'll burn her out—burn her out, poor thing! Old Siglen from Altair babbled. *Let us stick to our last—we dare not expose ourselves, no, no, no! The ET's would attack us then.*

Shut up, Ironpants, David said.

Shoulder to the wheel, you old wart, Capella chimed in waspishly. *Hit hard first, that's safest.*

Look, Rowan, Reidinger said. *Siglen's right. He could burn you out.*

I'll take the chance.

16

Damn Deneb for starting all this! Reidinger didn't quite shield his aggravation.

We've got to do it. And now!

Tentatively at the outset, and then with stunningly increased force, the unleashed power of the other FT & T Primes, augmented by the mechanical surge of the five stations' generators, was forced through the Rowan. She grew, grew and only dimly saw the puny ET bombardment swept aside like so many mayflies. She grew, grew until she felt herself a colossus, larger than ominous Jupiter. Slowly, carefully, tentatively, because the massive power was braked only by her slender conscious control, she reached out to Deneb.

She spun on, in grandeur, astounded by the limitless force she had become. She passed the small black dwarf that was the midway point. Then she felt the mind she searched for; a tired mind, its periphery wincing with weariness but doggedly persevering its evasive actions.

Oh, Deneb, Deneb, you're still intact! She was so relieved, so grateful to find him fighting his desperate battle that they merged before her ego could offer even a token resistance. She abandoned her most guarded self to him and, with the surrender, the massed power she held flowed into him. The tired mind of the man grew, healed, strengthened and blossomed until she was a mere fraction of the total, lost in the greater part of this immense mental whole. Suddenly she saw with his eyes, heard with his ears and felt with his touch, was immersed in the titanic struggle.

The greenish sky above was pitted with mushroom puffs, and the raw young hills around him were scarred with deflected missiles. Easily now, he was turning aside the warheads aimed at him.

Let's go up there and find out what they are, the Reidinger segment said. *Now!*

Deneb approached the thirty mile-long ships. The mass-mind took indelible note of the intruders. Then, off-handedly, Deneb broke the hulls of twenty-nine of the ET ships, spilling the contents into space. To the occupants of the survivor, he gave a searing impression of the Primes and the indestructability of the worlds in this section of space. With one great heave, he threw

17

the lone ship away from his exhausted planet, set it hurtling farther than it had come, into uncharted black immensity.

He thanked the Primes for the incomparable compliment of an ego-merge and explained in a millisecond the tremendous gratitude of his planet, based on all that Denebians had accomplished in three generations which had been so nearly obliterated and emphasized by their hopes for the future.

The Rowan felt the links dissolving as the other Primes, murmuring withdrawal courtesies, left him. Deneb caught her mind fast to his and held on. When they were alone, he opened all this thoughts to her, so that now she knew him as intimately as he knew her.

Sweet Rowan. Look around you. It'll take a while for Deneb to be beautiful again but we'll make it lovelier than ever. Come live with me, my love.

The Rowan's wracked cry of protest reverberated cruelly in both naked minds.

I can't! I can't! She cringed against her own outburst and closed off her inner heart so that he couldn't see the pitiful why. In the moment of his confusion, she retreated back to her frail body, and beat her fists hopelessly against her thighs.

Rowan! came his cry. *Rowan, I love you.*

She deadened the outer fringe of her perception to everything and curled forward in her chair. Afra, who had watched patiently over her while her mind was far away, touched her shoulder.

Oh, Afra! To be so close to love and so far away. Our minds were one. Our bodies are forever separate. Deneb! Deneb!

The Rowan forced her bruised self into sleep. Afra picked her up gently and carried her to a bed in a room off the station's main level. He shut the door and tiptoed away. Then he sat down, on watch in the corridor outside, his handsome face dark with sorrow, his yellow eyes blinking away moisture.

Afra and Ackerman reached the only possible conclusion: the Rowan had burned herself out. They'd have to tell Reidinger. Forty-eight hours had elapsed since they'd had a single contact with her mind. She had not heard, or had ignored, their tentative requests for her assistance. Afra, Ackerman, and the machines could handle some of the routing and freighting, but two liners were due in and that required her. They knew she was alive but that was all: her mind was blank to any touch. At first, Ackerman had assumed that she was recuperating. Afra had known better and, for that forty-eight hours, he'd hoped fervently that she would accept the irreconcilable situation.

"I'll run up the dynamos," Ackerman said to Afra with a reluctant sigh, "and we'll tell Reidinger."

Well, where's Rowan? Reidinger asked. A moment's touch with Afra told him. He, too, sighed. *We'll just have to rouse her some way. She isn't burned out; that's one mercy.*

Is it? replied Ackerman bitterly. *If you'd paid attention to her in the first place . . .*

Yes, I'm sure, Reidinger cut him off brusquely. *If I'd gotten her light of love his patrol squadrons when she wanted me to, she wouldn't have thought of merging with him mentally. I put as much pressure on her as I dared. But when that cocky young rooster on Deneb started lobbing deflected ET missiles at us . . . I hadn't counted on that development. At least we managed to spur her to act. And off-planet at that.* He sighed. *I was hoping that love might make at least one prime fly.*

Whaaa-at? Afra roared. *You mean that battle was staged?*

Hardly. As I said, we hadn't anticipated the ET. Deneb presumably had only a mutating virus plague to cope with. Not ET.

Then you didn't know about them?

Of course not! Reidinger sounded disgusted. *Oh, the original contact with Deneb for biological assistance was sheer chance. I took it as providential, an opportunity to see if I couldn't break the fear psychosis we all have. Rowan's the youngest of us. If I could get her to go to him—physically—I failed.* Reidinger's resignation saddened Afra, too. One didn't consider the Central Prime as a fallible human. *Love isn't as strong as it's supposed to be. And where I'll get new Primes if*

19

I can't breed 'em, I don't know. I'd hoped that Rowan and Deneb ...

As a matchmaker ...

I should resign ...

Afra cut the contact abruptly as the door opened, admitting the Rowan, a wan, pale, very quiet Rowan.

She smiled apologetically. "I've been asleep a long time."

"You had a tiring day," Ackerman said gently.

She winced and then smiled to ease Ackerman's instant concern. "I still am, a little." Then she frowned. "Did I hear you two talking to Reidinger just now?"

"We got worried," Ackerman replied. "There're two liners coming in, and Afra and I just plain don't care to handle human cargo, you know."

The Rowan gave a rueful smile. "I know. I'm all set." She walked slowly up the stairs to her tower.

Ackerman shook his head sadly. "She sure has taken it hard."

Her chastened attitude wasn't the relief that her staff had once considered it might be. The work that day went on with monotonous efficiency, with none of the byplay and freakish temperament that had previously kept them on their toes. The men moved around automatically, depressed by this gently tragic Rowan. That might have been one reason why no one noticed particularly when, toward the very end of the day, the young man came in. Only when Ackerman rose from his desk for more coffee did he notice him sitting there quietly.

"You new?"

"Well, yes. I was told to see the Rowan. Reidinger signed me on in his office late this morning." He spoke pleasantly, rising to his feet slowly and ending his explanation with a smile. Fleetingly Ackerman was reminded of the miracle of the Rowan's sudden smiles that hinted at some incredible treasure of the spirit. This man's smile was full of uninhibited, magnetic vigor, and the brilliant blue eyes danced with good humor and friendliness.

Ackerman found himself grinning back like a fool, and shaking the man's hand stoutly.

"Mightly glad to know you. What's your name?"

20

"Jeff Raven. I just got in from—"

"Hey, Afra, want you to meet Jeff Raven. Here, have a coffee. A little raw on the walk up from the freighting station, isn't it? Been on any other Prime stations?"

"As a matter of fact . . ."

Toglia and Loftus had looked around from their computers to the recipient of such unusual cordiality. They found themselves as eager to welcome this magnetic stranger. Raven graciously accepted the coffee from Ackerman, who instantly proffered cigarettes. The stationmaster had the feeling that he must give this wonderful guy something else, it had been such a pleasure to provide him with coffee.

Afra looked quietly at the stranger, his calm yellow eyes a little clouded. "Hello," he said in a rueful murmur.

Jeff Raven's grin altered imperceptibly. "Hello," he replied, and more was exchanged between the two men than a simple greeting.

Before anyone in the station quite realized what was happening, everyone had left his post and gathered around Raven, chattering and grinning, using the simplest excuse to touch his hand or shoulder. He was genuinely interested in everything said to him, and although there were twenty-three people vying anxiously to monopolize his attention, no one felt slighted. His reception seemed to envelop them all.

What the hell is happening down there? asked the Rowan with a tinge of her familiar irritation. *Why . . .*

Contrary to all her previously sacred rules, she appeared suddenly in the middle of the room, looked about wildly. Raven touched her hand gently.

"Reidinger said you needed me," he said.

"Deneb?" Her body arched to project the astounded whisper. *"Deneb? But you're . . . you're here! You're here!"*

He smiled tenderly and drew his hand across her shining hair. The Rowan's jaw dropped and she burst out laughing, the laughter of a supremely happy carefree girl. Then her laughter broke off in a gasp of pure terror.

How did you get here?

Just came. You can, too, you know.

21

No, no, I can't. No T-1 can. The Rowan tried to free herself from his grasp as if he were suddenly repulsive.

I did, though. His gentle insistence was unequivocable. *It's only a question of rearranging atoms. Why should it matter whose they are?*

Oh, no, no . . .

"Did you know," Raven said conversationally, speaking for everyone's benefit "that Siglen of Altair gets sick just going up and down stairs?" He looked straight at the Rowan. "You remember that she lives all on one floor? Ever wondered why all her furniture has short legs, Rowan?"

The girl shook her head, her eyes wonderingly wide.

"No one ever stopped to ask why, did they? I did. Seemed damned silly to me when I met the woman. Siglen's middle ear reacts very badly to free-fall. She was so miserably sick the first time she tried moving herself anywhere, she went into a trauma about it. Of course, it never occurred to *her* to find out why. So she went a little crazy on the subject, and *who* trained all the other Primes?"

"Siglen . . . Oh, Deneb, you mean? . . ."

Raven grinned. "Yes, I do. She passed on the trauma to every one of you. The Curse of Talent! The Great Fear! The great bushwah! But agoraphobia, or a middle-ear imbalance, is not a stigma of Talent. Siglen never trained *me*." He laughed with wicked boyish delight and opened his mind to the Rowan. Warmth and reassurance passed between them. Her careful conditioning began to wither in that warmth. Her eyes shone.

Now come live with me and be my love, Rowan. Reidinger says you can commute from here to Deneb every day.

"Commute?" She said it aloud, conscious of the overall value of Siglen's training, but already questioning every aspect.

"Certainly," Jeff said, approving her thoughts. "You're still a working T-1 under contract to FT & T. And so, my love, am I."

"I guess I do know my bosses, don't I?" she said with a chuckle.

"Well, the terms were fair. Reidinger didn't haggle for a second after I walked into his private office at eleven this morning."

"Commuting to Callisto?" the Rowan repeated dazedly.

"All finished here for the day?" Raven asked Ackerman, who shook his head after a glance at the launching racks.

"C'mon, gal. Take me to your ivory tower and we'll finish up in a jiffy. Then we'll go home. With two of us working in our spare time, Deneb'll be put to rights in no time ... *And when we've finished that* ...

Jeff Raven smiled wickedly at the Rowan and pressed her hand to his lips in the age-old gesture of courtliness. The Rowan's smile answered his with blinding joy.

The others were respectfully silent as the two Talents made their way up the stairs to the once-lonely tower.

Afra broke the tableau by taking the burning cigarette from Ackerman's motionless hand. He took a deep drag that turned his skin a deeper green. It wasn't the cigarette smoke that caused his eyes to water so profusely.

"Not that that pair needs much of our help, people," he said, "but we can add a certain flourish and speed them on their way."

A Meeting of Minds

IOTA AURIGAE WAS A BLAZE AT ZENITH, TO Damia's left, glinting off her tiny personal capsule. Capella's light, from the right nadir, was a pulsing blue-white. Starlight from the Milky Way bathed her, too, but the only sound was her even breathing as she allowed her mind to open fully to the mindless, echo-freedom of deep space.

It was as if she could feel the separate cerebral muscles relaxing, expanding, just as her tall slender body went gradually limp. But it was primarily the mental relief that Damia sought so far away from her control Tower at the Federated Telepath and Teleport installation on Aurigae. It was the utter peace of deep space she required as anodyne to the constant demands of her position as Psionic Prime, responsible for the flow of commerce and communication in this Sector of Federated Worlds, the Nine-Star League. She was young, true, barely twenty; but age is relative, particularly when the need is great, and her mental talents were unusually mature. Furthermore, she was of the Raven Clan, born into a tremendously talented family, carefully indoctrinated and trained to assume an executive role as the influence of Federated Worlds expanded into new star systems, needing more Prime Talents.

Occasionally, even her young mind felt the strain and required respite from the insistent murmur of broadcasting thoughts that beat, beat, beat against hers: little minds which could not conceive the forces that Damia, Aurigan Prime, could marshall in gestalt with the mighty dynamos of the Tower.

With a flick of a finger, Damia screened out the overbrilliant starlight and opened her eyes. The softened stargleams, points of gem fire in the black of space, winked and pulsed at her. Idly she identified the familiar patterns they made, these silent friends. Somehow the petty grievances that built up inside her were gently dispersed as the overwhelming impersonality of cold nothingness brought them into proper perspective.

She could even forget her present preoccupation for a moment: forget how lonely she was; how she envied her brother, Larak, his loving, lovely wife and their new son; envied her mother the company of her husband and children; envied her Afra's . . .

Afra! What right had he to interfere, to reprimand her! His words still seared. "You've been getting an almighty huge vicarious charge out of peeking in on Larak and Jenna. Scared Jenna out of her wits, lurking in her mind while she was in labor! You leave them both alone!"

She was forced to admit herself at fault. But how had Afra known? Unless Larak had told him. She sighed. Yes, Larak would have known she was eavesdropping. Though he was the only T-3 among her brothers and sisters, he had always been extremely sensitive to her mind touch. And she and Larak could always overwhelm any combination of the others, even if Jeran, Cera, and Ezro, all T-1s, teamed up against them. Somehow, she switched mental gears, doubling the capability of other minds within her focus.

But it had humiliated her to be reamed by Afra. Well, better by that yellow-eyed, green-skinned T-4 Capellan than her father, acting in his capacity as Earth Prime. She rather hoped that her father had not learned of her breach of T- etiquette.

Odd, though, she hadn't heard as much as a whisper from Afra since then. It must be over seven months. He had listened in as she'd apologized to both Jenna and Larak, and then silence. He couldn't be *that* angry with her.

Damia diverted her thoughts away from Afra, and went through the ritual of muscular relaxation, of mental wipeout. She must be back in the Tower very soon.

In a way, the fact that she could handle Prime duties with no higher ratings than a T-6 to assist had certain disadvantages. The Tower staff could handle only routine, planetary traffic, but she had to be on hand for all interstellar telepathic and teleportation commerce.

It would be wonderful to have a T-3 with her: someone who could understand. Not some*one* . . . be honest with yourself out here in space, Damia. Some *man*. Only men shy away from you as if you'd developed Lynx-sun cancers. And the only other unmarried Prime was her own brother, Jeran. Come to think about Jeran, the smug tone in his recent mind-touches as they exchanged cargoes and messages between Deneb and Auriga undoubtedly meant that he had found a likely mate, too.

It was no consolation to Damia that her mother had known and warned her of this intense, feminine loneliness. But Jeff Raven had appeared to breach the Rowan's tower and the Rowan had at least had Afra's company . . .

Afra! Why did her mind keep returning to *him?*

Damia realized that she was grinding her teeth. She forced herself through the rituals again, sternly making specific thought dissipate until her mind drifted. And, in the course of that aimless drifting, an aura impinged on her roving consciousness. Startled—for nothing could be coming in from that far quarter of space—she tightened her mind into a seeking channel.

An aura. A mere wisp of the presence of something. Something . . . alien!

Alien! Damia recomposed herself. She disciplined her mind to a pure, clear, uncluttered shaft. She touched the aura. Recognition of her touch, retreat, return.

The aura was undeniably alien, but so faint that she would have doubted its existence except that her finely trained mind was not given to error.

An exultation as hot as lust caused her blood to pound in her ears. She was not wrong. The trace was there.

Taking a deep breath, she directed an arrow-fine mental shout across the light-years, nadirward, to the

Earth Prime FT & T Tower, high above the Grand Canyon.

Alien spacecraft approaching our galaxy intercepting at Auriga, she informed Jeff Raven.

Damia, control, *damn it, girl. Control,* Jeff replied, keeping his own mental roar within tolerable bounds.

Sorry, Damia amended briefly without real contrition. Her father was capable of deflecting her most powerful thrust.

You are on a tight focus, I trust, with news like this? he asked in an official tone.

Of course, I am. But my first duty is to report to Earth Prime, isn't it?

Don't come over sweet innocence on me, missy. Now, give your full report.

Can't give a full one. The alien aura is barely detectible, four light-years galactic north-northeast, Sector 2. I arrowed in once I heard the trace and it responded.

It responded—

The aura.

You reported a spacecraft.

Father, how else could anything cross the intergalactic sea?

My dear child, in our galaxy, we have encountered many odd life forms that did not require light or oxygen to exist.

I say, spacecraft. I touched it.

Damia? and Jeff's tone was suspicious. *Where are you?*

I was only resting, she temporized, suddenly aware that she was doing something not quite circumspect.

Resting is permitted. But how far are you from the Tower? Jeff insisted.

A light-year.

With only a T-6 Station as control? Supposing, daughter, something happened to you? Supposing that alien aura decided to home in on you . . .

Oh, Dad, if I can't read more than an aura of Them, and they haven't changed position or rate since I informed you, they sure as hell don't pose any threat to me.

She carefully suppressed a giggle at her father's exasperation. She very seldom got the better of either her father or Afra—she erased that name and went on—but it didn't keep her from trying.

All right, missy, show me, Jeff demanded, still severe.

She allowed him to join her mind completely as she led him out beyond the blaze of stars. She led him directly to the alien trace. The aura was palpable but so far away that only the extraordinary perception of two powerful minds could sense it.

I caught anticipation, curiosity, Jeff told his daughter thoughtfully as he withdrew from the tight focus. *And caution, too. Whatever it is, is approaching our galaxy.*

I shall maintain a watch, Damia volunteered, unable to conceal her intense excitement at this momentous event.

Not at any time personally endangering yourself, Prime, Jeff abjured her, coloring the official concern with personal.

No, of course not. But I'd like to borrow Larak to maintain an augmented watch.

Larak's training T-3s to augment old Guzman on Altair. The old man sleeps most of the time but he's the only Prime we have for that Sector until Ezro's older, Jeff replied. *I'll send you Afra. He'd be better anyhow.*

Because Afra has already touched those aliens you and mother routed above Deneb twenty-odd years ago? Damia laughed, covering up her reaction to Afra's coming with a jab at her father's recall.

Jeff chuckled amiably, giving her credit for a deep perception.

Well, I'd rather wait until Larak's free. I can just hear mother screaming at being deprived of Afra.

Damia, Jeff's tone crackled with disapproval. *That is an irrational, childish and insulting remark. Repair your attitude.* His tone altered. *If you hadn't, at one time or another, intimidated every T-2, -3 and -4 in the Federated Worlds, I could send someone else—*

And matchmake into the bargain? She tinged her thoughts with derision, and then advised smugly, *Your dynastic plans will bear better fruit with Jeran. Only don't let him settle for anything less than a T-4.*

28

That was score two for her, she decided as she felt her father's startled pause.

You haven't been eavesdropping again, have you, Damia?

She parried that surprise with a quick, *After Afra reamed me for that with Larak? Not bloody likely.*

Oh, it was he who stopped you? Your mother thought it was Isthia.

The trouble with telepaths is sometimes they think too much, she remarked acidly, infuriated afresh to realize that her mother, also, knew of that incident.

Damia! Jeff's tone was unusually severe. *Your mother is the only person in the galaxy who has any inkling of your problems . . .*

Then why did she hand me over to Isthia to raise? Damia flashed back without thinking.

Because, my darling daughter, you were without doubt the most infuriating, incalcitrant, unmanageable four-year-old. Your mother was too ill with her pregnancy to keep track of you blithely teleporting all over the system. I sent you away, not your mother. It was not her decision and she resisted it every step of the way. I've told you that before. But you two are so bloody much alike . . .

Damia snorted. She was not the least bit like her mother. There was absolutely no resemblance between them. She was Jeff's daughter from her slender height to her black hair and vivid blue eyes. Ezro, yes, and Larak, too, took after the Rowan. But not she. Of course, Damia had to admit, her mother had an exceedingly strong and diverse psionic talent or she wouldn't be Callisto Prime, but Damia was just as strong, and she had the added advantage of that catalystic ability as well.

Well, Jeff was saying in a milder tone, *you'll see it one day, my dear, and I, for one, shall be immensely relieved. Your mother and I love you very much and we're damned proud of the way you've taken over your official responsibilities on Auriga. Professionally I have no quarrel with you.*

Damia basked in her father's praise. He didn't give it lightly.

If you were only able to relate more to the people

around you, he continued, spoiling the compliment, then added briskly, *I'll send Afra on directest. I can trust his impartiality,* and to Damia's amazement, her father chuckled.

She stabbed at his mind to find the basis for the amusement, but met a blankness as her father had turned his mind to some other problem.

"Impartiality? Afra?" The sound of her own voice in the little personal capsule startled her.

What on earth was that supposed to mean? Why would Afra's impartiality be trusted—above hers—in identifying or evaluating an alien aura?

But Afra was to come to Auriga.

After he had broken contact with Damia, Jeff did not immediately turn to other problems. He mulled over the subtler aspects of that vivid contact with his daughter. Damia's mind was as brilliant as Iota Aurigae, and about as stable as any active star's surface. He had caught the edges of her skillfully shielded reactions to several of his references. He was reassured to note growing evidence of emotional maturity, except where her mother and Afra were concerned.

Damia had unwittingly suppressed what Jeff recalled most vividly about the day he had sent her away to Isthia on Betelgeuse for fostering. It had been Afra the four-year-old Damia had clung to, cried for, not her mother. Jeff sighed. The decision to send Damia to Isthia had been one of the hardest he had ever had to make, personally and professionally. But Rowan had been extremely ill during her pregnancy with Larak, and Damia, coming early into her extraordinary mental powers, had made life pure hell for everyone in the Raven household: teleporting herself—and anything her fancies seized upon—indiscriminately around the system. Only Afra had any control over her, and he had had to be at Callisto Tower.

Under Isthia's calm, unruffled discipline, Damia had learned to control her waywardness. She became sincerely fond of Isthia. Strange that it was the Rowan whom Damia still blamed for that separation.

Rowan, Jeff called out to Callisto Tower, and sensed

30

that his wife was resting as the interchanges on Callisto's cargo decks filled from Earthside.

Her mind touched his gladly, with a delight that belied the fact they had breakfasted together a few hours earlier.

Open to me. Damia's made an alien contact. See it.

Alien? Near Damia? The fleeting maternal concern was quickly supplanted by professional curiosity as the Rowan scanned Jeff's recent experience beyond Auriga. *Of course, Afra can go. But why on earth would Damia think Afra couldn't be reassigned as you see fit. He often has, but it's true I never get on as well with other T-3's.*

Too true, Jeff replied teasingly, to divert Rowan from scanning recent conversations too deeply, *but if I didn't know Afra as well as I do . . .*

Jeff Raven, there has never been a single thought between me and Afra that—

Jeff laughed and she sputtered at him indignantly.

Actually, she continued, thoughtfully, *I'd be very relieved to have Afra with Damia. I know how lonely it must be for her . . .*

If she hadn't been so heavy-handed with every other high T young male, she wouldn't be lonely, Jeff said briskly, before Rowan got started on how she had failed her daughter. *Now, is Afra in gestalt with you?*

Right here. I'll leave you two men alone.

Refusing to placate her ruffled feelings, Jeff caressed her with a very affectionate thought before he felt Afra's mind touch his.

Are you sure you're only T-3? he asked, a little surprised at the firmness in the Capellan's touch.

I'm in gestalt, after all, Afra replied, good-naturedly. *And, in the course of twenty-odd years in the presence of the fine Raven touch, even a lowly T-3 learns a few tricks. From the expression on the Rowan's face, I'd hazard that Damia is being discussed. What's she up to now?*

Damia had just returned to Auriga when she heard the Rowan giving the Tower official warning of the transmission of a personal capsule.

31

Afra? Damia exclaimed, reaching back along her mother's touch to Callisto.

Damia! Afra said warningly but too late.

Without waiting for the Rowan to flip the capsule halfway to Auriga, Damia blithely drew the carrier directly from Callisto, ignoring her mother's stunned and angry reaction to such an abuse of protocol.

She regretted her impulsive action almost immediately. But Afra's capsule was opening and he was swinging himself over the edge. She could not have missed his trenchant disapproval if she'd been a mere T-15. He stood up, looking down at her, the same aloof, contained man. Now why, Damia wondered irritably, had she expected Afra to change? Had *she?* And would Afra condescend to comment on those changes in her?

She rose from her own capsule, instinctively standing very erect as if to minimize the differences in their heights. Tall as she was, inches taller than her mother, she came only to Afra's shoulder.

"You will apologize to your mother, Damia," Afra said, his unexpected tenor speaking voice a curious echo of his quiet mental tone. "Isthia taught you better manners even if we never could."

"You've been trying to lately, though, haven't you?" The retort came out before she could stop it. Would Afra always have this effect on her?

He cocked his head to one side and regarded her steadily. She sent a swift probe which he parried easily.

"You were distressing Jenna unnecessarily, Damia. She appealed to me as the nearest male of her Clan, and because she did not wish Jeff to know of your indiscretion."

"She chose well." Damia was so appalled at the waspishness of her tone that she extended her hand toward him apologetically.

She could feel him throw up his mental barriers and, for a second, she wondered if he might refuse what was, after all, the height of familiarity between telepaths. But his hand rose smoothly to clasp hers, lightly, warmly, leaving her with the essential cool-green-comfortable-security that was the physical/mental double-touch of him.

Then, with a one-sided smile, he bowed to indicate he was flattered but allowed a recollection of her as a nude baby on a bath towel to cross his public mind.

She made a face at him, and substituted Larak's son. Afra blandly put "her" back on the towel beside her nephew.

"All right," she laughed, "I'll behave."

"About time," he said with an affable grin, and looked beyond her to their surroundings.

He had seen Auriga in others' mind-eyes but the amber sunlight was easier on his eyes than Earth's bright yellow, so that Auriga was not a dark world to him, but a restful one. The sweet-scented breeze sweeping down from the high snowy mountain range was lightly moist and the atmosphere had a high oxygen content, exhilarating him.

"It's a lovely world you have here, Damia."

She smiled up at him, her blue eyes brilliant under the fringes of long black lashes.

"It's a lovely young vigorous world. Come see where I live," and she led the way from the landing stage to her dwelling.

The house perched on the high plateau above the noisy metropolis that was Auriga's major city, and Damia's Sector Headquarters. Its randomly sprawling newness had a vitality which the planned order of Earth lacked. Afra found the sight stimulating.

"It is, isn't it?" Damia agreed, following his surface thought. Then she directed his mind to her day's discovery, giving the experience exactly as it had happened to her. "And the touch is unlike anything I've ever met."

"You certainly didn't expect it to be familiar, did you?" Afra asked in dry amusement.

"Just because they come from another galaxy doesn't mean they *can't* be humanoid," she replied.

Afra snorted in disgust and went into her main living room.

"I'll fix your favorite protein," she volunteered in one of her mercurial shifts.

"Oh, don't go to any trouble for me."

33

"No trouble at all." Mischievously, she allowed him to see her reaching for supplies from his home world light-years away.

"Always the thoughtful hostess," he said, graciously inclining his head. "Have you estimated the alien's arrival?"

"I'll know better when I've had a chance to judge their relative speed," she said. "A day or two would give me some idea."

He watched her at the homey duties. Like most T-1s, she enjoyed manual work and performed the daily housekeeping herself, without relying on mechanical services most households considered necessities. In a few minutes she set before him a perfectly cooked attractively served meal which he greeted perfunctorily.

"Can't I ever impress you?" she asked, half wistful, half sharp.

"Why should you want to?" he asked, affecting mild surprise. "I knew you from your first incoherent thought."

"Familiarity breeds contempt, huh?"

"Contempt, no. Understanding, yes. Particularly at our levels. And, of course, confusion, wherever you are," Afra replied. "Very good, just the way I like it," he added appreciatively, indicating his dinner.

Damia made a face at him across the table, and with a deliberate disregard for T- manners, reached a portion of the sauce-steeped meat into her mouth without spilling a drop. When Afra continued to ignore her, she sighed and picked up her fork.

"Shall I take over the regular workload, Damia, and leave you free for surveillance?"

"We don't have a heavy traffic right now. It's between harvests in this system, and manufacturing is slow for the next few months. The usual amount of tourists, though."

"How have you covered your absences with the staff?"

"Just told them I've been resting. I'll account for your presence as a preliminary survey for FT & T. Right? As if any of those lamebrains could 'search' me," she concluded contemptuously.

"So true," Afra replied, indicating in his public mind his professional respect for her.

She was not deaf to the irony and was about to reply hotly, but went back to eating rather than give him further satisfaction.

It was unprecedented, this contact with sentient life from what was probably another galaxy, yet for all her capriciousness, Damia had not permitted a hint of panic or her own inner excitement to escape. In that she heeded one of the basic tenets of her position. Panic enough was fomented within the complex Federated Worlds in the normal course of power struggles, revolutions, ecological problems, and pioneer exigencies. By common consent, instantaneous communications between planets no longer meant instant hysteria of worlds unconcerned with the emergency. Federated World Government handled the reports of all local disputes which were, by law, reported to them by FT & T Primes. Interstellar political or natural disasters were not added to the emotional burdens already suffered by populations. Primes exercised the option to disperse or retain reports which might affect minorities within their jurisdiction, but digests of all communications were, by law, available on request.

Damia propped her chin in her hands and looked earnestly at Afra across the table. She sighed heavily.

"You were right to call me to task for 'tasting' Larak and Jenna. But I did want to know what it would be like to be in love and then bring forth a baby."

"And . . . ?"

"Apart from the pain, I guess it's rewarding enough."

"You don't sound too sure."

Damia cocked her head and traced an involved pattern on the table with her index finger.

"It must be different to do it yourself, no matter how deeply you scan."

A trace thought behind her shield, called forth by her remark, sent through Afra a bolt of terror which he barely managed to contain. She was unconsciously censoring, and it had to do with the alien aura and with her own desire for the experience of motherhood. But trace thought it was, and he had only that one-millisecond impression, tantalizing, terrorizing.

"Why, Afra, why?" Damia continued, unaware of the reaction she had produced in him, her own mind absorbed in self-pity. She launched herself physically from the table in one lightning move, and stood at the window wall, her back as expressive of her frustration and bitterness as her mind. "Why am I a loner? The Rowan found Jeff, but where, when will I find someone?"

"Damia, you've met every psionic prospect Talent above Class 7 in the Nine-Star League."

"Them," she dismissed those candidates scornfully.

"Young Nicos, the T-5 working with Jeran on Deneb, was mighty taken with you. Calm down a bit—"

"Nicos!" Damia's eyes flashed blue fire. "That post-adolescent mess! Why, it'd be five or six years before he's even presentable."

Afra was no stranger to such dismissals. He'd heard many since the time Damia had begun to be interested in the opposite sex as a precocious adolescent. There had been times when he wished he had followed his own deep-hidden desire. But he had given a great deal of thought to the variables, and knew that he could only wait. He knew how hard it must be for Damia to watch others pairing off, achieving the enviable total accord that telepaths enjoyed, and for which she was so eager. Her very brilliance and beauty caused many otherwise willing mates to shy away. Usually, she would talk herself out of her mood, but tonight there was a new undercurrent that was dangerous in its intensity.

"Is that why you so eagerly await the arrival of the aliens?" Afra said in a soft drawl, deliberately leaching all emotion out of his words. "On the off chance they're biologically compatible? Do you envision your soul mate winging across the void to you?"

She whirled to face him, her eyes wide with rage.

"Don't *you* taunt me, Afra," she said in a hoarse whisper.

He inclined his head in apology.

"Better get some sleep, Damia," he said gently, and gave her a little mental push toward her bedroom.

"You're right. I am tired, Afra, and excited, and

silly. It's just . . . just that sometimes I feel like nothing more than a useful mental stevedore: not a person at all. Then this happens . . . and I . . . I have the fantastic chance to establish communication with alien minds . . ."

Again Afra caught the unmistakable and unconscious suppression of a thought within the maelstrom of her weariness.

Damia turned on her heel and left the room. Afra watched the sunset turn the plateau a deep tangerine, then diminish in the east. Brooding over the evening's conversation, he waited until the roiling activity of Damia's mind subsided into the even beat of sleep. Then he, too, went to bed. Carefully, just as he was on the edge of sleep, he reinforced his mental screens so that none of his longing for her would escape. He wondered, in that honest interval between consciousness and dreaming, if he would have enough strength left to cope with a third generation of Raven women.

The next day they initiated the new routine. Damia handled the long-distance items first. Then after the incoming workload had been sorted out and there were no more demands on her talent, she departed into space, to "rest," leaving Afra to deal with the remaining tasks.

Although the function of a Prime was complex, a two-minute mental briefing by Damia supplied Afra with the background of immediate problems and all the procedures peculiar to that station. The memory bank would give any additional information. When the focal talents of the gestalt were exchanged, not even one-half a beat of the pulse of the Aurigean Sector Headquarters was missed. The allocation of duties pleased Afra because it would give him the opportunity to use the gestalt of the Station to reach Jeff without Damia knowing. She would be too busy "reaching" for the alien touch to be aware of Afra. The temporary breach of her trust in him was offset by the absolving knowledge of its necessity.

In terms of intergalactic distances, the aliens approached at a snail's pace: by interstellar references, faster than the speed of light. A week passed and then one evening Damia returned from her daily "rest" bursting with news. She moved from the landing area right into the living room, where Afra was lounging.

"I made individual contact," she cried. "And what a mind!" She was so excited that she didn't notice the flare of jealousy which Afra couldn't suppress. "And what a surprise *he* got," she went on.

From the moment she had entered, Afra had known that the mind was male.

"A Prime talent?" he asked, counterfeiting a show of genuine interest.

"I can't assess it. He's so . . . different," she exclaimed, her eyes shining and her mental aura dazzling with her success. "He fades and then returns. The distance is immense, and there isn't much definition in the thoughts. I can only reach the surface." Damia threw herself onto the long couch. "I'm exhausted. I shall have to sleep before I can reach Jeff with the news. I don't dare use the station."

Afra agreed readily, waiting until she relaxed into sleep. Ethics aside, he tried to reach this experience in her mind below the emotional level, only to find himself overwhelmed by the subjective. Damia was treating herself to a high emotional kick! Afra was afraid for her, with a fear deeper than any he had ever touched personally or vicariously. Afra withdrew troubled. She had better calm down and start acting like a Prime when she woke, instead of a giddy girl. If she didn't, he'd push the panic button himself.

After several hours' sleep, Damia's mental pyrotechnics were calmer. She "reached" Jeff with a professional report of the contact, only just a trifle high. When she had finished broadcasting, Jeff got a private thought to Afra but Afra could only confirm Damia's report. He did not yet comment on his vague forebodings.

The next day, Damia tossed off her necessary work as fast as she could, then went into space. And Afra waited as he had been waiting for Damia for years. She returned so shining from the second encounter, Afra had to clamp an icy hold over his mind.

The third morning, as Damia sat in the control tower, she worked with such haste Afra reprimanded her. She corrected herself, gaily, making far too light of her mistake, and then, eagerly, she propelled herself out toward the rendezvous. When she returned that evening so tired that she reeled into the living room, Afra took command.

"I'm going with you tomorrow, Damia," he said firmly.

"What for?" She sat bolt upright to glare at him.

"You forget that I have a direct order from Earth Prime to check the aura of these aliens. You've no way of knowing this isn't a reinvasion by the same entities that attacked Deneb twenty years ago."

"Sodan said they'd had no previous contact with any sentients," she said, half angry.

"Sodan?"

"That is how he identifies himself," she said with smug complacency. She lay back on the couch, smiling up at Afra.

It disturbed him to know that this entity had a name. It made the alien seem too human. Nor could Afra quite reason away the tenderness with which Damia spoke that name.

"Good enough," Afra said, with an indifference he didn't feel. "However, you don't need to introduce me formally. All I need is to check on the aura. I'll know in an instant if there's any familiarity. I won't jeopardize his confidence in your touch. He'll never know I've been there." Afra yawned.

"Why are *you* tired?"

"I've been stevedoring all day," he said with a malicious grin.

The remark had the desired effect of infuriating Damia. The very fact that he could so easily divert her conclusively proved to Afra that her emotions were unhealthily involved. It no longer mattered whether this Sodan was of the race that Jeff and the Rowan had fought. He was a menace in himself.

Somehow Afra got through the evening without a hint of his inner absorption spilling over. Damia, reliving the success of her day, wasn't listening to anything but her own thoughts.

The next day, after the necessary work was completed, Damia and Afra both took to their personal capsules. Afra followed Damia's thrust and held himself silently as she reached the area where she could touch the aura of Sodan. Damia then linked Afra and carried his mind to the alien ship. As soon as the alien touch impinged on Afra's awareness, much was suddenly clear to him: much seen, and worse, much unseen.

What Damia could not, would not, or did not see justified Afra's nagging presentiment of danger. *Nothing* out of Sodan's mind was visible: and nothing beyond his public mind was touchable. The alien had a very powerful brain. As a quiescent eavesdropper, Afra could not probe, but he widened his own sensitivity to its limit and the impressions he received were as unreassuring as his increasingly stronger intuition of disaster.

It was patent that this Sodan was not of the previous invasion species: that he had been traveling for an unspecifiable length of time far in excess of two Earth decades.

It would not occur to Damia that Afra would linger once he had established his facts. But Afra did linger, discovering other disturbing things. Sodan's mind, undeniably brilliant, was nevertheless augmented. Afra couldn't perceive whether Sodan was the focus for other minds on the ship or in gestalt with the ship's power source. Straining to his limit without revealing himself, Afra tried to pierce the visual screen or, at least, the aural one. All he received was a low stereo babble of mechanical activity, and the burn of heavy elements.

Defeated, Afra withdrew, leaving Sodan and Damia to exchange thoughts that he had to admit were the ploys of courtship. He returned to Auriga and lay in the Tower couch, summoning up the energy to call. Jeff Raven had moved young Larak nearer to Auriga to facilitate sub-rosa communications.

It was not, Afra assured himself, that Damia had deliberately hidden anything in her reports to himself or to Jeff: she was unaware that her usually keen perceptions were fuddled and distorted by her emotional involvement: she who had prided herself on her ability to assess dispassionately any emotionally charged incident.

Larak, Afra called, drawing heavily on the gestalt and projecting his own mental/physical concept of Larak to aid him in reaching the mind.

Man, you're beat, Larak came back, sharp, clear green.

Larak, relay back to Jeff that this Sodan . . .

It's got a name?

It's got more than that and Damia is responding on a very high emotional level, Afra sighed heavily. *Relay back to Jeff that I want him and the Rowan to remain on call at all times to me. I consider this an emergency. Get yourself pushed out here as soon as you can relay that message. I'll need you here so we can get through to Prime when we need to without going through Station or Damia.*

Coming, Larak responded crisply.

Afra leaned back in the couch and flicked off the generators, thanking the paradox that allowed Damia to run a Station on low T ratings; she would be unable to catch what he had just transmitted.

He would have given much to have been able to handle the Sodan mind by himself, without having to call on other Primes. All through Damia's life, Afra had been able to cope with her mercurial tempers and to direct her restless energies. And though his recent complete withdrawal from her had been painfully calculated, it meant that now he could neither further his cause, nor divert Damia from her headlong immersion in romance. Nor was he able to challenge Sodan and remove that competition.

"Galloping gronites, you look like a rough ride on a long ellipse comet," was Larak's cheery greeting as he bounced into the Tower.

"Your description is remarkably apt," Afra replied grimly, and gripped Larak's shoulder to convey the one impression he had not included in the broadcast.

Love has touched our fair sister at last, huh? Larak murmured sympathetically. *And with a total alien.*

A very dangerous alien, unfortunately, Afra added. "There is fissionable material aboard, mighty heavy stuff for a ship bound on an ostensibly peaceful exploratory mission. Heavy enough to suspect whoever

41

gave Sodan his mission *knew* our civilization is on an advanced level."

"More's the pity," Larak agreed thoughtfully, perching on the edge of the console. "Could you sense any communications with his own people?"

"Tremendous power source in the ship. Tremendous, but by the mighty atom, Larak, you can't get past the public mind. Anyhow, I couldn't. And Damia hasn't." Afra rose, paced restlessly back and forth in the narrow Tower.

"Then it's possible he has informed them of the contact?"

"I can't tell."

Larak held Afra's glance, and then sighed.

"It'll be a shame to have to destroy him," he said slowly.

"Ha! We'll be lucky if we can," Afra replied. "Oh, yes, Larak, that mind is the equal, if not the superior, of Damia's. It could destroy . . . all of us."

"Then we must act quickly before any suspicion leaks to Damia," Larak said in sudden resolution.

Together the two flicked on the generators and soberly presented to Jeff and the Rowan the action they deemed advisable.

But are we sure the evasions are deliberate? Maybe this alien is exercising caution? I would if I met a mind in outer space, the Rowan said in argument. She met absolute resistance to her position. *Why can't we destroy him then? Why must we ask her to do it?* She spoke as Damia's mother, not Callisto Prime.

For one thing, we can't reach that far without her. Nor can we draw, as Damia can, without prearrangement on other Talent reserves, Jeff replied. *We'll have to show her how dangerous Sodan is,* he added, disliking this as much as any of them.

Each day Damia returns to Auriga a little more tired than the previous one, Afra said slowly. *I suspect that he realized he must drain her before she suspects his intentions.*

Playing with her? The Rowan was angry now.

Don't be silly, mother, Larak said derisively.

Not in that sense, Rowan, Afra answered her. *I*

suspect Damia was as much a surprise to him as he has been to her.

Hurry, Larak cautioned him. *She's returning. And boy, is she exhausted!*

Afra suppressed a feeling of annoyance that the curious childhood link between Damia and Larak gave him the edge in sensing Damia's return. He turned his mind to the debate, as decision and strategy were settled in the moment before Damia's capsule landed back on Auriga.

"Larak. I thought I felt you near," she cried happily as she saw her brother, the picture of casual relaxation, perched on the edge of the console.

"Just thought? You usually know," he said, crowing with boyish delight. "This alien sure has got you wrapped up and tied like a present. See how the mighty have fallen."

When Damia flushed, Larak roared with laughter.

"I've got to meet this guy," he said.

"I've always felt that I was building experience and training for one special reason," Damia said, her eyes shining, "and now I know what it is!"

"The whole Sector will know in a moment if you don't lower your 'voice,' " Afra said, sharply, to give Larak a chance to control the shock the boy was feeling as he witnessed Damia's exultation.

Resentfully, Damia dampered her emotional outpouring.

"I suppose you arrived with an appetite like a mule," she said sourly.

Larak's face was a study in innocent hurt.

"I'm a growing boy, and while you're out courting, Afra's getting overworked, and leaner and hungrier."

Damia looked guiltily at Afra.

"You *do* look tired," she said with concern. "Let's all push over to the house and have dinner. Larak, why are you here?"

"Oh, Dad wants Afra to pinch-hit on Procyon. Two high T's are down with one of the local viruses and traffic is backing up. Say, what's this alien ship like? Crew or full automation for a void trek?"

Her hand poised over the cooking dials, Damia hesitated. She looked at her brother blankly.

"Oh, you men are all alike. Details, details!"

"Well, sure," Larak replied. "But if details like that bore you, they fascinate me. I'll ask him myself."

"You can't reach that far!"

"I planned to hop a ride with you tomorrow."

Damia hesitated, looking for assistance from Afra, who shrugged noncommittally.

"Oh, for glory's sake, Damia. This is no time to be coy," her brother said.

"I'm not being coy!" she exploded. "It's just that . . . just that . . ."

"Who're you kidding?" Larak wanted to know, letting his temper rise with hers. "You're gone on this guy, and how do you know he's even anything resembling a man?"

"His is a true mind, brilliant and powerful," she said haughtily.

"That's great for fireside chats, but no damned good in bed."

Damia reddened, half with fury and indignation, and half with sudden virginal embarrassment at her brother's accurate thrust.

"You're insufferable. If it weren't for me, we wouldn't have been warned at all."

"Warned?" Afra leapt on the choice of word. Perhaps she was not as completely bedazzled as they'd thought.

"Of this momentous meeting," she went on, oblivious to the implication. "You've touched him, Afra. Don't you agree?"

"That it's a brilliant mind? Yes," and Afra nodded judiciously.

Damia caught his sour undertone. "Oh, you . . . you're jealous, that's all." And then she frowned, looking at Afra with sudden suspicion.

"Hey, you're letting my dinner burn," Larak said, pointing.

"And you say that women gossip," Damia exclaimed, quickly lifting two pans from the heat. "It's a mercy nothing *is* burned."

They ate in strained silence, Larak and Afra concentrating hard to maintain a convincing surface of thought. They hardly needed to because Damia went off into her own private reverie, ignoring them completely.

"You may be infatuated with this Sodan," Larak said, "but it doesn't affect your cooking. Doesn't even taste scorched."

Too much a woman not to be pleased by even a brother's praise, Damia relaxed.

"He isn't an advance scout for a second invasion force, I gather," Larak addressed Afra.

"No. In the very brief touch I had," Afra replied quickly, "he's been traveling much longer than twenty years."

Larak whistled appreciatively, just as if he didn't know this already.

"Did you take a look around at the details my sweet sister is uninterested in?" he asked.

"No. There were no obvious visual images and I was only concerned with recognition."

"He has eyes," Damia replied loyally. "We've discussed the concept of sight. You must take into consideration that he is also the controller of the ship, and the drain on his energies reaching me and managing his crew and ship must be enormous. It certainly is on me."

"Yeah. You need your beauty sleep—bad," said Larak.

"I'd like to see you do half as well."

"Children! Cut it out!" Afra intervened authoritatively.

Larak and Damia glared at each other, but the long habit of obeying Afra held.

"Both of you, get to bed," he added. "Snarling at each other in the worst example of sibling rivalry I've seen since you returned from Isthia's an opinionated ten-year-old. Makes me wonder how your father dared put you in as Aurigan Prime."

"If there's anything that annoys me more than Larak acting fraternal, it's you, Afra, making like the older generation." She spoke coolly, but her flare of temper had subsided.

Afra shrugged, relieved that his diversion had worked before Larak inadvertently showed Damia why he was probing these particular areas.

"At least, this generation's representative has sense enough to go to bed when he's out on his feet," he muttered. As he passed Larak, the boy winked.

The next morning at breakfast, no one looked as if he had slept well. Afra kept a surface rumble going in his mind to mask both tension and anxiety. Larak delivered a running monologue on his son. Damia was also closely shielding. When they reached the Tower, Damia took the most cursory glance at Station business, and said "I'll take you out now, Larak."

"Fine. Dad wants Afra back at Callisto tonight."

Damia hesitated. "Afra had better come along, then, for a second look around." She looked challengingly at Afra, who shrugged.

This was, however, unexpected luck. Afra had thought he might have to follow Larak and Damia surreptitiously. He switched the boosters up to the top, and signaled Damia and Larak to get into their capsules. While they did so, he called Jeff and the Rowan to stand by, then settled into his own shell, reassured by their sustaining presence in his mind.

Is there any possible chance we're wrong about Sodan's intentions, or the depth of Damia's emotional commitment? pleaded the Rowan.

Less and less, Afra told her, grimly. *We'll know soon for certain. Larak needled her last night. She'll have to check to make sure he's wrong.*

Then he touched Damia and Larak, and all three went the mere half-light further to the ship and Sodan.

You have rested well and are strong today, was the cool greeting after an instant's welcoming flash.

Damia instinctively covered against the discovery of her co-riders, but the greeting stuck in her mind. There was the hint that Sodan did not wish her so strong, and yet a tinge of relief colored that fleck of thought.

You come nearer to physical contact with us every day, she began.

Us? Sodan queried.

My planet, my people . . . me.

I'm only interested in you, he replied.

46

But my people will be interested in you, she parried unable to censor from Afra and Larak the pleasure she felt in his compliment.

There are many people on your planets? he asked.

Planet.

At least, Afra concluded, she remembered to be politically discreet.

Doesn't your sun have several life-supporting satellites?

That is why I must know more about your physical requirements. Damia replied smoothly. *After all, my home world may not have the proper atmosphere . . .*

My physical wants are attended to, Sodan replied coldly, with a slight emphasis on the second word.

It was the Rowan who caught the infinitesimal break in his shielding, and simultaneously all four minds stabbed at the area to lay it bare. Sodan, torn by this powerful invasion, lashed back in self-defense with a vicious blow at Damia, whom he thought perpetrated the attack.

No, no! Not I, Sodan, she screamed. *Larak, what are you doing?*

Afra struggled frantically to become the focus of the other minds, only to find himself caught in Larak's mind with the Rowan and Jeff, as the curious bond between brother and sister snapped into effect.

He must be destroyed before he can destroy you, Damia, the Larak-focus said, tinging its inexorable decision with the regret it felt.

No! I love him. His mind is so brilliant, cried Damia, pitting her own strength against her peers to defend her lover. The Larak-focus staggered back, unable to prosecute and attack against such a combination.

Damia, he is only a mind!

Stunned, Damia hestitated, and the Larak-focus plunged forward again, battering against the shielded Sodan.

Only mind? She gasped, begging Sodan to deny it.

Why no vision? Why no sound? He is only a brain, devoid of all except remembered emotion. He is bound here to destroy. Feel the heavy stuff in the ship? Is that customary for a peaceful scouting expedition?

You're against me, against me. No one wants me to be happy, cried Damia, suddenly aware, terribly aware of her loving blindness. *He loves me. I love him.*

If he has nothing to hide, he will let you see, the Larak-focus continued implacably.

Let me see you, Sodan. Damia was pleading, desperately, hopefully.

For what seemed an eternity, Sodan hesitated.

If I could, I would, he said softly and with honest regret.

Like a vengeful sword, her mind, freed from the infatuation Sodan had artfully fostered, gathered and sprang with the others to destroy the aggressor. For Damia now understood the purpose behind Sodan's impersonality. The battle was waged in the tremendous space between two heartbeats. Sodan, his mind fortified by the nuclear power of his ship, was stronger than their conservative estimates. And almost negligently, he held the Larak-focus at bay, his mind laughing at what he considered their puny efforts.

Then Damia's pressure increased as she stripped away the veil of her romantic illusions to align herself with the Larak-focus to defend her Sector. Sodan called for more power within himself. The scorching blaze that fed through Damia's growing catalystic mind flashed through and stripped him bare, lashing beyond to trigger the atoms of the ship into instability. Involuntarily, and for a microsecond, Sodan's past flickered.

Once, generations ago, embodied, he had breathed an alien air, walked an alien road; until his brain had been chosen to undertake the incredible enterprise of crossing the galactic rift.

In my fashion have I loved you, he cried to Damia as he felt her reach the fuel mass. *But you never loved me,* he added with intense surprise as her mind, vulnerable in the instant of that massive thrust, was open to him. *And he shall not have you either!*

With his last strength, Sodan sent out one final jealous mental blast just as the ship exploded.

Frantically, even as she felt herself blacking out from the tremendous drain on her resources, Damia tried to deflect that blow.

As a kingpin flattens a row of its fellows, so Sodan's blast, striking through the Larak-focus, caused a wave of mental agony to roll backward to Auriga where Station personnel grabbed at their skulls in anguish, to Earth and Callisto where T-ratings cringed in pain, and on to Deneb and even Altair. Horrified crews found Jeffrey Raven and the Rowan unconscious in their Tower couches. Jeran, head aching, was hastily summoned, for FT & T command devolved to him in the emergency. Jeran took time out to assure himself that with sufficient rest his parents would recover, then he informed the Federated World Government of the event. He was requested to proceed with the defensive fleet to Auriga.

Isthia appeared at Earth Headquarters at his urgent bidding and, with her help, he was able to extract gently from Jeff's taxed mind the position of the three personal shells.

As they approached the orbit, they could "hear" nothing.

It is possible, Isthia said hopefully as they could find no discernible aura, *that all three have gone into very deep shock. The power in Damia's final thrust!*

Damia cannot be dead, Jeran tried to convince himself. *Sodan may have been powerful, but is there a T-rating in the galaxy who didn't feel her hit him? We cannot lose her!* He had already resigned himself to other losses.

"Ah!" Isthia gave a sharp gasp. *I have them.*

Jeran reached with her, signaling the flagship's T-3 to assist.

"She's alive," he cried in relief. *I thought I felt them all die.*

"Afra lives, too, but he's very faint. Larak . . ." and Isthia's voice faded. *Why did the focus have to snap through him?*

They brought Afra's capsule in first, and Jeran, who was at the head as the shell was opened, pressed fearful hands against the man's temples. Afra's body was drawn up in the fetal position of complete withdrawal.

"He's badly hurt, Isthia. God, will we save him? *Should* we, if he'll be psionically numb for the rest of his life?"

Isthia moved his hands aside, and applied her own, her touch naturally more delicate than Jeran's.

"I can't tell more than that he wants to die. The spark of life is very faint." She gave rapid mental orders to the medics standing by so that, within seconds, Afra's body was receiving emergency injections to stimulate the failing life signs.

Divorce your emotions Jeran, Isthia told him sharply. *Help me reach him. He wants to die. We must pull him back.*

Jeran shook himself and, holding his breath, placed his hands above Isthia's on Afra's head.

Together they probed, ignoring the mental anguish they experienced at having to touch so torn a mind. Uppermost was the thought that both Larak and Afra had shared: Sodan striking at them and Damia, exhausted, trying to block it.

He'll kill her, he'll kill her, was the repeated cry of terror, a curious melding of both Larak and Afra, swirling in the pain of Afra's mind. *No, Damia. Don't try. I waited too long. No, Damia.* Then the enigmatic sequence was repeated.

Damia lives, Damia lives, Jeran and Isthia told him.

Damia lives, damia lives damia lives, whispered the essence of Afra.

Isthia caught Jeran's eyes with surprised confusion. Hopeful now, they reinforced the will to live.

Afra, Damia lives. She rests. She waits for you, Isthia murmured soothingly.

Sleep, Afra, rest. Damia lives, Jeran urged.

Damia lives? Damia lives!

With a shudder, Afra's body untwisted from the fetal curl. For one terrifying moment, he was still. Gasping, Isthia dipped way down into the suddenly tranquil mind only to be reassured that Afra had merely slipped into deep sleep.

"He's very badly hurt, Jeran," Isthia admitted sadly as they watched the medics wheel Afra away to a tightly shielded room.

They opened Damia's capsule together. She lay on her side, looking very young, but there were marks that showed the effects of that meeting of minds. She had bitten through her underlip and a trickle of blood

50

ran in a scarlet line across her cheek. Her fingernails had cut into her palms when she had clenched her fists and her face was streaked with tears.

With infinite compassion, Isthia turned the girl onto her back and laid both her hands lightly on Damia's temples.

I can't reach them. I can't get there in time. I hurt. I've got to try. I hurt. Oh, will I lose them both? Isthia could hear the words faintly, deep in the tired mind.

With a sigh of relief, Isthia straightened.

Is she badly burned? Jeran asked impatiently, having waited outside Isthia's contact but aware it had been made.

Not burned but deeply hurt on several levels. Damia's been cut down to size, Isthia remarked ruefully, *the terrible way only the very bright and confident are. She'll never forget that she underestimated Sodan's potential because she became infatuated with him.*

For all of that, if she hadn't touched him first, where would we be with such a menace zeroing from space?

Isthia waved that aside as of incidental importance.

That won't matter to Damia, Jeran. Her initial lapse of judgment caused Larak's death and has seriously injured Afra.

Merciful God, Isthia, once the attack on Sodan began, nothing could have saved Larak, no matter where he was in the focus-mind. Death is far kinder than being burned out. She's not to blame.

Isthia shook her head sadly. *No, she isn't to blame and I hope it never occurs to her that, in the crisis, instinct overrode reason and it was Afra she struggled to save.*

Afra? What in hell? asked Jeran before he followed Isthia's thought to its source. *So that's why Sodan struck to kill. He was after Afra.*

He stepped back as Isthia signaled to the medics to administer deep-sleep drugs and intravenous nourishment to Damia.

With great reluctance they turned to Larak's silent shell. Because they had to, they opened it and saw with some little relief that there was no mark of his passing on the young face. A curiously surprised smile lingered on his lips.

Isthia turned away in tears and Jeran, too numb to display his own sorrow, put his arm around her to lead her away.

"Sir," the captain of the ship said respectfully when they entered the control room, "we have the location of the alien ship debris. Permission to recover fragments?"

"Permission granted. Isthia and I will return to the Tower."

"Very good, sir," the captain said, and stiffened to a rigid attention. The unashamed tears in his eyes and his very crisp salute expressed wordlessly his pride, his sympathy, and his sorrow.

Struggling against a will determined to keep her asleep, Damia fought her way to semi-consciousness.

"I can't keep her under. She's resisting," a remote voice called to someone.

As distant as the sound was, like a far echo in a subterranean cavern, each syllable fell like a hammer on her exposed nerves. Sobbing, Damia struggled for consciousness, sanity, and a release from her agony. She couldn't seem to trigger the reflexes that would divert pain, and an effort to call Afra to help her met with not only the resistance of increased agony but a vast blankness. Her mind was as stiff as iron, holding each thought firmly to it as though magnetized.

"Damia, do not reach. Do not use your mind," a voice said in her ear. The sound was like a blessing and the reassurance it gave her wavering sanity was reinforced by the touch of . . . Isthia's hands on hers.

Damia focused her eyes on the woman's face and clutched Isthia's hands to her temples in an unconscious plea for relief of pain.

"What happened? Why can't I control my head?" cried Damia, tears of weakness streaming down her face.

"You overreached yourself, destroying Sodan," Isthia said.

"I can't remember," Damia groaned, blinking away the tears so she could at least see clearly.

"Every rating in FT & T does."

"Oh, my head. It's all a blank and there's something I have got to do and I can't remember what it is."

"You will, you will. But you're very tired, dear," Isthia said crooningly as she stroked her forehead with cool hands. Each caress seemed to lessen the terrible pain.

Damia felt the coolness of an injection pop into her arm.

"I'm putting you back to sleep, Damia. We're very proud of you but you must allow your mind to heal in sleep."

" 'Great nature's second course, that knits the ravelled sleeve of care.' What's knitting, Isthia? I've never known," Damia heard herself babbling with a cool scalliony taste in her throat as the drug spread.

Again, after what seemed no passage of time at all, Damia was inexorably forced to consciousness by her indefinable but relentless need.

"I can't understand it," came Isthia's voice. This time it did not reverberate across Damia's pained mind like tympany in a small room. "I gave her enough to put a city to sleep."

"She's worrying at something and probably won't rest until she's resolved it. Let's wake her up and get the agony over."

Damia forced her mind to concentrate on identifying the second voice. With a grateful smile she labelled it "Jeff." She felt her face gently slapped and, opening her eyes, saw Jeff's face swimming out of the blurred mass about her.

"Jeff," she pleaded, not because he had slapped her but because she had to make him understand.

"Dear Damia," he said with such loving pride she almost lost the tenuous thought she tried to hold from him.

Her body strained with the effort to reach out only a few inches a mind that once had blithely coursed light-years, but she soon managed to communicate her crime.

I burned out Larak and Afra. I killed them. I linked

53

to the Larak-focus and killed them to destroy Sodan.
I saved myself and killed them.

Behind Jeff she heard Rowan's cry and Isthia's exclamation.

"No, no," Jeff said gently, shaking his head. He placed her hands on his forehead to let her feel the honesty of his denial. "In the first place, you couldn't. You don't *use* others. You sort of shift gears into high speed to make other minds work on a higher level. You drew power from the Larak-focus to destroy Sodan, yes. But the killing thrust was yours, Damia; you were the only one capable of doing it. And every T-rating in the Federated Worlds will vouch for that. Your touch, my dear, is indescribable. Further, without you to throw *us* into high gear, Sodan could have destroyed every Prime in FT & T."

Damia heard an approving, admiring murmur from Rowan.

"Will my touch come back? I can't feel anything," and in spite of her control Damia's chin quivered and she started to sob with fear.

"Of course it'll come back, dear," said the Rowan, who elbowed Jeff aside to kneel by her daughter and stroke her hair tenderly.

"You'd better go knit some more sleeves of ravelled care," Isthia suggested with therapeutic asperity. "You knit like this," and Isthia inserted a visual demonstration of the technique of knitting into Damia's mind. It was an adroit change of subject, but Damia, with a flash return of perception, saw the three were evading her.

"I must be told what has happened," she demanded imperiously. A wisp of memory nagged at her and she caught it. "I remember. Sodan made one last thrust." She closed her eyes against that recall, remembering too, that she had tried to intercept it and, "Larak's dead," she said in a flat voice. "And Afra. I couldn't shield in time."

"Afra lives," the Rowan said.

"But Larak? Why Larak?" Damia demanded, desperately striving to touch what she felt they must still be hiding from her.

"Larak was the focus," Rowan said softly, knowing,

54

too, that Damia would never absolve herself of her brother's death. "Afra was supposed to be the focus, being the experienced mind, but the old bond between you and Larak snapped into effect. You tried to shield Larak, but his mind was too unskilled to draw help from you. Jeff and I felt it because we were part of the focus, too, and we tried to help divert it. We could cushion only Afra in time. Sodan's was a very powerful mind."

Damia looked from her mother to her father and knew that that much was true. But another reservation hovered in their eyes. . .

"You're still hiding something," she insisted, fighting with exhaustion. "Where's Afra?"

"Okay, skeptic," Jeff said, lifting her into his arms. "Though why his snores haven't kept you awake, I don't know."

He carried her down the hall. Pausing at an open door, he swung her around so she could see into the room. A night light hung over the bed, illuminating Afra's quiet face, deeply lined with fatigue and pain. Denying even the physical evidence, Damia reached out, touching just enough for reassurance the pained mental rumble that meant Afra still inhabited his body.

"Damia, don't do that again," Jeff said, carrying her back to her room.

"I won't but I had to," she replied, her head ballooning with agony.

"And we'll see you don't again until you're well enough. Out you go, missy," and she slid into blackness.

An insistent whisper nibbled at the corners of her awareness and roused Damia from restoring sleep. Cringing in anticipation of the return of pain, she was mildly surprised to feel only the faintest discomfort. Experimentally, Damia pushed a depressant on the ache and that, too, disappeared. Unutterably pleased by her success, she sat up in bed. It was night and she was in her family's home. She stretched until a cramp caught her in the side.

Heavens, hasn't anyone moved me in months? she asked herself, noting that her mental tone was firm. She lay back in bed, deliberating. *Poor Damia,* she said in a self-derisive tone, *ever since that encounter with that dreadful mind-alien, she's been nothing but a T-4, T-9? T-3?* Damia tried out the different grades for size and then discarded them all, along with her histrionics.

You idiot, you'll never know till you try.

Tentatively, without apparent effort, she reached out and counted the pulses of three . . . no four, sleepers. Afra's was the faint one. But, Damia realized in calm triumph, it *was* there. Which brought her face to face with the second fact.

She slid from her bed to stand by the window. Beyond the lawn of evergrass, beyond the little lake, to the copse of evergreens her glance traveled. And stopped. Instinct told her that Larak was buried there and the thought of Larak buried and his touch forever gone broke her. She wept in loneliness, biting her knuckles and pressing her arms tightly into her breasts to muffle the sound of her mourning.

Out of the night, out of the stillness, the whisper tugged at her again. She stifled her tears to listen, trying to identify that sliver of sound. It faded before she caught it.

Resolutely now, she laid her sorrow gently in her deepest soul, a part of her but apart forever. No matter what Jeff and Rowan said, she had caused Larak's death and maimed Afra. Had she been less preoccupied, less self-centered, she would not have been so dazzled by the fancy that Sodan was her Prince Charming, her knight in cylindrical armor.

Such a pitiful thing she was: a spoiled, rotten-hearted child, demanding a new toy to dispel boredom when all the time . . .

The whisper again, fainter, surer. With a startled cry of joy, Damia whirled from her room, running on light feet down the hall. Catching at the door frame to brake her headlong flight, she hesitated on the threshold of Afra's room.

She caught her breath as she realized that Afra was sitting up. He was looking at her with a smile of disbelief on his face.

"*You've* been calling me," she whispered, half-questioning, half-stating.

"In a lame-brained way," he replied. "I can't seem to reach beyond the edge of the bed."

"Don't try. It hurts," she said quickly, stepping into the room to pause shyly at the foot of the bed.

Afra grimaced, rubbing his forehead. "I know it hurts but I can't seem to find any balance in my skull," he confessed, his voice uneven, worried.

"May I?" she asked formally, unexpectedly timid with him.

Closing his eyes, Afra nodded.

Sitting down cautiously, Damia lightly laid her fingertips to his temples, and touched his mind as delicately as she knew how. Afra stiffened with pain and Damia quickly established a block, spreading it over the damaged edges. Resolutely, regardless of the cost to her own recent recovery, she drew away the pain, laying in the tender areas a healing mental anesthesia. Jealousy, she noticed someone else had been doing the same thing.

Isthia . . . has . . . a . . . delicate . . . touch . . . too. He sent the thought carefully, slowly.

"Oh, Afra," Damia cried for the agony the simple thought cost him. "You *aren't* burned out. You *won't* be numb. I won't let you be. Together we can be just as powerful as ever."

Afra leaned forward, his face close to hers, his yellow eyes blazing.

"Together, Damia?" he asked in a low intense voice as he searched her face.

Her fingers plucking shyly and nervously at his blanket, Damia could not look away from an Afra who had altered disturbingly. Damia tried to comprehend the startling change. Unable to resort to a mental touch, she saw Afra for the first time with only physical sight. And he was suddenly a very different man. A man! That was it. He was so excessively masculine.

How could she have blundered around so, looking for a *mind* that was superior to hers, completely overlooking the fact that a woman's most important function in life begins with physical domination?

"Damia—speechless?" Afra teased her, his voice tender.

She nodded violently as she felt his warm fingers

closing around her nervous hand. Immediately she experienced a profoundly sensual empathy.

"Why did you wait so long, knowing that I needed you?" The words burst from her.

With a low triumphant laugh, Afra pulled her into his arms, cradling her body against his and settling her head in the crook of his arm.

"Familiarity breeds contempt?" he asked, mocking her gently with her own words.

"And how could you . . . a T-3 . . . manage to mask . . ." she went on, growing indignant.

"Familiarity also bred certain skills."

"But you were always so aloof and reserved. And Mother . . ."

"Your mother was no more for me than Sodan was for you," Afra interrupted her, his eyes stern as she stared up at him, shaken by his harsh voice.

His expression altered again, his arms tightened convulsively as he bent his head and kissed her with an urgent, lusty eagerness.

"Sodan may have loved you, in his fashion, Damia," Afra's voice said in her ear, "but mine will be far more satisfying for you."

Trembling and ready, Damia opened her mind to Afra without a single reservation. Their lips met again as Afra held her tightly in what would shortly be far more than a mere meeting of minds.

"Daughter" and "Dull Drums" were specifically slanted for the young adult market, but the original yarn concerning Nora Fenn and the futuristic university system is far, far out.

I had submitted a story called "A Pocket to Mend" at the Pennsylvania Milford SF Writers' Conference, chaired by Damon Knight and Kate Wilhelm. It was savaged by the assembled writers as sentimental, impossible, and stupid! And after I had the opportunity to try to explain my intentions, I was told that I had done all the wrong things for all the wrong reasons. They suggested I go home and really think the basic idea through. From the original premise I retained the term "Wendy," meaning a girl with tolerance and understanding (in my story, training), who acts as housemother to and bears the children of men with homosexual proclivities.

I had enough homosexual male friends—even before the Gay Liberation developed—who were bitter that they could not adopt children because of their sexual preferences. I have never felt capable of writing a full-length novel about this situation as it should be written. So only these three stories exist, and they involve a futuristic society in which *all* citizens may have a "legal" child.

"Changeling" has never before been published. This story deals with one aspect of the "Wendy" theme. I wrote it originally in response to Harlan Ellison's request for a story for his *Dangerous Visions* anthology. Frankly, I think this one has a far more dangerous vision than "The Bones Do Lie," the story Harlan finally accepted.

Daughter

THE MOMENT HER FATHER BEGAN TO YELL AT her twin brother Nick, Nora Fenn edged toward the door of the Complex office. George Fenn's anger always seemed to expand in direct proportion to the number of witnesses. She knew it humiliated Nick to be harangued in front of anyone, and this time there was absolutely nothing she could say in Nick's defense. Why hadn't he waited till she got back from school and could help him program the Planter?

"Fifty acres clearly marked corn," and Father viciously stabbed a thick forefinger at the corner of the room dominated by the scale model of the farm. He'd spent hours last winter rearranging the movable field units. In fact, Nora thought he displayed a lot more concern for the proper allocation of crops than he did for his two children. He certainly didn't berate the corn when the ears weren't plump or turned to ergot.

"And you," roared Father, suddenly clamping his hands tightly to his sides, as if he were afraid of the damage they'd do if he didn't, "*you* plant turnips. What kind of programmer are you, Nicholas? A simple chore even your sister could do!"

Nora flinched at that. If Father ever found out that it was she, not Nick, who did the most complex programming . . . She eased past the county maps, careful not to rustle the thin sheets of plastic overlay that Father had marked with crop, irrigation, and fertilizing patterns. The office was not small. One wall, of course, was the computer console and storage banks, then the window that looked out onto the big yard of the Complex, the three-foot-square relief model of the Fenn Farmlands on its stand. But two angry Fenns would diminish a Bargaining Hall.

Nora was struck by a resemblance between father and son, which she'd not really appreciated before. Not only were both men holding their arms stiffly against their sides, but their jaws were set at the same obstinate angle and each held one shoulder slightly higher than the other.

"I'm going to see that so-called Guidance Counselor of yours tomorrow and find out what kind of abortive computer courses you've been given. I thought I'd made it plain what electives you were to take."

"I get the course I'm able to absorb . . ."

Oh, please, Nick, breathed Nora, don't argue with him. The Educational Advancements will be posted in a day, two at the most, and then there's nothing he can do to alter the decision.

"Fenns are landsmen," Father shouted. "Born to the land, bred by the land!"

The dictum reverberated through the room, and Nora used the noise to mask the slipping sound of the office door. She was out in the narrow passageway before Father realized that he'd lost part of his audience. She half ran to the outer door, the spongyfiber flooring masking the sounds of her booted feet. When she was safely outside the rambling trilevel habitation, she breathed with relief. She'd better finish her own after-school chores. Now that Father'd got started on Nick, he'd be finding fault elsewhere. Since there weren't any apprentice landsmen on the Fenn Farm Complex right now, "elsewhere" could only be Nora. Mother never came in for Father's criticism, because everything she did in her quiet unspectacular way was perfectly done. Nora sighed. It wasn't fair to be so good at everything. When her children complained Mary Fenn would laugh and remark that practice made perfect. But Mother always had some bit of praise, or a hug or a kiss to hearten you when she knew you'd *tried*. Father . . . if Father would only say something encouraging to Nick . . .

Nora stayed to the left of the low, rambling, living quarters, out of the view afforded by the office window. She glanced across the huge plasti-cobbled yard which she had just finished hosing down. Yes, she had washed down the bay doors of the enormous barn that housed the Complex's Seeder, Plowboy, and Harvester. And done a thorough job of cleaning the tracks on which the heavy equipment was shunted out of the yard and onto the various rails leading to the arable tracts.

Turnips! If only Nick had blown the job with a high-priority vegetable, like carrots or beets. But turnips? They were nothing but subsistence-level food. Father cannily complied with Farm Directives and still managed to plant most of the Fenn lands to creditable crops like corn and beets. Fifty more acres of turnips this year might mean Nick would have that much less free credit at the university.

Nora sighed. When Educational Advancements were posted, the suspense would be over, the pressure off the graduating students. Who'd go on to Applied or Academic in her class, she wondered? But there was no way of finding out short of stealing Counselor Fremmeng's wrist recorder. You only got pass/fail decisions in elementary grades. An arbitrary percentile evaluation defeated the purpose of modern educational methods. Achievement must be measured by individual endeavor, not mean averages or sliding curves. Young citizens were taught to know that knowledge was required of contributing citizens. Computer-assisted drill constantly checked on comprehension of concept and use of basic skills. Educational Advancement, either Applied or Academic, depended as much on demonstrated diligence as inherent ability. Consequently, the slow student had every bit as much chance, and just as much right to education as the quick learner.

Well, Nora told herself briskly, it doesn't contribute anything to society to stand here daydreaming. You'll know in a day or two. In the meantime . . .

Nora went through the grape arbor toward the skimmer shed, near the far left compound wall. She had just turned in to the building when she felt the

62

reverberation of rapid thudding through the linked plasti-cobbles. Then Nick came pounding around the side of the building.

"Nora, lend me your skimmer?" he begged, un-racking it as he spoke. "Mine's still drying out from Saturday's irrigating."

"But, Nick . . . Father . . ."

Nick's face darkened the way Father's did when he met resistance.

"Don't give me any static, Nor. I gotta change state . . ."

"Oh, Nick, *why* didn't you wait until I could've checked you out?"

Nick set his jaw, his eyes blinking rapidly.

"You had to see Fremmeng, remember? And when I got home, the orders were waiting and I couldn't. I'm due over at Felicity's *now*." Nick turned up the pressure gauge, filling the tanks of the skim-mer. "Orders. Orders. That's all I ever get from him. That and 'Fenns are crop farmers,'" Nick snorted. "He thinks he can program kids like a computer. Well, I'm *not* a crop farmer. It switches me off. Off!"

"Nick, please. Keep unity. Once you get to the university, *you* choose the courses you want. He can't go against Educational Advancement. And if he tries, you can always claim sanctuary against parental co-ercion. There isn't anyone in the Sector who wouldn't support your claim . . ."

Nick was staring at her incredulously, but sud-denly the anger drained out of his face and was re-placed by an exaggerated expression of tolerant forbearance.

"Claim sanctuary? I haven't lost all sense of unity, Nora," he told her sternly. "Hey, what did Frem-meng want *you* for?"

"Me? Oh, he had the absolutely more irrelevant questions! About how you and I get along, my opin-ions on family harmony and social contributions, and pairing off."

Nick regarded her with an intent, impersonal stare.

"He did, huh? Look, Nor," and her brother's mood changed state completely, "I need to see Felicity. I gotta blow out of *here!*"

Nora grabbed his arm as he inflated the skimmer. "Nick, what *did* you say to Father?"

Nick gave her a sour look now. "I told him he'd better hold off making so many big plans for me to be the Fenn Complex's Master Ruralist, until he sees the Educational Advancements."

"Nick, if you don't get Advancement, Father will just . . . just . . ."

"Abort and sulk!" Nick finished for her. "No, I'll get Advancement, all right. On my terms! There's not a blasted thing wrong with Applied. It's Father who tried programming the university for me. But I've had different plans." Nick's look turned as hard as Father's could when he'd lost crops.

"What do you mean, Nick? What have you been doing?" Nora was suddenly scared. What had Father driven Nick to do?

"Nora, sweetie, Old Bates at the Everett Complex is about due for retirement. Felicity Everett and I want to pair off as soon as the E.A.'s have been posted. And it's just possible that Landsman Everett would opt for me as assistant." Nick's expression altered again, this time to enthusiasm, and Nora felt relief at the change.

"Oh, he would, Nick. You know what he said about your term paper on ovine gene manipulation." Then Nora caught the significance of his plan.

"Yes, indeedy, sister mine. Nick can cut a program on his own, without your help or Father's."

She was so astonished at the calculation in his smile that he was able to loosen her fingers from the handlebars. He was off on the skimmer at a high blow before she could stop him.

"Nick . . ."

"Give my love to our foul-feathered friends!" he called over his shoulder cheerfully, and launched the skimmer straight across the meadows toward the Everetts' Herd Complex.

Resolutely, Nora made for the distant poultry house on foot. Father proclaimed that chickens and turkeys were a woman's business. She hated tending them and usually swapped the chore with Nick. Nick found poultry a trifle more engrossing than the tedious crop programming.

Why couldn't Nick focus a little more attention on what he was doing instead of expending all his energies thwarting Father? Irritably, she scuffed at a vagrant pebble in the track that led straight from the low-rambling Farm Complex, set in the fold of the soft hills, toward the Poultry house. She could see the glitter of the round roof as she topped the next rise.

Educational Advancement! She so hoped that she'd qualify . . . at least for Applied Advancement. That would prove to Father she wasn't all that stupid, even if she was a girl. Maybe, if she could make Journeyman Class Computer . . . she really felt that she understood mathematics and symbolic logic. If she got Journeyman, Father mightn't be so disappointed when he finally realized that Nick was absolutely set against crop farming. While Father might feel that women were being educated far beyond society's profit, no contributing citizen could argue with the Advancement Board's decision. For the board was impartial, having the best interests of society *and* the individual at heart. Father might scoff at the premise that everyone had the constitutional right to shelter, food, clothing, *and* education as long as he maintained a class average. But then, Father disparaged a system that rewarded the diligent student with credit bonuses for something as intangible as academic excellence.

"That doesn't feed anyone, make anything, buy or sell anything," he'd say when he'd started on that tangent. There was no use explaining to such a pragmatist.

If Nora could get certified in computer logistics and was able to handle the Complex's Master Ruralist, then surely he'd be proud of her. He wouldn't mind that one of his children was a girl, not the second boy *he'd* printed into the Propagation Registration.

Father never let Nora, or her mother, forget that he had not computed twins, nor mixed sexes. *He'd* opted for both legal progeny to be male. Since early

65

sex education in school, Nora had wondered how her mother had managed not only a multiple birth but a split in sexes without Father's knowledge. For one thing, multiple births had been uncommon for the last hundred years, since Population Control had been initiated. Most duly registered couples opted for one of each sex, well spaced. Of course, George Fenn would complain about PC, too. Or rather, the provision which permitted only exceptional couples to have one or two more children above the legal number—in return for extraordinary contributions to society.

"They put the emphasis on the wrong genetic factors," Father would argue bitterly whenever the subject came up. "If you breed for brain, the species weakens physically, flaws develop." He'd always flex his huge biceps then, show off his two-meter-tall, one-hundred-kilo frame in support of his argument. He'd been disappointed, too, when Nick, scarcely an undersized man, stopped slightly short of two meters in height. Father'd glower at Nora, as if her slender body had robbed her twin of extra centimeters.

How had Mary Fenn, a woman of muted qualities, coped so long and amiably with her husband? Her quiet, uncritical voice was seldom raised. She knew when you were upset, though, or sick, and her capable hands were sure and soft. If anyone deserved Maternity Surplus, it was Mother. She was so good! And she'd managed to remain completely in control of herself, a presence unperturbed by her husband's tirades and intemperate attitudes, efficiently dealing with each season and its exigencies.

Of course, it was no wonder that Mother was quiet. Father was such a dominating person. He could shout down an entire Rural Sector Meeting.

"A fine landsman," Nora heard her father called. "But don't cross him," she'd heard whispered. "He'll try to program things his way, come hell or high water. He knows the land, though," was the grudging summation.

"Knows the land, but not humans," Nora muttered under her breath. "Not his children. Certainly he doesn't know what his son really wants."

Maybe once Nick gets away to university, harmony will be restored between father and son. Nick ought to have a stronger desire to maintain family unity . . .

Crop farming wasn't all that bad, Nora thought. By punching the right buttons, you could now mow a thousand-acre field, as Nora had done as a preteen, when the apprentices let her. You could winnow and cull with a vacuum attachment; grade, bag, clean your field far more efficiently than the most careful ancient gleaners. You could program your Plowboy to fertilize at five levels as the seed was planted. One Complex with two families or a couple of responsible apprentices could efficiently farm an old-time county-sized spread and still turn a luxury credit. Not to mention having fresh and ready supplies of any edible and some of those luxuries above the subsistence level that the City Complexes craved.

Now Nora could hear the pitiful muted honking of the geese in the Poultry House. She winced. There were certain aspects of farming that could not be completely automated. You can't tape a broody hen, and you can't computerize the services of a rooster. Cocks' crows still heralded sunrise over the fields, whether the clarion summons issued from a wooden slated crate or the sleek multipentangle that housed the poultry raised by the Fenn Complex. Eggs laid by hens in Nora's charge would be powdered and eventually whipped to edibility on the Jupiter station, or be flash-frozen to provide sustenance when the first colony ship set forth as it was rumored to do in the next decade. Turkeys from this Complex regularly made the one-way trip to the Moon bases for Winter Solstice celebrations, call them Saturnalias or Santa Claus if you would.

She entered the poultry pentangle through the access tunnel which led straight to the computer core that handled all watering, feeding, cleaning, egg collection, and slaughter operations. The Fenn Complex did not sell to dietary groups, so the market preparations were the standard ones.

She checked the tapes on the Leghorn fifth, replenished the grit supply, and tapped out a reorder sequence. She flushed out all the pen floors and re-freshed the water. Then she checked the mean weight of the tom turkeys, growing from scrawny, long-legged adolescence to plump-breasted maturity. A trifle more sand for digestion, a richer mash for firmer meats, and a little less of the growth hormones. Concentrated goodness, not size for size's sake anymore.

The geese were fattening, too, on their fixed perches. Goose livers on the rod. Nora hated the calculated cruelty that brought in credit margin for the Fenn Complex. Stuff the poor helpless fowl, engorge their livers for the delectation of the gourmet. The geese lived sheltered, circumscribed lives, which was not living at all, for they couldn't see out of their own quarters. Nothing distracted them from their purpose in life—death from enlarged livers. Nora was distracted from her chores by their shrill honking. She forced herself to read the gauges. Yes, the upper group were ready for market. Even their plaint registered the truth of their self-destruction. They'd been bred for one purpose. It was their time to fulfill it. She coldly dialed for a quotation on the price of geese and goose liver at the Central Farm Exchange. The European price printed out at a respectable high. She routed the information to the Farm's main console. It might just sweeten Father's cantankerous mood to realize a quick credit from the sale.

Nora took a detour on the way back, across the one-hundred-acre field. The willows her great-grandfather had planted the day the Farm Reforms were passed were tipped with raw yellow. Spring was an Earth-moment away. Soon the golden limbs would sprout their green filaments, to drape and float them on the irrigation ditch that watered their thirsty feet. Would *her* great-grandchildren admire the willows in their turn? The whimsy irritated her.

She walked faster, away from what the willows stood for. She didn't really have to be back at the Complex until mealtime, an hour or so away. Father always programmed too much time for her to tend the poultry house, which was an unflattering assessment of her ability but usually gave her more time for something she'd wanted to do that Father might not consider contributory. If only *once* he'd look at her as if she weren't something printed out by mistake. How in the name of little printed circuits *had* Mother dared to have twins?

Nora used her spare time to pick cress at the sluice gate beds. It was a soothing occupation and contributed to dinner's salad. When she finally got back to the house, she glanced into the office. The printout slot was clear, so Father had seen her report. She'd simply have to wait to find out if he'd acted on the data. The main console was keyed to his code only.

She heard the meal chime from the kitchen area and quickly brought the cress to her mother, who was taking roast lamb out of the oven. Did Mother know about Nick's quarrel? Lamb was her father's favorite protein.

"Oh, cress! That was a considerate thought, Nora. We'll put a few sprigs on the lamb platter for looks. There'll only be three of us for dinner, you know."

Nora didn't know, for surely Nick would be back from the Everett Complex; but just then Father came in, grim-faced, and sat down. Again Nora wondered just how far he had goaded Nick this afternoon. Why had she played the coward and left?

The tender lamb stuck in her throat like so much dry feed. Her stomach seemed to close up as if eating had been programmed out, but she forced herself to clear her plate. No one, in this day and age and especially at George Fenn's table, wasted real food. Once—and only once—as a child she had left real food on her plate. She'd spent the next two weeks trying to swallow common subsistence-level rations.

Conversation was never encouraged at Fenn meals, so the awkward meal dragged on. When Nora could finally excuse herself and make for the sanctuary of her room, her father stopped her.

"So, Nora, you've been doing Nicholas's programming for him, eh?" Father's voice was icy with disapproval; his eyes were specks of gray.

Nora stared back, speechless. Oh, Nick couldn't have!

"Don't gawk at me, girl. Answer!" Father's big fist

banged the table and a startled "Yes, Father," came from her.

"And how long has this . . . this deception gone on?"

Nora didn't dare look at him.

"How long?" Father repeated, his voice rising in volume and getting sharper.

"Since—since spring," she answered.

"*Which* spring?" was the acid query.

Nora swallowed hard against the sudden nauseating taste of lamb in her mouth.

"The first year of programming."

"You *dared* take over a task assigned your brother —by me? Designed to acquaint him with the problems he'll face as a landsman?"

Instinctively Nora leaned as far back in her chair, away from her father's looming body, as she could. Not even George Fenn would disrupt family harmony by striking a child, but he was so angry that it seemed to Nora he had become a terrible stranger, capable even of causing her physical harm.

"Nick couldn't seem to get the trick of it," she managed to say in her own defense. "I only helped a little. When he got jammed."

"He's a Fenn. He's got farming in his blood. Five generations of farming. You've robbed him of his heritage, of his proper contribu—"

"Oh, no, Father. Nick's always contributed. He'd do the poultry . . ." and her sentence broke off as she saw the bloated, red face of her father.

"You dared . . . *dared* exchange assignments?"

"You miss the point entirely, George," Mother interceded in her placid way. "The tasks were completed, were well done, so I cannot see why it is so wrong for Nick to have done which, and Nora what. They're both Fenns, after all. That's the core of the matter."

"Have you changed state, woman?" Father wanted to know, but astonishment had aborted his anger. "Nicholas is my son! Nora's only a girl."

"Really, George. Don't quibble. You know, I've been thinking of enlarging my contribution to society now that the children are about to advance. I'd really like to go back to the Agriculture Institute and update my credentials. Sometimes," Mother went on in the conversational way in which she was apt to deliver startling conclusions, "I think the children have studied a whole new language when I hear them discussing computer logic. Remember when I used to take an apprentice's place, George? Of course, it would be much more interesting for me if you'd diversify the Complex. I can't have any more children, of course, but if we bred lambs or calves, I'd've young things to tend again. Society does say it'll satisfy every individual's needs." She gave her husband an appealing smile. "Do try to compute that in your fall program, George. I'd appreciate it."

Looking at Mother as if she'd taken leave of her senses, Father rose and pushed back his chair. He mumbled something about checking urgent data, but stumbled out of the dining area, past the office, and out of the house.

"Mother, I'd no idea . . ."

The rest of Nora's words died in her throat because her mother's eyes were brimming with mischief and she looked about to laugh.

"I oughtn't to do that to George when he's had a big dinner. But there're more ways to kill a cat than choking him with butter—as my grandmother used to say. Although that's a shocking way to use butter —not to mention a good cat—but Grandmother was full of such dairy-oriented expressions. Hmmm. Now dairy farming might not be such a bad compromise, considering the printout quotes on milk and cheese this spring." Then she closed her lips firmly as if her own loquacity startled her as much as it did Nora. The laughter died in her eyes. "Nora?"

"Yes, Mother?"

"In this society, a person is legally permitted to develop at his own pace and follow his own aptitudes. Not even a stubborn atavist like your father has the right to inhibit another's contribution. Of course, the responsible citizen tries to maintain harmonious relations with his family unit up to that point of interference.

"You realized, I'm certain, that even if Nick has no love of crop farming, he is basically attuned to

71

rural life. I've been so grateful to you, dear, for . . . soothing matters between your father and brother." The words came out haltingly and though Mother didn't look directly at her, Nora could appreciate her difficulty. Mother had scrupulously avoided taking sides in the constant altercations between Nick and Father. She had somehow always maintained family unity. Her unexpected frankness was essentially a betrayal of that careful neutrality. "I had hoped that Nick might be a more biddable boy, able to go along with his father's ambitions. They may be old-fashioned—"

"Mother, you *know* Father is positively medieval at times." Nora regretted her flippancy when she saw the plea for understanding in her mother's eyes. "Well, he is, but that's his bit. And he does make a distinguished contribution as a landsman."

"Yes, Nora. Few men these days have your father's real love of the earth. It isn't every landsman," Mother added, her voice proud, "who runs a Complex as big as ours and makes a creditable balance."

"If only Father didn't *try* . . ."

But Mother was looking off into the middle distance, her face so troubled, her eyes so dark with worry, that Nora wanted to cry out that she really did understand. Hadn't she proved that with all she'd done to keep unity?

"You're a kind, thoughtful, considerate child, Nora," Mother said finally, smiling with unexpected tenderness. "You undoubtedly rate very high on interpersonal relationships."

"You must, too," Nora protested, glancing toward the office.

Mother gave a rueful little laugh. "I do, or I shouldn't have got on so well with your father all these years. But, right now, we both have to work together to maintain family harmony."

"You haven't had a deficiency notice on me, have you?"

"Good lands, no, child," and Mother was clearly startled at the notion. "But Nick had an interview with Counselor Fremmeng and he's reasonably certain, from the way the Counselor talked, that he is going to disappoint your father. You know that George has been positive Nick would receive Academic Advancement. And frankly, Nora, Nick not only doesn't want it, he's sure he won't get it."

"Yes, he mentioned something like that to me this afternoon after Father reamed him," Nora said sadly. "But what could Father possibly do in the face of E.A. postings except admit that he couldn't compute Nick into his own program?"

Mother gave Nora one of her long, disconcertingly candid stares.

"It's not a question, Nora, of what your Father would or would not do. It's a question of how we maintain family unity, and your father's dignity and standing in the Sector. With a little tactful and affectionate . . . handling, he can think it was all his own notion in the first place."

Nora stared at her mother with dawning respect and admiration.

"That's why you offered to update your credentials?"

Mother grinned. "Just thought I'd plant the notion. It *is* spring, you know."

"Mother, why on earth did you marry Father?" Nora asked in a rush. She might never get another chance to find out.

An unexpectedly tender expression on her mother's face made her appear younger, prettier.

"Land's sake, because he was the kind of man I wanted to marry," Mary Fenn said with a proud lift of her chin. "A man to do for, and George takes a lot of doing, you know. Keeps me on my toes. He has such tremendous vitality. I like that. He knows and loves and understands the land, and I wanted that, too. I knew that was good for me, to be close to the land, and I wanted to raise my children close to natural things. Sometimes I think there's too much dependence on technology. I'm a throwback, too, Nora, just as much as your father is with his antiquated notions of a son following in his father's footsteps on land that's been in the same family for generations." Mother looked down at her square-palmed strong-fingered hands as if they represented her inner self.

"I like to feel warm earth, to get dirty. I want to *do* with my hands, not just let them idly punch a button or two. I like growing things, young things. If I could've defied the Population Control laws, too, I'd've had a whole passel of brats to raise. As it was . . ." and her lips formed a glowing smile of love and compassion that could encompass a whole county.

"As it was," Nora said with a giggle, "you had twins in spite of Father."

"Yes," Mary Fenn chuckled, her eyes lit up with laughter, "I had twins. A boy for your father," and her face was both dutiful and mischievous, "and a girl for me."

"Well, Nick's not the son Father wanted. Mother—" and suddenly the answer was the most important thing in Nora's life. "—Mother, am I the daughter *you* wanted?"

The laughter died abruptly and Mother placed her square hands on either side of Nora's face.

"You're a good child, Nora. You never complain. You work hard and willingly. Yes, you're a good daughter."

But that wasn't the answer Nora wanted.

"But what do *you* want me to *be*?"

"Happy, Nora. I want you to be happy." Mary Fenn turned, then, to glance around the kitchen area, checking to see if all was in order. It was a dismissal, a tacit gesture not to pursue this subject further. Her mother often did that. Particularly with Father. She didn't actually evade a question, simply didn't answer it directly or fully.

"Mother, that isn't enough of an answer anymore."

Her mother turned back to her, her eyebrows raised in a polite question that turned to a frown when she'd studied her daughter's stern face.

"I only wanted a daughter, Nora, not a child in my own image, to follow in my path. Just a girl child to raise, to love, to delight in. A woman is proud to bear her son, but she rejoices in her daughter. You've given me much secret joy, Nora. I'm proud of you for many, silly little motherly reasons you'll understand when you have your own daughter. Beyond that . . ." Mother began to move away. "I believe that everyone must be allowed to determine his own life's course. In that respect I am completely modern. Do *you* dislike farm life as much as your brother, Nora?"

"No," but Nora realized as she said it that she was no longer sure. "It's not that I dislike it, Mother, it's just that I'd prefer to do something more . . ."

"More cerebral, less manual?" her mother asked teasingly.

Nora could feel the blush mounting in her cheeks. She didn't want Mother to think she felt farming wasn't a substantial contribution.

"Well," and her mother's voice was brisk again, "the Advancements will soon be posted. They'll decide the matter once and for all. In the meantime—"

"I'll be a good daughter."

"I know I can count on you," and there was a sudden worried edge to her mother's voice. "Now go. You've studying, I know. You want to achieve a good credit bonus at graduation."

Nora let her mother's gentle shove propel her toward the ramp up to the bedroom level. But she was far too disquieted to study. Her mother had never been so forthright, and yet Nora did not feel the reassurance which ought to have resulted from such frankness.

There'd been many nuances in the conversation, emotional undertones which her mother had never permitted her daughter to hear before. And so many shifts. Almost as if Mother had really been sounding her out. On what? Useless to examine emotions: they were too subjective. They weren't computable data.

Nora tapped out a request for a mathematics review, senior level, on her home-study console. She was still staring at the first problem, when the computer pinged warningly and then chattered out the answer. Nora turned off the console and sat staring at the printout.

Was she really the daughter Mary Fenn had wanted? How would she ever know? She was certainly not the second son her father had intended to sire, though she had all the capabilities he'd wanted. If Nick wouldn't crop farm the Fenn Complex, how were they going to get Father to accept a compromise?

Maybe Mother wanted her to prove to Father that she knew more about crop farming than Nick right now? No, George Fenn wanted his *son* to follow him at Fenn Complex. If not Nick, then some man, because George Fenn's atavistic temperament required him to pass land to a man, not a woman, even of his own genetic heritage.

This year's apprentices would be assigned here soon, fresh from their courses in Applied Agriculture at the Institute. Maybe she'd like one of them, pair off with him, and then the Fenn land would at least remain in partially Fenn hands for another generation. Was this what Mother had been hinting at when she mentioned Nora's rating in IPR?

No, the trick would be to get Father to agree to diversify. That way Nick, who was just as stubborn as his father, could follow his heart's desire and society would benefit all around. But, when Mother brought that notion up at mealtime, Father had rushed out of the house as if his circuits had jammed.

Nora looked disconsolately down at the console. Within the parameters of the programming, computers reacted to taped instructions, facts that could be ineradicably stored as minute bits in their memories. Only humans put no parameters on dreams and stored aspirations.

The sound of a vehicle braking to a stop broke into her thoughts. Nick had come back!

The angle of the house was such that Nora could only see the blunt anonymous end of a triwheel from her window. Nick had her skimmer. But—Nora grasped at the notion—Nick had gone to the Everetts. Maybe Landsman Everett was bringing him back. Father openly admired the breeder, said he was a sound husbandsman and made a real contribution to society.

Nora sat very still, straining to hear Nick's voice or Landsman Everett's cheerful tenor. She heard only the subdued murmur of her mother's greeting, and then Father's curt baritone. When she caught the second deep male rumble, she ceased listening and turned back to the console. She did have exams to pass, and eavesdropping did not add to family unity.

Nora usually enjoyed computer-assisted drill. It put one on the mental alert. She enjoyed the challenge of completing the drill well within the allotted time. So, despite her concerns, she was soon caught up in her studies. She finished the final level of review with only one equation wrong. Her own fault. She'd skipped a step in her hurry to beat the computer's time. She could never understand why some kids said they they were exhausted after a computer-assisted session. She always felt great.

"Nora!"

Her father's summons startled her. Had she missed his first call? He sounded angry. You never made Father call you twice.

"Coming!" Anxious not to irritate him, she ran down the ramp to the lower level, apologizing all the way. "Sorry, Father, I was concentrating on CAI review . . ." and then she saw that the visitor was Counselor Fremmeng. She muttered a nervous good-evening. This was the time of year for Parent Consultations, and deficiencies were usually scheduled first. She couldn't have made that poor a showing . . . A glance at her father's livid face told her that this interview was not going the way George Fenn wanted it.

"Counselor Fremmeng has informed me that *you* have achieved sufficient distinction in your schooling to warrant Academic Advancement."

The savage way her father spat the words out and the disappointment on his face dried up any thought Nora had of exulting in her achievement. Hurt and bewildered, unaccountably rebuked in yet another effort to win his approval, Nora stared back at him. Even if she was a girl, surely he didn't hate her for getting Academic . . . In a sudden change of state, she realized why.

"Then Nick didn't?"

Her father turned from her coldly so that Counselor Fremmeng had to confirm it. His eyes were almost sad in his long, jowled face. Didn't *he* take pride in her achievement? Didn't anyone? Crushed with disappointment, Nora pivoted slowly. When she met her mother's eyes, she saw in them something greater than mere approval. Something more like anticipation, entreaty.

"Your brother," Father went on with such scathing bitterness that Nora shuddered, "has been *tentatively* allowed two years of Applied Advancement. The wisdom of society has limited this to the Agricultural Institute with the recommendation that he study *animal husbandry.*" He turned back to face his daughter, eyes burning, huge frame rigid with emotion.

Serves him right, Nora thought, and quickly squelched such disrespect. He had been too certain that Nick would qualify for the university and become a Computer Master for the Fenn Complex. He'll just have to adjust. A Fenn is going on. Me.

"How . . ." and suddenly George Fenn erupted, seeking relief from his disappointment with violent pacing and exaggerated gestures of his big hands, "how can a girl qualify when her brother, of the same parentage, raised in the same environment, given the same education at the same institution, receives only a tentative acceptance? Tentative! Why, Nicholas has twice the brains his sister has!"

"Not demonstrably, Landsman," Counselor Fremmeng remarked, flicking a cryptic glance at Nora. "And certainly not the same intense application. Nick showed the most interest and diligence in biology and ecology. His term paper, an optional project on the mutation of angoran ovines, demonstrated an in-depth appreciation of genetic manipulation. Society encourages such—"

"But sheep!" Father interrupted him. "Fenns are crop farmers."

"A little diversity improves any operation," Counselor Fremmeng said with such uncharacteristic speciousness that Nora stared at him.

"My son may study sheep. Well then, what area of concentration has been opened to my . . . my daughter?"

Nora swallowed hard, wishing so much that Father would not look at her as if she'd been printed out by mistake. Then she realized that the counselor was looking at *her* to answer her father.

"I'd prefer to—"

"What area is she qualified to pursue?" Father cut her off peremptorily, again directing his question to the counselor.

The man cleared his throat as he flipped open his wrist recorder and made an adjustment. He studied the frame for a long moment. It gave Nora a chance to sort out her own thoughts. She really hadn't believed Nick this afternoon when he intimated he'd thwarted Father's plans. And she'd certainly never expected Academic!

The Counselor tapped the side of the recorder thoughtfully, pursing his lips as he'd a habit of doing when he was trying to phrase a motivating reprimand to an underachiever.

"Nora is unusually astute in mathematics and symbolic logic . . ." The Counselor's eyes slid across her face, again that oblique warning. "She has shown some marked skill in Computer Design, but in order to achieve Computer Technician . . ."

"Computer Tech— Could she actually make Technician status?" Father demanded sharply, and Nora could sense the change in him.

Counselor Fremmeng coughed suddenly, covering his mouth politely. When he looked up again, Nora could almost swear he'd been covering a laugh, not a cough. His little eyes were very bright. None of the other kids believed her when she said that the Counselor was actually human, with a sense of humor. Of course, a man in his position had to maintain dignity in front of the student body.

"I believe that is quite within her capability, Landsman," Counselor Fremmeng said in a rather strained voice.

"Didn't you say, Counselor, that Nora qualified for unlimited Academic Advancement?" Mother asked quietly. She held Nora's eyes steadily for a moment before she turned with a little smile to her husband. "So, a Fenn *is* going on to university this generation, just as you'd hoped, George. Now, if you could see your way clear to diversify— And did you notice the premium angora fleece is bringing? You know how I've wanted young things to tend and lambs are so

79

endearing. Why, I might even get Counselor Fremmeng to recommend updating for me at the Institute. Then, George, you wouldn't need to spend all those credits for apprentices. The Fenns could work the Complex all by themselves. Just like the old days!"

"It's an encouraging thing for me to have such a contributing family unit in my Sector. A real pleasure," Counselor said, smiling at the older Fenns before he gave Nora a barely perceptible nod.

"Well, girl, so you'll study Computology at the university?" asked Father. His joviality was a little forced, and his eyes were still cold.

"I ought to take courses in Stability Phenomena, Feedback Control, more Disturbance Dynamics . . ."

"Listen to the child. You'd never think such terms would come so easily to a girl's lips, would you?" asked Father.

"Mathematics is scarcely a male prerogative, Landsman," said Counselor Fremmeng, rising. "It's the major tool of our present sane social structure. That and social dynamics. Nora's distinguished herself in social psychology, which is, as you know, the prerequisite for building the solid familial relationships which constitute the foundation of our society."

"Oh, she'll be a good mother in her time," Father said, still with that horrible edge to his heartiness. His glance lingered on his wife.

"Undoubtedly," the Counselor agreed blandly. "However, there's more to maintaining a sound family structure than maternity. As Nora has demonstrated. If you'll come to my office after your exams on Thursday, Nora, we'll discuss your program at the university in depth, according to your potentials." His slight emphasis on the pronoun went unnoticed by George Fenn. Then the Counselor bowed formally to her parents, congratulated them again on the achievements of their children, their contribution to society, and left.

"So, girl," her father said in a heavy tone, *"you'll* be the crop farmer in this generation."

Nora faced him, unable to perjure herself. With his pitiful honking about farming Fenns, he was like a goose, fattening for his own destruction. She felt pity for him because he couldn't see beyond his perch on these acres. But he was doing what he'd been set in this life to do, as the geese were making their contribution to society, too.

Unlimited Academic Advancement! She'd never anticipated that. But she could see that it was in great measure due to her father. Because he had considered her inferior to Nick, she'd worked doubly hard, trying to win his approval. She realized now that she'd never have it, Father being what he was. And being the person she was, she'd not leave him in discord. She'd help maintain family unity until Father came to accept Nick as a sheep-breeder, diversification on the Fenn acres, a Fenn daughter in the university. Mother would step in to help with crop farming and there'd be no decrease in contribution.

"I'll do all I can to help you, Father," Nora said finally, realizing that her parents were waiting for her answer.

Then she caught her mother's shining eyes, saw in them the approval, the assurance she wanted. She knew she was the daughter her mother had wanted. *That* made her happy.

Dull Drums

THE TROUBLE WITH STUDENT-ISSUE CLOTHING was not its neutrality, thought Nora Fenn, but its instability. Did the suppliers think students doddered about the academic cloisters like pensioners? She fingered together the rent across her hip, hoping that no one would brush against her and widen the tear. She must have overstressed the fabric when she stamped out of Con's last night. Wouldn't you know it'd be on the left side, where her tights had run this morning?

Doggedly she continued along the pedestrian way, toward the Metropolis' Main Computer Block, twisting through and dodging clumps of slower-moving citizens.

It had been such an honor to qualify for the special Cybernetics course, given by Master Scholar Siffert himself, that Nora didn't mind the twenty-minute commute from the University Complex to the Computer Block no matter how the others in the class complained. (Not much suited them anyhow!) After nearly a year, she still reacted to the metropolitan life with added alertness. Just to walk the pedestrian ways, to look at the variety of faces and costumes and shops was a treat for a Farm Complexbred girl. She usually started for this class early so she'd have time to window-shop and people-watch. But today Con's mean words leapt about her mind.

"Yeah, you say you like people, Nora Fenn, but I never saw anyone communicate less in my life."

"Just because I'm not always gibbering . . ." she'd said in self-defense.

Con had thrown back his head and howled. "The very notion of you . . . *you* . . . gibbering! May I be around to see the day!"

There was nothing wrong, Nora told herself stoutly, in taking pleasure in just being among people. You didn't have to participate actively . . .

But last night's scathing accusations rang in her ears.

"You can't be a parameter cloddie forever, Nora. You'll never really know what life is about until you start communicating and experiencing actively. And don't tell me you're in computer programming because that's your aptitude. That's your cop-out so you won't have to live and feel. If your Guidance Officer had wit one about him, he'd have phased you out of Computer Science, and shoved you into the Humanities. And opened wide holes in your father's home-brewed homilies."

"My father . . ."

"Your father," and Con was so incensed the cords stood out in his neck, "your father is a throwback to all the parental autocracies, the chauvinistic, narrow-minded, sex-blocked, inhibiting, maladjusting, martyrizing, egotistical, possessiveness that our present system of social harmony is supposed to correct!"

"How dare you say such things!"

"Because you have! Only you're still too much under your father's domineering influence to realize how much you resent him."

"I don't resent my father. I understand his—"

"Understand?" Con threw his arms up in dramatic frustration. "Understand why he's refused to give you any decent credit allowance? By the printed circuits which feed us, every other Complex manager would do without so he could budget *something* for any youngster his unit can send on to Academic Advancement! And for a kid on *unlimited* Academic Advancement . . . Wake up, Nora. Your ever-loving father has never forgiven you, his daughter, much less the Educational Committee, for letting *you* go on to university instead of the male, his son, your brother."

"I don't need credit allowances." Nora tried to

sound convincing, but she'd been hurt and confused by her father's parsimony. "I got an academic bonus of a hundred credits first term."

Con shook his finger right under her nose.

"You can fool yourself, Nora Fenn, but you, sure as zero times zero is zero, don't fool me! Your paternal parent has royally screwed you, and why you persist in trying to prove you're worth his disdainful notice, even if you are female, I don't understand. He isn't worth the effort."

Con had stepped forward then, his expression hard and angry as he grabbed her arms and gave her a good shaking. His manner was frighteningly different from the jovial, joke-cracking clown pose he usually affected.

"Abort the Computer courses, Nora. Get into Humanities. Take some Behavorial Psych. See objectively how futile it is to try and win your father over. And then grow up and live as Nora Fenn instead of George Fenn's unwanted female child."

"Thank you, Connor Clarke, for your lecture and your advice. Send me the bill! But don't try my number. I'm writing you out of my program from now on."

She had grabbed up her cloak and strode from his room, racing down the hall to the anti-grav shaft. She'd entered it fast—that's probably when she'd torn her tunic—and cried all the way down the a.g. shaft to her own level, cursing Con under her breath and desperately trying not to remember what he'd said.

But his words haunted her now as she walked into the shadow cast by the Computer Block. It was cold in the shade and Nora pulled her shabby cloak tighter around her. It had been the one piece of Complex-issue clothing she'd been able to bring with her. Not that her father had ever let his family use more than farm issue.

"No need to put credits into fancy fabrics and silly clothes you wear once a month. People should take us for what we are, not what we wear. It isn't needful for us to show our status."

"Needful," that was her father's operative word.

What was needful was procured instantly, and ordered in the best quality, regardless of the cost. What was unnecessary was given scant consideration.

It hadn't been needful for Nora to have any credit allowance from the Fenn Farm Complex. She would, George Fenn had solemnly announced, have student quarters at the University Complex, adequate food since students did not eat subsistence-level but a high-calorie diet, and sufficient clothing to cover her decently. If Nora were as good a student as the Educational Committee (which had passed her for Advanced Study instead of her brother, Nick) had said, then she would earn credit bonuses with those brains of hers, wouldn't she? Privately, Nora had vowed she'd earn a bundle. And she had. But now she regretted her diplomacy—no, her subservient conciliatory gesture, as Con would say—in permitting her father to select a heavy CompSci program for her first year.

"That way you'll qualify as Computer Technician Grade II by spring instead of wasting your time on unnecessary trimmings," her father had said.

What he meant, Nora knew now, was it wouldn't be needful for the Fenn complex to pay the salary of the Grade II Comptech for the spring planting.

Six months at University and Nora Fenn knew that she wouldn't be able to go back to the Farm. It wasn't simply the knowledge that her father's basic sociological orientation was limited, but the realization that she'd hated her existence there, from fattening geese to the tractor work that all the automation in the world couldn't make much less bone-jarring. The glitter of bright lights and vapid entertainments in the Metropolis didn't attract her half as much as the people: crowds, mobs, groups, the antithesis of the lonely Farm Complex with its rigid society, seasons, and the so-well-known personalities.

She was gregarious—but she didn't have to be garrulous the way Con was—to enjoy a group situation. She didn't need to maul people with sweaty hands: she could enjoy the sound of voices, the play of emotions on faces, the interaction of brand-new combinations.

Deep in thought, she arrived at the great Computer building. And crossed the magnificent inner hall without gawking at the famous sculpture depicting Man overpowering the Laeconia of Science. She passed but did not re-examine the tri-dex models reviewing the significant events leading to the Dicta —Ecology, Economy and Society—in which the technical sciences had swung violently to alleviate the crushing social problems and foster the conservation of dwindling natural resources. She marched quickly past the programming desk with its lines of applicants and petitioners.

Every citizen had the right to Bank-storage: every citizen could apply for additional space, for more programming time, for re-programming: that was as much their right as subsistence, shelter, and education. Free access had ended citizen fear of a computer-controlled society and had proved to the doubtful that science worked for man's good, not his extinction or domination.

Nora took the anti-grav shaft up to the storage banks where the class was being held, and despite her depressing reflections, she experienced that curious sense of elation, of purpose, that usually gripped her on the way to this course.

She knew that as a first-year student she was incredibly lucky to be in Research Scholar Siffert's special course. Master Siffert was *the* man in Computer Programming. Each student had to be especially recommended by his or her Mentor and then passed on by Siffert himself. (Nora had lost pounds anticipating her qualifying interview with the man.) Their integrity had to be above reproach because the course included lift-lock privileges. All the laboratory work involved the erasure of private records to clear storage for new use, but lift-lock privileges meant the student would have access to any records in the memory banks. Hence the care with which the candidates were chosen.

To clear obsolete records from the memory the students had to cross-check references in Housing and Obituary, audit the old text, and check a variety of items on income, profession, and free individual use of computer access: the last chore was to provide statistical data for a fair apportionment of storage space to citizens. Nora wasn't certain of the exact goal of the course, although she'd learned a lot from the labs about data retrieval and erasure. Research Scholar Siffert was known for his eccentric methods, but undoubtedly all would be clear in the final lecture.

The one aspect of the course she disliked was the attitude of the other students. Granted they'd all passed the same integrity clearance, but she did feel their approach to the lab work was improper. It had become the fashion to try and top each other with ridiculous anecdotes drawn from their auditing. Callous and cruel, Nora thought, to ridicule the dead for their shortcomings and human follies.

As she entered the Data Erasure room, she heard Larry Asher's inane, cawing laughter above the general chuckles.

"Haven't you heard any good ones, Fenn?" Asher asked her as she slipped into a chair.

She shook her head.

"Fenn apparently specializes in dull drums," Clas Heineman said with a twitch of his lips for the pun.

"On the contrary," Nora replied, raising her voice above the laughter as she remembered Con's jibes, "I've had some very interesting ones. But I don't think they're ludicrous."

"Fenn also has no sense of humor," Clas remarked with a rueful grin.

"Humor has nothing to do with your quips, Clas Heineman. It's easy to mock something you've not the sensitivity to appreciate."

"Oho, Fenn's got opinions, too," Larry Asher said, chortling over the verbal tiff brewing between the two. Heineman was not only an upperclassman, with a high scholastic average, but also one of the university's dominant personalities. "Tell us more, Fenn."

Clas Heineman dared her, his eyes sparkling. The rest of the class waited, all too eager to see Heineman score her down.

She took a deep breath and stolidly addressed Heineman:

"What you don't appreciate, Clas Heineman, is what a panorama of the human condition you've been auditing."

"Go on," Clas said in that poisonously quiet tone she'd heard him use before he changed the state of some unwary underclassman.

"I know what you'd find hilarious—the woman who recorded her husband snoring so she could prove to him that he did. After he died, she'd have that played back every night so she could get to sleep." Someone guffawed and she glared in his direction. "That isn't *funny:* it's human. So's the man who programmed a report of his luxury credit standing to wake him up every morning and put him to sleep at night. Then he won the Index Lottery and canceled the instructions. Or the fat woman who had the words 'think thin' played back all day just below the audible level. It must have worked because three months later there's a stop-order. Of course, you're all so grand and well adjusted that you won't need to program such things. And all those would-be poets . . . *Why* are they so laughable? *You* all pinion your friends and make them listen to your sonnets. At least the dead poets only bored themselves!" She knew that the frustration and anger in her voice were not for the class alone but for her own personal situation. But she'd started to let go all those pent-up feelings. "And I'd just love to be around when someone, a hundred years from now, starts auditing your files. I wonder what will be risible to him."

The smirks had faded from some faces, but Clas Heineman's smile remained as fixed as the glittering eyes he focused on her.

"And for all your scholastic honors, I don't think you've realized just what all these so-funny incidents show."

"Since you're so acute, suppose you tell the rest of us obtuse clowns." Heineman's voice was deadly now and Nora was suddenly as scared as she'd been when she confronted her father and insisted on her student rights.

"The subtle change of fear and suspicion of his neighbors to fear and suspicion of the computer-based society: then a gradual acceptance of computer-assistance. We all started with records beginning in 1990 when the main Comp banks were switched on in this Metropolis, so you should all see what I mean. By mid-century I noticed a definite drop in the incidence of recorded paranoia, and the incidence and repetition of psycho-chem therapy. It's noticeable because people begin inputting the most deeply intimate secrets. They've realized that no one can break a privacy seal . . . until we come along with our sophomoric mentalities."

"Oh, come now, Nora," a girl said from the back of the room, "so much of it's pretty damned dull." But she sounded embarrassed.

"I don't agree. I think it's fascinating to watch a saner mental outlook emerge."

"Thank you for the lecture, Miss Fenn," Larry Asher said with a jeer.

"Thank you, indeed, Miss Fenn," repeated a deep voice.

The entire class swiveled about, startled. In the doorway stood the substantial figure of Research Scholar Siffert. The students leapt to their feet. "Thank you, class. Remain standing, Fenn."

She felt the hopeful aura of the class as they watched Master Siffert approaching her. She felt utterly miserable, but she held her chin up and her shoulders back. She was damned if she'd let anyone see her change state.

The Scholar closed the distance between them, with each step looming more and more forbiddingly. He isn't at all like Father, she told herself, half-heartedly. She steeled herself to look him in the eye and then realized that Master Siffert was by no means grim. His lined face was suddenly cut by an enormous grin. He seized Nora by the shoulder and turned her toward the expectant students, one arm proprietarily draped over her shoulder.

"Nora Fenn has just earned a scholarship bonus of three hundred luxury credits, and a distinctive honors scholastic credit."

There was an astonished mass gasp. Nora closed her mouth with a snap when she realized that her jaw had dropped open. Three hundred l.c.'s? He couldn't possibly mean that! And a d.h.? What on earth had she done?

"We will dismiss the rest of you from today's auditing. I do not believe that you would be able to keep your mind on your work after Fenn's astute summation. And then, too, you will need considerable time for the essay, the length of which I leave to your judgment," and he swept the room with the stern glance, "on the psychological trends in personal programming in the early twenty-first century. I believe that most of you have penetrated the fifty-year mark of that era. Nora Fenn," and he gave her a paternal hug, "has spared you what I imagine would have been an unwelcome surprise at term end when this essay normally would have been announced. You are dismissed."

The group rapidly dispersed. Nora made an attempt to follow, but the Scholar's heavy arm remained about her shoulders and to disengage herself would be improper.

When the room had cleared, the Scholar released her, gesturing toward a chair. He seated himself next to her, crossing his legs and beaming at her.

"I don't really deserve—"

"Nonsense, my girl. Not many students outsmart Siffert." His beam took on additional radiance.

Nora felt a blush rising in her cheeks. He chuckled and patted her hand.

"No, now. You were using your mind and your heart, which all too few computer programmers do. They tend to regard people as bits to be recorded or changed, instead of thinking, emoting humans with all the frailties of the human condition." He chuckled again. "I had rather counted, you know, on the notorious student irreverence toward the task to obscure the ultimate goal of the course."

Nora groaned, realizing that she had undone some very careful manipulating.

"I do so enjoy the look on their faces when these young scuts have to change state to the proper polarity. There ought to be some very stimulating essays. And," his eyes twinkled at Nora, "to have a student

90

capable of some independent evaluation—outguessing a Research Scholar—delightful!" He beamed. "Really delightful!"

There was no question that she'd pleased him, and Nora began to relax though she still couldn't believe in her good fortune. With an alacrity at odds with his size and age, the Scholar rose and strode to the master panel that dominated the classroom. Nora heard his lift-lock slide in and then the click of rapidly depressed input keys: the almost negligible pause before print-out occurred. Master Siffert grunted and turned, leaning against the control board and eying her thoughtfully.

"Really diverting but, my dear Fenn, whatever are you doing in Computer Sciences?" He waved a print-out sheet at her. "You'd be wasted on a Farm Complex. What on earth is your Complex Manager about? Not to say your Local Guidance Officer? And why have you been permitted to continue in a cross-aptitudinal course? Really, I shall have quite a deal to say to your Mentor. However could he encourage you in this gross misdirection of ability?"

"Sir, I applied for CompSci."

"What? How's that again? CompSci with your personality index? Good heavens, no! Won't do! I'd be going against the precepts of the Educational Act to condone that!" He strode over to her. "Don't look so woebegone, my dear. Do some serious re-evaluation yourself. I'd say you'd be much happier in socio-psych dynamics, for instance. Can't imagine how you've been permitted to continue almost a full academic year in the wrong field. I shall definitely have a word with your Mentor."

"Please, sir. It's not his fault. My Complex Manager needs a good Computer Technician . . ."

"You'd be wasted on a farm, my dear Fenn. Wasted. Surely your parents have seen your real aptitudes."

"Sir, my father is the Complex Manager and it's my wish to—"

Scholar Siffert pinned her with an astonished stare.

"Your father? Is the Complex Manager and . . . Good heavens, I thought such situations couldn't happen anymore." Siffert blinked and regarded her with outright horror. Then his expression softened. "You appear to me to be a very level-headed young woman, Nora Fenn."

"The situation has been difficult, sir. You see, my twin brother, Nick, opted for animal husbandry. He wasn't qualified for Academic Advancement, just Applied." Nora knew she was expressing things badly and stammered on: "Father'd always expected that Nick would be the Computer Technician and—well, it wasn't socially harmonious to do anything else just then."

Siffert regarded her sternly. "The situation is outrageous. Parents cannot be permitted to live vicariously through their children. Can't be permitted. You should not be in Computer Sciences. You're excused from the rest of the course."

"I'd really like to continue . . ."

The Scholar made a rueful noise and then smiled kindly at her. "Well, it wouldn't be good for class morale for you to stay on, my dear. Besides, you've already accomplished what the course was designed to effect: an understanding of the human condition behind the bits and program status. No, my dear. Use this course time to find out where you really belong. Consult your floor psychman." He gave her a warm, reassuring smile. "I'll register your scholastic rating and bonus. Why don't you ring up your boyfriend and sport him to a real-meal? And I warn you, I shall have a few words with your Mentor. In person." He wheeled, his Scholar's robe billowing behind him, to the master panel, in effect dismissing her. As she left the room, she heard him typing, heard the printout chatter a rebuttal.

She couldn't believe what had happened: a fantastic credit bonus *and* a distinctive honors. Just wait until she told Con! She could feed him . . . And then she realized that she couldn't tell Con for several very good reasons: Scholar Siffert supported Connor Clarke's opinion that she shouldn't be in CompSci at all . . .

"Nora . . ."

Clas Heineman blocked her path.

She ducked, ran to the grav shaft, and entered it fast. If Con was the last person she wanted to see right now, Clas Heineman was the next to last. She whipped out of the grav shaft on the ground level and dodged through the throng in the Main Hall. She underestimated Heineman's determination to intercept her.

He caught up at the entrance, grabbed her hand and, when she wrenched free, caught at her tunic, all but ripping the student-issue clothing from her.

"Hey, I'm sorry," he cried, dismayed. Before Nora could protest, he'd wrapped her tightly in his own cloak and bustled her onto the fast pedestrian way, speeding toward the edge of the metropolis. She couldn't struggle with her clothing in shreds and only his cloak saving her from an immodesty citation.

Shaken by the morning's events and last night's scene, Nora began to cry.

"Hey, don't get in that state, Fenn," Clas said, concerned. "I'm not polarized. In fact, I owe you an apology. Two." Clas Heineman grinned at her, his eyes anxious. His arm tightened reassuringly, his fingers pressing into her waist under the cloak. When he felt her bare flesh, he politely took a new hold. "I didn't mean to tear your clothes. This student issue isn't worth a discarded bit, is it? Good thing you've got three hundred lc's."

Clas reminded her in the nicest way that people were looking at them, even if they were on the fast belt and speeding by. It wasn't good manners to publicize intimacy.

"Oh, Clas, it's so far back to the U!"

"Back to the U? For more student issue? Don't be silly, Fenn. We're transferring . . . now!"

He half lifted her to the moderate-speed belt and then, with a second warning, to the slow one. At the next shopping center, he guided her off and straight into the clothing section.

"I've always wondered what you'd look like in a decent outfit," he said conversationally as he steered her into the shop. He gave her an appraising look. "Deep red . . . like that suit, for instance."

"Oh, no! That's fourteen credits." But Nora

couldn't help coveting the smart tunic suit with its silver piping, the ample sleeves, and the matching garnet cape. It was made of a tightly woven durable material.

"A first-year student who has copped a dh in Siffert's course cannot appear back on campus in tatters," Clas told her, and before she could protest, he dragged her up to the shop's computer and shoved her wrist ID disc into the slot, punching out a data request. She wasn't certain if Clas made a deliberate or an unconscious mistake in data retrieval. A credit balance was all that the shop required, but he'd punched for a credit check. The entries made a distressing picture of her economic status. There was the student bonus for her midterm and the shocking allowance of ten credits from her Complex.

"Clas, that's not fair . . ."

His eyes were thoughtful as he looked at her.

"You got a lousy Complex, girl. Well, you can tell 'em to feck off if that's all they can scrape up for a student with your ability. Why, my Complex . . . Change state! Let's get you dressed, girl."

The attendant had appeared, prompted by the use of the computer panel. Clas erased all but the credit balance and the attendant's smile was correspondingly affable.

"If you're going to feel guilty about spending for clothes, Nora Fenn, I'll drag you to the nearest psych machine," Clas Heineman said later as they emerged, socially apart, from the shop.

"I shouldn't have let you talk me into buying so much," Nora said, but she smiled at him. He'd overridden her objections and, neatly reinforced by the shop attendant, who had visions of a respectable commission, talked her into buying not only the garnet-red suit but two other outfits and some pseudo-leather boots: all completely unnecessary since Nora had maintained that the one good outfit would do for social occasions, and she could, after all, do well in student issue for classes.

"A d.h. has a certain position to maintain, Nora," Clas informed her, and told the attendant to airshoot the rest of the purchases to Nora's student quarters.

"Now, I'll do some spending," he said, and steered her to the nearest eating house.

He didn't consult her, just punched out a high-protein lunch, definitely luxury class.

"If I asked you what you wanted you'd probably insist on ordering basic standard, and this is not the day to be basic or standard. Not after your class performance."

That reminded Nora of the remarks she'd directed at him and, abashed, she stared down at her hands. He started to laugh.

"Nora," he said in a wheedling tone that surprised her into looking up, "do you know the real aim of Siffert's courses?" Then, before she could speak, he shook his head. "No, not the humanistic approach to computer programming. Think again?"

Nora shook her head, too confused by the day's events to be able to think logically.

"It's to puncture the pomposity of computer programmers. You were the only one," and Clas waggled a finger at her, "who wasn't trying to figure out what *technical* trick Siffert had up his sleeve this semester. The trick was not technical, of course, and the rest of us smart-ass d.h. and student programmers have been neatly deflated to size. By you and by Siffert. Oh, for the love of little apples, Nora Fenn, will you stop blushing? Ah, here's food. Real food! Not student pap or subbie wad."

Nora ate with as much relish as Clas, although she was shocked at such profligate expenditure of credit on food. Clas was amusing company, too, completely unlike Connor, whose single-minded intensity when ingesting food left no time for conversation. Naturally they discussed the course and Clas urged Nora to expand on her observations. Although it seemed to Nora that she was monopolizing the conversation, Clas gave no indication that he was bored by what she had to say. It wasn't until the lights began glowing on the walkways that Nora realized how late it was.

"I've got to get back to my Dormblock. I've an assignment to research," she said.

"Say, it is rather late. And I've work for tomorrow, too. Not to mention that essay next week."

"Well, you've more than enough material now to get an honors grade on Siffert's essay," Nora said as she settled her new cloak about her shoulders and smoothed the fabric with an appreciative hand. Then she noticed Clas staring at her in a guilty fashion.

"Did you think I'd—"

"Why not?" Nora was puzzled. "I was afraid you'd be furious with me for what I said in front of the class. And then you gave me this lovely treat . . ."

Why on earth did Clas look so stunned?

"Fenn . . . Nora, you've an alarming habit of changing state when no one expects it." He got to his feet.

It was difficult to talk on the fast belt back to the University Complex, but Clas kept one hand firmly about her waist and whenever she looked up at him, he smiled down at her and gave her a little squeeze. When they finally hopped over to the University Plaza, he took both her hands in his.

"What's your call sequence?"

She stammered it out, because she certainly hadn't expected him to ask for it. He gave her hands one more squeeze.

"You'll be hearing from me, Nora Fenn. *After* I've turned in that essay."

And somehow, to her surprise, she believed him.

She had to take the cross-campus belt to her dormitory quad, a trip she'd found rather chilling in the old cloak with the wet spring winds knifing around building corners. She pulled the new, windproof cloak more tightly around her, secure in its warmth and in the warmth of the day's miracles. Just wait till she showed Con . . .

The day's pleasures diminished. It'd been gratifying to have Clas Heineman interested in her, prod her into buying more clothes than were really needful, and luxuriating in a high-credit meal, but she'd rather have shared her triumphs with Con. He'd shared her miseries.

She was half tempted to go to the Commons and see if, by any chance, he might be about. But he wouldn't want to see her, not after the way she'd stormed out of his place yesterday. She'd even told him she'd canceled his number from her program. She hadn't, of course, but he wouldn't know that.

She cudgeled her brain to think of some way of apologizing to him, of making amends. She couldn't help him with any of his courses because he was in a different discipline. She'd darned all his socks and patched his good cloak where the fastening had torn. She'd . . .

"Hey, don't you speak to old friends now you're a d.h., with a five-hundred-credit bonus?"

Con's bony fingers clutched her arm and swung her about. She searched his long, doleful face, with the shock of bird's nest hair, the rather ludicrous black handlebar moustache, and saw only comic dismay in the wide-set intelligent grey eyes.

"You mean, you're still speaking to *me?*"

"Whaddya mean? Am I still speaking to you?" He frowned and then, seeing they were attracting attention, pulled her out of the walkway and into the angle of the building. "You mean, because of last night?"

She nodded, swallowing anxiously, watching the shift of expression on his mobile face. He was no Clas Heineman for looks, but she felt much more comfortable with Connor Clarke. He took her by both arms now and gave her a rough shake, his thin fingers biting into her flesh.

"Aw, Nora," he said in a cajoling tone, his eyes tender, "friends can get mad at each other, you know, without printing out a major disaster. Besides," and he recovered himself with a characteristic shrug, "I was right and you ought to know it today. Say, gal, have I been strutting for you since I heard. A d.h. and 500 lc's? And you scored off Clas Heineman and all those wire-brained plug-in artists . . ."

"The bonus was only three-hundred and Clas Heineman—"

"You watch that soft-soaper, Nora," and with one of his sudden switches, Con was in a sober phase again. "He may come trying to pick your brains 'cause he's got to maintain his—"

"He already has," Nora said, giggling. Now she knew what had disconcerted Clas Heineman in the food shop. He'd laid on the charm thick and figured he'd taken her in when he was pumping her about her files. Only it'd never occurred to her that that wasn't a fair exchange for the way she'd talked to him in class and for the meal he'd bought her. She did know more about people than programming.

"He has?" Con was nonplussed.

"He waylaid me after Siffert excused me and—"

"He didn't!"

"And," Nora giggled again, twirling on her toes to show off her cape and the tunic suit underneath, "he made me spend money on new clothes. D'you like 'em? The student issue just tore right off me."

"Huh? Oh, yeah, nice— Tore right off you!" Con looked angry enough to take Clas Heineman apart bit by bit.

"Mind your thoughts, Con. Really, you're over-reacting in a gross fashion. Besides which, you caused the first rip in my s.i. last night . . . All Clas wanted was to pump me and—well, after the way I rounded on him in front of the class . . ."

"Nora!" Con roared her name with a most reassuring possessiveness in his tone. "Nora . . ." Then he deflated with misery. "Nora, I was wrong last night. You don't have to gabble like me to relate to people. You *know*!"

"No, Con, *you* were right. And I am out of CompSci. Master Siffert is ordering me out," she said, patting Con's face to reassure him and grinning affectionately at his miserable expression.

"Well, then," and Con brightened immediately, putting his arm around her waist and drawing her over to the cross-campus walk, "since that's settled, let's go eat and you can tell me all about it. Mind you, I've heard some state-changing versions that don't sound like my Nora at all." He stopped in his tracks, so that she all but tripped over his feet. "That is, if you want to . . . after the way I treated you last night."

Nora smiled up at him. "Oh, go tell it to the computer. It *has* to listen to you!"

Changeling

CLAIRE GLANCED QUICKLY AT ROY AGAIN, HER mind churning with astonishment, fury, and confusion. She simply had to persuade him to bring her back to City. Prenatal instructions blithely stated that the first birth was apt to take longer, but never how long. Claire knew that she had a wide pelvis, and she'd done all the strengthening exer— She concentrated on deep-breathing as the uterine muscles contracted strongly.

Good God, was this why Roy had been so faithful in attending the prenatal courses? She and Chess had thought that it was only because this baby was Roy's and, because of his sexuality, likely to be his only issue. Had Roy planned *this* all along?

She swallowed, for the nausea was acute.

"Roy, I'm going to be sick," she said, amazed that she could speak so calmly.

"Don't!"

The order was frightening, almost as frightening as the speed with which he skipped the uneven terrain, barely skimming the low ridges as the helicar climbed higher and higher into the Alleghenies.

He must be taking me somewhere, but where? Claire thought desperately. And why? Why?

A short, strong contraction pulled at her and she gasped inadvertently. Roy looked at her then, his almond-shaped eyes narrowing slightly.

"That's too soon. Are they increasing?"

"Yes, yes. You've got to take me back to City, Roy."

"No."

A flat-out, inarguable negative.

"For your baby's sake, Roy . . ." The soft entreaty,

intense despite her quiet voice, caused the perfect curve of his wide mouth to flatten in anger.

Claire felt bereft of all courage. Roy was not going to be dissuaded from whatever insane course he had inaugurated. And that was very like Roy . . . and terribly unlike him. Why? *Why?* Where had she miscalculated with this brilliant, beautiful, complicated personality. What had she, after all, done wrong? Artificial insemination had solved his basic problem in the matter of becoming a father. Had he so little confidence in her after the years they'd lived so equably together? What maggot had got into his mind over this baby? He couldn't be jealous of Chess . . . or Ellyot? That was the prime reason for her having Roy's child first.

Claire had to stop thinking to concentrate on breathing as the contractions renewed. As she checked the sweep second hand on the heli's panel, she realized that Roy, too, was timing the spasms.

Oh, God, what is the matter with him? Why is he acting this way? We thought we'd covered every possible reaction. But to kidnap me? At the onset of labor? Roy, Roy, what did I do wrong?

Claire fought back tears, which would infuriate Roy. She wanted to scream but such a distressingly female reaction would not serve. It was the calm, rational quality of their relationship, the experts had told her, that was so essential to Roy's stability. The fact that Claire was always serene, so much the antithesis of the flamboyant feminine emotionalism which was repugnant to Roy Beach, had sustained this unusual experiment in human relationships. Now, every instinct in her rebelled noisily against his actions. But every last shred of disciplined rationality she had cried caution, patience, containment.

What had possessed him that he was compelled to act in this fashion? Things could go wrong, even at the last minute, and if they were so far from the City's obstetrical help, what could she do? Then Claire remembered again that Roy had attended every prenatal lesson and had read more books than she had. She bit her lips to contain an hysterical sob. Now she knew that it had not been complacent acceptance that Roy had exhibited, but twisted planning.

No, not twisted planning, she hurriedly corrected her thoughts. Roy wasn't twisted: he just saw things from a different angle. A very different angle, since he regarded women as a different species, useless in his environment. Up to the present moment, she'd been the sole exception. And how could she have been so dense as to imagine that he would react in any normally predictable fashion at the moment of parturition of the one child he was likely to sire?

The groan that issued from Claire's throat was part despair, part pain.

Roy glanced at her again, his eyes sliding around, through, beyond her, without seeming to pause long enough to admit her existence. He did note the contractions that rippled across her swollen belly. He frowned slightly as he looked back across the hills. Judging, Claire realized, whether he had enough time to make his destination before the birth occurred.

Where could he be taking her? Did Ellyot know? Or Chess? Ellyot surely, of the four of them, should have caught an inkling of Roy's plans. Roy barely noticed her these last few months, but he was constantly with Ellyot and Chess. The grotesqueness of her once slender, perfect figure would be repugnant to him: she'd expected that. Her physical perfection had first attached Roy to her. So it was reasonable for him to be revolted by her gravid condition even though it was his child that warped her body. She had dressed as concealingly and fashionably as possible and then kept out of his way—to the point of ducking into closets whenever she heard his quick light step in the house.

Unable to look at him or at the blurring green of the forest over which the heli passed, Claire closed her eyes and shuddered again. She forced herself to relax into the contractions. They were unquestionably stronger—and longer. She could tell that without recourse to the chronometer. And Roy was timing them, too. Let Roy take over. He had. Let him do his worst. He would be the biggest loser. By God and all the growing insight of modern psychiatry, she had done her best. Between pains, she cast back into memory and tried to reason out this extraordinary abduction.

Roy Beach, Praxiteles, Adonis, Apollo, call him Male Beauty in the classic mode, and adore him . . . at a distance. Always at a distance, please. He is not to be touched, he is untouchable. The crisp golden curls that fall in stylish sweeps across the high forehead; the wide-set, slightly slanting almond-shaped, green-green eyes over broad cheekbones, eyes that looked with such ruthless intensity at the wonders of the world, assessing its hidden beauties, disclosing its accepted horrors; the fine straight nose with sensitive flaring nostrils; the sensuous lips, neither too full nor too thin, graceful in the double curve of an Apollonian bow; the firm wide jaw. An incredibly beautiful face—and a beautiful body, tall, straight, deep-chested, muscular with graceful strength, hairlessly smooth. Then Nature compounded her gifts and gave him an intelligence that ranked him one of the most brilliant geopoliticians of the past three centuries. Nature, not always kind, added one final quirk to the psyche of Roy Beach, prince among men, to ensure that no princess would rouse tender, heterosexual feelings in his superb breast. And yet . . .

Claire Simonsen met Roy Beach in City University Complex. If they had not chanced to attend the same seminar, they would doubtless have been introduced by some meddler or other. As Roy Beach was a sleeping prince of godly perfection, Claire Simonsen was Snow White. Hair black as coal, skin white as snow, lips red as drops of blood on a queen mother's linen, she was gracious and gentle, and the fairest in the land—at least, in Penn City and its environs. She was also an extremely intelligent young woman: not equal to Beach as a theoretician—for her talent was in personal relationships which translated into human terms the geopolitical equations—but she was both able to follow and interpret his theories up to the point where he made the final ascent of intuitive genius.

At the time they met, Roy had not yet admitted his sexual preference and was intensely aggravated by the importunities of both sexes. Claire, for the same reason, saw in him the answer to her insistent suitors.

"I don't like females," Roy had told her that first

evening in his quarters. "But I also haven't found a man with whom I can form an attachment." Roy never equivocated. "I may never find someone congenial. If you do, you have my blessings. Until that time—" and one of his rare and beatific smiles touched the perfect lips "—be my guest?"

"With you, candor has become an art," Claire had replied.

"If we are to continue to deal pleasantly together, candor is essential."

Claire distinctly remembered that she had been strolling around his study room (even as a student, he rated status quarters), admiring the simplicity and elegance of its furnishings, the knowing placement of the few paintings, the Britton bronze, the Flock marble statuette. Unquestionably, Roy had been the model.

"You feel compelled to preserve the image of masculinity?" she had asked.

He had shrugged, his almond, green-green eyes expressionless.

"I am the image of masculinity."

"But not its substance."

He had frowned slightly, then he again awarded her that incredible smile. This time, it lit his eyes with humor.

"Sexuality in this day and age is, thank God, a personal, not a social choice. However, there is subtle pressure to pair off, and until this has been done, one is subjected to constant entreaties." He paused, nodding understandingly as Claire shuddered. Until Roy had blatantly annexed her that evening, she had been pestered by three quarrelsome and competitive fellow freshmen. "You are the most beautiful woman I have met. It is a pleasure to listen to your voice, to watch you move across a room." Roy smiled wryly. "Artistically, we complement each other."

"We do," Claire could not help grinning back at their reflections in the mirror surface of the darkened terrace doors. "God and witch. White and black."

"Are you always so tactful, Claire?"

She was a trifle startled at the laughter in his voice, at the definite twinkle in the intensely green eyes.

103

Whatever reservations she had faded. Without humor, Roy Beach would have been insufferable.

"Let us see how we deal together, then," she replied. "It'll be a relief, even if we split up next Saturday, to have those hot-handed louts off my . . . my back."

Smoothly, Claire had adapted herself to Roy's ways. It was never mentioned but it was obvious to a girl with Claire's perceptions that the weight of compromise in the arrangement would always be hers. However, it was a small price to pay for being left alone once the word got abroad that Roy Beach and Claire Simonsen were quartering together. There might have been intense private speculation, but custom forbade probing. They were welcomed everywhere and were soon the acknowledged leaders of their University class.

The key, Claire had discovered, to Roy's intricate personality was to accept him at his own evaluation, a fluid standard which she understood intuitively at first, then intellectually as she penetrated deeper into Human Behavorial Sciences, until she could not have said why she knew how to suit him but invariably did. Theirs could never be a physical relationship, but Claire occasionally thought she was his mental alter ego. However, in his own way, he was devoted to her and as aware of her emotional needs as she was of his; once to the point of being demonstrably tender with her when one of her brief love affairs dissolved painfully.

It had been a tempestuous affair and ended in a bitter quarrel. Claire had run blindly back to Roy's quarters to find him waiting for her, and patient with her distress.

"You appeared to enjoy him," Roy had remarked when she paused at one point in her harangue. "He's got a reputation for proficiency, at any rate. Or didn't he make a good lover, after all?"

Claire had pulled the remnants of her pride together and looked at Roy.

"He is certainly physically attractive," Roy had said thoughtfully, taking her by the arm and leading her toward her old room. "But not your intellectual equal. You'd've fought sooner or later. Here's a trank: it'll ease the worst of the withdrawal."

He had pushed her onto her bed, tugged off her

boots, gave her water to down the medication, and, to her immense surprise, had kissed her cheek lightly after he arranged covers over her.

With amazement, she detected a faint shadow of worry in his eyes.

"*We* understand each other, Claire. We complement each other. Do not settle for less than the best your own excellence can command."

As she drifted off to sleep, Claire was oddly comforted that Roy regarded her as a personality in her own right, and not as an adjunct or supplement to his own consequence.

There had been further brief associations for her, but always the standard that Roy had set for her governed the flare of sexual desire. On those occasions she had terminated the relationship—until Ellyot Harding was introduced to Roy at the Eastern Conference of Cities.

When Roy brought the slender dark man back to the flat Roy and Claire had moved, of course, to civilian quarters after obtaining their advanced degrees —Claire was instantly aware of the bond between the two men, and of her own attraction for Ellyot. She was also aware of the surprise that rocked Ellyot Harding at her presence in Roy's quarters. She could all but hear his startled thought, What's a *woman* doing with him?

But Ellyot was quick to perceive subtleties and, on the heels of the first shock, came comprehension. He had instantly stepped forward, to grip her hand, to place a cool kiss on her cheek.

"You *must* be Claire Simonsen," for Roy had not yet had a chance to introduce her. "I followed your programmed analysis of the Deprivation Advantage with intense interest. In fact, I have allowed for that factor in the renewal project currently planned in my City. Oh, I apologize . . . Roy is rescuing me from the sterility of Transient Accommodations, and the inevitability of having to talk shop with other victims trapped there."

Ellyot's good-natured smile never touched just his lips, his whole face was involved in it.

"Go right ahead," Roy urged, turning to dial drinks

at the console. "I rather thought you two would have overlapping interests. Explore them while I order a dinner suitable for this momentous occasion."

The look on Ellyot's face was mirrored in Claire's for both caught the nuance, the unspoken assumption in Roy's bland directive. Ellyot smiled, raised his eyebrows in a question.

"Yes, it is indeed an occasion," Claire said. "You might like our northern scallops, Ellyot—tender, sweet, delicious."

"The North has much to recommend it," Ellyot replied, leading Claire to the deep wall lounger. His manner was both triumphant and entreating.

Ellyot did not return to the Transient Accommodations or to the southern City which had sent him to the Conference. Claire's supervisor hired him immediately he made known his willingness to transfer. By the time City Management reviewed accreditation in the fall, the three had enough status to move to a larger single dwelling on the outskirts of the City. In fact, Claire was surprised at the outsized dwelling Roy chose for them.

"It's marvelous to have such space to spread out in, Roy, but it'll take every accommodation credit we own to manage this place," she had said.

"Not for long," was all Roy said, imperturbably.

He looked insufferably pleased with himself during the few weeks it took them to arrange and settle into the new house. Claire noticed that Ellyot was unusually irritable and put that down to Roy's insistence on each of them having a separate sleeping room. In fact, relations, up until then extremely harmonious, became strained.

"What is he up to?" Ellyot demanded of Claire one evening when Roy was at a meeting. "I know he's being coy about something."

"So do I, but I thought you'd know."

"Well, I don't. You've known him longer, Claire, can't you hazard what's on his mind?"

"Did you think I've some magic talisman to see into Roy's mind? I don't even sleep with him."

"That's the first catty thing I've heard you say."

"It wasn't catty, Ellyot, truly," she said in gentle

apology even as he blurted out a request for pardon.

"You're a remarkable woman, Claire. Why have you never cut out? Why aren't you—well, jealous or . . ." He hesitated and, to her surprise, blushed. "I mean, you're so obviously hetero, and yet . . ." He gestured vaguely around the high-ceilinged living room.

"It's as much Roy for me as for you, Ellyot," she heard herself say, and then stopped, having finally voiced that admission. "Yes, it is Roy. We have never been lovers—never—but there's nothing of misplaced maternity in my relationship with Roy, or sisterly affection for that matter. It's a relationship . . . of the spirit. No platonic nonsense, either. I honestly, truly, deeply admire, respect, and . . . and love Roy. I cannot live fully without him and I cannot—"

"I know exactly what you mean," Ellyot said softly, with a ghost of a smile on his lips, but none in his eyes. He leaned back against the couch. "You remember the day we met? I'd a hetero marriage contract set up in my old City, you know, but half an hour in Roy's company and that was all over." He grinned. "I wanted children, you see, but Roy was too much."

Now Ellyot turned his head toward her, his eyes reflecting her image. She felt his hand touch hers, spread her fingers against his palm.

"She was no match for Roy . . . or you." He dropped her hand and abruptly stood up, almost glaring at her. "And this is not fair to you, either. You've enough status to have a child of your own from a lover. Get out of here, have a child, marry, don't waste your life on us . . . on Roy. He doesn't *mean* to be exclusive. He just is."

His outburst surprised him as much as did her, for he dropped down on the sofa, one arm behind her, and scowled earnestly as he covered both her hands in a tight grasp.

"Yes, he just is," Claire said softly. "I cannot leave him, Ellyot, any more than I can leave you. There's no other company I'd rather keep, you know." She gently returned the pressure of his hand.

"But I *know* you want children. I've seen you pausing by the playyards. I've seen the longing in your face."

107

"I'm in no hurry. I'll find someone . . ."

Ellyot snorted his opinion of that naïveté. "You haven't even had a lover in the past year. All you've done is work . . . work."

"You've been keeping tabs on me?" Claire was touched by his sudden protectiveness. That was more Roy's role than Ellyot's.

"Neither of us wants you wasting your womanhood on just anybody . . . or no one."

Claire shook her head slowly, conscious of a deep and tender affection for Ellyot. "Did neither of you think to ask my opinion?"

Ellyot glanced sharply down at her. His eyes darkened and he pulled in a deep startled breath just as he bent to kiss her fully and passionately on the mouth.

When she and Ellyot emerged from her room the next morning, Roy merely nodded pleasantly and invited them to join him at the table. Breakfast for three had already been dialed.

Nor was there any embarrassment. Almost, Claire once mused, as if Roy had expected something of this sort and was relieved that it had finally taken place. After the first occasion, Claire had to be the aggressor with Ellyot, though he was never reluctant.

However, in the course of the next few months, Claire realized that the lovemaking she shared with Ellyot could become invidious. It was impossible to make love with Ellyot and not sense Roy, not make love with Roy through Ellyot, not hunger for Roy's magnificent body when Ellyot's covered hers.

Roy had brought Ellyot into their circle for his own ease and solace. Triangularity could deteriorate the relationship. Claire must find a fourth member. She wasn't getting any younger, and Ellyot was correct about how much she longed for a child.

Claire was convinced that Roy had perceived her turn of thought. Of course, they had been talking about building a real kitchen into the house the next time City Management raised their total income. Roy was intensely interested in raw food preparation and increasingly annoyed with the mass-produced combinations available from the public kitchens, despite the interesting variations he achieved with what came out of the dispensers. But it was Claire, restless, increasingly dissatisfied, who undertook to find an architect who would design a kitchen room for them.

The first firm she consulted laughed at the notion of an entire room devoted to the preparation of food for consumption. The second thought she wanted a rough arrangement such as could be installed in a retreat too far from a City or Center for regular facilities. They recommended another firm that did reconstruction work for museums. That was how she met Chess Baurio.

"He's very busy, you know," she was told over the telephone by the receptionist. "But the notion is bizarre enough that he might just like to try it." An appointment was made and she went directly to his office, not far from their home.

It could never be called love at first sight, for he was extremely antagonistic from the moment she introduced herself. Only because he'd never attempted to solve such a design problem did he reluctantly agree. And then, under the stipulation that it was done his way. He knocked down one after another of her plans, sarcastically deriding her painstaking research. In fact, when she had finally got him to agree to come to the house and examine the proposed site, Claire wondered why she had put up with his manner and attitude for one session, much less contemplate a further association.

Still, when he arrived the next morning, he was unexpectedly pleasant, even charming—until Roy walked in. If Roy Beach was the personification of the classic concept of the male manner, Chess Baurio was the twenty-first century's. Compact, lean, healthily attractive, alert, he was the antithesis of Roy's studied indolence. Roy was the aloof, detached, arrogant observer; Chess was the involved, enthusiastic, vital participator.

As Roy strode up to the terrace where she and Chess were discussing the location of the kitchen room, the air became charged with electric hostility.

Claire looked at Chess, saw that his eyes were snapping with anger, that the smile on his face was set, that his movements as he leaned forward slightly to shake Roy's hand were jerky. His manner became stilted, false. She glanced at Roy, who was his usual urbane self.

"Chess Baurio? You designed the new theater complex at Northwest 4," Roy said by way of greeting. "Now, why did you use polyfoam instead of Mutual's acoustical shielding?"

"Ever heard the wows in the Fine Arts Theater at Washington South?"

"Can't say that I've been in that theater, but wasn't it John Bracker, Claire, who was so vehement in his objections to playing in that hall?"

"He did mention he'd rather play under Niagara Falls," she said lightly, hoping to ease the tension.

"And polyfoam corrects wow?" Roy demanded of Chess.

"In that size building, or in amphitheater form." Baurio's voice had a bitten quality.

"I've been advised to use it in our music room," Roy went on, blandly, dialing out three coffees and passing them round as if Chess would naturally take his black as they did. "What's your opinion on its use in a small room?"

"As a consultant?"

The rudeness in Chess' tone surprised Claire. People were rarely rude to Roy. He simply didn't elicit that kind of response. She held her breath. Roy did not appear to notice.

"The kitchen room comes before the music room, but we always combine efforts. I believe that Ellyot . . . Ellyot Harding," and that was the first time Claire ever heard Roy qualify any acquaintance so pointedly, "is the third member of the house . . . has a preference for natural woods as acoustical materials, rather than manmade products."

Hostility fairly bristled from Baurio now.

"We have not really discussed the music room. I imagine, however, Designer Baurio, that if the kitchen room is successful, we'll get busy on the other," Claire said, trying to sound relaxed and gracious. Why was anything Roy said so offensive to this Baurio?

"I'm not at all sure," Baurio said icily, putting down his untouched cup of coffee, "if anything I designed would be successful in this . . . this kind of *ménage.*"

110

Not even Roy could ignore that, and he slowly turned toward Baurio, his eyes glittering.

"You object to polyandry?"

"I object . . . I object to such a monopoly, to the sheer waste of . . ." He broke off, glaring savagely from Claire to Roy before he spun around and strode out of the house.

"What on earth possessed you to come out with statements like that, Roy?" Claire asked. "He was . . . to design a kitchen room . . . What happened?"

Roy smiled down at her. "He'll be back. And *you* must make him stay."

After the most tempestuous three months in her entire life, she did, but only when their marriage contract had been registered in the City. And that came about only because Roy and Ellyot cornered Chess privately at the end of a particularly bitter quarrel.

The end of the mad abduction and the cessation of a particularly painful contraction—her muscles were beginning to hurt despite training and control—were simultaneous. Claire opened her eyes to a leafy vista, the tops of trees below the heli's landing gear. Startled, she peered down. The heli was perched on the edge of a sudden, sharp drop, the bottom of which was hidden by foliage. Wildly she turned to Roy. His eyes wouldn't focus on her, his breath was uneven.

"Can you move?" he asked.

"Where?" She couldn't control the quaver in her voice.

He threw up the hatch and jumped out, ignoring the gasp she made as she had a flash of him disappearing over the precipice, leaving her alone and at the mercy of her body's birth-drive in the cramped nose of the heli.

"Put your hands on my shoulders," he ordered, and she found herself obeying.

She moved as quickly as she could, knowing that a spasm was seconds away. It seized her as she reached out to him and sent her reeling into his arms. He had seen the look of pain on her face, and deftly caught her to him, holding her firmly despite the awkward position for them both.

111

It seemed an age until the contraction passed. She submitted weakly as he swung her up and strode off. She buried her face against his shoulder.

Does he intend for me to have the child in the woods, like an animal? she wondered.

"You'll have to open the door," he said in her ear.

She looked down and fumbled for the crude latch, surprised that there should be a door, for she had only the fleeting impression of the façade of the retreat, its rustic logs, the heli's floatons apparently resting on the surface which camouflaged the retreat. Vaguely, she hoped the roof was firmly supported against the heli's weight.

As Roy angled her through the doorway, she caught a glimpse of the superb view of the valley below them, the mountains beyond. When had he acquired such a retreat? Or who had lent it to him? Stupefied, Claire wondered if Ellyot had suspected this and kept silent.

A contraction. She couldn't suppress the groan, which deafened her to a statement Roy muttered under his breath. But, seemingly a century later, he laid her on a bed and was arranging her body in the best position to ease the strain.

"A hard one, huh?" he said as she lay, panting. She didn't resist as his hands turned her gently and stripped off her maternity sack, or as they felt her writhing abdomen.

How can he bear to touch me? He has scarcely looked at me for five months.

The next moment she became aware of other preparations for the coming birth and she began to struggle fastidiously.

"Don't resist. This has to be done. For the child's sake."

Hearing the anger and distaste in his voice for what he had to do, she forced herself to relax and endure his ministrations.

Her waters broke while she was on the toilet and she began to whimper, more from embarrassment and tension than pain.

"What is it?" His voice was clinical.

"The waters broke."

He got her back to the bed, on her back, and examined her with the deftness of her obstetrician.

"The head is in the birth canal," he said just as she experienced the first of the second-stage contractions. "That's right. Push down!"

She fought the hand that pressed down on the upper part of her belly.

"No, no Roy. Leave me alone. Get a doctor. Please, Roy!"

His face loomed suddenly above her so that she was forced to open her eyes wide and look at him.

"I know what to do, Claire. The child is *mine!*"

"But you could have assisted at the hospital, Roy," she cried, slowly perceiving through her pain and anxiety what motivated him.

"With Chess listed as your legal spouse? *We* haven't that right yet. No, Claire, this is *my* child."

"It's mine, too," she screamed.

"Is the pain unbearable? I'll fix the mask for you."

"Mask?"

"I have assembled everything that might be needed," he told her in that odd flat voice. "Do you need the mask now?"

"No, no. No!" She couldn't succumb to the desire for relief from the pain, though it was fierce now, fierce and inexorable, convulsing her body, seizing her with a steadily increasing rhythm, permitting her not so much as a moment to relax straining muscles.

"Good. Press harder. Press downward." She heard his voice through a mist of sweat and tears and pain.

She grabbed at the bed, flailed wildly around for something to hang onto and was rewarded with a strong wrist to grasp. But for that hand, she was lost in a nightmare of stretch, strain, pant and gasp, of a body that was not hers, that responded to primal urgings. The comforting hand, the reassuring voice were part of it and apart from it. The rhythm increased, unbearable, constant, exhausting, and then, wrenched by a terrible spasm, her body arched. She was sure she had been torn apart.

The pain was gone. Sweat dripped into her eyes. She felt almost lifeless, certainly weightless but . . . serene, strangely enough. Her legs were spread wide, the thigh muscles ached, her vagina throbbed, and all pain was replaced by the languor of exhaustion. She became conscious of movement within the room, of a harsh breathing, a wet splat, and then the tiny gasp as infant lungs sucked in air and complained mewlingly.

She raised herself on her elbow, one hand reaching for the sound.

"Roy?" She dashed sweat and damp hair from her eyes.

Roy's back was to her. When he turned, she was startled to see a surgical mask across his face, the translucence of plastic gloves high up his muscled forearms. And, dangling from his left hand, a tiny, arm-waving inverted form, the cord still attaching it to her.

"Oh, God, Roy, give him to me."

Roy's eyes were full of tears as he laid the child on her belly.

"I have delivered my son," Roy said in the gentlest voice. "Don't touch him," he added, knicking her hand away with the bare part of his forearm. "You're not sterile."

"He's mine, too," she protested, but did not reach out.

She watched as Roy deftly tied off the umbilical cord, swabbed the child's mouth, painted his eyes. As he tenderly oiled the reddish skin, Claire craned her neck to glimpse with greedy eyes at the perfection of the tiny form.

And the baby was perfect, from the delicate kicking feet to the twitching fists. His head bones were still pointed, but there was a fineness about the angrily screwed features. Despite the unconventionality of his birth, he was alive and obviously healthy. She did not protest when Roy swathed the child in a receiving blanket and laid him in the portable crib that he pushed gently to one side of the bed.

"Now, you." Again all emotion was leached from his voice.

With the heel of his hand, he pressed into her flattened belly. She screamed for the pain of it and was seized, to her horror, with another contraction that brought a flood of tears to her eyes.

"You leave me alone!" she cried, feebly batting at his arms.

"The afterbirth!"

And it was delivered.

Utterly exhausted, she lay back. She felt but did not move as he sewed the torn skin of her, only vaguely wondering that he knew how. She was too weary to help as he cleaned her, changed the soiled sheets. She was only grateful that the pain and the shame were over as he covered her tightly bound body with a light blanket. She could hear the baby snuffling somewhere in the room and his continuing vigor was more reassuring than anything else. She felt herself drifting off into sleep and tried to fight it. She must stay awake. She couldn't afford to sleep. He might try to leave her now he had the child he had wanted so desperately.

And that thought stuck in her mind. The child Roy wanted so desperately was born. That was why he had acted so rashly. His child. His child! She had, after all, and however deviously, become the mother of his child.

A tiny voice, insistent and undeniable for all its lack of volume, roused her. She felt hands turn back the covers that lay so comfortingly around her. She felt her upper body lifted, supported with pillows. Drowsily, she evaded full consciousness until she felt her arm crooked, felt the scrape of linen against her skin, the warmth of a small rounded form, hands against her right nipple, the coolness of a wet sponge, then the fumbling of small wet lips and the incredible pleasurable pain caused by a suckling child.

She opened her eyes to the dim light. Roy was sitting on the edge of her bed, his hand securing her lax hold on the child. She was fully aware in that instant, aware and awake. She glanced down at the tiny face, eyes tight, lips working instinctively for the nourishment she could feel it drawing from her breast.

Roy did not remove his hand, yet it was not as if he did not trust Claire. And suddenly she understood all that must have been driving him since she had blithely announced her desire to have his child first. She had taken him, of them all, by surprise. She had astounded and startled him. She had given him a hope, a promise that Roy Beach had never even considered, given the circumstances of his sexuality. She had given him the child of his own flesh, yet she had not soiled him with her femininity.

She understood now why he had been unwilling to trust anyone but himself with the responsibility of delivering his child.

The pressure in her other breast was painful. She disengaged the nipple from the searching, protesting mouth and quickly shifted the babe, taking a sensuous delight in the tug and pull of the eager lips as they fastened on the new food source.

Then she looked up at Roy. She smiled at him as their eyes met. She felt that she saw directly into his heart and soul for the first time in their long association. With her free hand, she reached for his and placed it on their son.

"I called Chess, and told him where you are. He said Ellyot made him understand."

Claire tried to tell him with her eyes that she did, too, but all she could say was, "Does he plan to come here?"

There was a quick start in Roy's body and his eyes plowed deep into hers as if he, too, had to know her heart, at least this once.

"It would be more peaceful," she added, holding onto his gaze, "to have the first few days alone, if you can stand it."

"If *I* can stand it . . ."

Claire had to close her eyes against the look of intense joy, of almost painful jubilation in Roy's face. She felt him lean toward her, across the child, so that the baby kicked against the constriction. She felt his lips on hers, her body responding unreasonably to his benediction.

When she opened her eyes again, he was smiling down at the babe with untroubled pride and affection.

And that was how it must be forever, Claire reflected and deliberately put aside that brief, tantalizing glimpse of the forbidden paradise.

"Weather on Welladay" stands alone. Judy-Lynn del Rey when she was *Galaxy Magazine*'s energetic Gal Friday-Monday-Tuesday-Wednesday-Thursday, gave me a future cover for the magazine around which to write a story. Not as easy as it might seem. A helicopter and a tall man stood among what looked like Christmas-tree decorations on the deck of a great whaleboat. Surrounded by lots of water! So pick up the ball and throw it, because you *have* to account for every element in that cover somewhere in your story.

It was a mystery to me how to do it, so I made the story a mystery.

Weather on Welladay

WELLADAY WAS INDEED A WATERY WORLD, Shahanna thought as the day side of the planet turned under her ship. Good thing that explorers were obstinate creatures; otherwise the hidden riches of this stormy world would have gone unnoticed.

She checked her location visually as the ship's computer began to print landing instructions.

"I'm not that stupid," she murmured, noticing the turbulence of several storm centers that blossomed in the northern hemisphere of Welladay. She tapped out *Locate* for the Rib Reefs, the rocky spine of the planet that stretched from north to south and broadened into the Blade, the one permanent installation on the watery world. "At sunrise, hmmm? Wouldn't you know. And right in the path of one storm. Well, let's beat it in." She began to punch out landing coordinates.

At that moment, the proximity alarm rang. She hit the *Enlarge* toggle of the screen control just in time to see two telltale blips—the small satellite that ought to be in orbit near her, and the larger one that certainly ought not to be in Welladan skies. Suddenly her ship rocked with the violence of a direct hit. Shahanna remained conscious just long enough to hit the survival button on the armrest.

Odis planted his flippered foot on the young whale's blunt snout and shoved.

"This is no time for nuzzling, nuisance," he roared, as the force of his thrust sent the baby backfinning. Whales liked to be talked to—roared at—though there was little chance they understood more than the tone

118

of voice. Some fishmen denied even that much comprehension. "Almost finished now, Mother," Odis bellowed reassuringly at the massive creature whose thyroid glands he was tapping.

The indicator dial of the long-beaked suction pump reached the red area, whereupon, with more deftness than others gave him credit for, Odis broke the connection and sealed the beaker. He closed the tap mouth and noted the date of this tap in paint-pen above the metal insert. Old tap-dates had faded but the new paint would glow for the three months necessary for a mature whale to generate more vital radioactive iodine in its thyroid gland.

Odis touched the zoom button on the drone's remote control, then scrawled the whale's registry number beside the luminous date on the beaker before holding it for the drone to record. That formality observed, he scratched the female's rubbery upper lip where the scales had been torn. What kind of a fight had she been in? Well, at least the wound had healed.

Once again her child tried to nose Odis' fishboat out of the way. Chuckling over the creature's antics, Odis climbed up the boat's ventral fin and over the back to the hatch. Ducking below, he stored the precious beaker of radioactive iodine in the chemfoam-protected carrier.

Back on the fishboat's snub-nosed brow, Odis frowned at the sight of the school of whales beginning to melt away from the neighborhood. He had been out since early morning, tracking them down, and spent a good hour easing into the herd before he had tried to tap one. First, he'd pounded affectionately on the snouts of the mammals he knew as well by scar marks as by registration code. Two had shied away from him so wildly that he began to worry that this group had already been milked by that fardling pirate. When he was finally able to draw alongside the old blue-scarred cow and do a light tap, he had decided that their weather-sense was all that was making them skittish.

Between the freakish storms of Welladay and the fardling pirates, Odis growled to himself as he squinted toward the darkening horizon, they might as well pull the plug on operations here. He frowned. Where else would he find a world more to his liking? A task more suited to him, a man born and bred on a high-gravity planet? Or creatures big enough not to suffer from his inordinate strength?

Pleased with himself, he stepped on the release for the outboard panel and began to beam toward Shoulder Blade for a weather report.

The instrumentation was on a pole that looked like a colorful Christmas tree when it was lit up—which was now. It was recording various local indications of the weather. But when he tried to reach Okker in his harbormaster's lookout at the Eye of the lagoon, the beam crackled with interference. So the easterly storm had hit them. Even with a band of weather satellites, one couldn't always be sure of weather on Welladay.

Odis tagged the playback in case Okker had broadcast while he was tapping the whale. He whistled as he listened to Okker's sour report of mach-storm warnings, the advice that all vessels return to Shoulder at cruising depth and hold at shelf-level until recall— the local storm over Shoulder seemed to be only a squall. The warning was repeated twice with additional ominous details on the mach-storm's wind velocity, estimated drift, and duration.

Odis grunted. He could just imagine Okker's disgust at relaying such a message. Tallav, the maggoty Planetary Administrator, had probably been at Okker's elbow. With the exercise of tolerance, Odis could understand the reasons for Tallav's ineffectualness. A meek man, he was not suited to a blustery, stormy world like Welladay, even if affairs proceeded normally. But Tallav was caught in a fladding bind. Someone was pirating the main source of Welladan wealth so that no substantial revenue had been garnered from the whales in months. Result: Supplies could not be paid for, and credit had been suspended. What with the depredations caused by pirates and various natural catastrophes, only three fishboats were operable. Requests from legitimate sources for the priceless radioactive iodine had become demands: Urgent! *Top Priority.* Gray phage was endemic and periodically epidemic. The only specific vaccine was a dilute suspension of the radioactive iodine. In addition to the risk of tapping to death the few whales they could now find, Welladan fishmen were constricted by lack of operable craft.

The two best fishmen, Odis and Murv—a newcomer on a Debt-Contract—had been sent out in an attempt to find and tap enough of the valuable substance to make up at least one critically needed shipment. Whatever Odis and Murv could get today, therefore, was crucial. Fleetingly, Odis wished they could charge a hardship premium, but the price of the iodine had been fixed by Federation officials who evidently were too concerned with other crises to pay attention to repeated Welladan requests to investigate piracy.

So here was timid Tallav, calling the fishmen back because there was a mach-storm brewing in the west. Odis ran a quick check of the instrumentation on the approaching storm, now boiling black and ochre on the horizon.

As he evaluated the readings, he maneuvered his ship toward the nearest adult whale. He could get one more tap completed before he would have to duck and run home. Fishboats were sturdily designed for Welladan waters, to race on hydrofoils with the scaly spawn of her seas, to plunge trenchward with the whales, to endure the savagery of a sudden squall, to wallow, whalelike, within the school itself without being attacked by a nervous male.

He coasted along the port side of the mammal, rather pleased that the creature was not shying off as did its schoolmates. The painted code above the tap-vent had faded completely, so Odis toyed with the idea of getting at least a beaker and a half, as he made his preparations to tap.

It was then that he noticed the strange color of the scales. At first, he thought it was caused by the light —the sky had already changed with the approach of the storm. As he looked around, there wasn't another whale in sight; they'd all raced away, north and south, deep from the storm center. This whale wasn't moving because it was close to death.

Cursing with pent-up anger, Odis stomped below, retrieved the beaker he had just drawn, and prepared to pump the contents into the sick mammal. Would it be enough? Was the gesture merely a waste of fluid now—fluid as precious to the life of Welladay as to this mammal? Odis refused to consider this a waste. In an angry scrawl he painted the date and the circumstances on the whale, adding a crude skull and crossbones.

He stepped back then, clenching his teeth, railing against the brutality of the pirates. He wondered bitterly just how many more beasts had been tapped dry, just how many more black, bloated corpses would roll in on the fresh tides after the storm?

He waited, hoping for some sign of change in the creature. There was no way of knowing how long ago the tap had occurred—hours, days? Or how swiftly the infusion would correct the whale's deficiency.

A fresh wind came up, and the outboard panel chattered metallically, then began to crackle with an authoritative noise. A craft approaching? Odis scanned the clouds. Suddenly a second drone broke into view, higher and north of him. He glanced down at the seaviewer, waiting for the indication that another fishboat approached. The drone whistled overhead, but the seaviewer remained empty.

Murv was the only other fishman out! Where was he that he would send his drone back alone? Had he been caught by mach-violence? A wilder shriek tore the air; and the whale reacted with a nervous bobbing, then pulled away from the fishboat.

Odis swung the Christmas tree, got a fix on the sound, and followed it. The intruder was high up but lancing downward, downward and right into the machstorm. He flipped the track toggle, keeping the outboard panel lined up with the visual trace of the spaceship until it disappeared into the clouds.

That boiling trail had come from nothing based on Welladay. And it was heading away from the only settlement on the water world. Odis retracted the outboard panel. As he climbed down the ladder, he shot a final look at the whale, now moving slowly in a northerly direction. No, the iodine had not been a waste. If the creature could just make it out of the storm's path, it could feed itself back to strength on the plankton in the northern waters.

Odis slammed the hatch down and searched the pilot's couch just as the computer printed out the intruder's course: straight into the storm, directly in line with the only other permanent landfall, Crown Lagoon. The realization was particularly bitter to Odis, for that was the direction from which Murv's drone had just come.

Slowly, Odis tapped out a new course for the fishboat. Not back to the safety of Shoulder Blade, but straight into the storm, directly on the intruder's tail. Then he fed into the computer the details that Okker had transmitted on the mach-storm. As the printout chattered, Odis sank back into the padded couch, his suspicions confirmed. In approximately five hours, the eye of the mach-storm would be centered over the gigantic old volcano whose mouth formed a twenty-kilowide lagoon. The shards and lava plateaus of its slopes were like a galactic–sized crown, thrown down just above the equator of Welladay in the shallow meadows of the western seas.

Murv could hold up in the deep beyond the island's shores—safe enough even with a mach-storm lashing deep into the ocean—until the eye of the storm covered Crown. Murv could then surface, deliver the stolen iodine to the ship which had sneaked in under cover of the storm. Well, Murv would do well to leave with that pirate. Once the Investigator got here—and the planet was registered as bankrupt and taken over by the Federation, Welladay would be no place for any freedom-loving man. *Flads!* Murv must have enough of the iodine on him to buy a planet. He sure had sold out Welladay!

Grimly Odis settled down for the long run. He'd stay on the surface and run on the hydrofoil as long as he could, at least until the storm's violence forced him to the relatively quieter, but slower depths. He had to intercept Murv before the traitor got the iodine off-planet.

But where had the man hidden the valuable substance all this time? Every possible crevice on Shoulder Blade had been searched repeatedly once the fishermen realized what was happening. Hadn't Tallav initiated

123

the drone-escort to prevent any fishman from tapping too deeply? How the flads had Murv managed?

True, he had sent his drone back. But you couldn't tap a whale in the midst of a storm and he was within his rights. Indeed, Tallav would have screamed if Murv had kept the drone.

Odis leaned forward, tapped his own drone's controls. He printed out a message for it to transmit once the squall lifted over Shoulder Blade, then sent it to track him miles above the coming storm. He might just find it useful to have a drone in the eye. He would risk Tallav's tantrums.

As there was nothing more he could do now, Odis settled down to a short nap.

The old survey charts had better be right about that underwater channel into the lagoon, Murv thought as he listened to the stress noises of the fishboat and grimly watched the danger lights blink warnings. The fathometer marked the unsteady ascent as the craft bucked tidal pulls and storm rips. He must be nearing the archipelago.

The straps that held Murv firmly to the pilot's seat cut into his flesh and he cursed absently as he began to match the chart to sea-viewer.

Blighted planet! The whole thing had appeared so fardling simple. He was used to risks, trained to surmount them. So he had opted to contract as a fishman, to look around for a while, spot the trouble, and then back out again, ready for more demanding work. On a watery planet, with only one permanent settlement, and only one product that was in great demand throughout the galaxy, what could have been simpler? He had not, however, counted on such a trivial detail as weather. Nor had he counted on the mimsy-pimsy fardling parasite of a Planetary Administrator coming up with a drone escort to prove *his* fishmen were not the murdering pirates. That wrinkle had restricted Murv's investigations, but it didn't make him trust Tallav. Murv knew better than to trust anyone.

Furthermore, Murv had not counted on sympathizing with the great whales. After he had been taught to milk them, after he had been assigned a school, it had annoyed the hell out of him to see the rotting carcasses of whales that had trustingly let humans tap them to death. They even lined up to get milked. No, the waste—the fladding waste of it—galled Murv the most.

He must be nearing the tunnel mouth; he could feel the fishboat being sucked relentlessly toward the basaltic shelf. His fingers flew over the pitch and yaw controls, decreased the play in the helm, and ignored the neck-jarring rolls. On the fathometer and on the roiled viewscreen in front of him, the bottom of the ocean met the ramparts of the old volcano in a solid wall of tortured lava!

Shahanna was roused by the shrieking hiss of the insistent wind. She opened her eyes to grayness, to the realization that the crash foam was dissipating, to the knowledge that she was still alive and breathing. In spite of the cushioning foam and the padding of her seat, she felt thoroughly wrung out. Motion was painful. She turned her head, groaning as stiff muscles protested. A solitary yellow light gleamed on the control panel, then blinked off as she watched. The ship had sent out its death knell, the last thing this type of spacecraft was programmed to do before all its systems failed.

Shahanna reached with an enfeebled hand to her side pouch, fumbled for a stimulant and a pain depressor. Clumsily, she jabbed the drugs into her arm and then, gasping at the discomfort even that slight motion caused, lay back. The drugs worked swiftly. She staggered to her feet and worked her muscles, relieved that nothing had broken or split. Her wrist chrono showed that some eight hours had elapsed since the unexpected attack. Automatically, she reached toward the log recorder.

"All systems dead, gal," she reminded herself, and looked out the plastight window.

Jagged black rock surrounded the nose of the scout and sheets of water scudded across the window.

How lucky can a gal get? She thought. I cracked up on land? Shahanna frowned. "Shoulder?" The Rib Reefs had been half a planet away when she had been

125

shot down. There was no possible entry she could have made that would land her on Shoulder. But she remembered some other semi-permanent land masses on the charts, if one could dignify a wayward archipelago or a transient volcano as land mass.

The lock was jammed solid, Shahanna discovered, but the escape hatch was clear. The little scoutship rocked under her feet, and she realized it had been rocking ever since she had come to. The pitch of the wind had risen a few notes, too, and water sloshed across the viewpane in a constant fall. If she were on an island in one of those archipelagos, she was on a very precarious one.

Shahanna wasted no further time on speculation. She quick-sealed her orders onto her ribs, slapped additional supplies to her belt, shrugged into an all-purpose suit. That done, she harnessed on a life-support tank and donned her headgear and the water-aids, then punched the destruct on her ship's instrumentation and threw open the escape hatch. She got a face full of wave and drew back sputtering and choking. Undaunted, she rearranged her mask and took a second look.

Gaunt black fingers of stone held the ship. But the rising tides, wind-lashed and moon-churned, rocked the boat resting in its impromptu dry dock, grabbed it with a greedy urgency. What remained of the aft section of the ship was rocking slowly down into the water.

"That guy was a good shot—cleared off my engine. But I'm a live one." Another wave slapped across her face. She ducked instinctively and then, with a deft movement, was over the side of the ship, its bulk protecting her from a worse battering.

She could see beyond her ship, through the spaces of the finger rocks. It wasn't a comforting view, for the huge expanse of water was equally wild. A grinding sound reminded her that she had little time for deliberation. The ship slipped further down the rocky palm. Shahanna saluted it, promising retribution, and clambered up through the rock fingers. She didn't see that an outcropping of rock caught and held the forward section of her sliding ship above the water.

"This is the damnedest terrain" Shahanna said aloud

as she scrambled higher, grateful for the tough fabric of her gloves as she found handholds on the razor-edged shards of rock. The rain was coming down in such heavy torrents that she could barely see a few feet in front of her. The wind pounded her with hammer blows. She would not last long in this maelstrom, Shahanna decided, peering around for some sort of shelter against a rocky ledge. Instinct directing her, she climbed doggedly to such a height as she could manage on rockpile. The absence of water pouring over her and the slackening of the wind indicated a sanctuary, and she was inside the little cave before she even realized it existed. With an inarticulate moan, she crawled far enough inside to be out of the reach of the elements. Sighing, she rolled onto her back as exhaustion claimed a battered mind and body.

Planetary Adminstrator Tallav watched anxiously as the nets drew the battered space craft into the safety of the Broken Rib Hangars. Almost on cue, rain in blinding sheets plummeted until the dome over the living quarters beyond the hangars looked like a waterfall and the storm drains began to fill with alarming speed. Tallav shuddered at the ferocity of the floods.

You'd think twelve-foot-deep dikes would be ample anywhere—except on Welladay, he thought as he started down the ramp to welcome the eagerly awaited Investigator.

It wouldn't do to appear nervous, Tallev thought. Might cause suspicion. Nor should he appear irritated that it had taken Federation such an unconscionably long time to dispatch an Investigator. Didn't they realize the consequences of letting this out-and-out piracy of the vital radioactive iodine go on for so long? Surely his messages had been explicit, his reports detailed. But to wait until Central Credit actually suspended all shipments to Welladay—that was disgraceful. Disgraceful and unjust.

Tallav slid back the portal and stepped out into the rock-hewn chamber that housed the drones and visitors' shuttles. Such noise as the crewmen made in securing the ship was lost in the vast room. Tallav was a little surprised at the Investigator's physical appearance.

Not that he expected a full-uniform for a minor planet like Welladay, but an Investigator ought to appear in something more than a faded one-piece shipsuit.

"I'm Tallav, Planetary Administrator, Grade 3-B," he said in a firm voice, saluting the new arrival with what he felt was the proper deference. Investigators were not exactly equal in status to Planetary Administrators but they had superplenary powers which they could invoke if circumstances warranted. "And you are Investigator . . ."

"Brack's the name."

Tallav was a little annoyed by the very casual return of his salute.

"Your arrival couldn't be more opportune," Tallav went on, indicating the exit to Brack. "We haven't so much as a drop of the radioactive iodine left, and two top-priority emergency capsules came in just before you got here. The tone was rather high-handed. You timed that a mite close, if I may say so."

The Investigator shot him an odd look as he ducked under the portal. Tallav dogged the lock wondering if the Investigator thought he was being critical.

"Storms on Welladay are unusually violent," he continued. "That's why we net down all craft."

Brack snorted and let Tallav lead the way to the office.

"If you'll just come this way, Investigator, my tapes and personnel are entirely at your disposal. We want this piracy stopped immediately—"

"In that storm?"

"Well, no, of course not. I mean, that is . . . surely my communications gave you ample facts from which to draw some conclusions? After all, there aren't very many places on Welladay from which a pirate could operate."

"No, there aren't."

"Now, here we are. May I offer you some refreshment? Or would you permit yourself to try some off-world stimulant? I'm afraid the commissary is a little low—tedious, this business of being boycotted until these pirates are apprehended and the iodine is collected properly."

"I could do with some hot protein. Natural . . . if you can supply it."

Tallav decided not to take offense at the suggestion that Welladay could not feed its population decently. He roused the mess hall personnel and ordered a meal from his private stores. No sooner had he turned, smiling, toward the Investigator, than the com unit beeped urgently.

His hand hovered over the unit to silence it. Then he saw it was Hangar calling. The dolts hadn't managed to damage the Investigator's ship, had they?

"Well, what is it?"

"Drone K-Star is back. Or rather, what's left of it is back," the hangarmaster reported.

"Who was that one assigned to?"

"Murv."

"Are all the other drones back?" he asked, inadvertently glancing at the waterfall that covered his plasglas wall.

"No, sir!"

"What? Who could still be afloat in this?"

"Odis."

"Odis? But he . . . Get off the line. I must talk to the harbormaster."

Angrily, he jabbed the new call. "Okker, has Murv got in yet?"

"No, nor Odis either. Just like that new-worlder to try and send his drone back through a storm," old Okker said.

"What were their destinations?"

"You ordered 'em out yourself. Told 'em to milk anything they could catch."

"Well, you knew a storm was coming up. Didn't you call them back?" It was difficult for Tallav to restrain his irritation with the old fool. No respect for status. Just because he had been one of the original fishmen of Welladay, he thought he knew more about everything than a trained Planetary Administrator.

"What do you think, Tallav? I know my job as harbormaster. Besides, Odis is smart enough to run submerged for the eye and drift back with it till it disperses."

Tallav shuddered inwardly, trying hard not to notice

129

the half-smile on the Investigator's lips at the impudence of his subordinate.

"And Murv?" Tallav was compelled to ask. He distrusted the new-worlder and would like nothing better than for him to turn out to be their pirate. He looked the part and he was obviously opting to go off-planet as soon as he could. That was the trouble with the Debt Contractees—men forced to accept undesirable-world employment never took any real interest in their work.

"I can't speak for him."

"Why didn't you report their absence when the storm broke?"

"Did. You weren't in. Down meeting that snooper you sent for so long ago."

"Investigator Brack is present in my office."

"Good for him," Okker replied, ignoring the frost in Tallav's voice. "Now let me get back to my Eye. That damned fool Sharkey's out, too."

Brack was suddenly very alert.

"The Chief?" Tallav was now fully alarmed. Losing Sharkey was unthinkable. The man was a sheer genius with the fishboats, able to repair absolute wrecks. If he lost the engineer, he might just as well resign. He would never get a replacement at the price he could force Sharkey to take.

"You can't test a patched hull in dry dock, you know," Okker was reminding him needlessly.

"Yes, yes. Keep me posted."

"Don't I always?" The connection was broken at the harbormaster's end and the meal arrived at the same instant.

"And you say there's not a drop of the radioactive iodine in store at the moment?" Brack asked as he attacked his food with more speed than manners.

"Not a drop. In an attempt to fill these . . . these demands," Tallav gestured toward the message capsule shells, "I sent out my two best fishmen."

"Into that?"

There was no doubt of the Investigator's disapproval.

"No, not into that. That storm developed some hours after they had cleared port. Even with weather satellites keeping constant guard, storms can come up with frightening speed. You see, when there are two or more moons in conjunction, particularly with one of the other planetary masses in the system . . ."

"Agreed, agreed. I know my meteorology. So that means that the only iodine is either still in your whales or preferably riding out a storm."

"And hidden somewhere in the possession of those pirates."

"You have proof of piracy?"

"Proof? Of course. Take, for example, the rotting hulks of whales who have been deliberately and wantonly milked to death."

"No more than that?"

"What more is necessary?" Tallav was appalled at the man's obtuseness.

"You've got . . . how many fishmen?" The Investigator's smile was condescending.

"No Welladan fishman would milk a whale to death!" Tallav sat up stiffly to protest that possibility.

"You're sure?"

"Very sure. And just to prevent such a ridiculous accusation being leveled against my subordinates, I took precautionary steps. You heard my hangarmaster report a drone's return? When it became apparent that someone was tapping the whales to death, I initiated a drone-escort for every fishboat. The drone is programmed to hover while tapping is in process, taking careful note of the quantity taken from the glands and making a record of the number of the mature whale. They all receive a tattoo, you see. There could be no way to escape such vigilance."

The Investigator shrugged. "But didn't I understand that two ships are still out, and only one drone back in? Murv, wasn't that the name? If there's no drone watching him right now . . ."

"In this weather? The turbulence covers the entire northern hemisphere. You couldn't possibly tap in this weather. Besides, the whales have undoubtedly sounded for protection."

"Northern hemisphere, you said? What about down south?"

"No whales in any great number. The sea is shallow

131

there except for the Great Longitudinal Trench, and that's too deep for fishboats anyway."

"Who's this Sharkey?"

"Our Chief Engineer. Marvelous talent with any kind of engine or vehicle. Keeps our boats afloat and our drones aloft. In fact, he helped rig the control device so that the drone hovers the instant its linked fishboat comes to a stop.

"Sharkey, huh? Appropriate name for a water worlder."

"Beg pardon? Oh, yes, I see. Ha ha."

"He's out without a drone."

"Oh yes, just checking a hull. You can't do that in dry dock, you know. And we're very low on vital materials until Central Credit releases our long-overdue shipment. Besides, he may be a genius with an engine but he couldn't tap a whale to save his life, even if the weather were calm enough to do so."

"How so?"

Tallav leaned back. These were questions he could answer. "Came here originally as a contractee. Whales didn't take to him. Couldn't even get near enough to them to do a tap. They got to the point of being able to identify the pulse of his fishboat, and they scattered whenever he approached." Tallav didn't believe that himself, but the other fishmen did and swore to it.

"The whales didn't take to him?" Brack echoed Tallav's skepticism.

"Oh, they've as much rudimentary intelligence as other forms of mammalian sea life. They evidently develop an affection—or dislike—for certain fishmen. Odis, for instance, and old Okker when he still tapped and even Murv, the contractee, have had no difficulty going deep into schools—until recently, that is."

"Very interesting." The investigator squinted thoughtfully at the watery plas-glas. "I'm sure you won't mind if I take a walk about."

"No, no," Tallav was on his feet too.

"On my own, Tallav. I'd like to talk to the harbormaster. Take a look at the docks and quarters. You know."

Tallav did know and, though he disliked the notion that a Central Worlds Investigator would be . . . snoop-

132

ing—there was no other word for it—if such activity resulted in the apprehension of the pirates, he must ignore his feelings.

"And have you a counter?" Brack added, smiling slightly, his hand outstretched.

"Counter? Whatever for?" Tallav was shocked. The very idea that he, the Planetary Administrator, might not have conducted the most extensive search for any radioactive iodine illegally hidden anywhere in Shoulder, that his estimation of the fishmen might be erroneous, that . . . Fumbling with indignation, he turned his own handcounter over to Brack.

"Now announce my presence," Brack pointed toward the com-unit.

Rather stunned, Tallav depressed the *All-stations* switch and informed Shoulder Blade that Investigator Brack was to be given aid and assistance in his efforts to uncover the pirates.

Shahanna stirred in her sleep, became aware first of the rough surface on which she was bedded and then of the closeness of the ragged walls. Other senses also registered information—the freshness of the air combined with moist rock, the curious yellow light that filtered in and the assault of complete silence. She sat up, then painfully aware of muscular discomfort and stiffness, crawled out of the shallow cave and looked around.

To the right and forward, massive black and gray clouds, their churning innards clearly visible, scudded beyond the outer rim of the old volcano. All around she saw the diffused vibrant yellow of cloud-strained light—bathing the surrounding area with a strange clarity that made the view of this archipelago and its lagoon crystal clear.

Far off on the left, Shahanna discerned the approaching rim of the other half of this storm. She looked back at the receding section, trying to estimate the extent of the eye and to figure out how much time she might have before the onslaught of the rest of the storm.

She shrugged. She had few options. Her shallow cave had sheltered her well enough up to now. If only it would protect her just a while longer. Suddenly something bobbed up on the waters of the mirror-sleek lagoon below her. Instinctively, Shahanna ducked down and peered cautiously over the obscuring rock.

"The size of it!" she gasped. The sea life of her home world boasted no monster like this whale of Welladay.

Quickly, she reviewed what she knew of the creatures. The fishmen of the planet milked their glands for precious radioactive iodine, by inserting a surgical tap into the gland-sac. Therefore, they must be used to humans. So, perhaps she could figure out a way to activate the tap herself. Her hand went to her belt and then fell. Even if she could tap the whale, with her ship a wreck on the bottom of the sea, how would she get the iodine off-world?

She stared at the floating monster, blinked as a piece of its head appeared to lift. "A fish*boat*." She watched as a man's figure became outlined blackly against the reflecting water.

She grabbed her hand weapon and dropped three shots forward of the fish snout, waving her arms in a broad semaphore to attract the Welladan's attention. To her amazement, he dove back into his ship. Within seconds the craft submerged.

Cursing her bad luck, wondering how else she could have attracted his attention, and annoyed at such a cowardly retreat, Shahanna began to pick her way down the basaltic rocks. She couldn't imagine that he would rather brave the storm than face one lone occupant of the volcano. Surely he'd surface again.

Of all the rotten luck, Murv was growling to himself. The air in the fishboat was rank with human and machine stenches. He was weary and sore from the rough transit of the old channel. The boat was leaking from half a dozen seams which he had better seal before the second half of the storm hit. Of course the lagoon would be quieter than the open sea and he had figured on having the chance both to air the boat and to patch it while the eye of the mach-storm passed Crown Lagoon.

His sonar indicated an overhang along the south coast of the lagoon. Good. He would be undetectable there and could find out who that trigger-happy ape was. And if it just so happened that he was the pirate —stranded?

Pirate? He was jumping to conclusions. Flads, who else would be on Crown Lagoon in the middle of a storm. Tallav had only ordered two fishboats out, and the figure on the rocks was too rangy to be Odis!

Murv's irritation quickly dissolved. He found himself eagerly scrambling into his gear. What luck! What sheer unadulterated luck! To find that passage into the lagoon itself and to spot the pickup. Flads, where had the pirate hid his ship? Crown Lagoon was one fardling big place.

The unmistakable triple cracks of a hand weapon had echoed around the lagoon, unnaturally amplified by the volcanic rock hollows, the water, and the curious flat calm of the storm's eye. The shots were distinctly audible to Odis, busy mooring his fishboat on the outer rim of the Crown. He tapped the outboard instrumentation button. Odis quickly called the drone down from its circling security above the stormy mass. If only he could actually catch the pirates in the act of transferring the stolen iodine! Even at speeds no human could tolerate, the distance was still too great for the drone to descend in time. So he slowed its descent. It wouldn't do for the drone to be observed from the ground.

Three shots, he reflected. A signal? He glanced upward at the yellow-clouded skies. There was plenty of time for them to make a transfer before the winds picked up again. And he would have plenty of time to find that space shuttle. There was more than one way to milk a whale!

He secured the outboard gear and went below for his suit and water-aids. He snapped a remote-control drone unit to his belt, a knife to his calf sheath and a buckle-and-line sphere to his shoulder harness. He carefully checked the assist-tanks before he strapped them on. Then, jumping into the water, he began to swim with rapid and powerful strokes around the southern edge of the outer Crown. He knew that he would find better mooring for a space shuttle on the lower south edge of the island.

When she finally reached the shores of the lagoon, Shahanna kicked impotently at the coarse black sands. Nowhere was there any trace of that fishboat—nary a wake nor a ripple, bubble or slag.

"Slimy coward. Twice coward! What were you running from?"

She paused. Maybe Welladans were under attack from the same ship that had fired on her. Maybe that's why the repeated demands for the iodine had been ignored. Perhaps that coward had merely acted with sensible caution. Oh ho, that put a new light on the fishman's retreat. And, if he thought she was one of the invaders, she'd never see him again. That was certain!

Disgusted, she sank down to the beach and leaned wearily against a convenient rock. She forced herself to rest, to drain off the poisons of fatigue caused by her difficult descent. Even though this planet did have a lighter gravity than her own, her efforts had been tiring.

Displacing enough water to inundate the narrow beach and half drown Shahanna, the fishboat suddenly surfaced alarmingly close to the shore. Choking from the unexpected drenching, the girl staggered to her feet, too furious to be frightened by the grotesque pseudo-fisheyes that glared at her from the boat's snout.

"That's the last, remember," a rough voice yelled at her. "And remember, if I'm not off this fardling world in five revolutions, I set the Investigators on you when they get here. And they're coming."

Shahanna jumped back as a large plas-foamed cube landed heavily at her feet.

"Wait," she cried as the fish-snout began turning away from her.

"Can't wait, you fool. And neither can you if you want to get off this fardling planet before the storm socks us in again. Grab that stuff and get off-world."

Shahanna watched as the hatch slammed down and water foamed over the fins of the fishboat. She looked back at the plas-foamed cube and saw its shock webbing—black triangles against the gray stuff. Was that the kind of protection given valuable space shipments?

She dropped to her knees, her arms involuntarily starting to grab up the cube. My God! She pulled back. It just had to be—*a cubeful of radioactive iodine!* Liters of it, just thrown at her feet. She threw back her head and laughed: "Well, I got what I came for, certainly. They've got to give me marks for that!"

She rose to her feet, absently brushed the clinging dark sands from her legs. Her ship had already sent out the death knell. That would eventually connect with a civilized agency which would be compelled to report it to the authorities, and then a search would be inaugurated. She had supplies in her belt for several weeks, in addition to what the sea could provide. Perhaps, and her chuckle was one of pure amusement now, she had only five revolutions to wait until the error in delivery was discovered.

Suddenly she felt much better. With a deft twist, she yanked the heavy cube to her back and began to retrace her steps to the shallow cave. That would be a difficult hole to find, but there she'd be safe from the storm. Her ascent was slower and far more treacherous than her descent because the cube was an unbalancing burden, its weight a strain even on her heavy-world strength. Shahanna had been chosen for this mission for many reasons, not the least of which was her often-demonstrated tenacity. She continued her climb upward.

Murv watched the delivery take place with a mixture of satisfaction and irritation. He was too far away to make out the features of either party, or the code letters of the fishboat fins. He took careful note of the odd gait of the receiver—definitely an off-worlder, someone used to a heavier gravitational pull. Murv knew to a kilogram how heavy that iodine cube was, yet the off-worlder had shouldered it with ease.

Muscles or not, Murv decided, that was going to be a fardling hard climb. The pirate must have ducked into the lagoon at the onset of the storm, probably in a small shuttlecraft. Must be a fladding good pilot, too, Murv grudgingly admitted, to land on a stormy Welladan sea, ride out a mach-storm and then trip along like that. Murv glanced over his shoulder toward the west. The black and ochre clouds were still low on the horizon but coming in fast. He grinned to himself. He *could,* of course, shoot the pirate now, take the radioactive iodine back to Shoulder, and get off this fardling world for good. Everything legal and above-board; no need to blow his cover. But that did not solve the second part of the puzzle: Who was the illegal tapper?

So a dead pirate informed on no one. But tackling an off-worlder presented other problems, even to a man adept at rough fighting from combats on a dozen outer planets. Well, there was more than one way to milk a whale, Murv decided, and started after the pirate.

Flads! Why hadn't the fishboat swung just slightly port or starboard so he could see at least one letter of the code? And why hadn't the fishman emerged further from the hatch? Murv could have identified him with one clear glimpse of profile. Murv cursed again, remembering that the only other man out when the storm broke was Odis. He was cynic enough to believe any man capable of any deed, given the right combination of pressure and opportunity. But Odis? His love for the great whales was exceeded only by his love of this drenched world. He was the last man Murv would have suspected of treachery. Still, you never knew what went on inside a man's head: everyone had a price.

That settled it for Murv. He could not kill the out-worlder until he had discovered the identity of both traitor and pirate—and learned, to his own satisfaction, why Odis tapped whales to death.

To Shahanna, time was shortened to the span involved in a simple physical effort. First one foot must lift, its toes finding a hold, somehow, on the treacherous rock. The toes must then grip long enough to tense the calf muscles which must inform the long thigh muscles of the effort required of them. Arms must, somehow, manage to retain their grip on the shock-webbing on the unquestionably valuable and impossibly heavy cube.

She was only vaguely aware of other pressures: the wind beginning to rise, gustily plucking at the overbalancing burden on her back now and then, or lightly cooling the sweat that trickled down her face and into her suit. The light was changing, darkening as the other side of the storm neared the island. She was completely unaware of being under observation or that her tenacity implied far greater familiarity with the terrain than she actually possessed. An innate sense of direction was another of her assets. Once she had been to any place on any world, she was able to retrace her steps to it, just as she was now heading toward the anonymous cairn hidden.

She dragged herself and her burden into the cave and then, with a sigh of complete fatigue, curled around the cube, one hand seemingly welded to the shock web. That protective reflex as well as the darkening skies prevented Murv from locating her when he finally realized that she was no longer climbing ahead of him.

He had followed cautiously, therefore slowly, and was not unduly alarmed when he could no longer see the straining figure with its awkward load. At first, he wondered how the pirate could have gotten so far ahead of him. Then he reached the highest ridge of the southern escarpment and realized that the pirate must have taken cover. From here, the island jutted outward and downward.

At that moment Murv caught sight of the half-submerged craft. "Fladding stupid fool. He isn't going anywhere." He laughed. "But then is he?"

Carefully Murv worked over to the ship, using the tumbled rockscape to cover his advance, keeping close watch on the open hatch lest the pirate discover him prematurely. He agilely reached the open lock, listening for any sounds of activity within. It wasn't a large vessel but a single cabin job. He gave the deserted interior one sweeping look. So, the guy hadn't made it back. He'd gone to ground somewhere up in the crags.

Murv began to pick his way up again, following Shahanna's original route so, his back to the sea, he was unaware that he was being observed.

Odis had allowed the tides to pull him back under water, deep enough so that his progress could not be seen. He surfaced again, twice, in fact, looking for a way up the rock face so that he could outflank Murv.

139

He was annoyed that it was Murv up there on the rocks. Annoyed but puzzled. Murv gave every appearance of a man hiding. But why should he hide if he were the pirate's contact? And where was the iodine?

Where, too, was Murv's fishboat?

Glancing up at the clouds scudding and boiling on the horizon, Odis considered his next move. He had kept the drone just above the cloud cover, but now he directed it down to the northern part of the island to take a skimming run, hopefully to detect Murv's craft. The wind was rising enough to cover the whistling sound of a drone. Odis flipped on the visor and blinked at the rushing ocean picture on the tiny screen. He sent it twice over the northern arc of the island and it spotted his own boat moored to the east. But he found no trace of another fishboat, either visually or sonically. So he sent the drone aloft, remembering to check the wind velocity to be sure the drone was at a safe altitude. Then he sat down to think.

No ship. Had Murv lost his fishboat in the storm? Murv had a tendency to be too quick. After all, he wasn't all that accustomed to Welladan storm conditions. Of course, Murv might have discovered a ledge and moored the boat under that. One thing was certain, the pirate was going no place.

But who had blown off the after-section of the pirate's vessel? Had the Investigator arrived, spotted the pirate ship, and blasted it? If so, the Investigator must surely be at Shoulder now, so all Odis need do was wait until the storm lifted enough to get a message back there. He settled down to wait, keeping a weather eye on the approaching storm front. He had no intention of cutting it too close back to the safety of his own boat.

So why was Murv hiding? Had those three space shots been hostile rather than for identification?

The rain-laden wind began to keen in the darkening sky. Gouts of lightning spat through the bilious clouds. Warm air masses were moving in, Odis thought with pleasure. Storm is breaking up a little. Weather was capricious: a real mach-storm like this one, despite the pull of two moons and the conjunction of another planetary mass, could break up with a crustal shift up north.

140

Murv was moving, not merely shifting position but moving forward, darting to cover as he worked his way back up the slope. The rising wind was bothering him, Odis decided, and followed him obliquely. A flash of a head beam and Odis saw that Murv was definitely searching among the hollows and crevices of the cliff. Odis climbed faster.

He arrived in time to hear raised voices echoing in an argument. But the sounds were so diffuse and the rising wind so noisy that he could not pinpoint their location. Odis cursed softly under his breath as he jumped from crag to block, flashing his own beam in and out the darker hollows.

The next thing he knew, Murv had emerged from a low ledge, his arms wrapped around a foam-cask. Since there was no chance for Murv to reach his hand weapon, Odis stunned him with a full charge, neatly catching the cube as Murv folded.

Keeping one hand on the cube, Odis knelt and flashed his beam into the cavern. He caught sight of a dark lump that was a prostrate body. He turned it over and was reassured by a groan.

Rain began to spray across his back as he crouched between the two unconscious forms. He could just leave them here; they'd both be out a while. No. He didn't know where Murv's boat was and he couldn't permit the man to escape. Resigned, Odis settled down to wait.

"I don't know what you expected to find here," Okker said, his seamed face flushed with anger, "but are you satisfied now?"

"I really don't understand, Investigator," Tallav put in with understandable anxiety as he picked his way across the debris. "You certainly cannot have suspected Okker here, and he is absolutely the only one permitted in the Eye."

Brack was sweating from his exertions. He had pulled out every drawer, shelf, and movable fixture in the rock chamber, rapped on every inch of the rock walls, trying to find a hollow. He had moved his geiger counter over everything without a crackle for his pains. He didn't mind alienating Tallav or the ancient, but he was furious over the fruitlessness of his search. He

141

glanced at the two men, somehow now allied against him. That wouldn't do.

"This is the only installation known as the Eye on Welladay, isn't it?" he demanded curtly.

"What's left of it," Okker replied.

"Unavoidable. I . . . I intercepted a message, obviously from the pirates, setting up a contact point. I caught only part of it due to the storm's interference. *Southern edge of the lagoon where the eye is centered.*"

Brack pointed to the lagoon harbor which the single big window of the harbormaster's control room overlooked. "Your control room is on the southern edge of the lagoon. This place is called the Eye. What other eyes are there on this fladding planet?"

Okker regarded him with a deep scowl, then slapped his thigh, and burst out into a cackle.

"You sure you heard *where,* and not *when?*" He pointed an accusing finger at the Investigator as he danced about in an excess of amusement.

"You fladding idiot, stop that!"

"I believe I can answer you, Investigator," Tallav said, his manner stiff as he waved Okker to be still. "Logical topical references are deceptive to a newcomer." He smiled at the Investigator. "You see, this is not the only lagoon on Welladay. It is therefore possible that the message, which you say you heard imperfectly due to faulty transmission, said *when,* not *where.* Therefore, I presume the contact point meant the southern edge of the Crown Lagoon, when the eye of the storm was centered on it. Really, most ingenious. With proper timing, the pirate could make contact, pick up the radioactive iodine, and be off without ever being detected through the storm."

Brack swung around toward the exit. "Let's go then!"

"To Crown?" Okker cackled, reinfected with ill-timed amusement. "Not now. Eye's over Crown right now so they've made contact and the radioactive iodine is no doubt off-world. You blew it, Investigator!"

Brack seemed about to explode. Then, with a massive effort, he controlled himself and began to smile ominously. "No, that's where you're wrong, Okker. There can have been no contact because I disabled a small spaceship just after I picked up the message. Got a direct hit and saw it tumbling out of control. So that iodine is still on this world, waiting to be picked up. And I intend to do just that!"

"Not till the storm has cleared Crown, you aren't. Drones can't handle that kind of turbulence, not unless they go above it; and that's got to be too high for non-pressurized cabins," Okker told him.

"I hadn't planned to use local transport." Brack's smile broadened.

"Couldn't. Ain't even a fishboat left with sound seams. And," Okker pointed a nobby finger at the Investigator, "you just forget trying to make it in your spacecraft between now and the time the rest of the storm hits Crown. You couldn't do it on the trajectory you'd need."

"If only Sharkey were back with the boat he was testing," Tallav muttered, "that vessel could stand the trip. We have to get that iodine." Tallav turned to Okker. "Hasn't that squall along the coast lifted enough for us to find Sharkey? Where could he be?"

Okker shrugged. "That squall came up sudden. He probably had the good sense to head for the open sea to avoid getting smashed. He doesn't like to go seaward though," he contradicted himself, "so it won't hurt to look for him, before the whales do."

"Before the whales do?" Brack queried.

"Like I said, the whales don't like Sharkey. I'll get a weather picture. We're clear enough to receive . . ."

A bleep made the rest of his sentence inaudible.

"Odis to Eye, Odis to Eye: Drone-relay transmission. Proceeding Crown Lagoon at 1930 hours. Checking out spacecraft trajectory plotted toward Crown." A second raucous bleep.

"Of all the nerve," gasped Tallav, the first to recover.

"Must be that ship you shot up," Okker said to Brack with more respect than he had previously shown.

"He ought not to take such risks," Tallav muttered.

"Then he should be at Crown by now?" Brack asked in a tight voice, glancing up at the main chrono.

"Contact that drone, Okker," Tallav ordered. "Maybe we can relay a message to Odis to search for the iodine."

143

"Not if the eye's passed Crown," Okker grumbled, but his gnarled fingers sped with unexpected agility across the communications board. "Crown's a mighty good place to hide something on—it's full of hollows, caverns, and boulders."

"Get him to search the southern edge," Brack snapped.

"Yeah, that's right, isn't it," Okker said, glancing sideways at the Investigator.

Another unit began to chatter and a sheet of relay paper extruded from a slot.

"Weather relay from a satellite," Okker said, and grabbed the print before Tallav or Brack could. "Hmmm. Weather's closed in again over Crown, but see here," his stubby forefinger following the wispy leading edge of the mach-storm, "it's breaking up." He moved his finger to the right. "And we got some of the bonuses. If you want to find Sharkey, you'd better git. I'll transmit to Odis's drone. This weather looks like it'll clear in another couple of hours and he can look for the iodine. Can't do more'n that now."

"Be sure to tell him to search diligently for the iodine," Tallav was saying as Brack urged him out.

Another alert blasted and Tallav hesitated, his eyes widening at the distinctive sound.

"C'mon," Brack snapped.

"A sublight message?" Tallav moved back into the eye. "Now what?"

"Come!" Brack insisted.

"This is Federation Cruiser DLT-85F, Based Mirfak. A d-k has been received from your planet, Welladay. Coordinates Frame BE-27|186. Search and recover. Search and recover. D-k assigned to Mercy Ship Seginus X. Advise!"

"That pirate ship you shot down was a mercy boat. And it is now on Crown Lagoon," Okker snapped in a hard voice.

Tallav turned slowly to Brack, his face pale.

"Your pirates are more ingenious than we've given them credit for. Using a mercy boat as a contact vessel. Very clever. We must outsmart them. Catch them red-handed. Let's go, Tallav!"

Then Brack pulled the stunned Planetary Adminis-

144

trator down the corridor. Okker stared after them, his expression bleak, his eyes thoughtful. He turned back to his board then, and began to broadcast a message for Odis's drone to transmit. Then he warmed up the sublight generator. If he was right, Tallav wouldn't scream at the power use.

"I'm glad it wasn't you, Murv," Odis shouted, trying to make himself heard above the storm.

Murv nodded, grinning at Shahanna, who was unselfconsciously taping her orders back to her bare ribs. A bit heavy-boned, Murv thought, but no more flesh on them than was needed to make her a soft handful.

"Who is it?"

Even with Odis's lips tickling his ear, Murv could barely hear above the keening wind. He shrugged, then put his mouth to Odis's ear. "Someone stealing a fishboat, sneaking out under cover of the squall at Shoulder?" He had to repeat his words twice before Odis caught the entire sentence.

"Not past Okker. Only two boats seaworthy, anyhow. No parts!"

"Okker might be in it!"

Odis stared at Murv for a long moment, then shook his head vehemently, denying that possibility. So Murv shrugged and patted the cube of iodine significantly. Odis grinned in comprehension.

Shahanna prodded Murv's possessive hand, then jerked her thumb backward toward herself, rubbing the place where her orders from Federation for a top-priority requisition of radioactive iodine were taped. She emphatically pantomimed the quantity of iodine needed. Odis continued to nod and patted her hand reassuringly. She glared at Murv, who just grinned back with sheer deviltry in his eyes. When she realized he wouldn't give her the satisfaction of an acknowledgment, she reached across and gripped Odis firmly on the shoulder in an ostentatious gesture of friendship. She almost wished Murv had been the pirate, instead of the agent. She wondered if the ID plate, indisputable evidence of his authenticity, ever ached the arm-bone in which it had been implanted. He needn't have walloped her so hard when he snatched the iodine. But

145

then, she mused, he had acted within the scope of the information he possessed at that time. Just as Odis had when he knocked Murv out. She was sorry that she couldn't describe the fishman who had thrown the cube at her feet. She had gotten the most fleeting glimpse of him but she was sure she would be able to recognize him. However, that time was long off, judging by the siren winds. Shahanna arranged herself into as comfortable a position as she could and closed her eyes.

"There's something over to starboard," Brack said, raising his eyes from the screen to squint through the plas-glas snout bubble of the drone.

Tallav flipped up the call switch. "Must be Odis. We're halfway to Crown. Tallav calling fishboat. Tallav here. Fishboat. Answer!"

"You're in the ship?" Surprise and relief colored the voice of the respondent.

"Sharkey? What are you doing midocean?"

"Between the storms and the whales, I'm lucky to be anywhere," the man snapped. "You don't see them on your screen, do you?"

"We've spent hours scanning the coast for you," Tallav interrupted, angry but relieved at finding his mechanical genius. "You've got the only seaworthy boat and the Investigator and I—"

"Investigator?" Sharkey's voice was sharp.

Brack elbowed Tallav back from the speaker.

"Brack here. I have reason to believe that the pirated radioactive iodine is still on this Crown Lagoon the P.A. has been telling me about. I intercepted a message arranging a contact point on the southern shore of a lagoon, only the reception was faulty and I missed the entire message. Do you read me?"

"Yeah, I read you, Investigator Brack."

"Good. Now, can that fishboat of yours make it back to Crown Lagoon. You realize, of course, that we must pick up the iodine before the pirate can retrieve it. Another fishman, named Odis, is presently believed to be in the vicinity of the lagoon."

"Odis, but . . ."

"Can your fishboat accompany us?"

"Yeah, if you can keep those fardling whales off my back."

"We cannot permit that iodine to fall into the wrong hands, now can we?" Brack cut across Sharkey's complaints, more threatening than suggesting, Tallav thought.

"No, we can't," Sharkey agreed flatly.

"Good man. Now, how fast can that fishboat go?"

"Long as those squalls don't hit us, as fast as that air bubble you're in." And, as they watched, they could see the fishboat rise slightly from the water on its hydrofoils, then take off in the plume of spray that arrowed northeast by east.

Before Brack could speak, Tallav banked the drone and poured on power to follow.

"Would they send another Investigator?" Odis asked Murv when Okker's transmission was completed.

Murv shrugged, grimacing. "It's possible. This has taken a lot longer than predicted. And, with the credit embargo and no ships touching down at Shoulder, I haven't been able to send in a report. They might think I'd been drowned here. Now, with Shahanna to identify the Welladan contact, we can finish this up in no time. First we've got to get this treasure safely to Shoulder." He patted the iodine cube.

"The traitor is Sharkey," Odis said gloomily.

Murv laughed. "I'm not sure of anything. Remember, I thought it was you and you thought it was me, and then we both suspected Shahanna of being the pirate."

"Yes, but your Okker said Sharkey was still missing," Shahanna reminded the men, "and when he'd last heard from the P.A., they'd given him up for lost and were heading here."

"Try Okker again, direct, Odis," Murv urged, glancing up at the clearing skies.

"Another squall between here and Shoulder," Odis reported after several minutes of fruitless calling.

"This planet's fardling weather is . . . is . . ." Murv broke off.

"Don't mind me," Shahanna suggested with a grin, "but shouldn't we leave here while we have a chance?"

147

She pointed to the fringe of dark clouds on the western horizon.

"Okay. I'll check my boat," Murv said.

"I'll wrestle this down the hill again," Shahanna volunteered with mock forbearance.

"I'll see if there's anything left of my ship, but I doubt it," Odis said with resignation as he started south down the rocks.

"I can give you a hand part of the way," Murv offered, grinning at Shahanna.

"If you think you can keep up with me." She grinned back.

"Sharkey! The cube's on the rocks on the lagoon shore. Just where the contact said it would be!" Brack roared through the speaker.

"Oh, oh," Tallav gasped feebly. "However did it survive the storm, unprotected like that!"

"You're seeing things, Brack!" Sharkey roared back. "You're seeing things, I tell you."

"Like your whales, I'm seeing things. You fladding fool, it's clearly visible. Are you through that passage yet?"

"How'n hell could I be beaming to you if I weren't. I'm surfacing!"

"We're landing," Brack countered.

"I'm not sure I can land on that," Tallav said, unable to see any likely surface on the tumbled rockscape.

"You'd better. I don't think I altogether trust this chief engineer of yours," Brack muttered betweeen clenched teeth, his eyes never leaving the cube, white against the black lava on which it sat. "In fact, I find it definitely suspicious that he knew such a convenient channel into this lagoon which even you, as Planetary Administrator, didn't know existed."

"Yes, but . . . how could he possibly . . . I mean . . ."

"There's a flat space big enough for this thing."

"It'd be so much easier for Sharkey. After all . . ."

"Land!"

"Good heavens, he's here already," Tallav exclaimed as he set the drone down on the flat-topped slab that was scarcely larger than the drone's landing feet.

"What do you mean?" Brack followed Tallav's gesticulations and saw the figure emerging from the water, heading toward the cube. "How'dya get out of this thing?" he demanded, fumbling with his tunic.

Tallav reached across him and flipped up the hatch release. Brack, his eyes on the figure, suddenly froze.

"That's not Sharkey!"

Tallav looked. "No, it isn't, is it. But who . . . and—" Tallav broke off, staring at the Investigator. "How would you know what Sharkey looks like?"

"Get out, Tallav," Brack ordered and turned his hand weapon on the startled man.

As the two men emerged from the drone, the figure on the shore reached for the cube and grabbed it, then started off, up the slopes with more speed than either observer thought possible.

"Halt!" Brack shouted and lobbed off a shot after the fleeing figure.

A fishboat broke surface, its hatch flipping open for the flying exit of a man. He also began to shoot, three short cracks, splitting rocks just ahead of the fugitive. The man turned and began to descend as fast as he had climbed in the direction of the fishboat, heading obliquely away from the men by the drone.

"You see," Brack shouted at Tallav, "there's the pirate! We must intercept."

Tallav's previous doubts were swept aside by the urgency in Brack's voice, and he didn't hesitate to follow the man down the torturous escarpment to the beach. Brack paused, whipping off a few shots in the hope of slowing the pirate, but he was closing the distance to the fishboat faster than they could jump down the rocks.

"Be careful of the iodine," Tallav jabbered when the pirate started to use it as a shield.

The man flung the cube into the water and dove in after it, pushing it ahead of him toward the fishboat. He was urged on by Sharkey, who was running down the ventral fin to assist.

When Shahanna, winded and half-blinded with watery eyes, grabbed the shock-webbing for a final heave into the waiting man, she got her first look at his face.

"You're not Murv. You're . . ." and she grabbed the

149

cube back, frantically kicking out and away from the fishboat.

"Give me that thing or I'll blow you out of the water," Sharkey snarled.

"Shoot and you'll destroy the iodine."

Shots whistled over Shahanna's head, and Sharkey backed behind the flaring dorsal fin. Shahanna heaved herself away from the fishboat and began treading water halfway between both contenders. She used the buoyant cube as a head shield.

"I'm Tallav, Planetary Administrator of Welladay," the shorter of the two men on the shore yelled at her. "Come ashore. If you turn yourself in, I promise you immunity."

Shahanna felt intense relief. They had probably mistaken her for the pirate; that was why they'd shot at her. She struck out to the beach with strong sweeps of her free arm and long legs.

Tallav jumped about in the shallows, splashing water in her face as he vacillated between grabbing the iodine or her hand until she finally shook him off.

"I'm not a pirate. I'm from Seginus. My ship . . ."

"You survived?" Tallav gasped. "We got the d-k relayed from Fleet."

"Your pirate shot my engine away," Shahanna said as Brack joined them, lobbing another shot at Sharkey, who was trapped behind the dorsal fin of the bobbing fishboat.

"Investigator Brack mistook you for a pirate," Tallav explained nervously. "Why didn't you identify?"

"I never had the chance," Shahanna protested. "I was checking coordinates . . ." she trailed off when she caught the look on Tallav's face. She whirled to see that Brack's weapon was trained on them.

"I'll take that iodine. Now," Brack said, smiling slightly. He grabbed it by the shock-webbing, then carefully stepped backward and moved up the rocks, his gun covering Shahanna, Tallav and Sharkey.

Suddenly they were distracted by violent whoshing splashing sounds from the lagoon and a whining whistle from above. Shahanna took the opportunity to launch herself, her body taking every bit of advantage from muscles that had been trained on a heavy-gravity planet as she leaped at Brack. He could not keep track of three attackers at once so his shots went wild. Shahanna ripped the valuable iodine from his hand, then rolled sideways and down. She ripped her suit against the jagged rocks, but managed to scramble away with the cube.

When she came to rest against a huge black fist of a rock, she dazedly saw Sharkey running up the ledge of his fishboat toward the hatch. Then she heard his despairing scream as half a dozen fishboats closed in on him and he was tumbled into the water to be ground against the converging hulls. A bolt lanced past her ear and she wrenched around, trying to put the rock fist between her and Brack.

Somewhere Tallav was shrieking. "They've got him. They got him. He's getting away. Stop him!" Then abruptly the sounds of the struggles ended and Tallav's exhortations ceased.

Battered and shaking with pain, Shahanna drew herself up. She saw Brack, spread across the rocks just below the drone. Odis was climbing down, hand over hand on the line which Shahanna could see had tangled Brack's feet and brought him down. In the lagoon, where roiling waters lapped around Tallav's knees, only two fishboats remained—one lay unbelievably sideways on the rocks; its belly was barnacle-covered, exposed to glisten in the sun. The second was cruising slowly in to shore near Tallav.

With a sigh Shahanna sagged and laid her scratched cheek against the cool cube.

"I really don't credit what I saw," Tallav protested as he watched Murv and Odis bandage the Seginan girl.

"When I reached my ship under the ledge," Murv said patiently, "I saw the school on sonar, flooding in through the passage after him."

"Then he was kept from Shoulder by the whales?" Tallav asked.

"Hardly matters," Murv remarked. "We've got to get you back to the hospital at Shoulder, Shahanna."

"And the iodine," Tallav said.

"Better get, then," Odis suggested, pointing toward the squall brewing in the west.

"This fardling planet and its fladding storms!" Murv growled.

"I've got to get iodine to Seginus," Shahanna insisted, struggling to rise.

"We will. Just as soon as we fix you up at Shoulder."

"But my ship's—" Shahanna began, looking over her shoulder.

"Brack won't require his spaceship anymore," Murv assured her, helping her up and then swinging the cube to his back.

"Now, wait a minute, Murv," Tallav ordered, blocking his path.

"Fair's fair, Tallav. Brack blew her *mercy* ship up," Murv said, "and considering her help today, that's the least you can do."

"Of course, of course," Tallav replied.

"And to be sure, you can return the iodine to Shoulder," Murv went on, dumping the cube into Tallav's arms, "in Odis's drone."

"I'm left with your fishboat?" Odis asked, slightly amused.

"You're the sailor, friend," Murv laughed, thinking of the rough passage out of the lagoon.

"And that's the only fishboat we've got left until the embargo's lifted," Tallav added. "You be careful with it."

By the time Odis had clambered into the fishboat, the drones were circling above him. He tapped on the outboard panel release, plotted a course across the lagoon. The drones were approaching him now as he cut across the lagoon toward the passage out. They waggled farewell. Odis responded and then began to read his gauges. A man had to keep an eye on the weather of Welladay.

The three stories which follow are basically humorous—or at least they exhibit my own notions of whimsy and proportion. Humor is one of the hardest things to carry off in a story or a novel and especially in sf. But there are many humorous incidents in every life, so I've included such episodes in all my books.

"The Thorns of Barevi" was an attempt to cash in on the lucrative market for soft- and hard-core pornography in the 60's. The market paid well for such stories and many sf writers earned their monthly rent from such submissions. I thought I'd give it a try. I didn't really succeed there. But there were seeds in the short story that could eventually germinate a full novel about the modus operandi of the Catteni in subjugating a planet and its inhabitants. But I haven't written that one yet, either.

"Horse from a Different Sea" was written after my three years as a Cub Scout Den Mother. In my youth I was a Girl Scout; my brothers were Boy Scouts. So I have nothing but respect for the work done by scout leaders, and for any woman brave enough to be a den mother. Furthermore, the scouting programs have helped train many responsible and marvelous adults.

We're still in my Wilmington years with "The Great Canine Chorus." Actually, we acquired Wizard in New Jersey. He became one of the first K-9's to serve the Wilmington Police Force. He was an unusually intelligent beast, about eighty-five pounds' worth and so fast on his feet that he never had to bite, even when it was all legal. He never needed to, his handler told me: he'd trip up the guy he was chasing. Wizard was honorably retired after three years of service when

153

it was discovered that he had displacia of the hip. He lived another five years in comfort before the condition worsened enough to cause him constant pain. He sired one litter of pups, and Chet kindly gave me one, Merlin, who is the hero of a novel, *The Mark of Merlin*.

Wilmington is often maligned by its residents as being a one-horse town because of the equestrian statue of Caesar Rodney (one of the signers of the Declaration of Independence), which inhabits the park in the center of town.

Although there's a lot of *good* music in Wilmington, and many fine semiprofessional singers, there never was a canine chorus . . . that I heard about it, at any rate! Who knows what's happened since I left?

The Thorns of Barevi

CHRISTIN BJORNSEN WONDERED IF SUMMER on the planet Barevi could possible be the *only* season. There had been remarkably little variation in temperature in the nine months since she'd arrived here. She'd been four months in what appeared to be the single, sprawling city of the planet when she'd been a slave, and now had racked up five months of comparative freedom—tooth-and-nail survival—in this jungle, after her escape from the city in a stolen flitter.

Her sleeveless, one-piece tunic was made of an indestructible material, but it would not be very warm in cold weather. The scooped neckline was indecently low and the skirt ended midway down her long thighs. It was closely modeled, in fact, after the miniskirted sheath she had been wearing to class that spring morning the Catteni ships had descended on Denver. One moment she was on her way to the college campus; the next, she was one of thousands of astonished and terrified Denverites being driven by forcewhips up the ramp of a spaceship that made the *Queen Mary* look like a bathtub float. Once past the black maw of the ship, Chris, with all the others, swiftly succumbed to the odorless gas. When she and her fellow prisoners had awakened, they were in the slave compounds of Barevi, waiting to be sold.

Chris aimed the avocado-sized pit of the gorupear she was eating at the central stalk of a nearby thicket of purple-branched thorn-bushes. The bush instantly rained tiny darts in all directions. Chris laughed. She had bet it would take less than five minutes for the young bush to rearm itself. And it had. The larger ones took longer to position new missiles. She'd had reason to find out.

Absently, she reached above her head for another gorupear. Nothing from good old Terra rivaled them for taste. She bit appreciatively into the firm reddish flesh of the fruit and its succulent juices dribbled down her chin on to her tanned breasts. Tugging at the strap of her slip-tight tunic, she brushed the juice away. The outfit was great for tanning, but when winter comes? And shouldn't she concentrate on gathering nuts and drying gorupears on the rocks by the river for the cold season? She wrinkled her nose at the half-eaten pear. They were mighty tasty, but a steady diet of them . . .

A low-pitched buzz attracted her attention. She got to her feet, balanced carefully on the high limb of the tree. Parting the branches, she peered up at the cloudless sky. Two of the umpteen moons that circled Barevi were visible in the west. Below them, dots that gave off sparkles of reflected sunlight were swooping and diving.

The boys have called another hunt, she mused to herself and, still standing, leaned against the tree trunk to take advantage of her grandstand seat.

Before her chance to escape had presented itself, Chris had picked up a good bit of the lingua Barevi, a bastardization of the six or seven languages spoken by the slaves. She had gleaned some information about her captors, the Catteni. They were not, for one thing, indigenous to this world but came from a much heavier planet nearer galactic center. They were one of the mercenary-explorer races employed by a vast federation. They had colonized Barevi, using it as a clearinghouse for spoils acquired looting unsuspecting non-federation planets, and as a rest-and-relaxation center for their great ships' crews. After years of the free-fall of space and lighter-gravity planets, Catteni found it difficult to return to their heavy, depressing home world. During her brief enslavement, Chris had heard the Catteni boast of dying everywhere in the galaxy except Catten. The way they "played," Chris thought to herself, was rough enough to insure that they died young, as well as far from Catten.

Huge predators roamed the unspoiled plains of Barevi, and the Catteni considered it great sport to stand up to the rhinolike monsters with only a single spear. That is, Chris remembered with a grim smile, when they weren't brawling among themselves over imagined slurs and insults. Two slaves, friends of hers, had been crushed under the massive bodies of Catteni during a free-for-all.

Since she had come to the valley, she had witnessed half a dozen encounters between rhinos and Catteni. Used to a much heavier gravity than Barevi, the Catteni were able to execute incredible maneuvers as they softened their prey for the kill. The poor rhinos had less chance than Spanish bulls and, in all the fights Chris had seen, only one man was slightly grazed.

As the flitters neared, she realized that they were not acting like a hunting party. For one thing, one dot was considerably ahead of the others. And by God, she saw the light flashes of the trailing flitters' forward guns firing at the "leader."

Hunted and hunters were at the foot of her valley now. Suddenly, black smoke erupted from the rear of the pursued flitter. It nosed upward. It hovered reluctantly, then dove, slantingly, to strike the tumble of boulders along the river's edge, not far from her refuge.

Chris gasped as she beheld a figure, half-leaping, half-staggering out of the badly smashed flitter. She could scarcely believe that even a Catteni had survived that crash. Wide-eyed, she watched as he struggled to his feet, then reeled from boulder to boulder to get away from the smoldering wreck.

With a stunningly brilliant flare, the craft exploded. Fragments whistled into the underbrush as far up the slope as her retreat, and the idiotic thornbushes she had recently triggered sprayed out their lethal little darts.

The smoke of the burning flitter obscured her view now, and Chris lost sight of the man. The other flitters had reached the wreck and were hovering over it, like so many angry King-Kongish bees, swooping, diving, trying to penetrate the smoke.

An afternoon breeze swirled the black clouds about and Chris caught glimpses of the man, lurching still further from the crash. She saw him stumble and fall, after which he made no move to rise. Above, the bees buzzed angrily, deprived of their prey.

Catteni don't hunt each other as a rule, she told herself, surprised to find that she was halfway down from her perch. They fight like Irishmen, sure, but to chase a man so far from the city?

The crash had been too far away for Chris to distinguish the hunted man's features or build. He might just be an escaped slave, like herself. If not Terran, he might be from one of the half-dozen other subjugated races that lived on Barevi. Someone who had had the guts to steal a flitter didn't deserve to die under Catteni forcewhips.

Chris made her way down the slope, careful to avoid the numerous thorn thickets that dominated these woods. She had once amused herself with the whimsy that the thorns were the gorupear's protectors, for the two invariably grew close together.

At the top of the sheer precipice above the falls of the river, she grabbed a long vine which she had hung there for a speedy descent. On the river bank she stuck to the dry, flat rocks until she came to the stepping-stones that allowed her to cross the river below the wide pool made by the little falls. Down a gully, across another thorn-bush-filled clearing, and then she was directly above the spot where she had last seen the man.

Keeping close to the brown rocks so nearly the shade of her own tanned skin, she crossed the remaining distance. She all but tripped over him as the wind puffed black smoke down among the rocks.

"Catteni!" she cried, furious as she bent to examine the unconscious man and recognized the gray and yellow uniform despite its tattered and blackened condition.

With a disdainful foot, she tried to turn him over. And couldn't. The man might as well have been a boulder. She knelt and yanked his head around by the thick slate-gray hair which, in a Catteni, did not indicate age. Maybe he was dead?

No such luck. He was breathing. A bruise mark on his temple showed one reason for his unconsciousness. For a Catteni, he was almost good-looking. Most of them tended to have brutish, coarse features, but this one had a straight, almost patrician nose, even if there was a lot more of it than an elephant would want to claim, and he had a wide, well-shaped mouth. The Catteni to whom she had been sold had had thick, blubbery lips, and she'd heard rumors—never mind about them!

A sizzling crack jerked her head around in the direction of the wreck. The damned fools were firing on the burning wreck now. Chris looked down at the unconscious man, wondering what on earth he had done to provoke such vindictive thoroughness. They sure wanted him good and dead.

The barrage pulverized the flitter, leaving the fire no fuel. The wind, laden with coarse dust, blew odorously from the wreckage. The man stirred and vainly tried to raise himself, only to sink back to the ground with a groan. Chris saw the flitters circling to land on the plateau below the wreck.

"Going to case the scene of the crime, huh?"

It was completely illogical, Chris told herself, to help a Catteni simply because there were others of his race out to get him. But . . . she backtracked, just in case he had left any trace for them to follow. She went back as far as she could on the raw rock. Where dirt began, ash had settled in a thick layer, obliterating any tracks he might have made. After all, the Catteni might stumble on her if they thought their victim had escaped the crash.

He had got to his feet when she returned. She tried to lend her support but it was like trying to guide a mountain.

"Come on, Mahomet," she urged softly. "Just walk like a nice little boy to the river, and I'll duck you in. Good cold water'll bring you round."

A sharp, distant gabble of voices made her start nervously. God, those Catteni had got up that rock

159

face in a hurry. She'd forgotten they could take prodigious leaps on this light-gravity planet.

"They're coming. Follow me," she said in lingua Barevi.

He groaned again, shaking his heavy head to clear his senses. He turned toward her, his great yellow eyes still dazed with shock. She would never get used to such butter-colored irises.

"This way! Quickly!" she said, urgently tugging at him. If he didn't shake his tree-stump legs, she was going to leave him. Good Samaritans on Barevi had better not get caught by Catteni.

She pulled at his arm and he seemed to make a decision. He lurched forward, one great hand grasping her shoulder in an incredible viselike grip. They reached the river bank, still ahead of the searchers. But Chris groaned as she realized that the barely conscious man would never be able to navigate the stepping-stones.

The shouts behind them indicated that the others were fanning out to search the rocks. Urgently she grabbed his hand, leading him to the base of the falls.

"If you don't float, it's just too damned bad," she said grimly, and taking a running start, she knocked him into the water.

She dove in, right beside him, and when he did indeed continue to sink, she grabbed and caught him by his thick hair. Fortunately the water made even a solid Catteni manageable. Exerting all her strength and skill as a swimmer, she got his head above water and held him up with a chin lock.

By sheer good luck, they came up in the space between the arc of the falls and the cliff, the curtain of water shielding them from view. As the Catteni began to struggle in her grasp, the five hunters leapt spectacularly into view in the clearing by the pool. Her "Mahomet" was instantly alert and, instead of struggling, began to tread water beside her.

The Catteni were arguing with each other, and each seemed to be issuing conflicting orders.

Mahomet released himself from her chinhold, his yellow eyes never leaving the party on the bank. They watched, keeping the swimming motions to a minimum, though the falls would hide any ripples.

One Catteni, after a heated argument, decided to cross the wide pool in a fantastic, to Chris, standing leap. He and another began to move downstream, carefully examining both banks and casually surmounting up-ended coffin-sized boulders with no effort. The other three went charging back the way they had come, arguing violently.

After an endless interval, during which the icy water chilled Chris to the bone, the refugee finally touched her shoulder and nodded toward the shore. But when she realized that he was going to head back the way they had come, she shook her head emphatically, pointing to the other side.

"I've a flitter. Over there," she shouted at him over the noise of the falls. He frowned. "Safer. That way!" she insisted, jabbing a finger in the direction of her hidden vehicle. Stunned as she suddenly realized what she had done, she stared at him. "Oh, God!"

He raised an eyebrow in surprise, and she hoped for one long moment that he had not understood what she had said. But he had, and now his yellow eyes gleamed at her in the gloom with a different sort of interest.

He's like a great lion, Chris thought, and almost choked on fear.

"You have aided a Catteni," he said, rumbling in a deep voice. "You shall not suffer for that."

Chris wasn't so sure when she tried to climb out of the river and found herself numb with cold, and strengthless. He, on the other hand, strode easily out of the water. He looked down at her ineffectual struggles, frowning irritably. Then, with no apparent effort, he curled the long fingers of one hand around her upper arm and simply withdrew her from the water, supporting her until she got her balance.

Shivering, she looked up at him. God, he was big: the tallest Catteni she had ever seen. She had inherited the height of her Swedish father and stood five foot ten in her bare feet. She had topped most of the Catteni she had seen by several inches, but his eyes were level with hers. And his shoulders were as broad as the scoop of a road-grader.

"Where's the flitter?" he demanded curtly.

She pointed, furious that she obeyed him so instantly, and that she couldn't control the chattering of her teeth or the trembling of her body. He reached for her hand, relaxing his grip a little at her involuntary gasp of pain.

Replace "grubby paws" with "high-gravity paws," she told herself in an effort to keep up her spirits as she stepped in front of him.

"I'll have to lead the way through the thorns," she said. "Or maybe thorns don't bother Catteni hides?" she added pertly.

To her surprise, he grinned at her.

"Catteni are always cautious."

As she turned, she realized that she had never seen a Catteni smile before. She noticed, too, that he was following carefully in her footsteps. It was good to know that he was no more anxious to disturb the thorn-bushes with their vicious little barbs than she was.

They were halfway to the hidden flitter when both heard, off to the right in the valley, the staccato volley of orders in loud Catteni voices.

Mahomet paused, dropping to a half-crouch, instinctively angling his body so that he did not touch the close-growing vegetation. He listened, and although the words were too distorted for Chris to catch, he evidently understood them. A humorless smile touched his lips and his eyes gleamed with a light that frightened Chris.

"They have seen movement here. Hurry!" he said in a low voice.

Chris broke into a jog trot; the twisting path made a faster pace unwise. When they broke into the dell just before the extensive thicket, she paused.

"Where? Are you lost?" he asked.

"Through those bushes. Watch. And when I say move, *move!*"

He frowned skeptically as she picked up a handful of small stones. With a practiced ease, she began casting at the thickets. Gauging carefully, she threw right and left, watching and counting the thorn sprays to be sure she had triggered every bush. To be on the safe side, she scooped up one more handful of pebbles and broadcast it. No further thorns showered.

"Move!" His reaction time was so much faster than hers that he was halfway across the clearing within seconds after the order escaped her lips. She rushed in front of him. "We have five minutes to cross before they rearm."

An expression that was almost respectful crossed his face. Impatiently, she tugged at him and then began to weave her way among the bushes, following no recognizable route. When she made the last turn and he saw the flitter, its nose cushioned in the heavy cluster of thorn-thicket limbs, he gave what Chris assumed was a Catteni chuckle.

She waved open the flitter door and bade him to enter with a regal gesture. He walked straight to the instrument panel, grunting as he activated the main switch.

"Half a tank of fuel," he muttered, and then checked the other dials. He seemed pleased as he flipped off the switch. He glanced up at the transparent top, camouflaged by the interwining leafy limbs, at the bed she had made herself on the deck, at the utensils she had fashioned from spare parts in the lockers.

"So it was you who stole the commander's personal car," he remarked, looking intently at her.

Chris jerked her chin up.

"At least I landed it in one piece," she replied.

At that he laughed outright, once.

"You're one of the new species?"

"I'm a Terran," she said with haughty pride, her stance marred by uncontrollable shivering.

"Thin-skinned species," he remarked. He looked down at her heaving chest, and slowly started to stroke her shoulder with one finger. His touch was feathery—and more. "Soft to the touch," he said absently. "I haven't bothered to try a Terran yet . . ."

Before she could draw back, his left hand cupped her breast and the other grabbed her tunic at the back, ripping the garment from her in one sharp,

163

powerful jerk. The fingers of his right hand pulled her inexorably toward him.

"I saved your life . . ." she said in protest, her heart beating in panic.

"And I intend to reward you suitably."

"Not that . . ."

"A Catteni's honor is involved," he said, both hands exerting such pressure on her body that his caresses were painful.

With no effort at all he picked her up and deposited her on the bed. When she tried to wiggle away, he laid a hand, like a ton of bricks, on her chest. With the other, he stripped off his tunic, exposing his immense chest, each well-defined muscle rippling sinuously under slightly olive skin. The rest of his clothing followed.

"Oh no!" Chris cried in desperation. "You're . . . I can't!"

He glanced down at her wide, curving hips, and shrugged.

"Catteni have been enjoying your race since you were discovered," he reassured her calmly.

"Yes, but have *we* enjoyed it?"

She made a frantic attempt to evade him as he leaned down. But there was no escape from that implacable male. She arched her back, only to realize that she had made it much easier for him. She continued to struggle out of pride.

"You enjoy pain?" he asked, a puzzled frown on his face. His fingers tightened just that much more so that she felt she'd been caught in a vise and, with a shuddering moan she relaxed, too exhausted to offer even token resistance. "Now we will both enjoy," he said, and proceeded to prove his point.

Just as she was certain she would be split apart, apprehension was replaced by a surging emotion far more powerful and overwhelming. Somewhere, in that flood of intense relief and unexpected ecstasy, she heard him exclaiming, too, in loud surprise.

A harsh curse broke the silence that had settled in the hidden flitter. The warm, strong body of the Catteni stiffened. Chris glanced up at him in alarm. He brushed his hand warningly across her lips, all his attention focused in the direction of that swearing. The flitter door was still open, and both Chris and Mahomet heard the *vrrh, vrrh* as the thorn-bushes released their darts. There were loud cries of pain and further curses. Chris saw the Catteni's eyes dance with malicious amusement.

An authoritative voice uttered a rough command, and even Chris understood the "Get the hell out of here, nothing can pass this way."

She and Mahomet lay still, almost breathless, although the flitter was buried a good hundred yards from the edge of the thickets and could not possibly be seen. They waited until they heard no sound except the brief sighing of the wind.

With a low laugh, the Catteni finally withdrew from Chris, stretching leisurely, his joints popping and cracking with startling loudness.

"I'd heard there was a run on Terran women, and now I can see why. They use their heads as well as their tails."

Chris slapped at his hand, feeling like a flea attacking a Great Dane, but determined to make a gesture. He began to stroke her body, gently exploring it rather than attempting to arouse passion. He was curious, like a small intrigued boy.

"Yes, I can see why," he repeated with a chuckle. He lay back, glancing about the flitter. "This car has been gone five months. Why have you stayed so long alone?" he asked. "Are there others of you here?" He propped himself up on one huge elbow, looking suspiciously out the windows.

"Just me."

He relaxed and smiled. Sensing his receptivity, she dared ask him why he had been chased by his own people.

"Oh," and he shrugged negligently, "a tactical error. I was forced to kill their patrol leader. He had insulted the accomplishments of my squadron. And, as I was without allies, I withdrew."

"He who fights and runs away, lives to fight another day?"

"The *next* day," he corrected her, absently.

"The next day?"

"Certainly. It is against the Catteni Law to continue a quarrel past the same hour of the following day. I have only to lie hidden," and he grinned at her, "until tomorrow at sun zenith and then I can return."

"Won't they be waiting for you?"

He shook his head violently. "Against the Law. Otherwise, we Catteni would quickly exterminate each other."

"You honestly mean to say that, if they can't find you before noon tomorrow, they have to give up?"

He nodded.

"Would that Law apply to slaves, too?"

He looked at her intently. "It can. And I shall personally see that in your case it does. However, while we're waiting for tomorrow . . ." And he reached purposefully for her.

Batting at his possessive hands, she squirmed to free herself.

"What? Was I not tender enough with you?" he asked, concern flitting across his face. "We Catteni pride ourselves that we are gentle with our women."

Chris could think of a hundred argumentative replies to that statement, and yet had to admit that he had been considerate, gentle, and that even at the height of his passion, he had not forgotten to adjust his strength. His hands were caressing her now, softly, and despite herself, she was responding to him, wanting more of that strong gentleness.

"It's just . . . well . . . you've had quite a day," she temporized, aware that her body was already conforming itself to his even as she protested, "you've been in a crash, half-frozen in icy water and . . ."

"Like the thorn-bushes of Barevi," he said, smiling, "it takes the Catteni little time to rearm."

Horse from a Different Sea

ARE WE BABES-IN-THE-WOODS? OR I SHOULD say, babes-in-space. I don't mean beating the Russians to a manned moonbase or setting up a space hospital or making Mars adaptable to our survival there to ease the population explosion here. Our problem is more basic than that: can man survive as *Homo sapiens* or a reasonable facsimile thereof. In that department, are we wetting our spacesuits!

I know what I'm talking about. Only I can't talk. Not yet, since my evidence hasn't come to light, so to speak. It's due soon and, as an ambulance chaser from way back, I've got to be there. I'd rather know right off what the competition makes out as.

We—that is, mankind, Earth-type—are in for one helluva jolt and this is one therapeutic pill that has no sugar coating—unless it's an LSD cube. I'm not the only one in the medical fraternity to realize that there's something queer in the conversion chamber. Some of us tumbled to it six months ago. The research is not the stuff of which AMA citations are made, but it will be handy when I-told-you-so time comes.

For me it started when my perennial maternity case phoned up and asked for an appointment.

"Buzzy-boy says I must be pregnant again," Liz Lattimore said with understandable grimness in her voice. She has six under six—well, one set of twins.

Buzz is a guy on a single track, business and monkey business. As a kind of moral justice, he has sympathetic reactions to each of Liz's pregnancies in the form of violent morning nausea. Oh yes, it happens. Liz may develop varicose veins, hemorrhoids, boils, hot flashes, heartburn, and high blood pressure during her gestations. Buzz gets the morning sickness.

"How long since you missed a period, Liz?" I asked her.

"That's just it, Ted. This time he must be sympathetic to someone else because I came regular as clockwork last week."

"On a possible sixth pregnancy, you'd better see me."

She did. She wasn't pregnant.

"We had a fight a while ago," she told me after she'd dressed. "Buzz flounced out of the house like an injured Cub Scout. When he came home, he wore that merchandise-better-than-thou expression. Sometimes, Ted, it's a pure relief to me when Buzz cats around so I don't whinge."

She paused, about to add something more but hesitated. Even if she had voiced her suspicion then, I doubt it would've made much difference.

"Anything I can do, Liz?"

"Outside of helping to suppress a paternity suit if the case arises, I don't think so. We made up our differences." She rolled her eyes with droll expressiveness.

"Seriously, Liz, I'm glad you're not freshening again. You're run ragged now. Send Buzz in for a checkup. *He* may need it."

Buzz came in the next day at noon, which proved that he was now worried about himself.

"How come you said Liz wasn't pregnant?"

"Because she isn't. Praise be!"

"Then how come I got this damned morning nausea? I only get it when she's got buns in the oven."

"Nausea is a symptom not necessarily exclusive to pregnancy. Especially in the male of the species."

As I mentioned, we're such babes-in-space.

"Off the record, Buzz, could you be sympathetic to someone else?"

Buzz flushed.

"Ted, I'm nuts about Liz no matter what I do or say. I only go catting when we've had a fight or she's too pregnant to screw. Hell, Ted, if I didn't love her so much, d'you think I'd go home every night to a house full of squalling brats?"

"Well, that was quite an imagination you projected the other afternoon at Casey's."

"At Casey's?" Buzz swallowed. "I didn't know you were there."

"Buzz, your voice'd carry to your funeral. Was it the girl at Lady Linda's?"

A strange look crossed Buzz's face and I could see him about to evade the question with some Lattimorian verbal embroidery. "She was the damnedest woman I ever screwed, Ted. Once was, by God, enough. But that once . . ." Buzz whistled slowly, shaking his head.

Something in his attitude inhibited further questions, so I changed the subject by getting him to strip. After a thorough physical I found only a little hard lump near the large intestine, but not situated where it could cause pressure that might result in nausea. I sent him to the hospital for a gastrointestinal series but the results were inconclusive. I saw no cause for alarm, so I told him that the nausea was caused by overwork—with a wink—and to give up smoking.

In the next few weeks I examined four more seriously nauseated males with small intestinal lumps. I also heard of seventeen more around town. Then I had a visit from the leading local Boy Scout and our little unprepared Explorer gave me my first definite lead.

"Doc, can I see you for a minute? I mean, you're not too tired or anything?"

When six feet two inches and 185 pounds of Explorer Boy Scout Horace Baker comes sneaking around after my nurse has left, I'd better not be too tired to see him.

"Now, what's wrong with you, Hoke? You look mighty pale for Glen Cove's answer to a maiden's prayer?"

The boy literally cringed away from my buddy-type arm.

"Hey, feller, did I strike too close to home?" I led him to the surgery table.

"Aw, Doc, I'm in awful trouble." He groaned and averted his head.

"You mean," and I put on my best Ben Gazzara pose, "you've got some girl in trouble?"

"Naw," and he was momentarily indignant, "I wear my pants too tight. No, Doc, it's me. Ever since I went . . . to . . . Mrs. Linda's . . ." His voice failed him.

A kaleidoscope of impressions overwhelmed me for a moment at this confession. Kids grow up so fast. A few flashes of the red squally baby I'd delivered from Mrs. Baker merged into Explorer Hoke complete with merit badge sash, approaching in best Indian fashion Lady Linda's modestly situated house of seven delights. I wasn't sure whether I was glad or sorry that Hoke had taken his lustiness to Linda's. I was relieved that his experiments hadn't taken root, as it were, in any of his peers. Hoke needn't worry about VD: Linda's girls were clean. I had no remedy for his conscience, however.

"Well, now, Hoke, I don't think you have anything more to worry about than overactive sex glands. Linda's girls are—"

"Oh, it's not that, Doc. It's just that I can't eat. Nothing stays down. It's worse in the mornings, and Mom notices that I don't pack it away—hey!"

Past the first sentence I had dropped the TV medic pose and stretched him out flat. My fingers dug into his big gut and, sure enough, the precocious Explorer had joined the Group.

I gave him some dramamine and told him it was indigestion caused by a guilty conscience and to eat spaghetti for breakfast. He fortunately didn't argue because I had no more quick answers. I hurried him out, locked up, and went on a professional call.

Linda herself opened the door.

"Dr. Martin! You're psychic," she said by way of greeting. "I hate to mix pleasure with business and I'll expect your bill . . ."

"You won't get one because I *am* here on business, Linda," I said, trying not to be too brusque. "I'd appreciate seeing your new girl for a brief professional inquiry."

Linda looked stunned, an expression I never thought to see on her face.

"She's who I was calling you for." And Linda gestured me to follow her up the stairs. "She's been losing weight steadily. She's skin and bones and you know that doesn't bed easy."

"Nausea?"

"Doesn't mention it. Until three days ago she had the appetite of an elephant, but you'd never guess it to look at her." Linda was slightly jealous.

"How long's she been with you?"

"About five weeks. A friend sent her to me from Chicago. She's got a sister in the business there. She's good but funny, no one wants her steady. She's educated, too: speaks very good English."

"She's foreign?"

"Must be, but I can't place her accent and I never ask too many personal questions."

The room Linda gestured me to enter was dark and rank with a heavy, musty, unaired-attic odor. A dim light shone on the gaunt face of the dying girl. She *was* dying. It's an indescribable but recognizable look which I've seen too often in my years of practice. The pulse in her spider-thin wrist was barely discernible; her heartbeat muffled and erratic. She opened her eyes at my touch, then smiled wanly at Linda standing behind me.

"Too much at once. Now too little, too late. But thanks, Linda. I won't be much trouble, I promise." She spoke in a raspy voice, but her phrases were oddly inflected. "You see, Doctor, I'm dying and there's no cure for my ailment."

"No, you just rest easy," I began, but her knowing eyes mocked me for the specious words.

"A cigarette, please?"

I offered my case, tacitly admitting my helplessness. She was sinking so visibly that it would have been heartless to bother her. An autopsy would give me more specifics anyhow.

"Thanks. Now, would you please go? Both of you." This one was different all right. No last-minute confessions of inadequacy, no wailing for repentance

171

and salvation, and no real bravura. She just wanted to be left alone. I guided Linda out.

"Hell, Doc. Someone should stay with the poor kid," Linda said.

"You see too much TV."

"So does she," Linda replied with an irritated snort. "She's never smoked before."

The hall was suddenly flooded with a very bright light and an acrid formic acid stench like burning ants. I threw the door open but it was too late. The bed was a blazing funeral pyre.

I know now why, but at the moment I was aghast with remorse at this mystifying incineration. I couldn't understand how a cigarette, no matter how carelessly held by a novice smoker, could have caused as violent a combustion as this. I didn't have much time to think about it because it was all we could do to keep the blaze from spreading until the fire department got there. Neither Linda nor I mentioned that we'd only been out of the room three seconds when the fire started. No one would have believed us.

So my primary clue went up spectacularly in smoke. A little judicious inquiry uncovered a veritable epidemic of smoking-in-bed fire deaths in fifteen cities. One incident got a lot of publicity because the victim was a call girl. She was to have appeared before a board of inquiry the next day so her death was considered a grisly form of suicide. Seventeen such incidents on the East Coast scared me sufficiently not to want to know the odds against us in the rest of the world.

Linda gave me the names of all the men who had patronized the girl. If the others of her ilk had got around as much as she had . . . wow! Five of the men were patients of mine. Buzz was the furthest along—as far as I could tell—but then, it had been his tale in Casey's that had prompted others to visit the girl. The chief of police shouldn't have accepted payola in trade but that's his lookout. I almost wish I could morally allow the old fool to carry to "term." Jerry Striker's a poor enough character, but it'd serve his wife right. Martin Tippers? I hadn't guessed him for the type. Must have been drunk. And our precocious Explorer.

What a queer collection of males to be chosen to propagate an unknown race on a new world. *That's* what I mean about adapting to survive. Those gals, if females they were, used equipment to hand, not fancy life-support systems.

Now that I know the game, I can't just ingenuously suggest to any one of my equally puzzled colleagues that their patients got invited into a lady spider's nest. Or maybe they had a hurry call from a passing sea mare? The least bizarre examples of male incubation on this planet are spiders and sea horses, and those comparisons are quite enough to inhibit further speculation. Give the imagination full rein and there are endless possibilities. You pays your money and you takes your choice. Of course, if I let one of the men carry to term, I'd find out more. But, hell, neither my conscience nor my professional integrity will permit me.

The most I can do is spread out the curious unorthodox operations on my five pregnant males so that I'll have some interesting embryos for my babes-in-space theory. Even then I might goof. I don't know how long gestation takes, what would serve as a birth canal or, if you know what spiders do . . . well, you can see my problem. What form will the progeny ultimately assume? That of their hosts? The two foeti I've removed show different stages of freak-out evolution. I'm letting Hoke Baker go longest because he's adjusted best to the changes in his physiology. But I've got to arrange for his abortion soon—before he becomes eligible for an Explorer's Maternity Badge.

The Great Canine Chorus

PETE ROBERTS OF THE WILMINGTON, DELAware, K-9 Corps has as his partner a German shepherd named Wizard. One night, just after they took the beat, Wizard started acting itchy, nervous, whiny. He was snappish, not like himself at all. He kept trying to pull Pete toward Seventh Street.

That wasn't the beat, as Wiz well knew. But Pete decided there might be a good reason. Wizard was a canny dog; he could pick a culprit out of a crowd by the smell of fear the man exuded. And he'd saved Pete from two muggings already this year. So, protesting, Pete let Wizard lead him to a block of buildings being torn down as part of an urban renewal program.

Wizard became more and more impatient with Pete's apprehensive, measured pace, and tried to tug him into a jog. Pete began to feel worried, kind of sickly scared. Suddenly the dog mounted the worn stairs of one of the buildings about to be demolished. He pawed at the door, whining.

Who's that? a voice asked, high and quavering like an old lady's. *Pa?* It couldn't be too old a female, then.

Wizard barked sharply three times in the negative signal he'd been taught.

Hi, dog. Do you see my pa?

Wiz got down from the steps, looked up and down the street, then barked again three times.

Pa's so late, and I'm so hungry, the voice said.

Pete, who had eaten well an hour earlier, was suddenly overwhelmed with hunger—a sullen kind of

174

stomach cramp that he'd experienced in Korea when his unit was cut off for four days. The kind of gripping pangs you get when you're hungry all the time.

"Lady, I'm going down to the deli on the corner. I'll be right back with something to tide you over till your pa gets back." Pete made the announcement before he realized it. He left Wizard to guard the door.

He ordered a sub with no onions (somehow he knew she wouldn't want them), two cokes and a banana.

I'm in the back room, said the voice when he and Wizard entered the hall.

Pete had had the distinct impression the voice had come from the front of the building. It was too thin to have carried far. The stench in the filthy hall sickened Pete. No matter how many years he might spend on the force, he'd never get used to the odor of poverty. Maybe it was the stink that brought a growl from Wizard.

Pete pushed open the back door and entered the pitifully furnished room. On an old armchair by the window was a wasted little figure, like a broken doll thrown down by a careless child, limbs askew. By now he expected a girl, a child, but this was such a *little* girl!

Wizard got down on his belly, licking his lips nervously. He crawled carefully across the dirty floor. He sniffed at the tiny hand on the shabby arm of the chair, whined softly. The little hand did not move away, nor toward him, either.

What kind of a father, Pete fumed to himself, would leave a kid, a mere baby, alone in a place like this?

I'm no baby, mister. I'm nine years old, she informed him indignantly.

Pete apologized contritely, blaming his error on the glare from the single window. He wouldn't have thought her more than five, six at the outside. She was so pitifully underdeveloped. She was clean, as were her shred of a dress and the old blanket on which she lay, but the rest of the room was filthy. Her pinched face had a curious, calm beauty to it. When Pete knelt beside her, he saw her eyes were filmed and sightless. And when she spoke, her mouth did not move.

He found himself breaking off small pieces of the sub and feeding them to her. She sipped the Coke through a straw and a look of intense pleasure crossed her face.

I knew I remembered how wonderful it tasted, she said. But not with her lips.

The truth dawned on Pete; this child was a telepath. Impossible? He hadn't actually believed any of that crap. But there was no other explanation.

"You aren't talking," he said. "You don't make a sound."

I am too talking, answered the child soundlessly. *And you're answering.*

Pete gulped, hastily trying to mend matters. "You just don't speak the usual way."

I do everything kind of different. At least my pa's always complaining I do. Her head turned slowly toward him. *You don't suppose something's happened to Pa, do you? I can't hear very far away when I'm hungry.*

Guiltily, Pete fed her another bite. "When did you eat last?"

Pa was home this morning. But all we had was bread.

Pete vowed passionately to himself that he was going to see Welfare immediately.

Oh, you mustn't! pleaded the soundless voice. Wizard, ears flattened, growled menacingly at Pete. She was clearly frightened of Welfare. *They'd take me away, like they took my sister, and put me in a barred place and I'd never hear any birds or see Pa. They might cut me up 'cause my body doesn't work right.* She still spoke without sound.

"Aw, honey . . ."

My name's Maria, not honey.

"Maria, you got it all wrong. Wizard, you tell her. Welfare helps people. You'd have a clean bed and birds right outside the window."

It'd be a hospital. My ma died in a hospital because no one cared. Pa said so. They just let her die.

Wizard whimpered. Pete felt frightened himself.

176

He soothed Maria as best he could with promises of no hospitals, no cutting, plenty of birds. What she didn't finish of the sandwich, he wrapped up and put beside her. He started to peel the banana for her but she refused it.

It's a treat for Wiz for bringing you here. She laughed. *He listens to people.*

Pete grinned.

"How on earth did you know that fool dog loves bananas?"

Nothing could have been funnier to Maria, and her laughter was so contagious Pete grinned foolishly. Even Wizard laughed in his canine way, his tongue lolling out of one side of his mouth. Suddenly the atmosphere changed.

I hear Pa coming. You'd better leave. He wouldn't like having the fuzz in here.

"Then why did you let me in?"

Wizard. Dogs always know. I talk to dogs all the time. But I've never talked to one as smart as Wizard before. You get out now. Quick.

Pete felt a violent compulsion to take to his heels. Once they were around the corner the impulse vanished, so he waited a few moments and then peered out at the building. He saw a shambling figure go into the house where they had found Maria.

Pete was shaken by his encounter with the girl: shaken, confused, and frightened. She had taken him over, used him to suit her needs, and then cut him off in fear when all he wanted to do was help her. He worried about her all the way to the hospital: her pitiful life in those awful surroundings . . . and that strange talent.

He had a friend, a drinking buddy, who was interning at Delaware Hospital. Finding Joe Lavelle on duty in the emergency ward that night, Pete told him a little about the girl. "And what's going to become of her, living like that?"

"I'd say she was dead already and didn't know it," Joe snorted.

The thought of Maria dead choked Pete up. Her fragile laugh, her curious calm beauty gone? No!

"Hey, Pete!" The intern watched the cop's gut

reaction with amazement. "I was only kidding. Why, I couldn't even guess what was wrong with her without an examination. She could have had polio, meningitis, m.s., any variety of paralysis. But I'd say she needed treatment, fast. And I'd certainly like to see this kid who can make a stalwart defender of this one-horse town quake in his boots like this."

Pete growled and Wizard seconded it.

Laughing, Joe warded off an imaginary attack with his arm, just as his phone rang. Pete resumed his patrol.

The next morning, resolved to help Maria in spite of herself, he bought a frilly dress, bundled it and food and Wizard into his car, and went back to the house. He "talked" to let her know he was coming.

There was no answer. The back room was deserted. Except for the de-stuffed armchair by the window and two Coke bottles on the floor under it, Pete could have sworn no one had been in the house for months.

"Find Maria, Wiz," Pete ordered.

Wizard sniffed around and, with a yelp, raced out the door. He sniffed around outside and seemed to find a trace. Pete followed him in the car. Wizard acted just as if he knew exactly where he was going. He got halfway down the next block, then stopped as if he had run into an invisible wall. He lay down on the sidewalk, put his head on his paws, and whined. Then he slunk back to Pete at the curb.

"Find her, Wizard!" The dog crouched down and laid his ears back. It was the first time he had ever disobeyed that tone of voice.

"Maria! We're your friends! We want to help!" Pete called, oblivious to the stares. He was sure she could hear him. He waited, apprehensive, unsure.

No! came the one disembodied word, filling his skull till his head rang. There was no arguing with it.

"At least tell Wiz if you're hungry, Maria. He can bring you food. I promise I won't follow."

Twice in the next three weeks, Wizard darted into a deli, whining pathetically. The first time, it took Pete a minute or so to grasp what the big dog wanted.

Then he'd get a sandwich and a Coke to go, put it in a bag, roll the top into a handle for Wizard to carry. Then he'd wait till the dog returned. He was determined to prove to Maria that he'd keep his promise. He didn't want to lose contact with her.

In the meantime, he did a little library research on telepathy, but the textbooks were too much for him. When he asked the librarian for something a guy could understand, he was shown the science fiction shelves.

Maria didn't act like fictional telepaths. According to the stories, she should be able to get food when she wanted it, commit robberies undetected, start fires, transport herself and anyone else anywhere, aid society, and perform minor miracles. Like heal herself, even. The prospects were magnificently endless. Yet she was stuck in some hideous, hot horrible back room, half-starved and slowly dying of neglect.

The one thing Pete had to accept was the fact that Maria kept in touch with Wizard but excluded him. Since Pete considered Wizard every bit as smart as most men, he wasn't offended; but he felt powerless to help her as only another human could.

The next set of inexplicable incidents began about four weeks after Pete and Wizard first encountered Maria. They were pacing the beat on the hotel side of Rodney Square when the dog got restless. He strained against the leash until Pete let him go to see where he'd head. At a dead run, Wizard streaked down Eleventh Street, right over into Harry West's beat.

Harry walked with Pirate, the biggest dog on the force. Pete couldn't figure Harry in trouble. But he was wrong. He heard the sullen rumble of an angry crowd by the time he reached French Street. Wiz was already around that corner and in the middle of a fight. Pete whistled for squad cars as he broke into the edge of the crowd, swinging his nightstick. He could hear Wizard growling angrily. He heard a yelp and then the growling of a second dog. He stumbled over Harry, bleeding from a head wound. Pete got Harry clear of the stampede just as the squad cars arrived.

Both dogs were at work, snapping, snarling, darting around, and the crowd thinned rapidly. In a matter of minutes, all but the bitten, bruised, and brained had evaporated into the hot night.

"How'd you get here so fast?" Harry demanded as he came to. "I heard Wiz just as some kook pelted me with a bottle."

"Well, Wizard just took off," was Pete's unenlightened reply.

"Glad he did. We came down on a Code One, but when Pirate and I got to the edge of the mob to get them moving, they closed in like we was Christmas in July. Somebody got Pirate in the head and I couldn't turn anywhere without getting clobbered." Harry dabbed at the cuts on his hands. "I'd sure like to know what set them off."

Wizard and the bigger dog were wandering around the street, nervously sniffing. The paddy wagon arrived, and Wiz and Pirate assisted in rounding up the incidentals, just begging for one legal bite. Then they started whiffling around again.

"What's with the dogs?" Harry asked Pete as he helped him into a car. "Look at old Wiz pumping."

Wizard's tail was wagging like he was on his way to a steak fry.

"Maria!" Pete gasped and called Wizard to heel. The dog came bounding over, wriggling with delight. "Find Maria!" But Wizard barked three times, sneezed, and shook his head. Pirate came up, nuzzled Harry, sniffed Wizard, and then *he* barked three times.

"I got a girl that only talks to dogs yet," Pete said in bitter disgust.

Back on their own beat, Pete tried to figure out why Maria would have called Wizard. Harry and Pirate weren't in trouble at the time Wiz took off. Maria must have been worried . . . yeah, that was it! Worried about her old man! She'd called Wizard because her old man had been in that crowd.

And that explained why Wizard was so happy-acting. He'd found Maria's father's trail leading away from the rumble.

Pete left a note for Harry to keep an ear and an

eye open for any crippled kids on his beat and to let him know if Pirate ever acted . . . strange. She might keep in touch with Pirate, too, since the big dog had been involved in getting her father out of a tough scrape.

Two of the men picked up that day were known numbers runners. They stuck to their story that the cop had come busting in where he wasn't wanted and his damn dog had spooked the crowd into the rumble. They just "happened" to be there.

For the next few weeks Pete got no signs from Wizard that Maria was in any distress. This bothered him almost as much as hearing from her when she *was* hungry. At headquarters they were hearing nasty rumors about a new numbers racket. Certain hoods were being seen in new cars, in new quarters, acting up. Two runners were picked up on suspicion, in the hope of cracking them. They had to be released twenty-four hours later, clean, but one of them had bragged a little. Pete heard one of the detective lieutenants complaining bitterly about it.

"Yeah, the punk says, 'You gotta have evidence, Lootenant, and this time there ain't any, Lootenant. Not unless ya can read minds.' That's what he says, s'help me."

Maria! Pete thought with a sense of shock.

What was it Maria had said? When she was hungry, she didn't have the strength to hear far away. If she were well fed, how far could she hear? All the way to Chicago? To grab the numbers?

The conclusion just couldn't be dodged. Maria and her pa were involved. But how would she know she was doing something wrong? Whoever had latched onto her would be jubilant over the fact they were able to put something over on the cops. To Maria, cops were just the fuzz. Cops spelt trouble for her father. Cops meant Welfare, and hospitals, and she didn't know which one scared her the most.

"At least," Pete said to Wizard, "she's not in that crummy room. She's cared for. That was all I wanted, wasn't it? And she is a minor, so even when the gangs gets pulled in, she wouldn't be booked. Why, those

hoods might even get a doctor to try and fix her up."
He groaned. "And I sure as hell can't go to the Chief
and say, 'Look, there's a kid telepath running the
numbers.' Not even if I *knew* where to find her."

Wizard nuzzled his hand.

"Now what would Al Finch be wanting with a
high-priced specialist from Minneapolis?" the desk
sergeant asked Pete when he came on duty the next
night. "He's got medics and nurses hopping in and
out of his pad like he had the Asian crud."

"Better him than you," said Pete, automatically
laughing. But he was thinking *Maria!*

Pete found out where Al Finch was living. Outside
the building, Pete saw a truck from a pet shop deliver
a triple cage of singing birds, and he knew his hunch
was right. Finch was making book with Maria's mind-
reading ability.

"Maria," Pete called in his head, "Maria, answer
me. I know you're there. What you're doing, reading
numbers, is wrong. It's causing a lot of trouble. It'll
get you in trouble, too."

Pete, came Maria's voice in his head, sweetly, happily, *Pete, I'm not hungry anymore and I have so
many pretty birds. And you should see how nice Pa
looks now he's got a good job. I'm clean, and my
whole room is clean. I've got pretty dresses.*

Her giggle was light and tinkling. *Smelly men come
and poke me around. They say they want to fix me.
They can't, of course. Some of them say it out loud
and some tell Al they can. Then they say inside they
can't, that I'm a hopeless case.* She giggled again, as
if this were the funniest thing she'd ever said.

"Maria, I won't say Al isn't trying to help you and
make you happy. But he gets more out of you than
you get out of him. He's just using you. You miss getting the numbers through once and he'll hurt you."

Maria's laugh bubbled up. *I don't let myself get
hurt. And Al's all right. He thinks the damnedest
things sometimes.* She giggled naughtily. *He says he's
my sugar daddy.*

"Maria, you shouldn't use such words."

Maria's incredible laugh chimed through his head.

Al says it's cute the way I talk. And he really does like me.

"I'll bet," Pete said in a harsh tone. "Look, Maria, you can have the birds, and the good food, and a good job for your father, but get them from the right sort of people. Al Finch is dangerous! He's got a record for assault, attempted homcide, you name it. I'm afraid he'll hurt you."

He wouldn't dare, Maria replied with complete self-assurance. *I'm very important to him, and I know he means it. Do you know I have my own Coke machine?*

"Maria, Maria," Pete said with a groan. *Oh God, how do I explain? How, please, do I have the nerve to try?* "Maria," he called as loud as he could in his mind, "Maria, promise me one thing. You get scared of Al, or worried, just call Wizard or Pirate. Any of the dogs. They'll protect you. Just call the dogs!"

Wizard barked twice, paused, barked twice again. So did three stray dogs across the street. And a cat walking on a nearby fence meowed in the same sequence.

Pete tried not to worry. But she was so frail; well-fed or not, she couldn't have great reserves of energy. Finch might kill her without meaning to. He'd have to find a way to stop Finch using her.

On his day off, following a strong hunch, Pete hung around the betting windows at the Brandywine Raceway. Sure enough, Maria's father shuffled up to the ten-dollar window, just before the second race. Pete sidled up to him.

"You tell Al to be careful with Maria," he said. "He can use her too much, you know. He could kill her. And the cops'll tumble to Finch soon enough. They got a lead."

"Who're you?" the little man asked nervously, his face twitching as his red-rimmed eyes slid over Pete's face. "Fuzz?" He scurried away.

Pete had had a good look at his face, though, and was able to identify him in the rogue's gallery as Hector Barres. He had a record; vagrancy, drunk and disorderly, petty larceny.

No appeal based on Maria's frailty would reach

Barres. Right now he had all he wanted from life. Barres' thoughts were only for the money rolling in today. Tomorrow, and Maria's welfare, were far from his mind.

Now that he had Maria's last name, Pete checked hospital records and found her date of birth. Her mother had been picked up unconscious, already in active labor, and brought into the emergency ward. The intern who had delivered Maria had expressed doubts that the infant would survive, due to prenatal malnutrition.

Maria's mother had died in the same hospital two years later. The cause was neglect. Not on the part of the hospital. She had had tuberculosis, diabetes, and a coronary condition. She had been severely beaten about the abdomen and died of internal hemmorrhaging before they could operate.

Pete took to talking to Wizard on the beat at night, hoping that Maria would overhear him. He told Wizard all about Maria's mother, about her father's record, about how Maria could use her great gift to help people. He told her all he knew about paranormal powers, his feeling that she must conserve her energies; and he repeatedly cautioned her to call Wizard or Pirate if she felt endangered. Sometimes he had the feeling she listened to him. He knew she often talked to Wizard.

Then Al Finch stepped up his operations to include narcotics, apparently having approached and reached an agreement with the local drug pushers in an unprecedented crossover in vice. Pete and the police went quietly berserk. No known pushers were suddenly in evidence. There was no direct contact with or indirect approach to Finch. All known pushers were clean when they were picked up on routine searches. Not a sniff on them. But the stuff was circulating in greater quantities than had ever reached Wilmington before.

"Maria," Pete called resolutely to her from the corner opposite Al's apartment. "Do you know what drugs do to people?"

Sure. They have the coolest dreams to read.

"Do you take it?" He gasped, frightened.

I don't need to, Maria laughed with a mirth that no longer chimed. Her voice—the essence of the voice she sent—was hard and brassy. *I dig it from others. It's boss, man.*

"Then dig what happens when they can't pay to get it, Maria. When they have withdrawal. Dig that and see how boss it is!"

But, Pete honey: you gave me the idea yourself. It's much easier to grab the stuff from . . . well, never mind where. Her voice was sickeningly smug. *Easier than reading numbers out of Chicago. You said I was to take care of myself. I am.*

"I don't know why I bother with you. You know you're doing wrong, Maria. And when you get hurt, it'll be your own fault." Then . . .

He didn't know what hit him. When he came to, he was in the emergency ward with Joe bending over him anxiously.

"Brother, you've been out three hours and there isn't a mark on you."

Pete carefully touched his sore head with exploratory fingers. He hurt all over, every nerve felt twisted, his head half unscrewed.

"I got clobbered." The phrase had never seemed so apt.

"Yeah, I know," Joe replied drily. "But with what?"

"Would you believe a girl telepath?" Pete asked in a plaintive voice.

"Right now," Joe said wearily, "I'd believe an invasion of little green men."

Pete looked up at him, startled by the credulous bitterness in the young doctor's voice.

"What'd you mean, Joe?"

Annoyed with himself, Joe grimaced, then swore under his breath. He stepped to the door, looked up and down the hall. Closing the door tightly, with one final cautious look through the small glass insert, he asked, "Do you know where Al Finch is getting narcotics, Pete?"

The policeman groaned. "From the locked pharmacy cabinets of the hospitals."

Joe's eyes widened in stunned amazement. "How in hell did you know? Hahlgren didn't report it until noon and you've been in dreamland since then."

It was a relief to Pete to be able to tell someone his secret. When he finished, Joe shook his head slowly from side to side.

"Believe you, I must. The drug cupboard was bare at eight this morning. The question is, what do we do now?"

A few days later, Hector Barres was admitted to the hospital, stricken with a paralysis of the spine. Some of the drugs Maria had lifted from the hospital shelves were not pure opium. One was a thebaine compound which acted like strychnine and commonly caused spinal paralysis. Her father died of a heart attack shortly after his admission.

Suddenly all the dogs began to howl. Every dog in Wilmington added his note to the clamor. The dogs howled for a full ear-splitting hour despite every attempt to silence them. The SPCA and the Humane Association, police and firemen were called in—unsuccessfully—to disband a huge pack of hysterical dogs, cats, and tree beasts congregated in Maria's neighborhood.

Only when Maria released them, did the animals disband, melting away in a matter of moments. Pete and Joe took up a position across from her windows.

"Maria," Pete said. "I brought Joe with me. He did everything he could to save your father. But you've been stealing the wrong kind of drugs. It was one of those that killed your father."

I know, Maria said in a flat, hard tone. There was an odd blur to her projected voice that had always rung so clear and true in Pete's mind. *I've been . . . experimenting a little.*

There was a long pause. Pete suddenly experienced wild grief, a sense of terrified guilt which was quickly overlaid by a sullen resentment; and, finally, an irrational feeling of satisfaction.

He was a nasty old man. He was mean to me. He killed my mother.

186

Joe caught Pete's arm, his eyes wide with repugnance and dread.

You go away, Pete, Maria said. *Or I'll set my friends on you.*

"Maria, I don't care how much you threaten me," Pete said stolidly. "I have to tell you you're doing wrong."

Bug off, fuzz, Maria snapped. *I'm having fun. I never had fun before in my life. I'm living it up good now. You go away.*

"Pete," Joe cautioned urgently.

"Damn it, Maria . . ."

This time when Pete woke up in the emergency ward, Joe was in the next bed. They managed to talk the intern on duty into entering "heat prostration" on their charts as the cause of collapse. They promised faithfully to go to their respective homes and rest for the next twenty-four hours. Out on the hot street, Pete suggested that a couple of beers would start their unexpected holiday the right way, so they adjourned to the nearest air-conditioned bar.

The dogs began to howl again as they crossed the street.

"If we'd told anyone why the dogs howled," Pete said, moodily doodling in the moisture on the beer glass, "they would send us to the funny farm."

"Would you believe a hopped up preadolescent telepath?" Joe asked wistfully, and raised his glass in a mock toast.

"I only told her the truth."

"For truth she puts holes in our heads."

"All right, wise guy, what should I have done?"

"How do I know?" Joe asked with a helpless gesture of his hands. "My specialty's going to be internal medicine, not head-shrinking or pediatrics. I'm as lousy at this sort of work as you are." He thought for a while, holding his head. "The trouble, Pete, lies in neither you nor me . . . nor Maria. The trouble is the situation and the circumstances. If she'd had the sense to get born a Dupont instead of a Barres . . ." And he made a slicing motion with one hand.

They got drunker and drunker, somehow agreeing on only one thing: they were both so sensitive in the head bone that they couldn't give a j.d. brat the spanking she so richly deserved.

Or rescue her from hell.

Success on a small scene went to Al Finch's head. He decided that Wilmington offered too little scope for his operation's potential. Pete got the word from the desk sergeant that Finch had hired a private plane and a private ambulance.

Pete called Joe Lavelle, told him to meet him across from Maria's at once. Joe arrived in time to watch Maria being carried from the apartment on a stretcher.

"God Almighty, look," Pete cried. "Al Finch, framed by canaries."

Executing an intricate shuffle step, the gang leader was maneuvering the elaborate five-foot cylindrical triple birdcage through the door, all the while bellowing conflicting orders at his subordinates. That kept them bobbing so solicitously between Al and Maria that they all got royally in each other's way.

Then the rear stretcher-bearer tripped on the uneven sidewalk. He went down on one knee, losing his grip on the handles. Maria, her tiny body strapped to the stretcher, was jolted. The forward bearer, unaware for a moment of the accident, continued on and pulled the handles out of his companion's grip so that Maria, head downward, was dragged jouncingly along the sidewalk. With a yelp, Al leaped forward, unceremoniously depositing the canary cage on the lawn, where it rested at a dangerous tilt. He collided with one of his cohorts who had also jumped to the rescue. The two of them succeeded in startling the forward bearer and the front end of Maria's stretcher dropped with a second jarring jolt.

Like the incredible noise that issues from a cyphering organ played full through faulty stops, a chorus of strident howls arose. Starting with the piercing yelps of nearby dogs, it grew in intensity and volume as Maria, battered and pain-racked, summoned aid. It came bounding in answer to her call. With uncharacteristic ferocity, three poodles and a terrier launched themselves at the stretcher men. Before Finch could touch Maria, a collie and two boxers cut him off, snapping and snarling. The indignant doorman was tripped by a frantic cocker, who plunged at him from the lobby.

"Christ Almighty, she's called *all* the dogs," Joe cried.

A yelping, yapping, yipping vortex of sound with a rumbling, roaring ground-bass enveloped the area. The street soon became a seething mass of dogs, from ragged Scotties to leaping Dalmatians. More kept arriving on the scene, many dragging snapped ropes and chains, towing stakes, one even hauling a doghouse.

"She's called too many! She'll get hurt," Pete groaned.

As one, Pete and Joe started across the street, stepping on and over dog bodies. Pete caught a glimpse of a protective ring forming around Maria's man-abandoned stretcher.

"Maria! Maria!" he shouted over the tumult. "Call off the dogs. Call them off!"

The sheer press of numbers would overrun her. Kicking, flailing, Pete waded on. A cat, leaping from a stopped car roof, raked him with her claws. Joe reached the curb and fell, momentarily lost under the bounding bodies.

Suddenly, as if cut off by an invisible conductor, all sound ceased. The silence was as terrifying as the noise, but now the momentum of the charging animals faltered. Pete made it to the sidewalk in that hiatus. Neither Maria nor stretcher nor sidewalk was visible under the smooth and brindled, spotted, mottled, rough and smooth blanket of dogs and occasional cats.

Cursing wildly, Pete and Joe labored, throwing the stunned animals out of the way until a space was cleared around the overturned stretcher. The upset bird cage rolled down to the sidewalk, coming to rest with the bent door uppermost. A flurry of orange and yellow feathers, frightened canaries flew hysterically aloft, their frantic chirps ominous and shrill.

Unable to move, Pete watched as Joe carefully

turned the stretcher over. The two men stood looking down at Maria's crushed and bloodied body, trampled by the zeal of her would-be protectors. Then, moved by some obscure impulse, Pete joined her hands.

At this point, the dogs, released from the weird control that had summoned and then immobilized them, remembered ancient enmities. The abortive rescue mission turned into a thousand private battles.

Out of the corner of his eyes, Pete saw Wizard coming hell-for-leather down the street. Finch staggered to his feet, clawing his way up, using the bird cage as a support. With a howl, Wizard knocked him down again. Pete grabbed the man and arrested him for disturbing the peace. Wizard stood guard, in much better shape than any of Maria's other protectors, thanks to his late arrival.

The news story never mentioned that a human had been killed in the great dog riot. But it was noted that the unearthly canine choruses that had been plaguing Wilmington ended with that unscheduled concert.

But sometimes now when Pete Roberts is walking the beat with his K-9 partner, Wizard will suddenly start acting itchy and nervous. He whines and pulls, straining against the lead.

"Heel," Pete says stolidly, pretending nothing's happened.

One of these days I'll really put on the pressure.

"Finder's Keeper," "A Proper Santa Claus," and "Smallest Dragon-boy" were written at Roger Elwood's behest. He wanted short stories by McCaffrey. My estimable agent, Virginia Kidd, said that it was best not to limit McCaffrey, so I had to. The original ending of "A Proper Santa Claus" did not suit its intended market. I have reinstated *my* downbeat ending because *it* is logical.

Finder's Keeper

PETER TURNED IN FOUR DOZEN GOLF BALLS including the monogrammed ones that Mr. Roche had been yelling about. The course manager was almost cheerful as he counted out Peter's finder's fee.

"You've got a positive genius for scrounging balls, Pete. Don't know how you do it."

"My mother says everyone's got something they're good at," Peter replied, and began to edge out the door of the stuffy office. Comments like that made him nervous: he half-expected he'd given away his secret, and that he and his mother would be forced to run away again.

The manager only grunted and muttered about keeping the members happy. Peter ducked out, running home with his pocketful of dollars. Mother would be pleased, although she didn't like him using his trick of "finding" for "material gain," as she put it. But since she'd been too sick to work at the diner, they had precious little choice. Peter had wanted to get a full-time job as a caddy but his mother had resisted.

"You can't be like me, Peter. You got to have education and training. Your father was a smart man, but he didn't have enough education." Dedication made her eyes burn in her thin face. "It's education that matters in this world, Peter. You got to go to school." She emphasized her last statement by stringing the words out and enunciating them clearly.

Peter adored his mother but he hated her attempts to imitate a "country club" accent: her habit of quoting country clichés only ruined the effect she wanted to produce.

Seven dollars he was bringing home today. Not bad, added to the twenty-two he'd made caddying over the weekend. This week's rent, food, and some of the medicine were now paid for. If he could just talk Mother into letting him take a week off school now that the rains had stopped and spring sun was drying the greens, he'd really make some money! Mr. Roche always tipped a fiver, especially when Peter kept track of those monogrammed balls of his that he always swatted into the rough.

"Son, if you could patent that ball-homing instinct of yours," Mr. Roche had said more often than Peter liked, "you'd be a millionaire!"

It had made Peter almost scared to continue caddying for Mr. Roche, but the money was too tempting.

He came around the corner of their house trailer and skidded to an abrupt stop in the mud. Ken Fargo's green Mustang was parked on the concrete apron. The only good thing about his mother being sick, in Peter's estimation, was that she didn't have to be pleasant to creeps like Ken Fargo.

"He's pleasant enough and all that," his mother had said and then shuddered, smiling quickly to reassure Peter. "There's just something . . . slippery about him." She sighed. "I suppose he can't help being sour and suspicious. People do and say the most awful things to collect insurance! And he's lonely."

His mother would understand being lonely. And she'd understand the awful things people do and say —particularly if you're different in any way. But the knowledge hadn't made her sour, just more lonely, and sad, and cautious. Why she called Peter's knack of finding things a "gift," he didn't know. He felt it was a curse. It had brought them more grief, kept them moving around in the period before he'd learned not to "find" everything lost . . .

And why did Ken Fargo have to get unlost? They had thought him well gone when the insurance company that used him as an investigator had called off the search for the hijacked furs. There had been a reward of $15,000 for the return of those coats. Try as he would, Peter hadn't been able to figure out a legitimate way to "find" those furs. He hadn't been with the searchers when they'd looked in the old lead mine, or he'd have "found" the furs under the concealing layer of rubble in the ore carts. He couldn't go there alone now. That old shaft was dangerous, the supports worm-ridden and damp-rotted. Every kid in town had been warned, on pain of a strapping, to stay away.

Peter paused at the front of the house. He didn't want to go in. He didn't like the way Ken Fargo looked at his mother, and there wasn't much a thirteen-year-old boy could do to a six-foot man who'd fought his way out of some nasty corners (Fargo's words), and *looked* it from the scars on his face and knuckles. Peter took a deep breath and stomped up the two boxes that made steps into the trailer.

Peter knew the moment he walked in that Fargo had been badgering his mother. She was flushed and wringing her hands.

"Peter!" She all but swooped down on him. "Did you have a good day?" She was terribly relieved to see him.

"Sure did, Mother." He held out the seven dollar bills. "Hello, Mr. Fargo." He had to acknowledge the man's presence or his mother would chew him out for bad manners no matter how much she disliked Fargo.

"Long time no see," the man replied, jerking his shoulders to settle a flashy gold sports jacket. He sauntered toward the back of the caravan. "Sorry your ma's been ill. Should've let me know."

Peter blinked at him in surprise.

"Seven dollars," his mother was saying, her voice more natural now. "Oh, Peter, that's wonderful. Were you caddying?"

"That's just for scrounging golf balls."

Something happened in the room, some indefinable change in the air that registered against Peter's senses. When he looked at Ken Fargo, the man was occupied in lighting a cigarette. Peter glanced at his mother but she was proudly smoothing out the bills and arranging them all face up before she put them in her handbag.

"Peter's such a help," she said to Fargo, an artificial heartiness in her soft voice. "We've been just fine. I'll be back at work this week, but it was very nice of you to drop by and see us." She took two steps toward Fargo, her hand extended.

Fargo ignored the hand and sat down as if he meant to make a long visit. The knock at the door was a welcome diversion and Peter nearly collided with his mother as they both answered the summons.

"Oh, Mrs. Kiernan, have you seen my Victor?" It was Mrs. Anderson from two trailers down. Her three-year-old had such a perverse habit of straying that the distraught mother had taken to tying him to an old dog run. "I told Henry the rope was frayed. I was doing the wash and I just didn't notice. I suppose I should've checked when I didn't hear him fretting, but I wanted to finish . . . so I don't know how long he's been gone. Have you seen him? What with being home and all?"

Peter bristled at the implied insult, but his mother shot him a look, for she'd often let him "find" Victor. Mrs. Anderson was a nice woman, his mother had said, and had more than a wayward child to burden her.

"No, Mrs. Anderson, I haven't seen Victor this morning," his mother replied.

"Which way is he likely to go, Mrs. Anderson?" Ken Fargo asked.

"Oh, I just dunno. He could be halfway to town by now." The woman twisted back the lock of lank bleached hair that had escaped its pins. She swiveled her body slightly, looking pointedly at the green Mustang.

"Well, that's no problem. C'mon, Pete, you and me will take a little spin and see if we can locate the lady's wandering boy."

Peter gave his mother a swift look, and she gave him a barely perceptible nod.

"Shouldn't be no time at all before we have him safely back in your arms, Mrs. Anderson. Now don't worry. For one thing I'm an insurance investigator, and finding lost things is my *business*."

Again that electric feeling charged the air, but before Peter could appeal to his mother, Ken Fargo had hustled him out the door and into the car, all the time driveling reassurances to Mrs. Anderson.

"Roll down that window, Petey boy," the man said, and Peter set his teeth against the irritating familiarity.

"Keep a sharp eye out on your side. I'll take care of mine."

Fargo's tone, smugly confident, gave Peter fair warning. Somehow Fargo thought that Peter could "find" things. Somehow Peter had to discourage him.

"You just sing out when you see that brat, Pete. This car'll stop on a dime and hand you back six cents—inflation, you know, ha ha ha." Fargo deftly turned the Mustang into the road to town. Peter didn't protest although he knew that Victor Anderson was moving steadily in the opposite direction. "And I've got a bone to pick with you."

Startled, Peter looked around, but the man's frown was bogus.

"You should've let me know your mother was ill. She's a fine woman, your ma, and deserves the best. She could've had it if you'd let me know."

"We got along all right."

"Yeah, but she'd be much better now with the kind of food and care I could've provided. And I'd like to provide for her; you get what I mean?" An elbow prodded Peter in the ribs.

"We prefer to do for ourselves, thank you."

"You're a good kid, Peter, but there're things a man can do that a boy can't."

Peter wanted to wipe that look from Fargo's face.

"Hey, you keep your eyes peeled for that kid. Let's find him in a hurry and get back. I got something to ask your ma and you might as well hear it, too."

Peter obediently faced the window, but they reached the middle of the town without a sight of any child.

"How about that? We gotta search the whole town. I thought you said the kid went into town."

"No, sir. Mrs. Anderson said she thought he'd be halfway to town by now.

"Well, goddammit, where is he?"

Peter looked Ken Fargo straight in the eyes. "I don't know."

The man's face turned grim, then as suddenly assumed a forced good humor. "All right, kid. If he didn't go into town, maybe he went out of town?"

"Maybe someone's found him already. There's Officer Scortius."

The policeman was not the least bit pleased to hear that the Anderson kid was missing again, and his remarks confirmed Peter's private opinion that Mrs. Anderson was a prime nuisance in the tiny community of Jennings, Colorado. Fargo brandished his investigator's credentials, an additional irritant to Scortius, who'd been forced to muck around the countryside trying to find the lost shipment of furs "alleged" to have been stashed somewhere near Jennings.

"Well, I'll see who we can find to help track the brat."

"I'll do the main road out of town."

Officer Scortius grunted and waddled off.

As they drew alongside her trailer, Mrs. Anderson was hanging over the bottom half of her door, the picture of maternal anxiety. Clearly Victor had not been recovered, but Fargo assured her heartily that it was only a matter of moments, and gunned the Mustang countryward.

"Okay, Pete, let's find that kid and end this soap opera," Fargo said between his teeth. "How far up the road is he?"

"Gee, how would I know?"

"How would you know? Because you'd *know!*" The man's tone emphasized his certainty and Peter felt sick fear curl up from the pit of his belly. "I get around the country, Petey boy. And I hear things, interesting things." He paused and his voice took on a conciliatory tone. "Look, Petey boy, I like your mother. I want to take care of her the way a man can. She shouldn't have to work herself sick to give you a decent place to live and a good education. I know how set she is to see you educated. But you don't need much book learning to get ahead. Not you. You know, with your trick, we could be a team, you and me. In fact, we would be a top-drawer unbeatable team of private investigators."

That insistent, persuasive voice was bad enough; the arguments were worse. Fargo knew exactly how to get to Peter.

"Wouldn't that be great? Your ma not having to work anymore? And you, kid, you've been handicapped. You've made mistakes. It was foolish, you know, to find Lyle Grauber's missing stocks! To say nothing of that Cadillac in Colorado Springs!" Fargo's laugh was unpleasant and Peter cringed. That Cadillac business had meant they'd had to leave one of the nicest apartments they'd ever had. That was when they had decided that Peter better check with his mother before he "found" anything. There'd been a fortune in old five-dollar bills hidden in that Cadillac—and he couldn't tell the authorities how he'd known where it had been hidden.

"Yes," Fargo was saying in an ominously casual way, "the police are still looking for the kid who told them where to find that Caddy—and skipped. They want him bad."

The Mustang, like the Cadillac, had become a trap.

"You're mistaking me for someone else, Mr. Fargo," Peter managed to say in a steady, apologetic voice.

"Oh, no, I'm not. I'm a top-flight investigator because I'm smart. I put isolated clues together and come up with open-and-shut convictions."

If you looked adults in the face, they tended to think you couldn't be lying; but it took every ounce of self-control that Peter had learned in thirteen years to look Ken Fargo squarely in the eyes.

"You are wrong, Mr. Fargo. I've never been in Colorado Springs. And gee, if I could find things like you do and get reward money, I sure would have tried to for my mother's sake."

"How do you know about reward money, kid?"

"Mother told me that your company gives you ten percent of the value of anything you recover for them."

Fargo grunted at that, but just on the other side of the town limit sign, he braked, swearing with impatience.

"Where's that brat? C'mon, kid, where is he? You know!"

And Peter did. Victor was cutting across the Omers' meadow, out of sight of the road, and heading toward the old mines. Peter knew he'd better find the kid soon, but he'd have to get rid of Ken Fargo first and how was he going to manage to do that?

"No, Mr. Fargo, I don't know." Peter stared the man straight in the eyes. "I wish I did because Mrs. Anderson always tips fifty cents when someone brings Victor home."

"You made seven bucks today finding golf balls. What about that?"

Peter forced himself to grin. "All you have to do is watch where Mr. Roche slices his balls and then go bring 'em in when he isn't looking. Half the ones I brought in today were in the pond anyway."

Doubt flickered across Ken Fargo's face.

"Honest, Mr. Fargo, you're wrong about me."

A big Olds came piling down the road toward town. Cursing under his breath, Fargo pushed himself out of the Mustang and flagged the big car down.

"Yeah? What's the trouble, fella? No gas?" asked the driver, sticking his head out the window. Peter saw, with sinking heart, that it was Mr. Roche. He tried to squinch down in the seat. "Hi there, Peter. Find any more of my balls for me?" He flicked his cigarette to the roadside and gave Fargo his attention. "Kid's a genius finding m'balls in the grass. Like he could home in on them or something. Caddy for me, Saturday, Peter? Ten sharp?"

Limp with defeat, Peter nodded and sank down in the bucket seat, swallowing fiercely against the lump in his throat.

"Seen anything of a kid, too young to be off on his own?" Fargo asked.

"Kid? No. Nothing on the road from here to Hibernia."

Mr. Roche drove off in the Olds, leaving Peter at Fargo's mercy.

" 'Kid homes in on them or something,' huh? 'No, Mr. Fargo, you're wrong about me.' " Fargo's voice was savage as he slid into the driver's seat. "All right, Peter me lad. Now, unless you want some trouble, real trouble, with the cops in Colorado Springs, because they're looking for you, you'd better tell me where those furs are!"

"Furs?"

Fargo grabbed Peter by the wrist. He was as strong as he'd boasted, and the bones in Peter's arm rubbed together painfully in his grip. Blunt fingers gouged into the tendons until Peter had all he could do not to cry out.

"You *know,* don't you?"

The pain had caught Peter off guard and his face must have given away his secret knowledge, for Fargo swore.

"How long have you known?" Each word was punctuated by a flexing of those implacable fingers on his wrist. "D'you realize you done me out of fifteen thousand dollars?" Just as Peter was certain Fargo would break his arm, the man's attitude altered. "Okay, kid. I understand. You and your mother got scared after that Cadillac caper. Well, you don't have to be scared anymore. I said we'd be a team and we will. No one will think it funny if *I* find things. I'm a first-rate investigator to begin with. But with you . . . okay, where're the furs?"

"In the old lead mine." Peter pointed toward the hills. And Victor.

"We searched there already." Fargo's expression was suspicious and menacing. "You lead me on, kid . . ." and he raised his hand warningly.

"The furs are hidden under the rubble in the old ore carts."

"How do you know? You seen 'em?"

"No, but that's where they are."

"You mean, we walked up and down past that loot?"

If they were mice, they would've bit you, Peter recited one of his mother's off-quoted phrases to himself. Thinking of his mother gave him a second hold on his courage. Fargo knew, but if his knowledge went no further than an old mine shaft . . .

"The road to that mine's around here, isn't it?"

Peter told Fargo the way.

"Now you're using the old noggin, Petey boy." Cooperation made Fargo good-natured. "Say, kid, how do you do it?"

"What?"

"No more of the innocent act." Fargo's voice took on its dangerous edge. "How do you find things you've never seen?"

"I can't always," Peter replied, trying to sound dubious. "It's just when things are on people's minds a

200

lot, like that Cadillac or the furs, I sort of get a picture where they are. Sometimes the picture is clearer than other times, and I know the location."

"What's with the golf balls? You must've found hundreds of stupid golf balls these past coupla months. Penny-ante stuff—when I think of the lists of lost, or strayed, items on the company's records . . . I can make a fortune!"

Peter swallowed. "I", not the more diplomatic "we." The Mustang swerved up the last bend to the mine. "It's getting dark, Mr. Fargo," Peter said. "We should get Victor. He's up there. We can come back tomorrow for the . . ."

"Forget that stupid brat! I want those furs . . . now!" Fargo pulled a huge handlight from under his seat and gestured with it for Peter to lead the way.

"The mine's dangerous, Mr. Fargo. And the ore carts are pretty far down . . ."

There was no reprieve in Fargo's eyes. Peter turned toward the shaft and started walking.

The walls were dripping with the recent spring thaws, and the tunnel had a clammy chill as they penetrated slowly down, turning the gentle bend that led into the bowels of the mine.

"That's a new fall," Peter said nervously as they scrambled over a soggy pile of mud.

Fargo shined the spotlight at the sagging supports. "Yeah, so let's get this business over with. Fifteen thousand will do a lot for us, Petey boy. For you, your mother, and me."

"Why don't you just take the furs and leave us alone, Mr. Fargo? It's not right for me to find things for money."

"Who says?" Fargo snorted at his altruism. "Like the old saying, Petey, 'Finders keepers, losers weepers.' And, Petey boy, I'm the finder's keeper from now on."

The smile on Fargo's face chilled Peter worse than the tunnel's cold. But the smile disappeared when they both heard the groaning of wood and the dribbling sound of dirt falling from a height.

"How much further?" Fargo asked. "This place isn't safe."

The ore carts were right up against the old fall which

had closed the mine. Fargo hoisted Peter into the first cart. The boy dug into the loose earth layering the cart, and Fargo swore as Peter unearthed the first of the plastic sacks. "They all that big? Christ, we can't pack those up that tunnel. Take all night." He heaved the plastic bags to the ground and the air puffed them up. He glanced up the tunnel, measuring its width. "I bet I can just get the Mustang down here." And he started off.

"Mr. Fargo, would you leave me the light?"

With the torch pointed forward, Fargo's smile was malevolent in the dim tunnel. "What? A big kid like you afraid of the dark? What could *find* you here?" He laughed. "Just think of all the things fifteen thousand will buy!"

Peter watched with a rapidly increasing anxiety as the gleam of the spot disappeared around the bend, leaving him in a total blackout.

"Afraid of the dark?" The taunt frightened him not half as much as the life looming with grim certainty before him. Not all the warmth of the pelts on which he crouched could have thawed the fear in Peter's heart.

An ominous creak, almost overhead, startled him further. "The finder's keeper," Fargo had said. There were darker death traps than an old mine shaft, and bleaker lightless vistas.

Nonetheless Peter cried aloud when he saw the return of light and heard the sound of the Mustang bumping along the cart tracks.

"Okay, move your butt and haul these furs into the car, Petey. On the double."

Another warning rumbled overhead and a gout of water spewed from the support directly above the ore carts. Peter grabbed the plastic bags, tripping over the trailing length of them.

"Keep 'em off the wet ground, you stupid jerk. They're worth a fortune."

Peter mumbled an apology as he crammed the bags into the car trunk. The plastic refused to give up its supply of air, and Fargo was cursing as he helped. Then he stormed down the tunnel for more furs, dragging Peter with him. The light from the Mustang's headlights helped relieve the gloom, although its exhaust was a blue plume in the cul-de-sac of the rockfall. Two loads and the trunk was full. Peter stood with an armful of plastic sacks wondering how they could possibly get them all in the sports car.

"Don't stand there, stupid, Dump 'em on the back seat."

That, too, was full shortly, so Peter heaved his next load onto the passenger seat, falling over it as he lost his balance. Accidentally he hit the wheel, and the horn. The noise startled Fargo into dropping his load, but his curses were covered by a long low rumble. Mud and ooze rained down.

Peter screamed, gesturing frantically to the bulging overhead beam. Then, suddenly he found himself stumbling over plastic bags, desperately pulling at Fargo's arm to get the man to move. Peter remembered scrambling and clawing through wet heavy mud. Then something struck him across the head.

His skull was on fire, his body rigid. Certain he was buried in the tunnel, he tried to move but his arms were held to his side. His fingers clawed but met fluffy soft warm blanketing. There was noise and confusion around him. He was aware of breathing fresh air, and yet . . . there was thudding and rumbling underneath him which echoed through his pain-filled head.

The mine had collapsed! But he was wrapped in a blanket. He was safe.

"Yeah, you wouldn't believe how fast that Mustang went into reverse. The surprising thing is I made it out in one piece at all. 'Course the company will see to the body work. All in the line of duty, Scortius! And I got what I went after. I found the furs."

"I" found the furs? Peter cringed at Fargo's arrogance.

"Considering you were out looking for the Anderson kid, you got double luck," the officer was saying enviously.

Fargo chuckled. "Two finds in one day. Not bad, huh? Say, Doc, how long does it take that ambulance to get here? I want Petey boy given the best of care.

I'll foot the bill myself. And, of course, we should get the little feller back to Mrs. Anderson, too."

"The ambulance's coming," Dr. Wingard said, and there was something in his voice that made Peter think that the doctor didn't much like Ken Fargo. "I'm just as anxious as you are about Peter's condition. I want an x ray of that skull . . ."

"I thought you said he had just a flesh wound?"

"There's a possibility of concussion—"

"Concussion?" Fargo was startled.

"Yes, it was a wound caused by a falling object. Sufficient force to crack the skull. And I want to run an EKG on Peter. I don't like the sound of that heart . . ."

"Heart?"

A fierce pounding in Peter's chest echoed the panic in Fargo's voice.

"Yes. Molly Kiernan's got enough on her mind, but I spotted an irregularity in Peter's heartbeat when I gave him a physical in school. Might be nothing at all. No mention of rheumatic fever on his school record."

"Rheumatic fever?"

"I'm the cautious type. I'd just like to check."

"Oh."

Peter was somewhat encouraged by the dubious sound of Fargo's rejoinder. Then he remembered Jorie Grant. She'd had a rheumatic heart and couldn't take gym; stayed out of school in hard weather, in general was a real twerp. Be like her? Peter groaned.

"Hey, he's coming to," Fargo cried.

The air about Peter seemed to press in on him and he had a sense of suffocation. A hand grabbed his chin and shook him.

"Hey, Petey. Speak to me!"

There was a scuffle and an exclamation of surprise from Fargo.

"If you don't mind, Mr. Fargo," Dr. Wingate said in a hard icy voice. "I'm the doctor here." A firm hand turned back the blanket and found Peter's wrist. "And for your information, you don't shake concussion cases." Boy, was Dr. Wingard angry! "Peter? Peter? Can you hear me?" His voice was gentle again.

"Concussion." That word again. It triggered a series of associations in Peter's mind and eventually made him think of TV shows he'd seen. Maybe . . . as his mother used to say, there were more ways to kill a cat than choking him with butter.

"Where am I?" He fluttered his eyelids like patients did on "Dr. Kildare." The act became real for the searchlights of the police cars were trained in his direction, bright enough to stun his eyes.

"Peter, it's Dr. Wingard. How're you feeling?"

"My head hurts."

"I know, boy. We'll soon fix that. Can you open your eyes again? And tell me how many fingers I'm holding up?"

Peter blinked. He could see that the doctor was holding up three fingers. He blinked again, made his eyes stay wide with fear.

"Who are you?" he asked, looking directly at the doctor as if he'd never seen him. Then he looked unseeingly at Fargo. "Where am I?"

"How many fingers, Peter?"

"Fingers? Fingers?" Peter couldn't think how many he ought to see if he didn't see the right number. But he could see the dawning of disappointed frustration and the fury of loss in Ken Fargo's face.

Losers weepers. Peter essayed a sob. After all, his head hurt—and he wasn't supposed to be as brave as Peter Kiernan.

"Who are you? Where am I? My head hurts." But the first sob was abruptly followed by deep hurtful ones which Peter hadn't ordered.

"There, there, boy. Take it easy. You'll be all right," the doctor said. He stood up, pulling Fargo aside. Peter strained his ears. "That head injury seems to be causing a little amnesia."

"Amnesia?"

"Oh, I don't think it's anything to worry about. A few weeks' rest in the hospital, a careful regime for a few months, and he'll be right as rain."

"Amnesia? And a bum heart?" Fargo glanced sourly at Peter, who gave a weak groaning sob. "Look, Doc, I've got to report to my company about finding those furs. You just send the bills for the kid to Midwestern. Least we can do for him!"

"You'll be looking in on Peter?"

Peter kept his eyes tightly shut, but he was thinking with all his strength: Go away, Ken Fargo!

Fargo cleared his throat and began to move away.

"Well, now, I'll certainly try to. You let me know when he's completely recovered. If he gets his memory back. And check out that bad heart, too."

Well now, Peter thought, Petey boy just wouldn't ever recover from his amnesia. Not completely. And not that part of his mind that made him valuable to Fargo. Finder's keeper indeed!

Weariness settled in along with pain and Peter closed his eyes tightly. It was reassuring to hear little Victor Anderson blubbering somewhere. But what did he have to cry about? He was found, wasn't he?

Peter would have to stop "finding" anything for a while. Even Mr. Roche's golf balls. But he could blame that on the crack on the head, too. He could still caddy.

Then, when he grew up, and without Mr. Ken Fargo interfering with him and his mother, why *he'd* become the toppest-flight insurance investigator. And nobody would consider it odd that he could find anything he needed to.

As his mother often said, it was an ill wind that blew nobody any good.

A Proper Santa Claus

JEREMY WAS PAINTING. HE USED HIS FINGERS instead of the brush because he liked the feel of paint. Blue was soothing to the touch, red was silky, and orange had a gritty texture. Also he could tell when a color was "proper" if he mixed it with his fingers. He could hear his mother singing to herself, not quite on pitch, but it was a pleasant background noise. It went with the rhythm of his fingers stroking color onto the paper.

He shaped a cookie and put raisins on it, big, plump raisins. He attempted a sugar frosting but the white kind of disappeared into the orange of the cookie. So he globbed up chocolate brown and made an icing. Then he picked the cookie out of the paper and ate it. That left a hole in the center of the paper. It was an excellent cookie, though it made his throat very dry.

Critically he eyed the remaining unused space. Yes, there was room enough, so he painted a glass of Coke. He had trouble representing the bubbles that're supposed to bounce up from the bottom of the glass. That's why the Coke tasted flat when he drank it.

It was disappointing. He'd been able to make the cookie taste so good, why couldn't he succeed with the Coke? Maybe if he drew the bubbles in first . . . he was running out of paper.

"Momma, Momma?"

"What is it, honey?"

"Can I have more paper? Please?"

"Honest, Jeremy, you use up more paper . . . Still, it does keep you quiet and out of my hair . . . why, whatever have you done with your paper? What are those holes?"

Jeremy pointed to the round one. "That was a cookie with raisins and choc'late icing. And that was a Coke only I couldn't make the bubbles bounce."

His mother gave him "the look," so he subsided.

"Jeremy North, you use more paper than—than a..."

"Newspaperman?" he suggested, grinning up at her. Momma liked happy faces best.

"Than a newspaperman."

"Can you paint on newspaper?"

His mother blinked. "I don't see why not. And there's pictures already. You can color them in." She obligingly rummaged in the trash and came up with several discarded papers. "There you are, love. Enough supplies to keep you in business a while. I hope."

Well, Jeremy hadn't planned on any business, and newsprint proved less than satisfactory. There wasn't enough white spaces to draw *his* paintings on, and the newspaper soaked up his paints when he tried to follow the already-pictures. So he carefully put the paints away, washed his hands, and went outside to play.

For his sixth birthday Jeremy North got a real school-type easel with a huge pad of paper that fastened onto it at the top and could be torn off, sheet by sheet. There was a rack of holes for his poster paint pots and a rack for his crayons and chalk and eraser. It was exactly what he wanted. He nearly cried for joy. He hugged his mother, and he climbed into his father's lap and kissed him despite his prickly beard.

"Okay, okay, da Vinci," his father laughed. "Go paint us a masterpiece."

Jeremy did. But he was so eager that he couldn't wait until the paint had completely dried. It smeared and blurred, brushing against his body as he hurried to find his dad. So the effect wasn't quite what Jeremy intended.

"Say, that's pretty good," said his father, casting a judicious eye on the profferred artwork. "What's it supposed to be?"

"Just what you wanted." Jeremy couldn't keep the disappointment out of his voice.

"I guess you're beyond me, young feller me lad. I can dig Andy Warhol when he paints tomato soup, but you're in Picasso's school." His father tousled his hair affectionately and even swung him up high so that, despite his disappointment, Jeremy was obliged to giggle and squeal in delight.

Then his father told him to take his painting back to his room.

"But it's your masterpiece, Daddy. I can fix it . . ."

"No, son. You painted it. You understand it." And his father went about some Sunday errand or other.

Jeremy did understand his painting. Even with the smears he could plainly see the car, just like the Admonsens', which Daddy had admired the previous week. It *had* been a proper car. If only Daddy had *seen* it . . .

His grandmother came, around lunchtime, and brought him a set of pastel crayons with special pastel paper and a simply superior picture book of North American animals and birds.

"Of course, he'll break every one of the pastels in the next hour," he heard his grandmother saying to his mother, "but you said he wants only drawing things."

"I like the book, too, Gramma," Jeremy said politely, but his fingers closed possessively around the pastels.

Gramma glanced at him and then went right on talking. "But I think it's about time he found out what animals really look like instead of those monstrosities he's forever drawing. His teacher's going to wonder about his home life when she sees those nightmares."

"Oh, c'mon, Mother. There's nothing abnormal about Jeremy. I'd far rather he daubed himself all over with paint than ran around like the Reckoffs' kids, slinging mud and sand everywhere."

"If you'd only *make* Jeremy . . ."

"Mother, you can't *make* Jeremy do anything. He slides away from you like . . . like a squeeze of paint."

Jeremy lost interest in the adults. As usual, they ignored his presence, despite the fact that he was the subject of their conversation. He began to leaf through the book of birds and animals. The pictures weren't proper. That brown wasn't a bird-brown. And the red of the robin had too much orange, not enough gray. He kept his criticism to himself, but by the time he'd catalogued the anatomical faults in the sketch of the mustang, he was thoroughly bored with the book. His animals might *look* like nightmares, but they were proper ones for all of that. They worked.

His mother and grandmother were engrossed in discussing the fixative that would have made the pictures "permanent." Gramma said she hadn't bought it because it would be dangerous for him to breathe the fumes. They continued to ignore him. Which was as well. He picked up the pastels and began to experiment. A green horse with pink mane and tail, however anatomically perfect, would arouse considerable controversy.

He didn't break a single one of the precious pastels. He even blew away the rainbow dust from the tray. But he didn't let the horse off the pad until after Gramma and his mother had wandered into the kitchen for lunch.

"I wish . . ."

The horse was lovely.

"I *wish* I had some . . ." Jeremy said.

The horse went cantering around the room, pink tail streaming out behind him and pink mane flying.

". . . Fixative, Green Horse!" But it didn't work. Jeremy knew it took more than just *wishing* to do it proper.

He watched regretfully as Green Horse pranced too close to a wall and brushed himself out of existence.

Miss Bradley, his first-grade teacher, evidently didn't find anything untoward about his drawings, for she constantly displayed them on the bulletin boards. She had a habit of pouncing on him when he had just about finished a drawing so that after all his effort, he hadn't much chance to see if he'd done it "proper" after all. Once or twice he managed to reclaim one from the board and use it, but Miss Bradley created so much fuss about the missing artwork that he diplomatically ceased to repossess his efforts.

On the whole he liked Miss Bradley, but about the first week in October she developed the distressing habit of making him draw to order: "class assignments," she called it. Well, that was all right for the ones who never knew what to draw anyhow, but "assignments" just did not suit Jeremy. While part of him wanted to do hobgoblins, and witches, and pumpkin moons, the other part obstinately refused.

"I'd really looked forward to *your* interpretations of Hallowe'en, Jeremy," Miss Bradley said sadly when he proffered another pedantic landscape with nothing but ticky-tacky houses. "This is very beautiful, Jeremy, but it isn't the assigned project. Now, look at Cynthia's witch and Mark's hobgoblin. I'm certain you could do something just as original."

Jeremy dutifully regarded Cynthia's elongated witch on an outsized broomstick apparently made from 2 x 4s instead of broom reeds, and the hobgoblin Mark had created by splashing paint on the paper and folding, thus blotting the wet paint. Neither creation had any chance of working properly; surely Miss Bradley could see that. So he was obliged to tell her that his landscape was original, particularly if she would *look* at it properly.

"You're not getting the point, Jeremy," Miss Bradley said with unaccustomed sternness.

She wasn't either, but Jeremy thought he might better not say that. So he was the only student in the class who had no Hallowe'en picture for parents to admire on Back-to-School Night.

His parents were a bit miffed since they'd heard that Jeremy's paintings were usually prominently displayed.

"The assignment was Hallowe'en and Jeremy simply refused to produce something acceptable," Miss Bradley said with a slightly forced smile.

"Perhaps that's just as well," his mother said, a trifle sourly. "He used to draw the most frightening nightmares and say he 'saw' them."

"He's got a definite talent. Are either of you or Mr. North artistically inclined?"

"Not like he is," Mr. North replied, thinking that if he himself were artistically inclined he would use

Miss Bradley as a model. "Probably he's used up all his Hallowe'en inspiration."

"Probably," Miss Bradley said with a laugh.

Actually Jeremy hadn't. Although he dutifully set out trick-or-treating, he came home early. His mother made him sort out his candy, apples, and money for UNICEF, and permitted him to stay up long past his regular bedtime to answer the door for other beggars. But, once safely in his room, he dove for his easel and drew frenetically, slathering black and blue poster paint across clean paper, dashing globs of luminescence for horrific accents. The proper ones took off or crawled obscenely around the room, squeaking and groaning until he released them into the night air for such gambols and aerial maneuvers as they were capable of. Jeremy was impressed. He hung over the windowsill, cheering them on by moonlight. (Around three o'clock there was a sudden shower. All the water solubles melted into the ground.)

For a while after that, Jeremy was not tempted to approach the easel at all, either in school or at home. At first, Miss Bradley was sincerely concerned lest she had inhibited her budding artist by arbitrary assignments. But he was only busy with a chemical garden, lumps of coal and bluing and ammonia and all that. Then she got the class involved in making candles out of plastic milk cartons for Thanksgiving, and Jeremy entered into the project with such enthusiasm that she was reassured.

She ought not to have been.

Three-dimensionality and a malleable substance fascinated Jeremy. He went in search of anything remotely pliable. He started with butter (his mother had a fit about a whole pound melted on his furry rug; he'd left the creature he'd created prancing around his room, but then the heat came up in the radiators.) Then he tried mud (which set his mother screaming at him). She surrendered to the inevitable by supplying him with Play-Doh. However, now his creations thwarted him because as soon as the substance out of which the proper ones had been created hardened, they lost their mobility. He hadn't minded the ephemeral quality of his drawings, but he'd begun to count on the fact that sculpture lasted a while.

Miss Bradley introduced him to plasticine. And Christmas.

Success with three-dimensional figures, the availability of plasticine, and the sudden influx of all sorts of Christmas mail order catalogues spurred Jeremy to unusual efforts. This time he did not resist the class assignment of a centerpiece to deck the Christmas festive tables. Actually, Jeremy scarcely heard what Miss Bradley was saying past her opening words.

"Here's a chance for you to create your very own Santa Claus and reindeer, or a sleigh full of presents . . ."

Dancer, Prancer, Donner, Blitzen, and Dasher and Comet and Rudolph of the red nose, took form under his flying fingers. Santa's sack was crammed with full-color advertisements clipped from mail order wishbooks. Indeed, the sleigh threatened to crumble on its runners from paper weight. He saved Santa Claus till the last. And once he had the fat and jolly gentleman seated in his sleigh, whip in hand, ready to urge his harnessed team, Jeremy was good and ready to make them proper.

Only they weren't; they remained obdurately immobile. Disconsolate, Jeremy moped for nearly a week, examining and re-examining his handiwork for the inhibiting flaw.

Miss Bradley had been enthusiastically complimentary and the other children sullenly envious of his success when the finished group was displayed on a special table, all red and white, with Ivory Snow snow and little evergreens in proportion to the size of the figures. There was even a convenient chimney for the good Santa to descend. Only Jeremy knew that that was not *his* Santa's goal.

In fact Jeremy quite lost interest in the whole Christmas routine. He refused to visit the Santa on tap at the big shopping center, although his mother suspected that his heart had been set on the Masterpiece Oil Painting Set with its enticing assortment of brushes and every known pigment in life-long-lasting color.

Miss Bradley, too, lost all patience with him and became quite stern with his inattentiveness, to the delight of his classmates.

As so often happens when people concentrate too hard on a problem, Jeremy almost missed the solution, inadvertently provided by the pert Cynthia, now basking in Miss Bradley's favor.

"He's naked, that's what. He's naked and ugly. Everyone knows Santa is red and white. And reindeers aren't gray-yecht. They're brown and soft and have fuzzy tails."

Jeremy had, of course, meticulously detailed the clothing on Santa and the harness on the animals, but they were still plasticine. It hadn't mattered with his other creations that they were the dull gray-brown of plasticene because that's how he'd envisaged them, being products of his imagination. But Santa wasn't, or so he thought.

To conform to a necessary convention was obviously, to Jeremy, the requirement that had prevented his Santa from being a proper one. He fabricated harness of string for the reindeer. And a new sleigh of balsa wood with runners of laboriously straightened bobby pins took some time and looked real tough. A judicious coat of paint smartened both reindeer and sleigh. However, the design and manufacture of the red Santa suit proved far more difficult and occupied every spare moment of Jeremy's time. He had to do it in the privacy of his room at home because, when Cynthia saw him putting harness on the reindeer, she twitted him so unmercifully that he couldn't work in peace at school.

He had had little practice with needle and thread, so he actually had to perfect a new skill in order to complete his project. Christmas was only a few days away before he was satisfied with his Santa suit.

He raced to school so he could dress Santa and make him proper. He was just as startled as Miss Bradley when he slithered to a stop inside his classroom door, and found her tying small gifts to the branches of the class tree. They stared at each other for a long moment, and then Miss Bradley smiled. She'd been so hard on poor Jeremy lately.

"You're awfully early, Jeremy. Would you like to

help me . . . Oh! How adorable!" She spotted the Santa suit which he hadn't had the presence of mind to hide from her. "And you did them yourself? Jeremy, you never cease to amaze me." She took the jacket and pants and little hat from his unresisting hand, and examined them carefully. "They are simply beautiful. Just beautiful. But honestly, Jeremy, your Santa is lovely just as he is. No need to gild the lily."

"He isn't a proper Santa without a proper Santa suit."

Miss Bradley looked at him gravely, and then put her hands on his shoulders, making him look up at her.

"A *proper* Santa Claus is the one we have in our own hearts at this time of year, Jeremy. Not the ones in the department stores or on the street corners or on TV. They're just his helpers." You never knew which of your first-graders still did believe in Santa Claus in this cynical age, Miss Bradley thought. "A proper Santa Claus is the spirit of giving and sharing, of good fellowship. Don't let anyone tell you that there isn't a Santa Claus. The proper Santa Claus belongs to all of us."

Then, pleased with her eloquence and restraint, she handed him back the Santa suit and patted his shoulder encouragingly.

Jeremy was thunderstruck. *His* Santa Claus had only been made for Jeremy. But poor Miss Bradley's words rang in his ears. Miss Bradley couldn't know that she had improperly understood Jeremy's dilemma. Once again the blight of high-minded interpretation and lady-like good intentions withered primitive magic.

The little reindeer in their shrinking coats of paint would have pulled the sleigh only to Jeremy's house so that Santa could descend only Jeremy's chimney with the little gifts all bearing Jeremy's name.

There was no one there to tell him that it's proper for little boys and girls of his age to be selfish and acquisitive, to regard Santa as an exclusive property.

Jeremy took the garments and let Miss Bradley push him gently toward the table on which his figures were displayed.

She'd put tinsel about the scene, and glitter, but they didn't shine or glisten in the dull gray light filtering through the classroom windows. They weren't proper snow and icicles anyway.

Critically, he saw only string and the silver cake ornaments instead of harness and sleigh bells. He could see the ripples now in the unbent bobby pins which wouldn't ever draw the sleigh smoothly, even over Ivory Snow snow. Dully, he reached for the figure of his Santa Claus.

Getting on the clothes, he dented the plasticene a bit, but it scarcely mattered now. After he'd clasped Santa's malleable paw around the whip, the toothpick with a bright, thick, nylon thread attached to the top with glue, he stood back and stared.

A proper Santa Claus is the spirit of giving and sharing.

So overwhelming was Jeremy's sense of failure, so crushing his remorse for making a selfish Santa Claus instead of the one that belonged to everyone, that he couldn't imagine ever creating anything properly again.

The Smallest Dragonboy

ALTHOUGH KEEVAN LENGTHENED HIS WALKing stride as far as his legs would stretch, he couldn't quite keep up with the other candidates. He knew he would be teased again.

Just as he knew many other things that his foster mother told him he ought not to know, Keevan knew that Beterli, the most senior of the boys, set that spanking pace just to embarrass him, the smallest dragonboy. Keevan would arrive, tail fork-end of the group, breathless, chest heaving, and maybe get a stern look from the instructing wing-second.

Dragonriders, even if they were still only hopeful candidates for the glowing eggs which were hardening on the hot sands of the Hatching Ground cavern, were expected to be punctual and prepared. Sloth was not tolerated by the Weyrleader of Benden Weyr. A good record was especially important now. It was very near hatching time, when the baby dragons would crack their mottled shells, and stagger forth to choose their lifetime companions. The very thought of that glorious moment made Keevan's breath catch in his throat. To be chosen—to be a dragonrider! To sit astride the neck of a winged beast with jeweled eyes: to be his friend, in telepathic communion with him for life; to be his companion in good times and fighting extremes; to fly effortlessly over the lands of Pern! Or, thrillingly, *between* to any point anywhere on the world! Flying *between* was done on dragonback or not at all, and it was dangerous.

Keevan glanced upward, past the black mouths of the weyr caves in which grown dragons and their chosen riders lived, toward the Star Stones that crowned the ridge of the old volcano that was Benden Weyr. On the height, the blue watch dragon, his rider mounted on his neck, stretched the great transparent pinions that carried him on the winds of Pern to fight the evil Thread that fell at certain times from the skies. The many-faceted rainbow jewels of his eyes glistened fleetingly in the greeny sun. He folded his great wings to his back, and the watch pair resumed their statuelike pose of alertness.

Then the enticing view was obscured as Keevan passed into the Hatching Ground cavern. The sands underfoot were hot, even through heavy wher-hide boots. How the bootmaker had protested having to sew so small! Keeven was forced to wonder why being small was reprehensible. People were always calling him "babe" and shooing him away as being "too small" or "too young" for this or that. Keevan was constantly working, twice as hard as any other boy his age, to prove himself capable. What if his muscles weren't as big as Beterli's? They were just as hard. And if he couldn't overpower anyone in a wrestling match, he could outdistance everyone in a footrace.

"Maybe if you run fast enough," Beterli had jeered on the occasion when Keevan had been goaded to boast of his swiftness, "you could catch a dragon. That's the only way you'll make a dragonrider!"

"You just wait and see, Beterli, you just wait," Keevan had replied. He would have liked to wipe the contemptuous smile from Beterli's face, but the guy didn't fight fair even when a wingsecond was watching. "No one knows what Impresses a dragon!"

"They've got to be able to *find* you first, babe!"

Yes, being the smallest candidate was not an enviable position. It was therefore imperative that Keevan Impress a dragon in his first hatching. That would wipe the smile off every face in the cavern, and accord him the respect due any dragonrider, even the smallest one.

Besides, no one knew exactly what Impressed the baby dragons as they struggled from their shells in search of their lifetime partners.

"I like to believe that dragons see into a man's

218

heart," Keevan's foster mother, Mende, told him. "If they find goodness, honesty, a flexible mind, patience, courage—and you've got that in quantity, dear Keevan —that's what dragons look for. I've seen many a well-grown lad left standing on the sands, Hatching Day, in favor of someone not so strong or tall or handsome. And if my memory serves me"—which it usually did: Mende knew every word of every Harper's tale worth telling, although Keevan did not interrupt her to say so—"I don't believe that F'lar, our Weyrleader, was all that tall when bronze Mnementh chose him. And Mnementh was the only bronze dragon of that hatching."

Dreams of Impressing a bronze were beyond Keevan's boldest reflections, although that goal dominated the thoughts of every other hopeful candidate. Green dragons were small and fast and more numerous. There was more prestige to Impressing a blue or brown than a green. Being practical, Keevan seldom dreamed as high as a big fighting brown, like Canth, F'nor's fine fellow, the biggest brown on all Pern. But to fly a bronze? Bronzes were almost as big as the queen, and only they took the air when a queen flew at mating time. A bronze rider could aspire to become Weyrleader! Well, Keevan would console himself, brown riders could aspire to become wingseconds, and that wasn't bad. He'd even settle for a green dragon: they were small, but so was he. No matter! He simply had to Impress a dragon his first time in the Hatching Ground. Then no one in the Weyr would taunt him anymore for being so small.

Shells, Keevan thought now, but the sands are hot!

"Impression time is imminent, candidates," the wingsecond was saying as everyone crowded respectfully close to him. "See the extent of the striations on this promising egg." The stretch marks *were* larger than yesterday.

Everyone leaned forward and nodded thoughtfully. That particular egg was the one Beterli had marked as his own, and no other candidate dared, on pain of being beaten by Beterli at his first opportunity, to approach it. The egg was marked by a large yellowish splotch in the shape of a dragon backwinging to land, talons outstretched to grasp rock. Everyone knew that bronze eggs bore distinctive markings. And naturally, Beterli, who'd been presented at eight Impressions already and was the biggest of the candidates, had chosen it.

"I'd say that the great opening day is almost upon us," the wingsecond went on, and then his face assumed a grave expression. "As we well know, there are only forty eggs and seventy-two candidates. Some of you may be disappointed on the great day. That doesn't necessarily mean you aren't dragonrider material, just that *the* dragon for you hasn't been shelled. You'll have other hatchings, and it's no disgrace to be left behind an Impression or two. Or more."

Keevan was positive that the wingsecond's eyes rested on Beterli, who'd been stood off at so many Impressions already. Keevan tried to squinch down so the wingsecond wouldn't notice him. Keevan had been reminded too often that he was eligible to be a candidate by one day only. He, of all the hopefuls, was most likely to be left standing on the great day. One more reason why he simply had to Impress at his first hatching.

"Now move about among the eggs," the wingsecond said. "Touch them. We don't know that it does any good, but it certainly doesn't do any harm."

Some of the boys laughed nervously, but everyone immediately began to circulate among the eggs. Beterli stepped up officiously to "his" egg, daring anyone to come near it. Keevan smiled, because he had already touched it—every inspection day, when the others were leaving the Hatching Ground and no one could see him crouch to stroke it.

Keevan had an egg he concentrated on, too, one drawn slightly to the far side of the others. The shell had a soft greenish-blue tinge with a faint creamy swirl design. The consensus was that this egg contained a mere green, so Keevan was rarely bothered by rivals. He was somewhat perturbed then to see Beterli wandering over to him.

"I don't know why you're allowed in this Impression,

220

Keevan. There are enough of us without a babe," Beterli said, shaking his head.

"I'm of age." Keevan kept his voice level, telling himself not to be bothered by mere words.

"Yah!" Beterli made a show of standing in his toe-tips. "You can't even see over an egg; Hatching Day, you better get in front or the dragons won't see you at all. 'Course, you could get run down that way in the mad scramble. Oh, I forget, you can run fast, can't you?"

"You'd better make sure a dragon sees *you*, this time, Beterli," Keevan replied. "You're almost overage, aren't you?"

Beterli flushed and took a step forward, hand half-raised. Keevan stood his ground, but if Beterli advanced one more step, he would call the wingsecond. No one fought on the Hatching Ground. Surely Beterli knew that much.

Fortunately, at that moment, the wingsecond called the boys together and led them from the Hatching Ground to start on evening chores. There were "glows" to be replenished in the main kitchen caverns and sleeping cubicles, the major hallways, and the queen's apartment. Firestone sacks had to be filled against Thread attack, and black rock brought to the kitchen hearths. The boys fell to their chores, tantalized by the odors of roasting meat. The population of the Weyr began to assemble for the evening meal, and the dragonriders came in from the Feeding Ground on their sweep checks.

It was the time of day Keevan liked best: once the chores were done but before dinner was served, a fellow could often get close enough to the dragonriders to hear their talk. Tonight, Keevan's father, K'last, was at the main dragonrider table. It puzzled Keevan how his father, a brown rider and a tall man, could *be* his father—because he, Keevan, was so small. It obviously puzzled K'last, too, when he deigned to notice his small son: "In a few more Turns, you'll be as tall as I am —or taller!"

K'last was pouring Benden wine all around the table. The dragonriders were relaxing. There'd be no Thread attack for three more days, and they'd be in the mood to tell tall tales, better than Harper yarns, about impossible maneuvers they'd done a-dragonback. When Thread attack was closer, their talk would change to a discussion of tactics of evasion, of going *between,* how long to suspend there until the burning but fragile Thread would freeze and crack and fall harmlessly off dragon and man. They would dispute the exact moment to feed firestone to the dragon so he'd have the best flame ready to sear Thread midair and render it harmless to ground—and man—below. There was such a lot to know and understand about being a dragonrider that sometimes Keevan was overwhelmed. How would he ever be able to remember everything he ought to know at the right moment? He couldn't dare ask such a question; this would only have given additional weight to the notion that he was too young yet to be a dragonrider.

"Having older candidates makes good sense," L'vel was saying, as Keevan settled down near the table. "Why waste four to five years of a dragon's fighting prime until his rider grows up enough to stand the rigors?" L'vel had Impressed a blue of Ramoth's first clutch. Most of the candidates thought L'vel was marvelous because he spoke up in front of the older riders, who awed them. "That was well enough in the Interval when you didn't need to mount the full Weyr complement to fight Thread. But not now. Not with more eligible candidates than ever. Let the babes wait."

"Any boy who is over twelve Turns has the right to stand in the Hatching Ground," K'last replied, a slight smile on his face. He never argued or got angry. Keevan wished he were more like his father. And oh, how he wished he were a brown rider! "Only a dragon —each particular dragon—knows what he wants in a rider. We certainly can't tell. Time and again the theorists," K'last's smile deepened as his eyes swept those at the table, "are surprised by dragon choice. *They* never seem to make mistakes, however."

"Now, K'last, just look at the roster this Impression. Seventy-two boys and only forty eggs. Drop off the twelve youngest, and there's still a good field for the hatchlings to choose from. Shells! There are a couple of weyrlings unable to see over a wher egg much less a dragon! And years before they can ride Thread."

"True enough, but the Weyr is scarcely under fighting strength, and if the youngest Impress, they'll be old enough to fight when the oldest of our current dragons go *between* from senility."

"Half the Weyr-bred lads have already been through several Impressions," one of the bronze riders said then. "I'd say drop some of *them* off this time. Give the untried a chance."

"There's nothing wrong in presenting a clutch with as wide a choice as possible," said the Weyrleader, who had joined the table with Lessa, the Weyrwoman.

"Has there ever been a case," she said, smiling in her odd way at the riders, "where a hatchling didn't choose?"

Her suggestion was almost heretical and drew astonished gasps from everyone, including the boys.

F'lar laughed. "You say the most outrageous things, Lessa."

"Well, *has* there ever been a case where a dragon didn't choose?"

"Can't say as I recall one," K'last replied.

"Then we continue in this tradition," Lessa said firmly, as if that ended the matter.

But it didn't. The argument ranged from one table to the other all through dinner, with some favoring a weeding out of the candidates to the most likely, lopping off those who were very young or who had had multiple opportunities to Impress. All the candidates were in a swivet, though such a departure from tradition would be to the advantage of many. As the evening progressed, more riders were favoring eliminating the youngest and those who'd passed four or more Impressions unchosen. Keevan felt he could bear such a dictum only if Beterli were also eliminated. But this seemed less likely than that Keevan would be turfed out, since the Weyr's need was for fighting dragons and riders.

By the time the evening meal was over, no decision had been reached, although the Weyrleader had promised to give the matter due consideration.

He might have slept on the problem, but few of the

candidates did. Tempers were uncertain in the sleeping caverns next morning as the boys were routed out of their beds to carry water and black rock and cover the "glows." Twice Mende had to call Keevan to order for clumsiness.

"Whatever is the matter with you, boy?" she demanded in exasperation when he tipped blackrock short of the bin and sooted up the hearth.

"They're going to keep me from this Impression."

"What?" Mende stared at him. "Who?"

"You heard them talking at dinner last night. They're going to turf the babes from the hatching."

Mende regarded him a moment longer before touching his arm gently. "There's lots of talk around a supper table, Keevan. And it cools as soon as the supper. I've heard the same nonsense before every hatching, but nothing is ever changed."

"There's always a first time," Keevan answered, copying one of her own phrases.

"That'll be enough of that, Keevan. Finish your job. If the clutch does hatch today, we'll need full rock bins for the feast, and you won't be around to do the filling. All my fosterlings make dragonriders."

"The first time?" Keevan was bold enough to ask as he scooted off with the rockbarrow.

Perhaps, Keevan thought later, if he hadn't been on that chore just when Beterli was also fetching black rock, things might have turned out differently. But he had dutifully trundled the barrow to the outdoor bunker for another load just as Beterli arrived on a similar errand.

"Heard the news, babe?" Beterli asked. He was grinning from ear to ear, and he put an unnecessary emphasis on the final insulting word.

"The eggs are cracking?" Keevan all but dropped the loaded shovel. Several anxieties flicked through his mind then: he was black with rock dust—would he have time to wash before donning the white tunic of candidacy? And if the eggs were hatching, why hadn't the candidates been recalled by the wingsecond?

"Naw! Guess again!" Beterli was much too pleased with himself.

With a sinking heart, Keevan knew what the news

must be, and he could only stare with intense desolation at the older boy.

"C'mon! Guess, babe!"

"I've no time for guessing games," Keevan managed to say with indifference. He began to shovel black rock into the barrow as fast as he could.

"I said, guess." Beterli grabbed the shovel.

"And I said I have no time for guessing games."

Beterli wrenched the shovel from Keevan's hands. "Guess!"

"I'll have that shovel back, Beterli." Keevan straightened up, but he didn't come to Beterli's bulky shoulder. From somewhere, other boys appeared, some with barrows, some mysteriously alerted to the prospect of a confrontation among their numbers.

"Babes don't give orders to candidates around here, babe!"

Someone sniggered and Keevan, incredulous, knew that he must've been dropped from the candidacy.

He yanked the shovel from Beterli's loosened grasp. Snarling, the older boy tried to regain possession, but Keevan clung with all his strength to the handle, dragged back and forth as the stronger boy jerked the shovel about.

With a sudden, unexpected movement, Beterli rammed the handle into Keevan's chest, knocking him over the barrow handles. Keevan felt a sharp, painful jab behind his left ear, an unbearable pain in his left shin, and then a painless nothingness.

Mende's angry voice roused him, and startled, he tried to throw back the covers, thinking he'd overslept. But he couldn't move, so firmly was he tucked into his bed. And then the constriction of a bandage on his head and the dull sickishness in his leg brought back recent occurrences.

"Hatching?" he cried.

"No, lovey," Mende said in a kind voice. Her hand was cool and gentle on his forehead. "Though there's some as won't be at any hatching again." Her voice took on a stern edge.

Keevan looked beyond her to see the Weyrwoman, who was frowning with irritation.

225

"Keevan, will you tell me what occurred at the black-rock bunker?" asked Lessa in an even voice.

He remembered Beterli now and the quarrel over the shovel and . . . what had Mende said about some not being at any hatching? Much as he hated Beterli, he couldn't bring himself to tattle on Beterli and force him out of candidacy.

"Come, lad," and a note of impatience crept into the Weyrwoman's voice. "I merely want to know what happened from you, too. Mende said she sent you for black rock. Beterli—and every Weyrling in the cavern—seems to have been on the same errand. What happened?"

"Beterli took my shovel. I hadn't finished with it."

"There's more than one shovel. What did he *say* to you?"

"He'd heard the news."

"What news?" The Weyrwoman was suddenly amused.

"That . . . that . . . there'd been changes."

"Is that what he said?"

"Not exactly"

"What did he say? C'mon, lad, I've heard from everyone else, you know."

"He said for me to guess the news."

"And you fell for that old gag?" The Weyrwoman's irritation returned.

"Consider all the talk last night at supper, Lessa," Mende said. "Of course the boy would think he'd been eliminated."

"In effect, he is, with a broken skull and leg." Lessa touched his arm in a rare gesture of sympathy. "Be that as it may, Keevan, you'll have other Impressions. Beterli will not. There are certain rules that must be observed by all candidates, and his conduct proves him unacceptable to the Weyr."

She smiled at Mende and then left.

"I'm still a candidate?" Keevan asked urgently.

"Well, you are and you aren't, lovey," his foster mother said. "Is the numbweed working?" she asked, and when he nodded, she said, "You just rest. I'll bring you some nice broth."

At any other time in his life, Keevan would have

relished such cosseting, but now he just lay there worrying. Beterli had been dismissed. Would the others think it was his fault? But everyone was there! Beterli provoked that fight. His worry increased, because although he heard excited comings and goings in the passageway, no one tweaked back the curtain across the sleeping alcove he shared with five other boys. Surely one of them would have to come in sometime. No, they were all avoiding him. And something else was wrong. Only he didn't know what.

Mende returned with broth and beachberry bread.

"Why doesn't anyone come see me, Mende? I haven't done anything wrong, have I? I didn't ask to have Beterli turfed out."

Mende soothed him, saying everyone was busy with noontime chores and no one was angry with him. They were giving him a chance to rest in quiet. The numbweed made him drowsy, and her words were fair enough. He permitted his fears to dissipate. Until he heard a hum. Actually, he felt it first, in the broken shin bone and his sore head. The hum began to grow. Two things registered suddenly in Keevan's groggy mind: the only white candidate's robe still on the pegs in the chamber was his; and the dragons hummed when a clutch was being laid or being hatched. Impression! And he was flat abed.

Bitter, bitter disappointment turned the warm broth sour in his belly. Even the small voice telling him that he'd have other opportunities failed to alleviate his crushing depression. *This* was the Impression that mattered! This was his chance to show *everyone,* from Mende to K'last to L'vel and even the Weyrleader that he, Keevan, was worthy of being a dragonrider.

He twisted in bed, fighting against the tears that threatened to choke him. Dragonmen don't cry! Dragonmen learn to live with pain.

Pain? The leg didn't actually pain him as he rolled about on his bedding. His head felt sort of stiff from the tightness of the bandage. He sat up, an effort in itself since the numbweed made exertion difficult. He touched the splinted leg; the knee was unhampered. He had no feeling in his bone, really. He swung himself carefully to the side of his bed and stood slowly.

The room wanted to swim about him. He closed his eyes, which made the dizziness worse, and he had to clutch the wall.

Gingerly, he took a step. The broken leg dragged. It hurt in spite of the numbweed, but what was pain to a dragonman?

No one had said he couldn't go to the Impression. "You are and you aren't," were Mende's exact words.

Clinging to the wall, he jerked off his bedshirt. Stretching his arm to the utmost, he jerked his white candidate's tunic from the peg. Jamming first one arm and then the other into the holes, he pulled it over his head. Too bad about the belt. He couldn't wait. He hobbled to the door, hung on to the curtain to steady himself. The weight on his leg was unwieldy. He wouldn't get very far without something to lean on. Down by the bathing pool was one of the long crook-necked poles used to retrieve clothes from the hot washing troughs. But it was down there, and he was on the level above. And there was no one nearby to come to his aid: everyone would be in the Hatching Ground right now, eagerly waiting for the first egg to crack.

The humming increased in volume and tempo, an urgency to which Keevan responded, knowing that his time was all too limited if he was to join the ranks of the hopeful boys standing around the cracking eggs. But if he hurried down the ramp, he'd fall flat on his face.

He could, of course, go flat on his rear end, the way crawling children did. He sat down, sending a jarring stab of pain through his leg and up to the wound on the back of his head. Gritting his teeth and blinking away tears, Keevan scrabbled down the ramp. He had to wait a moment at the bottom to catch his breath. He got to one knee, the injured leg straight out in front of him. Somehow, he managed to push himself erect, though the room seemed about to tip over his ears. It wasn't far to the crooked stick, but it seemed an age before he had it in his hand.

Then the humming stopped!

Keevan cried out and began to hobble frantically across the cavern, out to the bowl of the Weyr. Never had the distance between living caverns and the Hatch-

228

ing Ground seemed so great. Never had the Weyr been so breathlessly silent. It was as if the multitude of people and dragons watching the hatching held every breath in suspense. Not even the wind muttered down the steep sides of the bowl. The only sounds to break the stillness were Keevan's ragged gasps and the thump-thud of his stick on the hard-packed ground. Sometimes he had to hop twice on his good leg to maintain his balance. Twice he fell into the sand and had to pull himself up on the stick, his white tunic no longer spotless. Once he jarred himself so badly he couldn't get up immediately.

Then he heard the first exhalation of the crowd, the oohs, the muted cheer, the susurrus of excited whispers. An egg had cracked, and the dragon had chosen his rider. Desperation increased Keevan's hobble. Would he never reach the arching mouth of the Hatching Ground?

Another cheer and an excited spate of applause spurred Keevan to greater effort. If he didn't get there in moments, there'd be no unpaired hatchling left. Then he was actually staggering into the Hatchling Ground, the sands hot on his bare feet.

No one noticed his entrance or his halting progress. And Keevan could see nothing but the backs of the white-robed candidates, seventy of them ringing the area around the eggs. Then one side would surge forward or back and there'd be a cheer. Another dragon had been Impressed. Suddenly a large gap appeared in the white human wall, and Keevan had his first sight of the eggs. There didn't seem to be *any* left uncracked, and he could see the lucky boys standing beside wobble-legged dragons. He could hear the unmistakable plaintive crooning of hatchlings and their squawks of protest as they'd fall awkwardly in the sand.

Suddenly he wished that he hadn't left his bed, that he'd stayed away from the Hatching Ground. Now everyone would see his ignominious failure. So he scrambled as desperately to reach the shadowy walls of the Hatching Ground as he had struggled to cross the bowl. He mustn't be seen.

He didn't notice, therefore, that the shifting group of boys remaining had begun to drift in his direction.

229

The hard pace he had set himself and his cruel disappointment took their double toll of Keevan. He tripped and collapsed sobbing to the warm sands. He didn't see the consternation in the watching Weyrfolk above the Hatching Ground, nor did he hear the excited whispers of speculation. He didn't know that the Weyrleader and Weyrwoman had dropped to the arena and were making their way toward the knot of boys slowly moving in the direction of the entrance.

"Never seen anything like it," the Weyrleader was saying. "Only thirty-nine riders chosen. And the bronze trying to leave the Hatching Ground without making Impression."

"A case in point of what I said last night," the Weyrwoman replied, "where a hatchling makes no choice because the right boy isn't there."

"There's only Beterli and K'last's young one missing. And there's a full wing of likely boys to choose from . . ."

"None acceptable, apparently. Where is the creature going? He's not heading for the entrance after all. Oh, what have we there, in the shadows?"

Keevan heard with dismay the sound of voices nearing him. He tried to burrow into the sand. The mere thought of how he would be teased and taunted now was unbearable.

Don't worry! Please don't worry! The thought was urgent, but not his own.

Someone kicked sand over Keevan and butted roughly against him.

"Go away. Leave me alone!" he cried.

Why? was the injured-sounding question inserted into his mind. There was no voice, no tone, but the question was there, perfectly clear, in his head.

Incredulous, Keevan lifted his head and stared into the glowing jeweled eyes of a small bronze dragon. His wings were wet, the tips drooping in the sand. And he sagged in the middle on his unsteady legs, although he was making a great effort to keep erect.

Keevan dragged himself to his knees, oblivious of the pain in his leg. He wasn't even aware that he was ringed by the boys passed over, while thirty-one pairs of resentful eyes watched him Impress the dragon.

The Weyrmen looked on, amused, and surprised at the draconic choice, which could not be forced. Could not be questioned. Could not be changed.

Why? asked the dragon again. *Don't you like me?* His eyes whirled with anxiety, and his tone was so piteous that Keevan staggered forward and threw his arms around the dragon's neck, stroking his eye ridges, patting the damp, soft hide, opening the fragile-looking wings to dry them, and wordlessly assuring the hatchling over and over again that he was the most perfect, most beautiful, most beloved dragon in the Weyr, in all the Weyrs of Pern.

"What's his name, K'van?" asked Lessa, smiling warmly at the new dragonrider. K'van stared up at her for a long moment. Lessa would know as soon as he did. Lessa was the only person who could "receive" from all dragons, not only her own Ramoth. Then he gave her a radiant smile, recognizing the traditional shortening of his name that raised him forever to the rank of dragonrider.

My name is Heth, the dragon thought mildly, then hiccuped in sudden urgency. *I'm hungry.*

"Dragons are born hungry," said Lessa, laughing. "F'lar, give the boy a hand. He can barely manage his own legs, much less a dragon's."

K'van remembered his stick and drew himself up. "We'll be just fine, thank you."

"You may be the smallest dragonrider ever, young K'van," F'lar said, "but you're one of the bravest!"

And Heth agreed! Pride and joy so leaped in both chests that K'van wondered if his heart would burst right out of his body. He looped an arm around Heth's neck and the pair, the smallest dragonboy and the hatchling who wouldn't choose anybody else, walked out of the Hatching Ground together forever.

The late Hans Stefan Santesson approached me at a party to see if I could contribute to his proposed Walker Anthology on crime prevention in the future. I had nothing completed but I'd just finished "A Womanly Talent," in which parapsychics got made respectable. I'd proposed that there'd be such talents as 'finders' employed by law enforcement officers to locate lost persons and objects. Happily, that background generated this story, almost in one sitting . . . rewarding me in many ways. Authors dream yearningly of stories that'll write themselves. It happens infrequently and is regarded, at least by me, as a minor miracle—the good apple in the barrel of imagination, juicy, tart, memorable.

Apple

THE THEFT WAS THE LEAD MORNING 'CAST and ruined Daffyd op Owen's appetite. As he listened to the description of the priceless sable coat, the sapphire necklace, the couture-model gown, and the jewel-strap slippers, he felt as if he were congealing in his chair as his breakfast cooled and hardened on the plate. He waited, numbed, for the commentator to make the obvious conclusion: a conclusion which would destroy all that the North American Parapsychic Center had achieved so slowly, so delicately. For the only way in which such valuable items could have been removed from a store dummy in a scanned, warded, very public display window in the five-minute period between the fixed TV frames was by kinetic energy.

"The police have several leads and expect to have a solution by evening. Commissioner Frank Gillings is taking charge of the investigation.

" 'I keep my contractual obligations to the City,' Gillings is reported to have told the press early this morning as he personally supervised the examination of the display window at Coles, Michaels' and Charny Department Store. 'I have reduced street and consensual crimes and contained riot activity. Jerhattan is a safe place for the law-abiding. Unsafe for law-breakers.' "

The back-shot of Gillings' stern face was sufficient to break op Owen's stasis. He rose and strode toward the com-unit just as it beeped.

"Daffyd, you heard that 'cast?" The long, unusually grim face of Lester Welch appeared on the screen. "Goddammit, they promised no premature announce-

233

ment. Mediamen!" His expression boded ill for the first unwary reporter to approach him. Over Les's shoulder, op Owen could see the equally savage face of Charlie Moorfield, duty officer of the control room of the Center.

"How long have *you* known about the theft?" Op Owen couldn't quite keep the reprimand from his voice. Les had a habit of trying to spare his superior, particularly these days when he knew op Owen had been spreading himself very thin in the intensive public educational campaign.

"Ted Lewis snuck in a cautious advice as soon as Headquarters scanned the disappearance. He also can't 'find' a thing. And, Dave, there wasn't a wrinkle or a peak between 7:03 and 7:08 on any graph that shouldn't be there, with every single Talent accounted for!"

"That's right, boss," Charlie added. "Not a single Incident to account for the kinetic 'lift' needed for the heist."

"Gillings is on his way here," said Les, screwing his face up with indignation.

"Why?" Daffyd op Owen exploded. "Didn't Ted clear us?"

"Christ, yes, but Gillings has been at Coles and his initial investigation proves conclusively to him that one of our people is a larcenist: One of our women, to be precise, with a secret yen for sable, silk, and sapphires."

Daffyd forced himself to nullify the boiling anger he felt. He could not afford to cloud reason with emotion. Not with so much at stake. Not with the Bill which would provide legal protection for Talents only two weeks away from passing.

"You'll never believe me, will you, Dave," Les said, "that the Talented will always be suspect?"

"Gillings has never caviled at the use of Talents, Lester."

"He'd be a goddamned fool if he did." Lester's eyes sparkled angrily. He jabbed at his chest. *"We've* kept street and consensual crime low. Talent did his job for him. And now he's out to nail us. With publicity like this, we'll never get that Bill through. Christ, what luck! Two bloody weeks away from protection."

"If there's no Incident on the graphs, Les, even Gillings must admit to our innocence."

Welch rolled his eyes heavenward. "How can you be so naive, Dave? No matter what our remotes prove, that heist was done by a Talent."

"Not one of ours." Daffyd op Owen could be dogmatic, too.

"Great. Prove it to Gillings. He's on his way here now and he's out to get us. We've all but ruined his spotless record of enforcement and protection. That hits his credit, monetary and personal." Lester paused for a quick breath. "I told you that public education program would cause more trouble than it's worth. Let me cancel the morning 'cast."

"No." Daffyd closed his eyes wearily. He didn't need to resume that battle with Les now. In spite of this disastrous development, he was convinced of the necessity of the campaign. The general public must learn that they had nothing to fear from those gifted with a parapsychic Talent. The series of public information programs, so carefully planned, served several vital purposes: to show how the many facets of Talent served the community's best interests; to identify those peculiar traits that indicated the possession of a Talent; and, most important, to gain public support for the Bill in the Senate which would give Talents professional immunity in the exercise of their various duties.

"I haven't a vestige of Talent, Dave," Les went on urgently, "but I don't need it to guess some dissident in the common mass of have-nots listened to every word of those 'casts and put what you should never have aired to good use . . . for him. And don't comfort me with how many happy clods have obediently tripped up to the Clinic to have their minor Talents identified. One renegade apple's all you need to sour the barrel!"

"Switch the 'cast to the standard recruiting tape. To pull the whole series would be worse. I'm coming right over."

Daffyd op Owen looked down at the blank screen for a long moment, gathering strength. It was no precog that this would be a very difficult day. Strange, he mused, that no pre-cog had foreseen this. No. *That* very omission indicated a wild Talent, acting on the spur of impulse. What was it Les had said? 'The common mass of have-nots'? Even with the basic dignities of food, shelter, clothing, and education guaranteed, the appetite of the have-not was continually whetted by the abundance that was not his. In this case, hers. Daffyd op Owen groaned. If only such a Talent had been moved to come to the Center where she could be trained and used. (Where had their so carefully worded programming slipped up?) She could have had the furs, the jewels, the dresses on overt purchase . . . and enjoyed them openly. The Center was well enough endowed to satisfy any material yearning of its members. Surely Gillings would admit that.

Op Owen took a deep breath and exhaled regret and supposition. He must keep his mind clear, his sensitivities honed for any nuance that would point a direction toward success.

As he left his shielded quarters at the back of the Center's extensive grounds, he was instantly aware of tension in the atmosphere. Most Talented persons preferred to live in the Center, in the specially shielded buildings that reduced the "noise" of constant psychic agitation. The Center perferred to have them here, as much to protect as to help their members. Talent was a double-edged sword; it could excise evil but it neatly divided its wielder from his fellow man. That was why these broadcasts were so vital. To prove to the general public that the psychically gifted were by no means supermen, able to pierce minds, play ball with massive weights, or rearrange the world to suit themselves. The "Talented" person who could predict events might be limited to Incidents involving fire, or water. He might have an affinity for metals or a kinetic skill enabling him to assemble the components of a microscopic gyro, to be used in space exploration. He might be able to "find" things by studying a replica, or people by holding a possession of the missing person. He might be able to receive thoughts sent from another sensitive or those around him. Or he might be able to broadcast only. A true telepath, sender and receiver—Daffyd op Owen was only one of ten throughout the world— was still rare. Research had indicated there were more people with the ability than would admit it. There were, however, definite limitations to most Talents.

The Parapsychic had been raised, in Daffyd's lifetime, to the level of a science with the development of ultra-sensitive electroencephalographs which could record and identify the type of "Talent" by the minute electrical impulses generated in the cortex during the application of psychic powers. Daffyd op Owen sometimes thought the word "power" was the villain in perpetuating the public misconceptions. Power means "possession of control" but such synonyms as "domination", "sway," "command" lept readily to the average mind and distorted the true definition.

Daffyd op Owen was roused from his thoughts by the heavy beat of a copter. He turned onto the path leading directly to the main administration building and had a clear view of the Commissioner's marked copter landing on the flight roof, to the left of the control tower with its forest of antennal decorations.

Immediately he perceived a reaction of surprise, indignation, and anxiety. Surely every Talent who'd heard the news on the morning 'cast and realized its significance could not be surprised by Gillings' arrival. Op Owen quickened his pace.

Orley's loose! The thought was as loud as a shout.

People paused, turned unerringly toward the long low building of the Clinic where applicants were tested for sensitivity and trained to understand and use what Talent they possessed; and where the Center conducted its basic research in psionics.

A tall, heavy figure flung itself from the Clinic's broad entrance and charged down the lawn, in a direct line to the tower. The man leaped the ornamental garden, plunged through the hedges, swung over the hood of a parked lawn-truck, straight-armed the overhanging branches of trees, brushed aside several men who tried to stop him.

"Reassure Orley! Project reassurance!" the bullhorn from the tower advised. "Project reassurance!"

Get those cops in my office! Daffyd projected on his own as he began to run toward the building. He hoped that Charlie Moorfield or Lester had already done so. Orley didn't look as if anything short of a tranquilizer bullet would stop him. Who had been dim-witted enough to let the telempath out of his shielded room at a time like this? The moron was the most sensitive barometer to emotion Daffyd had ever encountered and he was physically dangerous if aroused. By the speed of that berserker-charge, he had soaked up enough fear/anxiety/anger to dismember the objects he was homing in on.

The only sounds now in the grounds were those of op Owen's shoes hitting the permaplast of the walk and the thud-thud of Orley's progress on the thick lawn. One advantage of being Talented is efficient communication and total comprehension of terse orders. But the wave of serenity/reassurance was not penetrating Orley's blind fury: the openness dissipated the mass effect.

Three men walked purposefully out of the administration building and down the broad apron of steps. Each carried slim-barreled hand weapons. The man on the left raised and aimed his at the audibly panting, fast-approaching moron. The shot took Orley in the right arm but did not cause him to falter. Instantly the second man aimed and fired. Orley lost stride for two paces from the leg shot but recovered incredibly. The third man—op Owen recognized Charlie Moorfield —waited calmly as Orley rapidly closed the intervening distance. In a few more steps Orley would crash into him. Charlie was swinging out of the way, his gun slightly raised for a chest shot, when the moron staggered and, with a horrible groan, fell to his knees. He tried to rise, one clenched fist straining toward the building.

Instantly Charlie moved to prevent Orley from gouging his face on the course-textured permaplast.

"He took two double-strength doses, Dave," Moorfield exclaimed with some awe as he cradled the moron's head in his arms.

"He would. How'n'ell did he get such an exposure?"

Charlie made a grimace. "Sally was feeding him on the terrace. She hadn't heard the 'cast. Said she was concentrating on keeping him clean and didn't 'read' his growing restlessness as more than response to her until he burst wide open."

"Too much to hope that our unexpected guests didn't see this?"

Charlie gave a sour grin. "They caused it, boss. Stood there on the roof, giving Les a hard time, broadcasting basic hate and distrust. You should've seen the dial on the psychic atmosphere gauge. No wonder Orley responded." Charlie's face softened as he glanced down at the unconscious man. "Poor damned soul. Where is that med-team? I 'called' them when we got outside."

Daffyd glanced up at the broad third floor windows that marked his office. Six men stared back. He put an instant damper on his thoughts and emotions, and mounted the steps.

The visitors were still at the window, watching the med-team as they lifted the huge limp body onto the stretcher.

"Orley acts as a human barometer, gentlemen, reacting instantly to the emotional aura around him," Les was saying in his driest, down-eastest tone. To op Owen's wide-open mind, he emanated a raging anger that almost masked the aura projected by the visitors. "He has an intelligence factor of less than fifty on the New Scale which makes him uneducable. He is, however, invaluable in helping identify the dominating emotion in seriously disturbed mental and hallucinogenic patients which could overcome a rational telepath."

Police Commissioner Frank Gillings was the prime source of the fury which had set Harold Orley off. Op Owen felt sorry for Orley, having to bear such anger, and sorrier for himself and his optimistic hopes. He was momentarily at a loss to explain such a violent reaction from Gillings, even granting the validity of Lester Welch's assumption that Gillings was losing face, financial and personal, on account of this affair.

He tried a "push" at Gillings' mind to discover the covert reasons and found the man had a tight natural shield, not uncommon for a person in high position, privy to sensitive facts. The burly Commissioner gave every outward appearance of being completely at ease, as if this were no more than a routine visit, and

239

not one hint of his surface thoughts leaked. Deep-set eyes, barely visible under heavy brows, above fleshy cheeks in a swarthy face missed nothing, flicking from Daffyd to Lester and back.

Op Owen nodded to Ted Lewis, the top police "finder" who had accompanied the official group. He stood a little to one side of the others. Of all the visitors, his mind was wide open. Foremost was the thought that he hoped Daffyd would read him, so that he could pass the warning that Gillings considered Orley's exhibition another indication that Talents could not control or discipline their own members.

"Good morning, Commissioner. I regret such circumstances bring you on your first visit to the Center. This morning's newscast has made us all extremely anxious to clear our profession."

Gillings' perfunctory smile did not acknowledge the tacit explanation of Orley's behavior.

"I'll come to the point, then, Owen. We have conclusively ascertained that there was no break in store security measures when the theft occurred. The 'lectric wards and spy-scanner were not tampered with nor was there any evidence of breaking or entering. There is only one method in which sable, necklace, dress, and shoes could have been taken from that window in the five minutes between TV scans.

"We regret exceedingly that the evidence points to a person with psychic talents. We must insist that the larcenist be surrendered to us immediately and the merchandise returned to Mr. Grey, the repesentative from Coles." He indicated the portly man in a conservative but expensive gray fitted.

Op Owen nodded and looked expectantly toward Ted Lewis.

"Lewis can't 'find' a trace anywhere so it's obvious the items are being shielded." A suggestion of impatience crept into Gillings' bass voice. "These grounds are shielded."

"The stolen goods are not here, Commissioner. If they were, they would have been found by a member the instant the broadcast was heard."

Gillings' eyes snapped and his lips thinned with obstinacy.

"I've told you I can read on these grounds, Commissioner," Ted Lewis said with understandable indignation. "The stolen . . ."

A wave of the Commissioner's hand cut off the rest of Lewis's statement. Op Owen fought anger at the insult.

"You're a damned fool, Gillings," said Welch, not bothering to control his rage, "if you think we'd shelter a larcenist at this time."

"Ah yes, that Bill pending Senate approval," Gillings said with an unpleasant smile.

Daffyd found it hard to nullify resentment at the smug satisfaction and new antagonism which Gillings was generating.

"Yes, that Bill, Commissioner," op Owen repeated, "which will protect any Talent *registered* with a parapsychic center." Op Owen did not miss the sparkle of Gillings' deep-set eyes at the deliberate emphasis. "If you'll step this way, gentlemen, to our remote-graph control system, I believe that we can prove, to your absolute satisfaction, that no registered Talent is responsible. You haven't been here before, Commissioner, so you are not familiar with our method of recording incidents in which psychic powers are used.

"Power, by the way, means 'possession of control', personal as well as psychic, which is what this Center teaches each and every member. Here we are. Charles Moorfield is the duty officer and was in charge at the time of the robbery. If you will observe the graphs, you'll notice that the period—between 7:03 and 7:08 was the time given by the 'cast—has not yet wound out of sight on the storage drums."

Gillings was not looking at the graphs. He was staring at Charlie.

"Next time, aim at the chest first, mister."

"Sorry I stopped him at all . . . mister," replied Charlie, with such deliberate malice that Gillings colored and stepped toward him.

Op Owen quickly intervened. "You dislike, distrust, and hate us, Commissioner," he said, keeping his own voice neutral. "You and your staff have prejudged us guilty, though you are at this moment surrounded by incontrovertible evidence of our collective innocence.

241

You arrived here, emanating disruptive emotions—no, I'm *not* reading your minds, gentlemen (Daffyd had all Gillings' attention with that phrase). That isn't necessary. You're triggering responses in the most controlled of us—not to mention that poor witless telempath we had to tranquilize. And, unless you put a lid on your unwarranted hatred and fears, I will have no compunction about pumping you all full of tranks, too!"

"That's coming on mighty strong for a man in your position, Owen," Gillings said in a tight hard voice, his body visibly tense now.

"You're the one that's coming on strong, Gillings. Look at that dial behind you." Gillings did not want to turn, particularly not at op Owen's command, but there is a quality of righteous anger that compels obedience. "That registers—as Harold Orley does—the psychic intensity of the atmosphere. The mind gives off electrical impulses, Gillings, surely you have to admit that. Law enforcement agencies used that premise for lie detection. Our instrumentation makes those early registers as archaic as spaceships make oxcarts. We have ultra-delicate equipment which can measure the minutest electrical impulses of varying frequencies and duration. And this p.a. dial registers a dangerous high right now. Surely your eyes must accept scientific evidence.

"Those rows of panels there record the psychic activity of each and every member registered with this Center. See, most of them register agitation right now. These red divisions indicate a sixty-minute time span. Each of those drums exposes the graph as of the time of that theft. Notice the difference. Not one graph shows the kinetic activity required of a "lifter' to achieve such a theft. But every one shows a reaction to your presence.

"There is no way in which a registered Talent can avoid these graphs. Charlie, were any kinetics out of touch at the time of the theft?"

Charlie, his eyes locked on Gillings, shook his head slowly.

"There has never been so much as a civil misdemeanor by any of our people. No breach of confidence,

242

nor integrity. No crime could be shielded from fellow Talents.

"And can you rationally believe that we would jeopardize years and years of struggle to become accepted as reliable citizens of indisputable integrity for the sake of a fur coat and a string of baubles? When there are funds available to any Talent who might want to own such fripperies?" Op Owen's scorn made the Coles man wince.

"Now get out of here, Gillings. Discipline your emotions and revise your snap conclusion. Then call through normal channels and request our cooperation. Because, believe me, we are far more determined—and better equipped—to discover the real criminal than you could ever ever be, no matter what *your* personal stake in assigning guilt might conceivably be."

Op Owen watched for a reaction to that remark, but Gillings, his lips thin and white with anger, did not betray himself. He gestured jerkily toward the one man in police blues.

"Do not serve that warrant now, Gillings!" op Owen said in a very soft voice. He watched the frantic activity of the needle on the p.a. dial.

"Go. Now. Call. Because if you cannot contain your feelings, Commissioner, you had better maintain your distance."

It was then that Gillings became aware of the palpable presence of those assembled in the corridor. A wide aisle had been left free, an aisle that led only to the open elevator. No one spoke or moved or coughed. The force exerted was not audible or physical. It was, however, undeniably unanimous. It prevailed in forty-four seconds.

"My firm will wish to know what steps are being taken," the Coles man said in a squeaky voice as he began to walk, with erratic but ever quickening steps, toward the elevator.

Gillings' three subordinates were not so independent but there was no doubt of their relief as Gillings turned and walked with precise, unhurried strides to the waiting car.

No one moved until the thwapping rumble of the

243

copter was no longer audible. Then they turned for assignments from their director.

City Manager Julian Pennstrak, with a metropolis of some four millions to supervise, had a habit of checking up personally on any disruption to the smooth operation of his city. He arrived as the last of the organized search parties left the Center.

"I'd give my left kidney and a million credits to have enough Talent to judge a man accurately, Dave," he said as he crossed the room. He knew better than to shake hands unless a Talented offered but it was obvious to Daffyd, who liked Pennstrak, that the man wanted somehow to convey his personal distress over this incident. He stood for a moment by the chair, his handsome face without a trace of his famous genial smile. "I'd've sworn Frank Gillings was pro Talent," he said, combing his fingers through his thick, wavy black hair, another indication of his anxiety. "He certainly has used your people to their fullest capabilities since he became L E and P Commissioner."

Lester Welch snorted, looking up from the map he was annotating with search patterns. "A man'll use any tool that works . . . until it scratches him, that is."

"But you could prove that no registered Talent was responsible for that theft."

" 'A man convinced against his will, is of the same opinion still," Lester chanted.

"Les!" Op Owen didn't need our sour cynicism from any quarter, even one dedicated to Talent. "No *registered* Talent was responsible."

Pennstrak brightened. "You did persuade Gillings that it's the work of an undiscovered Talent?"

Welch made a rude noise. "He'll be persuaded when we produce, both missing person and missing merchandise. Nothing else is going to satisfy either Gillings or Coles."

"True," Pennstrak agreed, frowning thoughtfully. "Nor the vacillating members of my own Council. Oh, I know, it's a flash reaction but the timing is so goddamned lousy, Dave. Your campaign bore down heavy on the integrity and good citizenship of the Talented."

"It's a deliberate smear job—" Welch began gloomily.

"I thought of that," Pennstrak interrupted him, "and had my own expert go over the scanner films. You know the high-security-risk set-up: rotating exposures on the stationary TV eyes. One frame the model was clothed; next, exposed in all its plastic glory. It was a 'lift' all right. No possibility of tampering with that film." Pennstrak leaned forward to Dave, though there was scarcely any need to guard his statements in this company. "Furthermore, Pat came along. She 'read' everyone at the store, and Gilling's squad. Not Gillings, though. She said he has a natural shield. The others were all clean . . . at least, of conspiracy." Pennstrak's snide grin faded quickly. "I made her go rest. That's why there's no one with me."

Op Owen accepted the information quietly. He had half-hoped . . . it was an uncharacteristic speculation for him. However, it did save time and Talent to have had both store and police checked.

It had become general practice to have a strong telepathic receiver in the entourage of any prominent or controversial public figure. That Talent was rarely identified publicly. He or she usually performed some obvious service so that their constant presence was easily explicable. Pat Tawfik was overtly Pennstrak's chief speechwriter.

"I have, however," Pennstrak continued, "used my official prerogative to supervise the hunt. There're enough sympathetic people on the public media channels to play down the Talent angle—at my request. But you know what this kind of adverse publicity is going to do to you, this Center, and the Talented in general. One renegade can discredit a hundred honest Injuns. So, what can I do to help?"

"I wish I knew. We've got every available perceptive out on the off chance that this—ah, renegade happens to be broadcasting joy and elation over her heist."

"Her?"

"The consensus is that while a man might lift furs and jewels, possibly the dress, only a woman would

245

take the shoes, too. Top finders are coming in from other Centers . . ."

"A 'find' is reported, boss," Charlie said over the intercom. "Block Q."

As Pennstrak and op Owen reached the map, Welch announced with a groan, "Gawd, that's a multilayer apartment zone."

"A have-not," op Owen added.

"Gil Gracie made the find, boss," Charlie continued. "And the fur is not all he's found but he's got a problem."

"You just bet he has," Les muttered under his breath as he grimaced down at the map coordinates.

"Charlie, send every finder and perceptive to Block Q. If they can come up with a fix . . ."

"Boss, we got a fix, but there's one helluva lot of similarities."

"What's the problem?" Pennstrak asked.

"We'll simply have to take our time and eliminate, Charlie. Send anyone who can help." Then op Owen turned to Pennstrak. "In reporting a 'find,' the perceptive is aware of certain particular spatial relationships between the object sought and its immediate surroundings. It isn't as if he has seen the object as a camera sees it. For example, have you ever entered a room, turned down a street, or looked up quickly and had the feeling that you had seen just"—and Daffyd made a bracket of his hands—"that portion of the scene before, with exactly the same lighting, exactly the same components? But only that portion of the scene, so that the rest was an indistinguishable blur?"

Pennstrak nodded.

" 'Finding' is like that. Sometimes the Talent sees it in lucid detail, sometimes it's obscured or, as in this case, there are literally hundreds of possibilities . . . apartments with the same light exposure, same scene out the window, the same floor plan and furnishings. Quite possible in this instance since these are furnished, standard subsistence dwellings. Nothing to help us single out, say Apartment 44E, Building 18, Buhler Street."

"There happens to be a Building 18 on Buhler Street,

boss," Les Welch said slowly, "and there are forty-eight levels, ten units per floor."

Pennstrak regarded op Owen with awe.

"Nonsense, this office is thoroughly shielded and I'm *not* a pre-cog!"

"Before you guys took the guesswork out of it, there were such things as hunches," Pennstrak suggested.

For op Owen's peace of mind and Lester's pose of misogyny, it was neither Building 18 nor Buhler Street nor Apartment 44. It was Apartment 1E, deep in the center of Q Block. No one had entered nor left it—by normal means—since Gil Gracie and two other finders had made a precise fix. Gil handed op Owen the master key obtained from the dithering super.

"My Gawd," Pennstrak said in a voice muted with shocked surprise as they swung open the door. "Like an oriental bazaar."

"Indiscriminate pilfering on a wholesale basis," op Owen corrected, glancing around at the rich brilliant velvet drapes framing the dingy window to the wildly clashing pillows thrown on the elegant Empire loveseat. A marble-topped table was a jumble of pretty vases, silver boxes, and goblets. Priceless china held decaying remains of food. Underneath the table were jaggedly opened, empty cans bearing the label of an extremely expensive caterer. Two empty champagne bottles pointed green, blind eyes in their direction. A portable color 'caster was piled with discarded clothing; a black-lace sheer body stocking draped in an obscene posture across the inactive screen. "A magpie's nest rather," he sighed, "and I'd hazard that Maggie is very young and has been poor all her life until . . ." He met Pennstrak's sympathetic gaze. "Until our educational program gave her the hints she needed to unlock her special Talent."

"Gillings is going to have to work with you on this, Dave," Pennstrak said reluctantly as he reached for the intercom at his belt. "But first he's going to have to apologize"

Op Owen shook his head vigorously. "I want his cooperation, Julian, grudged or willing. *When* he really believes in Talent, then he will apologize voluntarily . . . and obliquely," he couldn't resist adding.

To op Owen's consternation, Gillings arrived noisily in the cowlike lab copter, sirens going, lights flashing.

"Don't bother now," op Owen advised Pennstrak, for he could see the City Manager forming a furious reprimand. "She might have been warned by the finders' activity anyhow."

"Well, she's certainly been warned off now," Pennstrak stalked off, to confer with one of his aides just as Gillings strode into the corridor with his technicians.

According op Owen and Gracie the merest nod, Gillings began issuing crisp orders. He knew his business, op Owen thought, and he evidently trusted *these* technicians, for he didn't bother to crowd into the tiny apartment to oversee them.

"As soon as your men have prints and a physical profile, Commissioner, we'd like to run the data through our computer. There's the chance that the girl did take advantage of the open Talent test the Center has been advertising."

"You mean you don't *know* who it is *yet?*"

"I found the coat since I *knew* what it looked like," Gil Gracie said, bristling at Gillings' manner.

"Then where is it?" Gillings gestured peremptorily to the sable-less apartment.

"These are the shoes, Commissioner," said one of his team, presenting the fragile jeweled footwear, now neatly sealed in clear plastic. "Traces of dirt, dust, fleck of nail enamel and from the 'scope imprint, I'd say they were too big for her."

Gillings stared at the shoes disinterestedly. "No sign of the dress?"

"Still looking."

"Odd that you people can't locate a girl with bare feet in a sable coat and a bright blue silk gown?"

"No odder than it is for your hundreds of patrolmen throughout the city, Commissioner, to overlook a girl so bizarrely dressed," op Owen said with firm good humor. "When you 'saw' the coat, Gil, where was it?"

"Thrown across the loveseat, one arm hanging down to the floor. I distinguished the edge of the sill and the tree outside, the first folds of the curtain, and the wall heating unit. I called in, you sent over enough finders so that we were able to eliminate the similarities. It took us nearly an hour . . ."

"Were you keeping an 'eye' on the coat all the time?" Gillings demanded in a voice so devoid of expression that his contempt was all the more obvious.

Gil flushed, bit his lip, and only partially inhibited by op Owen's subtle warning, snapped back, "Try keeping your physical eye on an object for an hour!"

"Get some rest, Gil," op Owen suggested gently. He waited until the finder had turned the corner. "If you are as determined to find this criminal as you say you are, Commissioner Gillings, then do not destroy the efficiency of my staff by such gratuitous criticism. In less than four hours, on the basis of photographs of the stolen objects, we located this apartment . . ."

"But not the criminal, who is still in possession of a sable coat which you found once but have now unaccountably lost."

"That's enough, Gillings," said Pennstrak, who had rejoined them. "Thanks to your arrival, the girl must know she's being sought and is shielding."

Pennstrak gestured toward the dingy windows of the flat, through which the vanes of the big copter were visible. A group of children, abandoning the known objects of the development play-yard, had gathered at a respectful but curiosity-satisfying distance.

"Considering the variety of her accomplishments," op Owen said, not above using Pennstrak's irritation with his Commissioner to advantage, "I'm sure she knew of the search before the Commissioner's arrival, Julian. Have any of these items been reported, Commissioner?"

"That console was. Two days ago. It was on 'find,' too."

"She has been growing steadily bolder, then," op Owen went on, depressed by Gillings' attitude. And depressed that such a Talent had emerged twisted, perverted, selfish. Why? Why? "If your department ever gets the chronology of the various thefts, we'd appreciate the copy."

"Why?" Gillings turned to stare at op Owen, surprised and irritated.

"Talent takes time to develop—in ordinary persons.

It does not, like the ancient goddess Athena, spring full-grown from the forehead. This girl could not, for instance, have lifted that portable set the first time she used her Talent. The more data we have on . . . the lecture is ill-timed."

Gillings' unspoken "you said it" did reach op Owen, whose turn it was to stare in surprise.

"Well, your 'finders' are not novices," the Commissioner said aloud. "If they traced the coat once, why not again?"

"Every perceptive we have is searching," op Owen assured him. "But, if she was able to leave this apartment after Gil found the coat, taking it with her because it obviously is not here, she also is capable of shielding herself and that coat. And, until she slips that guard, I doubt we'll find it or her."

The report on the laboratory findings was exhaustive. There was a full set of prints, foot and finger. None matched those on file in the city records, or Federal or Immigration. She had not been tested at the Center. Long coarse black hair had been found. Skin flakes analyzed suggested an olive complexion. Thermo-photography placed her last appearance in the room at approximately the time the four "finders" fixed on her apartment, thus substantiating op Owen's guess. The thermal prints also revealed that she was of slender build, approximately five-four, weighing 105 pounds. Stains on a kitchen knife proved her to possess blood type O. No one else had occupied the apartment within the eight-day range of the thermography used.

From such records, the police extrapolator made a rough sketch of Maggie O as she was called for want of a better name. The sketch was taken around the neighborhood with no success. People living in Block Q didn't bother people who didn't bother them.

It was Daffyd op Owen who remembered the children crowding the police copter. From them he elicited the information that she was new in the building. (The records indicated that the apartment should be vacant.) She was always singing, dancing to the wall-'caster, and changing her clothes. Occasionally she'd play with them and bring out rich food to eat, promising they could have such good things if they'd think hard about them. While the children talked, Daffyd "saw" Maggie's face reflected in their minds. The police extrapolator had been far short of the reality. She was not much older than the children she had played with. She had not been pretty by ordinary standards but she had been so "different" that her image had registered sharply. The narrow face, the brilliant eyes, slightly slanted above sharp cheekbones, the thin, small mouth, and the pointed chin were unusual even in an area of ethnic variety.

This likeness and a physical description were circulated quickly to be used at all exits to the city and all transportation facilities. It was likely she'd try to slip out during the day-end exodus.

The south and west airstrips had been under a perceptive surveillance since the search had been inaugurated. Now every facility was guarded.

Gil Gracie "found" the coat again.

"She must have it in a suitcase," he reported on the police-provided hand unit from his position in the main railroad concourse. "It's folded and surrounded by dark. It's moving up and down. But there're so many people. So many suitcases. I'll circulate. Maybe the find'll fix itself."

Gillings gave orders to his teams on the master unit which had been set up in the Center's control room to coordinate the operations.

"You better test Gil for pre-cog," Charlie muttered to op Owen after they'd contacted all the sensitives. "He *asked* for the station."

"You should've told me sooner, Charlie. I'd've teamed him with a sensitive."

"Lookit that," Charlie exclaimed, pointing to a wildly moving needle on one of the remotes.

Les was beside it even as the audio for the Incident went on.

"Not that track! Oh! Watch out! Baggage. On the handcart! Watch out. Move, man. Move! To the right. The right! Ahhhh." The woman's voice choked off in an agonized cry.

Daffyd pushed Charlie out of the way, to get to the speaker.

"Gil this is op Owen. Do not pursue. Do not pursue that girl! She's aware of you. Gil, come in. Answer me, Gil. . . . Charlie, keep trying to raise him. Gillings, contact your men at the station. Make them stop Gil Gracie."

"Stop him? Why?"

"The pre-cog. The baggage on the handcart," shouted Daffyd, signaling frantically to Lester to explain in detail. He raced for the emergency stairs, up the two flights, and slammed out onto the roof. Gasping for breath, he clung to the high retaining wall and projected his mind to Gil's.

He knew the man so well, trained Gil when an employer brought in the kid who had a knack for locating things. Op Owen could see him ducking and dodging through the trainward crowds, touching suitcases, ignoring irate or astonished carriers; every nerve, every ounce of him receptive to the "feel" of a dense, dark sable fur. And so single-minded that Daffyd could not "reach" him.

But op Owen knew the instant the loaded baggage cart swerved and crushed the blindly intent Talent against an I-beam. He bowed his head, too fully cognizant that a double tragedy had occurred. Gil was lost . . . and so now was the girl.

There was no peace from his thoughts even when he returned to the shielded control room. Lester and Charlie pretended to be very busy. Gillings was. He directed the search of the railway station, arguing with the stationmaster that the trains were to be held and that was that! The drone of his voice began to penetrate op Owen's remorse.

"All right, then, if the Talents have cleared it and there's no female of the same height and weight, release that train. Someone tried the johns, didn't they? No, Sam, you can detain anyone remotely suspicious. That girl is clever, strong, and dangerous. There's no telling what else she could do. But she damn well can't change her height, weight, and blood type!"

"Daffyd. Daffyd." Lester had to touch him to get his attention. He motioned op Owen toward Charlie, who was holding out the hand unit.

"It's Coles, sir."

Daffyd listened to the effusively grateful store manager. He made the proper responses, but it wasn't until he had relinquished the hand unit to Charlie that the man's excited monologue made sense.

"The coat, the dress, and the necklace have reappeared on the store dummy," op Owen said. He cleared his throat and repeated it loud enough to be heard.

"Returned?" Gillings echoed. "Just like that? Why, the little bitch! Sam, check the ladies' rooms in that station. Wait, isn't there a discount dress store in that station? Have them check for missing apparel. I want an itemized list of what's gone, and an exact duplicate from their stock shown to the sensitives. We've got her scared and running now."

"Scared and running now." Gillings' smug assessment rang ominously in Daffyd's mind. He had a sudden flash. Superimposed over a projection of Maggie's thin face was the image of the lifeless store dummy, elegantly reclad in the purloined blue gown and dark fur. "Here, take them back. I don't want them anymore. I didn't mean to kill him. I didn't mean to. See, I gave back what you wanted. Now leave me alone!"

Daffyd shook his head. Wishful thinking. Just as futile as the girl's belated gesture of penance. Too much too soon. Too little too late.

"We don't want her scared," he said out loud. "She was scared when she toppled that baggage cart."

"She *killed* a man when she toppled that baggage cart, op Owen!" Gillings was all but shouting.

"And if we're not very careful, she'll kill others."

"If you think I'm going to velvet glove a homicidal maniac . . ."

A shrill tone issuing from the remote unit forced Gillings to answer. He was about to reprimand the caller but the message got his stunned attention.

"We can forget the paternal bit, Owen. She knocked down every one of your people and mine at the Oriole Street entrance. Your men are unconscious. Mine and about twenty or more innocent commuters are afflicted with blinding headaches. Got any practical ideas, Owen, on catching this monster you created?"

253

"Oriole? Was she heading east or west?"

"Does it matter?"

"If we're to catch her it does. And we must catch her. She's operating at a psychic high. There's no telling what she's capable of now. Such Talent has only been a theoretic possibility . . ."

Gillings lost all control of himself. The fear and hatred burst out in such a wave that Charlie Moorfield, caught unaware, erupted out of his chair toward Gillings in an instinctive defense reaction.

"Gillings!" "Charlie!" Les and Daffyd shouted together, each grabbing the whilom combatants. But Charlie, his face white with shock at his own reaction, had himself in hand. Sinking weakly back into his chair, he gasped out an apology.

"You mean, you *want* to have more monsters like her and him?" Gillings demanded. Between his voice and the violent emotions, Daffyd's head rang with pain and confusion.

"Don't be a fool," Lester said, grabbing the Commissioner by the arm. "You can't spew emotions like that around a telepath and not get a reaction. Look at Daffyd! Look at Charlie! Christ, man, you're as bad as the scared, mixed up kid . . ." Then Les dropped Gillings' arm and stared at him in amazement. "Christ, you're a telepath yourself!"

"Quiet, everybody," Daffyd said with such urgency he had their instant attention. "I've the solution. And there's no time to waste. Charlie, I want Harold Orley airbound in the Clinic's copter heading south to the Central Station in nothing flat. We'll correct course en route. Gillings, I want two of the strongest, most stable patrolmen on your roster. I want them armed with fast-acting, double-strength trank guns and airborne to rendezvous near Central Station."

"Harold?" Les echoed in blank astonishment and then relief colored his face as he understood Daffyd's intentions. "Of course. Nothing can stop Harold. And no one can read him coming."

"Nothing. And no one," op Owen agreed bleakly.

Gillings turned from issuing his orders to see an ambulance copter heading west across the sky.

"We're following?"

Daffyd nodded and gestured for Gillings to precede him to the roof. He didn't look back but he knew what Les and Charlie did not say.

She had been seen running east on Oriole. And she was easy to follow. She left people doubled up with nausea and crying with head pains. That is, until she crossed Boulevard.

"We'll head south-southeast on an intercept," Gillings told his pilot and had him relay the correction to the ambulance. "She's heading to the sea?" he asked rhetorically as he rummaged for the correct airmap of the city. "Here. We can set down at Seaman's Park. She can't have made it that far . . . unless she can fly suddenly." Gillings looked up at op Owen.

"She probably could teleport herself," Daffyd answered, watching the Commissioner's eyes narrow in adverse reaction to the admission. "But she hasn't thought of it yet. As long as she can be kept running, too scared to think . . ." That necessity would ever plague Daffyd op Owen: that they must run her out of her mind.

Gillings ordered all police hovercraft to close in on the area where she was last seen, blocks of residences and small businesses of all types.

By the time the three copters had made their rendezvous at the small park, there were no more visible signs of Maggie O's retreat.

As Gillings made to leave the copter, Daffyd op Owen stopped him.

"If you're not completely under control, Gillings, Harold will be after *you*."

Gillings looked at the director for a long moment, his jaw set stubbornly. Then, slowly, he settled into the seat and handed op Owen a remote com-unit.

"Thanks, Gillings," he said, and left the copter. He signaled to the ambulance to release Harold Orley and then strode across the grass to the waiting officers.

The two biggest men were as burly as he could wish. Being trained law enforcers, they ought to be able to handle Orley. Op Owen "pushed" gently against their minds and was satisfied with his findings. They possessed the natural shielding of the untemperamental which made them less susceptible to emotional storms. Neither Webster nor Heis was stupid, however, and they had been briefed on developments.

"Orley has no useful intelligence. He is a human barometer, measuring the intensity and type of emotions which surround him and reacting instinctively. He does not broadcast. He only receives. Therefore he cannot be harmed or identified by . . . by Maggie O. He is the only Talent she cannot 'hear' approaching."

"But, if he reaches her, he'd . . ." Webster began, measuring Harold with the discerning eye of a boxing enthusiast. Then he shrugged and turned politely to op Owen.

"You've the double-strength tranks? Good. I hope you'll be able to use them in time. But it is imperative that she be apprehended before she does more harm. She has already killed one man . . ."

"We understand, sir," Heis said when op Owen did not continue.

"If you can, shoot her. Once she stops broadcasting, he'll soon return to a manageable state." But, Daffyd amended to himself, remembering Harold sprawled on the ground in front of the building, not soon enough. "She was last seen on the east side of the boulevard, about eight blocks from here. She'd be tired, looking for someplace to hide and rest. But she is also probably radiating sufficient emotion for Harold to pick up. He'll react by heading in a straight line for the source. Keep him from trying to plow through solid walls. Keep your voices calm when you speak to him. Use simple commands. I see you've got hand units. I'll be airborne; the copter's shielded but I'll help when I can."

Flanking Harold, Webster and Heis moved west along Oriole at a brisk even walk: the two officers in step, Harold's head bobbing above theirs. His being out of step was a cruel irony.

Daffyd op Owen turned back to the copter. He nodded to Gillings as he seated himself. He tried not to think at all.

As the copters lifted from the park and drifted slowly

west amid other air traffic, op Owen looked sadly down at the people on the streets. At kids playing on the sidewalks. At a flow of men and women with briefcases or shopping bags, hurrying home. At snub-nosed city cars and squatty trucks angling into parking slots. At the bloated cross-city helibuses jerking and settling to disgorge their passengers at the street islands.

"He's twitching," Heis reported in a dispassionate voice.

Daffyd flicked on the handset. "That's normal. He's beginning to register."

"He's moving faster now. Keeps wanting to go straight through the buildings." Reading Heis' undertone, op Owen knew that the men hadn't believed his caution about Orley plowing through solids. "He's letting us guide him, but he keeps pushing us to the right. You take his other arm, Web. Yeah, that's better."

Gillings had moved to the visual equipment along one side of the copter .He focused deftly in on the trio, magnified it, and threw the image on the pilot's screen, too. The copter adjusted direction.

"Easy, Orley. No, don't try to stop him, Web. Stop the traffic!"

Orley's line of march crossed the busier wide north-south street. Webster ran out to control the vehicles. People turned curiously. Stopped and stared after the trio.

"Don't," op Owen ordered as he saw Gillings move a hand towards the bullhorn. "There's nothing wrong with her hearing."

Orley began to move faster now that he had reached the farther side. He wanted to go right through intervening buildings.

"Guide him left to the sidewalk, Heis," op Owen advised. "I think he's still amenable. He isn't running yet."

"He's breathing hard, Mr. Owen." Heis sounded dubious. "And his face is changing."

Op Owen nodded to himself, all too familiar with the startling phenomena of watching the blankness of Orley's face take on the classic mask of whatever emotions he was receiving. It would be a particularly un-nerving transition under these conditions.

"What does he show?"

"I'd say . . . hatred." Heis' voice dropped on the last word. Then he added in his usual tone, "He's smiling, too, and it isn't nice."

They had eased Orley to the sidewalk heading west. He kept pushing Webster to the right and his pace increased until it was close to a run. Webster and Heis began to gesture people out of their way but it would soon be obvious to the neighborhood that something was amiss. Would it be better to land more police to reassure people and keep their emanations down? Or would they broadcast suppressed excitement at police interference? She'd catch that. Should he warn Heis and Webster to keep their thoughts on Harold Orley? Or would that be like warning them against all thoughts of the camel's left knee?

Orley broke into a run. Webster and Heis were hard put to keep him to the sidewalk.

"What's in the next block?" op Owen asked Gillings.

The Commissioner consulted the map, holding it just above the scanner so he could keep one eye on the trio below.

"Residences and an area parking facility for interstate trucking." Gillings turned to op Owen now, his heavy eyebrows raised in question.

"No, she's still there because Orley is homing in on her projection."

"Look at his face! My God!" Heis exclaimed over the hand-unit. On the screen, his figure had stopped. He was pointing at Orley. But Webster's face was clearly visible to the surveillers; and what he saw unnerved him.

Orley broke from his guides. He was running, slowly at first but gathering speed steadily, mindlessly brushing aside anything that stood in his way. Heis and Webster were after him but both men were shaking their heads as if something were bothering them. Orley tried to plunge through a brick store wall. He bounced off it, saw the unimpeded view of his objective, and charged forward. Webster had darted ahead of him, blowing his whistle to stop the oncoming traffic. Heis alternately yelled into the hand unit and at startled bystanders. Now some of them were afflicted and were grabbing their heads.

"Put us on the roof," op Owen told the pilot. "Gillings, get men to cover every entrance and exit to that parking lot. Get the copters to hover by the open levels. The men'll be spared some of the lash."

It wouldn't do much good, op Owen realized, even as he felt the first shock of the girl's awareness of imminent danger.

"Close your mind," he yelled at the pilot and Gillings. "Don't think."

"My head, my head." It was Heis groaning.

"Concentrate on Orley," op Owen advised, his hands going to his temples in reaction to the knotting pressure. Heis's figure on the scanner staggered after Orley, who had now entered the parking facility.

Op Owen caught the mental pressure and dispersed it, projecting back reassurance/help/protection/compassion. *He* could forgive her Gil Gracie's death. So would any Talent. If she would instantly surrender, somehow the Centers would protect her from the legal aspects of her act. Only surrender now.

Someone screamed. Another man echoed that piercing cry. The copter bucked and jolted them. The pilot was groaning and gasping. Gillings plunged forward, grabbing the controls.

Op Owen, fighting an incredible battle, was blind to physical realities. If he could just occupy all the attention of that overcharged mind . . . hold it long enough . . . pain/fear/black/red/moiled-orange/purples . . . breathing . . . shock. Utter disbelief/fear/loss of confidence. Frantic physical effort.

Concrete scraped op Owen's cheek. His fingers bled as he clawed at a locked steel exit door on the roof. He could not enter. *He had to reach her* FIRST!

Somehow his feet found the stairs as he propelled himself down the fire escape, deliberately numbing his mind to the intensive pounding received. A pounding that became audible.

Then he saw her, fingers clawing for leverage on the stairpost, foot poised for the step from the landing. A too thin, adolescent figure, frozen for a second with indecision and shock; strands of black hair like vicious scars across a thin face, distorted and ugly from the tremendous physical and mental efforts of the frantic will. Her huge eyes, black with insane fury and terror, bloodshot with despair and the salty sweat of her desperate striving for escape, looked into his.

She knew him for what he was; and her hatred crackled in his mind. Those words—after Gil Gracie's death—had been hers, not his distressed imagining. She had known him then as her real antagonist. Only now was *he* forced to recognize her for what she was, all she was—and regrettably, all she would not be.

He fought the inexorable decision of that split-second confrontation, wanting more than anything else in his life that it did not have to be so.

She was the wiser! She whirled!

She was suddenly beyond the heavy fire door without opening it. Harold Orley, charging up the stairs behind her, had no such Talent. He crashed with sickening force into the metal door. Daffyd had no alternative. She had teleported. He steadied the telempath, depressed the lock bar, and threw the door wide.

Orley was after the slender figure fleeing across the dimly lit, low-ceilinged concrete floor. She was heading toward the down ramp now.

"Stop, stop," op Owen heard his voice begging her.

Heis came staggering from the stairway.

"Shoot him. For Christ's sake, shoot Orley, Heis," op Owen yelled.

Heis couldn't seem to coordinate. Op Owen tried to push aside his fumbling hands and grab the trank gun himself. Heis's trained reflexes made him cling all the tighter to his weapon. Just then, op Owen heard the girl's despairing shriek.

Two men had appeared at the top of the ramp. They both fired, the dull reports of trank pistols accentuated by her choked gasp.

"Not her. Shoot Orley. Shoot the man," op Owen cried, but it was too late.

Even as the girl crumpled to the floor, Orley grabbed her. Grabbed and tore and beat at the source of the emotions which so disturbed him. Beat and tore and stamped as she had assaulted him.

Orley's body jerked as tranks hit him from several sides, but it took far too long for them to override the adrenal reactions of the overcharged telempath.

There was pain and pity as well as horror in Gillings' eyes when he came running onto the level. The police stood at a distance from the blood-spattered bodies.

"Gawd, couldn't someone have stopped him from getting her?" the copter pilot murmured, turning away from the shapeless bloodied thing half-covered by Orley's unconscious body.

"The door would have stopped Orley, but he," Heis grimly pointed at op Owen, "opened it for him."

"She teleported through the door," op Owen said weakly. He had to lean against the wall. He was beginning to shudder uncontrollably. "She had to be stopped. Now. Here. Before she realized what she'd done. What she could do." His knees buckled. "She teleported through the door!"

Unexpectedly, it was Gillings who came to his aid, a Gillings whose mind was no longer shielded but broadcasting compassion and awe, and understanding.

"So did you."

The phrase barely registered in op Owen's mind when he passed out.

"That's all that remains of the late Solange Boshe," Gillings said, tossing the file reel to the desk. "As much of her life as we've been able to piece together. Gypsies don't stay long anywhere."

"There're some left?" Lester Welch asked, frowning at the three-inch condensation of fifteen years of a human life.

"Oh there are, I assure you," Gillings replied, his tone souring slightly for the first time since he had entered the office. "The tape also has a lengthy interview with Bill Jones, the cousin the social worker located after Solange had recovered from the bronchial

261

pneumonia. He had no idea," Gillings hastily assured them, "that there is any reason other than a routine check on the whereabouts of a runaway county ward. He had a hunch," Gillings grimaced, "that the family had gone on to Toronto. They had. He also thought that they had probably given the girl up for dead when she collapsed on the street. The Toronto report substantiates that. So I don't imagine it will surprise you, op Owen, that her tribe, according to Jones, are the only ones still making a living at fortune-telling, palm-reading, tea leaves and that bit."

"Now, just a minute, Gillings," Lester began, bristling. He subsided when he saw that his boss and the Commissioner were grinning at each other.

"So . . . just as you suspected, op Owen, she was a freak Talent. We know from the ward nurses that she watched your propaganda broadcasts during her hospitalization. We can assume that she was aware of the search either when Gil Gracie 'found' the coat, or when the definite fix was made. It's not hard to guess her motivation in making the heist in the first place nor her instinctive desire to hide." Gillings gave his head an abrupt violent jerk and stood up. He started to hold out his hand, remembered, and raised it in a farewell gesture. "You are continuing those broadcasts, aren't you?"

Lester Welch glared so balefully at the Commissioner that op Owen had to chuckle.

"With certain deletions, yes."

"Good. Talent must be identified and trained. Trained young and well if they are to use their Talent properly." Gillings stared op Owen in the eye. "The Boshe girl was bad, op Owen, bad clear through. Listen to what Jones said about her and you won't regret Tuesday too much. Sometimes the young are inflexible, too."

"I agree, Commissioner," Daffyd said, escorting the man to the door as calmly as if he hadn't heard what Gillings was thinking so clearly. "And we appreciate your help in the cover yarns that explained Tuesday's odd occurrences."

"A case of mutual understanding," Gillings said, his eyes glinting. "Oh, no need to see me out. *I* can open this door."

That door was no sooner firmly shut behind him than Lester Welch turned on his superior.

"And just who was scratching whose back then?" he demanded. "Don't you dare come over innocent, either, Daffyd op Owen. Two days ago that man was your enemy, bristling with enough hate and distrust to antagonize me."

"Remember what you said about Gillings Tuesday?"

"There's been an awful lot of idle comment around here lately."

"Frank Gillings *is* telepathic." Then he added as Lester was choking on the news. "And he doesn't want to be. So he's suppressed it. Naturally he'd be antagonistic."

"Hah!"

"He's not too old, but he's not flexible enough to adapt to Talent, having denied it so long."

"I'll buy that. But what was that parting shot '*I* can open this door'?" Lester mimicked the Commissioner's deep voice.

"I'm too old to learn new tricks, too, Les. I teleported through the roof door of that parking facility. He saw me do it. And *she* saw the memory of it in my mind. If she'd lived, she'd've picked my mind clean. And I didn't want her to die."

Op Owen turned abruptly to the window, trying to let the tranquility of the scene restore his equilibrium. It did—until he saw Harold Orley plodding along the path with his guide. Instantly a white, wide-eyed, hair-streaked face was superimposed over the view.

The intercom beeped and he depressed the key for his sanity's sake.

"We've got a live one, boss," and Sally Iselin's gay voice restored him. "A strong pre-cog with kinetic possibilities. And guess what?" Sally's excitement made her voice breathless. "He said the cop on his beat told him to come in. He doesn't want any more trouble with the cops so he . . ."

"Would his name be Bill Jones?"

263

"However did you know?"

"And that's no pre-cog, Sally," op Owen said with a ghost of a laugh, aware he was beginning to look forward again. "A sure thing's no pre-cog, is it, Les?"

For those of you who have consistently asked for more Helva stories, here is "Honeymoon." Only it's an un-story. I call it that because it cannot stand without a lot of explanation which really makes the minor incident that is the meat of the story much too top-heavy. You really ought to have read at least "The Ship Who Sang," the story, if not the full novel, to understand what is left out.

I have often called Helva my alter ego. "The Ship Who Sang" is my favorite story; I still cannot reread it without weeping, for I wrote it in an unconscious attempt to ease my grief over the death of my father, the Colonel. The other yarns in the novel were therapy for other personal problems, none of which actually figure in the plots. So, although this tale should have been the starting point of a new volume about Niall Parollan and Helva, I don't really yet know if Helva will sing again. "Honeymoon" does tie up the one loose end which the majority of my readers have complained to me about.

Honeymoon

"MAY I COME ABOARD, HELVA?"

Helva said yes without thinking because the traffic in technicians and Base officials attending to her refitting was constant. Then, she checked identity because while the voice was familiar, no technician would have couched such a formal request.

Rocco, Regulus representative for Mutant Minorities, was her unexpected caller. With the easy manner of one used to the protocol of brain-brawn ships, the Double M man saluted her behind the central column and sauntered into the lounge, looking about him with interest at the choice artifacts Niall had introduced, the circuit prints and cables draped about the control console, the pattern of dust and grit leading toward her engineering and cargo compartments.

"I've stopped apologizing for the mess," Helva said, "but the galley's intact if you don't mind serving yourself while Niall's not here . . ."

"I'm here because he isn't, Helva," Rocco said, refusing her hospitality with a courteous gesture and seating himself facing her panel.

"In which capacity? Double M, or Rocco?"

"Unofficially, but Rocco is always willing." Then he hesitated, biting the corner of his lip while Helva waited, amused that the suave, fashionably attired troubleshooter for Double M was at a loss for words. He'd had no block a scant seven days ago when he'd been needling Chief Railly before she'd extended her Central Worlds contract. "Let's just say that I had an interesting conversation yesterday which leads me to

beg the indulgence of a chat—an unofficial chat—
with you."

"On what subject?"

"Coercion?"

"Whose?" Helva was amused.

"Yours, primarily. Parollan's . . . well, that young
man can take care of himself."

Helva chuckled. "Now, Mr. Rocco, you *were* in
Chief Railly's office that day."

Rocco impatiently brushed that side. "Yes, I heard
the official line. They got you to extend your original
contract with them . . . which was almost legal."

"Very legal, Rocco. I did some surreptitious checking myself. And I got them . . ."

Rocco held up his hand, peremptorily cutting her
off. "Did or did not Railly deploy a detachment around
you, effectively preventing you from lifting off if you'd
so desired? And did or did not Parollan have to short
out a perimeter fence to get to you?"

"There was a little misunderstanding . . ."

"Little?" Rocco's swarthy face darkened to empha-
size that single explosion. "My dear Helva, I have my
sources, too. Railly had the entire planetary security
force, civilian *and* service, looking for Parollan."

"I had Broley on my side." Helva chuckled for the
city shell person's cooperation had been involuntary.
Broley still wasn't speaking to her because she hadn't
opted for independent status and taken on one of the
clients he had lined up for her.

"So you did. Do you now?"

"Oh, he'll sulk a while longer, I expect."

Rocco hitched himself to the edge of the couch.
"Now, look, Helva, I know what it says on paper but
I also know that Parollan's resignation from the Service
is still in effect. Oh, he's brawning you to Beta Corvi,
but there isn't anything contractual after that."

"So?"

"Helva, I don't mean for you to be left high and
dry. Especially with an incredible extension of debt
which you must work off. And with Chief Railly overtly
your enemy because of Parollan. Now that guy may
have been a brawn-brain ship supervisor for the last
twelve years, and bloody good at it from what I hear,

but that doesn't mean he's going to be a good brawn. By anything left holy, Helva, it's a long way from telling to doing."

"Do you remember my last brawn, Teron of Acthion, that well-trained, physically stalwart twithead?"

Rocco gave a long sigh that ended with a grudging grin. "Okay, so he was a dud that BB School turned out by mistake. You can go too far in the opposite direction." Obviously Rocco felt she had with Parollan. "Seriously, Helva, that contract extension makes my skin crawl. You're committed to repaying almost 600,000 credits . . . by the latest figuring."

"You do have good sources, Rocco."

He grinned again, maliciously. "In Double M, I've got to. Look, there's a lot more to this whole affair than the fact that in a scant ten years you paid off your original indebtedness to Central Worlds for your early childhood care, the initial shell, education, the surgery needed to fit you into this ship, maintenance, and so forth."

"I paid off partly due to Niall Parollan, remember?"

"Granted, granted."

"And when this cycle-variant drive we're taking back to Beta Corvi gets approved, we'll be out of debt in next to no time."

"Not when, Helva. *If.* If wishes were horses, beggars would ride. I saw the reports on that cycle-variant drive, Helva. I heard what happened to the manned test ship."

Helva snorted with contempt. "Ham-handed fools."

Rocco would not be diverted. "I don't mean the fact that they inadvertently cycled the power source too high, Helva, I mean that curious discharge that is worrying the nuclear boys juiceless."

"Why do you think we're taking it back to Beta Corvi?"

"And thank the gods that *you* are." Rocco recrossed his neatly booted legs in a nervous fashion. "Whatever that particular force is, it's bloody dangerous. *And* no one seems to know why or how."

"They'll tell me." At least, she amended privately, she thought they would. If only because the use to which humans put their minor form of stabilized energy

268

amused them. (And what did you do on Beta Corvi for an encore, Helva?) She was far from happy about having to go back to Beta Corvi, but the ends justified the means . . . she hoped.

To have a warp drive in her bowels! To soar when she'd been forced to plod in a plebeian fashion. And the hell with Rocco's "if" . . . although the if was a valid consideration. Still, she trusted the Corviki: she'd *been* a Corviki.

"Look, Rocco, that drive is worth a great deal of hassling and stress. Niall knows it. I know it."

"Why?"

"The cycle-variant is faster than light drive, it's warp. By being able to stabilize an unstable isotope at just the moment it is releasing its tremendous quantity of energy, the cycle-variant drive captures all that energy because the isotope doesn't dwindle downscale to a useless half-life. It remains at the constant high-energy peak. That output is controlled in its cycle of peak energy, and the rate of thrust—the speed of the ship powered that way—is determined by the ratio of cycles used at any given time. True, you can't lift off-planet on c-v drive, and a ship has to be structurally reinforced."

"And that odd trail of particles?" Rocco asked sardonically. "Those unknown thingies that have thrown communications haywire, loused up astrogational equipment, not to mention the solar phenomena recorded in the systems through which that test ship ran?"

Helva was silent. She was less certain of how the Beta Corviki could cope with those emissions. Unless there'd been a simple perversion of the data?

"Then there's the old philosophical question: Is this trip *really* necessary? Is man ready for this sort of progress?"

"Rocco! I'd thought better of you." Helva was surprised as well as scornful. " 'If man were meant to fly, he'd've been given wings.' "

Rocco regarded Helva with great tolerance and some sadness. "Helva, in my job, I become painfully aware that some progress costs too much in terms of human

269

adjustment, or emotional, psychological, or even physiological stress."

"On the pro side, look at the exploration potential for a hundred different minorities."

Rocco sighed. "I suppose we're committed to progress at any cost. Onward and upward for bigger, better, faster, smaller, tougher. However, back to my original topic, your coercion."

"There isn't any, Rocco."

"Oh? Have you any idea, Helva, how many circuits lead into this?"

"I know of a few, but I think you're going to tell me."

"Setting aside your understandable yearning to be the fastest virgin in the Galaxy—and you'll need the speed with Parollan aboard . . ."

"Tsk, tsk, jealous?"

"Or Parollan's wish to prove himself a better brawn than the prototype, we have dear Chief Railly, all set for that jump onto Central Worlds Council."

"Is that why he's been on our backs like a leech?"

"You didn't know? Tsk! Tsk on you, Helva. Yesiree ma'am! Since the civilian branch has blown it with their manned ship, think of all the glory accruing to one Chief Railly for getting the drive approved, of getting *you,* the very valuable and very well known 834 to extend her contract, thanks to his masterful handling of the negotiations."

Helva made a rude noise. "Parollan masterminded it."

"Undoubtedly he did, but Railly gets the official credit. Not only does Railly have a finger in your pie to be gold-plated; Dobrinon has first whack at the biggest Xeno plum in psychological history; Breslaw is frankly starry-eyed with visions of commanding the warp-drive squadrons."

"Rocco? What's in it for you?"

"Me?" Rocco made his eyes innocently wide.

"I'd've thought you'd be flogging me, too, to rescue the four I left behind me. —Oh, so that's it. Yes, they would be classed as mutant minorities."

"That's the kindest designation." Rocco cleared his throat.

270

"Yes, there was a lot of unfavorable publicity about them. I'd've thought the news value long since exhausted."

"It wasn't so much publicity, Helva," said Rocco, again biting the corner of his lip thoughtfully. One booted toe swung up and down. "No, society just doesn't like its members opting out of its grasp, particularly into a total alien form."

"Not to mention leaving their bodies behind." Helva had always wondered what had happened to the empty husks of Kurla Ster, Solar Prane, Chaddress of Turo, and . . . Ansra Colmer. But not so much that she could bring herself to ask. When she and the rest of the dramatic troupe had presented *Romeo and Juliet* to the Beta Corvi—in exchange for the stabilization of isotopes—they had had to use "envelopes" suitable to the methane-ammonia atmosphere of the planet. A timer had been rigged in the transfer helmets to insure that that consciousness returned to its proper environment. After the final performance, four people had not returned and were encapsuled in the Beta Corvi envelope. For very good and understandable reasons, or so Xenologist Dobrinon would like her to believe.

"There has been considerable pressure, you know," Rocco was saying, "on both SPRIM and Double M to investigate their defection/emigration/temptation . . ." He shrugged at the euphemisms employed. "Or at least to bring back conclusive evidence that they are happy in their new lives."

"I know two who are—three. Solar Prane has a new body; Kurla couldn't care less about hers so long as it was near his; Chaddress had nothing to look forward to in retirement, and Ansra Colmer . . ."

Rocco eyed Helva keenly, expectantly. "And Ansra Colmer . . ."

"Oh, the Corviki knew how to handle her."

"Hmmm."

"But aren't you slightly in conflict with yourself, Rocco? I mean, *you* class shell people as mutant minorities, though strictly speaking I'm a cyborg—"

"Yes, Helva," Rocco sounded purposefully pathetic, "the boot does pinch." His foot in fact was swinging, which was an unconscious gesture that would intrigue

271

the good Dobrinon. "I cannot reconcile coercing you to find out if the . . . flitting four were in any way coerced."

"I quite appreciate your dilemma, so I'll lift you off one horn. I do not, not even after all your interesting disclosures, consider myself coerced. Ah ah," for Rocco began to protest. "Pressured? Possibly, but I've been conditioned to a fine sense of responsibility, you see. I brought the equations for that nardy drive back to Regulus, and I inadvertently misplaced four passengers who were, you must admit, essentially my responsibility to convey thither and hither safely. I'd like some peace of mind on both counts."

"I'll forego knowing about our lost souls if you'll forego that drive."

"No way. I want that drive. How else can we pay off my indebtedness?"

"I'll call foul for you?"

"Rocco, I'm surprised. Shocked! This cannot be the incorruptible . . ."

"Damn it, Helva, I want you out of that contract and out away from Parollan. He's dangerous!" Rocco was on his feet and pacing.

"Good heavens! Why?"

"He's got a fixation on you, a brawn fixation."

"Who told you that? Broley? Oh, fardles, Rocco! Because he had the Asurans extrapolate a solido of me from my genetic background?"

"You knew?"

"He had a set made of every BB ship he supervised."

Rocco pointed a finger at her. "You're different."

"Quite likely. He's *my* brawn. Bluntly, Rocco, you're making a tempest in a teacup."

"A fixation could be dangerous to you in space, Helva, in a man of Parollan's sexual appetite."

"That fixation reached critical . . . and passed. That's why Niall became my brawn. He's far more aware of the inherent dangers of a brawn fixation than you are, Rocco. Or Broley."

Rocco affected a shrug, but Helva suspected he was unconvinced.

"All right, Helva, we're back to Square One and I'll

rephrase my initial question: Do you want what you now have, or were you *made* to want it?"

"Hey, Helva," Niall said into the com-unit, "let the lift down."

"Think on it, Helva, and remember that you can count on my support if you feel that you have actually been constrained against your own best interests."

Niall's hearty "Helva, I got 'em," as he waved the grapelike cluster of circuit guards, dwindled off in surprise at seeing their guest. "Well, we're honored, Rocco?"

"My congratulations on your appointment, Parollan. I'll be following the exploits of the NH-834 with renewed interest."

"I'll just bet you will." Niall's smile took the sting out of his slightly aggressive words.

"Fair enough," replied the Double M official, his own expression sardonic. He moved toward the airlock. "You are, you realize, very definitely in a minority."

"How so?" asked Niall, amused, as he neatly arranged the circuit guards on the gutted console and turned to face Rocco.

"My good Parollan, you are the only man who ever resigned from BB ship service to become a brawn."

"I'm no mutant."

Helva could hear the edge in Niall's voice, although generally his small stature didn't bother him.

"What is the definition of a mutant?" That was Rocco's exit line as the lift took him down, looking entirely too pleased with himself.

"Well, hump me, what was he after?" Niall asked.

"I gather he's been listening to Broley's gossip."

"And what is the gospel according to City Manager Shell Person Broley?"

"We're being coerced."

Niall scratched his ear, screwed up his face, and gazed out of the open airlock. Helva was situated by the immense Engineering sheds of the Regulus Base Complex. Niall had a clear view of the distant administration buildings at the opposite end of the plain. There were, as always, tremendous comings and goings of small ground vehicles and light helis. as well as slim BB ships.

Niall looked away from the airlock, toward her. Fleetingly Helva wondered if Niall Parollan "saw" the titanium column behind which her encapsulating shell rested, or the solido the Asurans had made, extrapolating a mature human body from her genetic background.

"You should have asked Rocco what's the definition of 'coercion,' " he said.

Helva gave a snort. "Well, *you've* never been restrained, either morally or physically."

"Balls," Niall replied in disgust. "And I don't need Rocco on my tail, too."

"Speaking of tails," Helva said gently because she caught the pulse of the comset about to light up, "here's our daily Railly now."

"Fardles! He's two minutes late. Railly," said Niall before the Chief could speak, "I'm up to my crotch in circuit guards that I should have had two days ago. Go way now and I'll call you back when I've finished."

"Parollan, there's isn't a Guild on this Base that isn't . . . Come out from under that console while I'm addressing you!"

Helva realized that all Railly could see of Parollan was his rear end.

"As you're constantly addressing me, and I know what you look like, my position provides no impediment to hearing every word you say. Besides which, I'm busy."

"Parollan, I'm warning you . . ."

"Which you do hourly. But I thought you wanted this expensive ship to lift ass and cease to offend your eyes, so what are you complaining about now?"

"You are not, I repeat, you are not to walk into any other section of this Base and badger, bully, or beat any other section leader or supervisor into giving *your* request top priority!"

"And if I don't comply, what'll you do? Throw me off Base?" Niall suddenly reversed his position and glared up at the comscreen. "Good, then Helva does not have to complete this mission if I am not her brawn." He made as if to quit his task.

274

"Parollan! You get on with the job! But I'm warning you . . ."

"Let's see, that's the fourth warning today, isn't it, Helva?"

"I don't keep track, Niall," she said gently, hoping her tone would warn him to be a shade more diplomatic. They'd be completely at Railly's mercy if the c-v drive weren't approved by the Corviki.

Fortunately Railly broke the connection. Chuckling, Niall ducked back under the panel.

"You know, Niall, if . . ."

"Helva!" His tone was slightly exasperated but reassuring. "The Raillys of this world can take a lot more backtalk than you think. Particularly, my girl, with all he stands to gain with you . . ."

Helva would rather he'd said "us."

"Even without that drive vetted, you're twice the ship. And with me to keep you from going soft with the likes of Railly, we'll make out one way or the other."

Helva was grateful for the plural pronoun. Now why had Rocco come to disturb her with his questions? While it was flattering to think she had so many friends, willing to do battle for her, she'd prefer to rely on her brawn.

Just then Supply arrived with an order of emergency rations to be stowed away.

"Why the fardles get in 'fortified coffee'? Yecht!" Niall was disgusted when the invoice was screened in.

"*If* we try that drive and can't manage it, or the particular emissions disqualify that application . . ."

"Think positively, my dear, and besides you're not ham-handed, gal, like those cloddies on the manned test ship."

"You might need concentrated supplies . . ."

"That coffee bubka is for—"

"It's better than no coffee. And half the supply hold *is* coffee. I wish I could figure out why everyone wants that stuff."

"Which reminds me," said Niall, crawling out from under the console and heading for the galley.

"Ah yes, you haven't had a cup in the last fifteen minutes."

"Longer. I had to extrude these things myself, you know. And we're having a party tonight."

"We've had a party every night."

Niall shot an overly innocent glance at her. "All work and no play . . ."

"What'll you do when we're aspace?" The question slipped out of her, probably due to Rocco's crack about enforced celibacy and Niall Parollan.

"The modern man is *not* dominated by his gonads, love. Think of the memories I'll have to sustain me." He cracked the seal on the coffee container as neat emphasis.

The lift buzzer rang. "If that isn't Breslaw, I'll have him arrested on board."

It was indeed the engineering officer, panting from the run across the huge engineering field. Helva was certain that Commander Breslaw had never, since he reached that rank, worked as hard as he was in overseeing each detail of her refitting, his computer cassette overheating from his constant demands. He was losing weight, too, Helva noticed with a critical eye. Do him good; make him look better in uniforms if he won his gamble on Helva's future.

"Do you two appreciate me?" asked Breslaw, leaning against the lock bulkhead to catch his breath. "Anyway, the ceramic coating is scheduled for tomorrow at 0900."

"About bloody time."

"Parollan . . ." And there was a slight edge to Breslaw's mock animosity. "One of these days I'm going to— "

"Get that final stripe for doing some work for a change," Niall finished. "You've only been promising that ceramic coating for the past three days. Fardles, how do you guys run this Base at all?"

"Look, Parollan, I want to run a final check on those tolerances in the drive room."

"Bloody right. I don't want something coming adrift at the speeds we'll be traveling."

"You hope," Breslaw amended gloomily.

Niall ignored him but the Commander's pessimism did not reassure Helva, not after Rocco's disturbing visit.

"Helva," her brawn said, "when those electricians appear—"

"I'll assemble them."

"Make 'em do it right the first time."

No sooner had he and Breslaw disappeared down the hatch to the drive room than the four tech ratings arrived, tremendously relieved that Parollan was not in evidence.

"He's a bugger to work for," muttered one of the men as he surveyed the console.

"Then use the luck," said another, "and let's get cracking before he does come back or we'll have to do the job over to prove we did it properly."

"Then do it right the first time," said Helva.

"Fardles," exclaimed the first man, looking nervously around him. "I forgot she was here."

"Where else did you think Helva would be?" asked the oldest of the quarter. "Sorry, ma'am. Now these green circuits have to be laid in first. Get with it, Sewel."

Helva turned on microvision, focusing it on Sewel's hands. Once she was certain he knew what he was about, she scanned the others. That panel had to be wired with the utmost precision or a cross-circuit could short out the entire panel at a crucial time. Further, the work was done with a minimum of waste motion. Niall Parollan may have been a bugger to work for, but work for him, and her, was well and expeditiously completed.

When they'd finished, she broached some of the party spirits for them in appreciation.

"Sun's over the yardarm for you, too, Commander," said Niall, returning with a dusty but pleased Breslaw. "Well worth it," he said after he'd inspected the console wiring. "I appreciate it, men," he said, toasting them: "my partner appreciates it," and he raised the glass to Helva's column: "Commander Breslaw appreciates it, and the Service will undoubtedly not bother to appreciate this unusual and prompt performance of your duties."

Sewel and the others were not certain that they should appreciate his toast, but the spicy Vegan liquor was far too palatable to resist.

After a third round from the bottle, Breslaw suddenly remembered that he was the supervisor of the Engineering Section of Regulus Base and that there were other matters for his attention as urgent as refitting the NH-834.

"But not as rewarding," Niall said, and restrained Breslaw.

When Sewel tried to leave, he and his men were all told to stay until the party had begun.

"Hell, your work day's over. We can't do anything more to Helva until tomorrow when she gets her unbreakable, unheatable, unwarpable, fusion-resistant coat, so let's have some fun."

The tech ratings were far too flattered to think of going and Helva was certain that the next time Niall Parollan needed an urgent electrical systems job done, these same men would leap at the chance to work on it.

The lift signal went just then as the duly invited members of the party began to arrive.

As usual during one of Niall's parties, the lounges, the cabins, the galley, the passageways soon filled with people prepared to enjoy and give enjoyment. Several brawns arrived, two of whom Helva knew were awaiting assignment and very envious of Niall's luck, but the majority of visitors were not service personnel. Therefore Helva was not only pleased but flattered that every new arrival first directed attention to the hostess, coming to her panel and either introducing themselves if this were their first appearance, or renewing their acquaintance with a chat. They tended to treat her as if she were visible and as mobile as themselves. She would have expected such courtesy from service-trained people, but in her travels Helva had regrettably discovered that the average person found it hard to cope with the concept, much less the reality, of a shell person. She'd used that to her advantage, but it was a welcome change to be considered a real person. How much of this was Niall's pre-party instruction or the good manners of intelligent, well-traveled men and women, she didn't know. But she enjoyed it.

278

A youngish art dealer, Permut Capiam from Ophiuchus Minor, gave her one explanation.

"Actually, I met Niall when he commissioned those Asuran solidos he used to get done for his BB ships. He used to complain that he had to spend a fortune keeping solidos of your partners because you changed so often. Seen yours?" Permut frowned. "No, I don't suppose that'd be good or rather . . ." he giggled, "a bit too good for your old ego." He waggled a finger at her exact position behind the panel. "Can't blame old Parollan for having a fix on *you*, Helva. You 'strapolated out the best of the lot. Must say, though, that it makes it easier to think of your solido than all this tinplating."

So, Niall's emotional attachment to her was public knowledge? Was this a good sign or a bad one?

Permut rattled on knowledgeably about Asuran extrapolations as he'd handled quite a few commissions. "Prehistory Roman and Greek statues are the rage right now. The Asurans merely need a fragment to do the whole sculpture, you know. They do it up in whatever material the client wishes—anything inanimate. There's a law now against low-life constructs." He became very serious. "That way lay madness . . . ugh! Zombie things. I was ever so relieved when the whole business was interdicted by CWC. The sort of low-life restoration is very dangerous." He stressed the syllables of the last two words.

"Have you tri-ds of the work you've handled?" Helva asked, curiously.

"You mean of the realities?" Permut was startled.

"No, tri-ds of, say, your latest showing. I don't fit in most galleries . . ."

"Oh my word, my gallery'd fit in you."

"And lately I've been so busy I've not had time to revise my library."

"My dear Helva, what an appalling omission. What's wrong with Parollan? It's the least he could do for you. Man doesn't live by bread alone, nor exist on a diet of pure physical sensation. Really. Say, I know just the person to give you. —Abu, honey girl, don't you have some spares of those marvelous tapes you did of the Ceta tour? You do like ET dance forms, don't you,

Helva? I mean, you've done your stint on the boards, so to speak. Abu has some perfectly magnificent free-fall performers."

Abu was an incredibly lithe albino who had capitalized on her genetic inheritance. She did wear remedial contacts for light sensitivity and, Helva noticed on fine vision, the girl also utilized a skin film so artfully applied that only magnification detected it.

Abu spoke with the lilt of one whose first language was pitched. The gently musical voice and her extreme grace fascinated Helva. Abu was equally entranced by Helva and the three of them chatted about new dance and art forms.

Suddenly Niall exploded back into the main lounge, carrying two long flaming skewers with bits of meat and vegetables. Behind him danced triplet girls, a dance team from Betelgeuse now the rage of Regulus City, dangerously brandishing their lighted skewers.

"Ancient earth recipe," Niall announced. "Shish kebabs. Have 'em while they're hot. There're plenty more where these came from. Don't burn your tongue."

Helva had wondered where he'd gone.

"Three of them?" Permut said with a rueful laugh. "No wonder he declared the galley out of bounds."

Helva caught the implication that more than culinary arts had been practiced there.

"With *three* of them?" asked Abu, taking the same interpretation. The gleam of regret in her eyes was not completely masked by her protective lenses.

"You know Parollan, my dear."

"Not as well as I'd like."

Then Niall was proffering them the still smoking meats.

"Oooh, this is good," Abu said, nibbling delicately and then rolling her eyes with appreciation. "This can't be mutton?"

"Regulan mutton!" Niall replied.

"It can't be," protested Permut, licking his fingers and grabbing more.

"All in the marinade, all in the marinade."

"Is that a new position?" Permut asked archly.

Niall laughed tolerantly and moved on to serve

280

other guests, but the ambiguous ribaldry disturbed Helva.

"Do you have olfactory senses, Helva?" Abu asked. "It seems rude to be so . . . so . . . rapacious in front of you."

"I don't smell as you do but I am able to sense fairly minute alterations in the composition of the air within and about me that would indicate odor."

"That's not quite what Abu meant," Permut said.

"I know but it's all I got."

"And you can't taste either?"

"No."

Abu's sensitive face registered dismay at this lack. "I thought you shell people could do everything we could."

"Not . . . everything," Permut said, and then some unuttered thought convulsed him with laughter.

Abu regarded him blankly for a moment and then with growing impatience and disgust.

"Everything comes back to sex with you, Permut."

"Not . . . not everything," he managed to say between gasps of laughter.

"Actually, Abu, the programming of the olfactory sensors does give me an indication of a human's reception of smells. If there's sulfur in the air, I'd know it, I assure you, as something distinctly unpleasant. As for taste, I can't miss what I haven't had," Helva said, hoping that Permut would stop being so prurient. He'd been good company up till now. "I would like to *know* how coffee tastes. Everyone seems to fancy it so above all other beverages."

Abu laughed. "I think it smells better than it tastes. Especially if you've got roasted beans and grind them fresh," her tone of voice dripped with gustatory pleasure.

"You know, I'd forgot that coffee is brewed from beans. I've only the container-type aboard."

"The best beans come from Ipomena in the Alphecan sector. I've a small supply given me by an admirer that I keep for special occasions."

"You do?" Permut asked, abruptly recovering his composure. "You do?" he repeated, sidling up to Abu and making such absurd expressions that she began to

281

laugh. "I tell you what, Abu, purely to aid in Helva's education, I will partake of your Ipomenan brew and give her a critical opinion of the quality, aroma, flavor, savor . . ."

"Oh, you!"

Suddenly Niall's voice rang out in happy surprise. "Davo Fillaneser? But of course, twice welcome. Come on up, Davo. Helva!"

Niall's clarion greeting had effectively silenced the babble and all eyes were on the newcomer appearing from the air lock. Davo smiled and so played up his entrance, bowing with such elaborate flourishes of nonexistent cape and hat, that everyone applauded.

"Fillaneser played Beta Corvi with Helva. Only he came back," Niall said by way of introduction, and the actor was quickly surrounded. Davo cast a humorously despairing glance toward Helva, mouthing "I want to talk to you later," as he was borne away.

It wasn't until after Niall mendaciously declared that Railly'd imposed a one o'clock curfew on his parties and started shoving people out the hatch as quick as the lift could make the trip, that Davo had a chance to approach Helva.

"Any chance of speaking to you, Helva?"

"You mean, privily?"

Davo nodded with a mirthless smile for her Shakespearean language.

"That is, if Niall can clear the deck . . ."

"Preferably of himself as well. Or is that too much to ask?"

Circumstances, in the persons of the triplets who helped to clean up the party debris, abetted Davo's wish. Niall found himself, or so he said, obliged to be sure the girls had transport into the City.

"It is past pumpkin time for Cinderellas," she said, and Niall commended her to Davo's company, and disappeared with his giggling trio.

"Does he mean to take on all three of them, Helva?" Davo asked.

"I'm under the impression that they've got something cooked up," she replied, and then chuckled over her phrasing. How would Dobrinon interpret that Freudian

282

slip? Davo guffawed, so Helva decided he'd been told about the shish kebab episode.

The actor's laughter faded though, and he took to pacing around the lounge. Helva waited. The next line was all his.

"I'd heard you'd paid off, Helva."

"Great heavens to Betsy, does everyone in the Galaxy know that?"

"You don't know how many friends you have, Helva, who make it their business to keep track of you."

"I'd heard you'd volunteered to go back to Beta Corvi for Dobrinon," she said, starting her own offensive.

Davo winced. "That's when they were sending that manned test ship with the c-v drive."

Helva laughed. "Just as well you didn't go, Davo, you'd be coming back for the next nine years."

"That wasn't why I didn't go, Helva. I copped out at the last moment. Did Dobrinon tell you that?" Davo looked directly at her now, and she could see the excited glitter in his eyes, the tenseness of his jaw muscles. "I turned coward. I *couldn't* go through that again. As much as I wanted to find out how Kurla and Prane . . . and Chaddress were. Helva . . ." Davo's voice shook with barely contained emotion, "is it true? That you're being forced to go back?" The question tumbled out of his mouth and his tone was distraught. "How can they let you put yourself in jeopardy like that again? I mean, Helva, you have many important friends, powerful ones. All you have to do is let us know . . ."

Helva was so flabbergasted at Davo's concern, at his suggestion that she almost laughed.

"Davo, my very good friend, I am in no jeopardy."

"Now, look, Helva," Davo assumed a man-to-man stance, "I don't care how many circuits are being tapped, who I have to buy or suborn, *you*—"

"Davo, where are you getting this notion from? Broley?"

"Broley?" Davo's surprise suggested that the City Shell Manager was not his informant.

"No, I don't guess you'd have any contact with the City Manager."

"I have spoken with him. He goes to all the plays," Davo admitted, "but not this trip."

"Well, then, where did you get this wild notion that I'm in any danger?"

"It's all over," and Davo made an expansive gesture. "You can't *want* to go back to Beta Corvi?" His convulsive shudder was not feigned; nor was the glint of terror in his eyes.

"Truthfully, no. But it's the only way I'll find out."

"Find out what, for the love of reason?"

"Oh, if the c-v drive works or will blow the cosmos to bits with the particular emissions, if our friends . . . exist. Take it easy, Davo," she added gently as she saw the man working himself up to another explosion. "Let's say I'm willing to take a gamble . . . with my eyes wide open to the probabilities. Which do, after all, favor me. The stakes are high, and when you get right down to the welded seam, there's more than that c-v drive to be vetted and lost souls accounted for. Tell me, in all this wild talk, what's the gen on Niall Parollan?"

Davo looked uncomfortable for a split second, and then only hesitant. He took a sharp deep breath and regarded her frowningly.

"I tell you, Helva, Parollan had a lot to do with our debriefing when we got back here after Beta Corvi. I liked what I saw of the man then. He had real sympathy for all of us—and he was very worried about the effects of the mission on you. Get right down to it, most of his questions during his interview with me had to do with you."

Helva fondly remembered Niall's abrasively diverting and restorative presence the night she'd come back . . . an empathy utterly shattered days later when he made known his opinion of her choice of Teron of Acthion as brawn: a well-substantiated opinion.

"What I hear about Regulus City now . . ." Davo summarized that in a long low whistle.

"Tell me, what's the betting on our length of partnership? On the success of our mission? On Railly's mak-

284

ing CW Council? And Breslaw hitting Chief?" With each of her questions, Davo's eyes opened wider.

"Damn it, Helva, the whole tone about you and Parollan, not to mention those others, is so . . . so disgustingly commercial, so sordid, that I had to see you. What I heard doesn't jibe with the Helva I know."

"Or the Parollan you've met."

"Right!"

"Do you agree that people under stress react more honestly than people in a party or gossip situation?"

"Certainly."

"So. Don't think I'm not highly flattered and touched by your concern, Davo. I am. But I think we, Niall and I, the NH-834, are a winning combination."

"I certainly hope so, Helva. I certainly hope so."

Amusement bubbled up in Helva. "I wish you'd read that line with more convincing sincerity, Davo."

"I wish I felt it myself. I don't favor this part for you, Helva. And I'm not alone. Remember, gal, all you gotta do is shout."

"Shout in an ammonia-methane atmosphere?"

"Don't tell me *you* want to play a return engagement there, Fillaneser?" Niall asked from the lock.

"No entrance cues, Helva?" asked Davo, annoyed.

"This team can't operate on two levels, Davo, not and succeed."

The actor nodded. He extended his hand to Niall.

"I'll wish goodspeed and a safe trip home, Helva, Parollan."

That line did have the ring of sincerity.

"You weren't long about it," Helva said, relieved by Niall's return for several reasons she didn't care to probe.

Niall was peering out at the night, at Davo's descent, so Helva left the lock open until he gave a snort and turned back to the lounge, frowning as he surveyed it.

"No, when I got to the gate, the Yerries had been refueling so I let them take the girls on in. Besides," he stretched and yawned mightily, "I need my beauty sleep." He bent down to scoop up a container tucked against the end of a couch, lobbed it toward the disposal chute, dusting his hands as his shot hit dead center.

"And tomorrow, we skin you, m'love. And then . . ." He rubbed his hands with anticipation as he moved toward his quarters.

"Up, up, and away?"

"Yup!"

He stripped and washed with his usual neat despatch and then lay on his bunk, hands clasped behind his head.

"That was a real good bash," he murmured, eyes closed, a happy smile on his face. "Good night."

"Good night, sweet prince, and may . . ."

Niall's eyes flew open and he made a mock-exasperated noise in his throat. "Will you never rid me of your Shakespeare saws? When I think of a perfectly good, well-behaved ship consorting with ribald, rowdy actors . . . I cringe." But he yawned again and was asleep before his jaw closed.

Helva chuckled as she secured the lock, lowered all but her safety lights, and began her habitual nightly check. Suddenly it was too silent; too empty of Niall and his energy. He was sort of like having one's own private hurricane and he probably expended as much energy as the nardy c-v drive could.

Would that thing work? And what accounted for Breslaw's pessimism? Had he rechecked some factor to a lower probability? Or was it the particle emission that troubled everyone? Even if the c-v drive were feasible, the emissions could make it highly impractical in settled space, which would rule out its use as far as Helva was concerned. Unless of course they detached her to Search and Survey. But would that kind of long-distance lonely travel suit Niall Parollan?

Why had she been plagued with both Rocco and Davo today? And why had Abu asked about her two missing senses? She'd had them in the Beta Corvi envelope. Not that "coffee" would be anything tastable by a Corvikan. Did they have its equivalent, Helva wondered?

Had Niall really overcome that brawn fixation? More corrosive to her peace of mind, if ruthlessly suppressed, was her own disquieting wish to see that Asuran solido. Shell people were conditioned not to think about physical appearance. They were told that their bodies were physically stunted to fit in the shells. They knew that they were necessarily immersed in nutrient fluids, that there were masses of wires connecting the various sections of their brains to the sensors that allowed them to operate their particular vehicle or mechanisms. It was tacitly understood that a shell person was a grotesque in a civilization that could ensure physical perfection and pleasing looks.

Only now had it become important to Helva to know that, but for the birth defect that had destined her to be a shell person, she would have been beautiful. She wanted to be, she could have been, but she wasn't. And it was possible that Niall, deprived of all feminine companionship on long trips, might succumb to the temptation to open her shell. Illegally he had obtained the release words, a sequence and pitch unique and supposedly known only to one person, which would open the panel and give access to her titanium shell beyond. As Rocco had said, a brawn fixation was dangerous.

The unbidden thought of Niall sporting with the three nubile girls in the galley exacerbated her mind. Had he suggested to Permut and Abu that they keep her occupied while he was ...?

You ... are a jealous bitch! Helva told herself in measured tones of surprise and self-repugnance. A shell person jealous of a mobile? For a sexual reason? Ridiculous and yet, she'd all the symptoms of sheer flaming jealousy.

She'd loved Jennan, but there'd been no trace of that utterly human vice in their relationship.

Well, Helva thought sternly, you didn't have to worry about sharing Jennan with half the female population of the Galaxy. And you didn't love him this way: you loved Jennan with a purity equal to Juliet's, with not a care as to things-as-they-are. You'd've changed your tune if Jennan had lived.

Or would I?

Jennan, at least, had been discreet. Unlike the stud she'd aboard her now.

Had Niall passed the danger point of his fixation? Or, when his libido reached the unendurable in space, would the temptation to open her panel return?

287

How much did Niall count on the Corvikis approving the drive? How long would he stay her brawn if they didn't?

It was scant consolation to realize that the cycle-variant drive wasn't the only one undergoing a test run.

By the time the immense crane had swung her back on her tail fins, Helva was evaluating her new suit of superfine superskin.

"You gleam, baby, you glisten, you shine in the sun like a jewel," Niall said into his combutton. In the company of Breslaw and Railly and several of the ceramicists, he was standing at a distance from her on the apron of the kiln building. "By god, you're blue in some lights. Is that stuff iridescent, Breslaw?"

Helva increased the magnification of her scanner on the group. Breslaw was beaming fatuously, for the process was a new application of old techniques and the coating had been accomplished with relatively no halts or snags. Certainly the finished product was impressive.

"How d'you feel, Helva," Niall asked.

"How's one supposed to feel after a face-lifting?"

"Bruised. Stop being so eternally female, woman. Are all your systems go? We don't need a clogged pore where we're going."

Helva'd been doing a rapid check of her exterior installations. Everything was in operating order, but she felt differently. Not uncomfortable, merely altered.

"So," Railly was saying to Niall in a steely, teeth-clenched voice, "now how soon can you lift?"

"Why, Chief, we'd've been away two days ago if I could've got any decent cooperation from servicing personnel." Blithely unaware of Railly's pop-eyed reaction, Niall turned to the startled ceramicists. "Do we need to wait until her skin cools?"

The senior technician stammered out something about temperature variations and tolerances, and then shrugged assent.

"Great. Good-bye all. See you sometime yesterday!"

With an insolent salute, Niall strode across the permatarm toward Helva. She let down the lift for a quick getaway, keeping one eye on Railly, who was apoplectic at the calculated insolence. Breslaw began speaking to his superior, though Helva couldn't tell if he were pacifying Railly or diverting him with other matters. The ceramicists had certainly departed quickly.

No sooner was Niall within than he brusquely signaled her to secure for lift-off. She started to get clearance from the Control Tower before she remembered a minor detail.

"We've no supervisor."

"Oh yes, we have. Railly!" The name came out as a growled curse. Niall bounced into the pilot's seat, strapped down. "Let's get off this fardling base. Now!"

She began lift-off, sluggish because of the extra weight in drive chamber, strut, and skin.

"It's heavy going, Niall," she warned him and then piled on thrust.

Once clear of Regulus's service satellites, Niall spun himself away from the console.

"One more moment down there listening to Railly and I'd've done my nut!" He heaved himself out of the pilot chair and floated across the lounge, his expression bleak and weary.

As she felt rather elated to be finally away, she was momentarily dumbfounded by the transformation in her private whirlwind. She was even more surprised when he bypassed the galley and hand-pulled himself into his cabin.

"Wake me, girl, if anything startling occurs."

He kicked off his boots, stripped off the shipsuit, rolled under the cover, pulling the free-fall strap across him, and was asleep before his arm dropped slowly back.

And so he slept and slept and slept. Which was no consolation to Helva.

She occupied herself at first by space-testing all her functions, did a bit of jockeying on thrusters to get the feel of how the modifications in her hull affected her maneuverability. She felt like a scow, and wondered if the now inert mass of the c-v drive would lighten once it was operative.

Asleep, Niall Parollan did not resemble his waking self: there was a curious vulnerability about his mouth, the sweep of rather long eyelashes on wide cheekbones. He looked altogether too young to be his chronological age and rather defenseless. He did not twitch, toss, or snore, moving less than usual in what she understood were normal sleep patterns. Economical that. She watched him for quite a long time, as if memorizing the very pores of his rather coarse skin, the way his hair pattern took an abrupt turn at the back of his head.

She firmly closed off that scanner and searched about her for sleeptime occupation. She dialed for Abu's dance tapes and viewed the first five minutes of one before it occurred to her that the dance forms were highly erotic and far too suggestive for her present state of mind. She flipped over to Permut's latest showing and, although she tried to be completely objective, discovered phallic symbols of one flagrant sort or another were the themes of all the art forms he was currently exhibiting. Exhibition indeed!

Rather appalled at the prominence of sexual motifs, she sought refuge in the good Solar Prane's nighttime occupation, but she had scarcely got into *Julius Caesar,* a play that ought to have been safe, when the tone of jealousy began to make itself obvious. *King Lear* was not much better, nor *Coriolanus.* She switched to comedy and got a good way into *The Comedy of Errors* before the stupidity of the lovers became too ironic. *The Tempest* was no good: she felt akin to poor Caliban and that did her morale no good.

She decided that the only safe subject was the specs of the c-v̄ drive, and tried to imagine that she were a Corviki examining the data and how it/she/they/he would react. The exercise was not felicitous because she began to think the c-v drive *wouldn't* work: it was an appallingly wasteful use of energy because the thrust had to be directed away from the goal to protect frail human bodies. Her conclusion depressed her so she turned back to Abu's tapes. There must be some dances that did not depict love-erotic or love-denied or . . .

Yes, the fifth tape was of a formal insect dance from the Lyrae IV system: color, motion, almost mesmerizing, very soothing certainly to Helva's distressed sensibilities. Gratefully, she gave herself up to the play of form and color. Halfway through the tape and much calmer, she wondered idly if it were *Niall's* sex drive she'd have to worry about.

Sixteen hours later Niall Parollan awoke, stretched, catapulted out of the bunk in one movement, and sang merrily away in the shower.

"What's our running time to Beta Corvi?" he asked as he was dressing. "And let's put on a bit of grav, love."

"Fourteen standard days, twelve hours, and nine minutes. How much grav, three-quarters?" She began to apply gravity as he settled himself in the galley.

"That's it exactly," he said, holding up his hand, and making a cut-off gesture. He bounced a little as he made for the coffee cupboard. With a warming container in one hand, he prepared a staggering protein meal.

"What? No shish kebabs?"

"That junk's for show." He took a long swig of the now hot coffee. "Ah, that's the stuff. Gotta keep up the image." He snorted as if repudiating that same image. "I think what recommends you most to me, dear girl, is that I don't have to *be* anyone but Niall Parollan within your stately walls." He stretched again until his shoulder bones cracked. "God, I'm still tired, riding those ship monkeys to get us out of there. Say, how's your nutrient balance?"

"Just great."

"What'd you do to amuse yourself last night?"

"Actually, I settled on some tapes Abu sent on board . . . formal insect dances from Lyrae."

Niall stared at her. "Great jumping puddles of fardle! Couldn't you find anything more exciting?"

"Quite likely," and Helva giggled without explanation. "But you know, the dances were very soothing."

"Do you always do something like that?" The notion evidently distressed Niall, as if she'd suddenly sprouted facial hair.

"Oh no. If I'm near enough, I can chat up another ship."

He chuckled. "Yeah, you BB ships are divvils for knowing gossip before groundstaff."

They talked amiably about other inconsequentialities while he consumed his enormous meal. He stretched out on the couch, then patted the bulge of stomach.

"Do you eat like that often?"

"Fardles, no. I'd be fat. That'll last me a long while." He yawned. "Did you get any new music on board? Abu was talking about some new reels . . ."

He was asleep within half an hour. At first concerned, Helva came to the decision that one of the reasons Niall Parollan seemed indefatigable around people was because he could conserve energy at other times. He woke up refreshed several hours later, ate lightly, did isometrics "to get rid of some breakfast," and then settled down to browsing through the technical journals he'd had her collect from Regulus Central Information. They discussed the article on polymer extrusions from alien silicates, he studied the c-v drive specs yet another time, relaxed over a coffee while the two worked a crossword puzzle in Deltan symbology, and then he bade her a fond goodnight and went to bed again.

That set the pattern for their trip as far as activity was concerned, exactly in accord with what could be expected from any trained brawn. Two evenings from Beta Corvi, it dawned on Helva that she had allowed herself to be influenced too much by people who did not know Niall Parollan at all . . . who knew of him and about his reputation. She, Helva the 834, knew another side of the man "himself," without image or affectation, and that personality was very likable, too likable. She sighed as she watched, for the twelfth time, the Lyraen dances and let herself be soothed. She could carry her true love through the stars and never touch him. But she could be more to Parollan than any other female in the entire galaxy, and woe unto her who tried to part them now!

Beta Corvi pulsed a vivid orange-red on the viewscreen as Helva picked up the first Corviki space buoy on her scanners. Instantly it colored, a microsun in the carpet of blackness.

She roused Niall, who was sleeping in eagle-spread abandon. Simultaneously the psyche-transfer circuit in

292

her mind was activated and she felt the query of the alien mind.

In the time it took Niall to rise from his bunk, the Corviki had established the identity of their visitors, the reason for their return, the alterations in her hull and the inactive core of the new drive, and issued her orbital instructions.

"Hey," Niall protested as a surge of power, uninitiated by Helva, sent him lurching into the door frame.

"Sorry, pal, they just took over."

"Took over?" Niall padded into the main cabin, rubbing his right arm. "I thought you'd wake me when we reached their first buoy."

"I did." She turned on the rear screen, focused on the fast-receding marker. "The Corviki don't waste time, which they consider another form of energy."

"Hmmm. An interesting concept."

"We're approaching orbit," she told him.

He blinked in astonishment. "One thing sure: those modifications of yours can sure take speed."

"A point."

"Hey, will they give me time to eat? A cup of coffee, at least?" He gestured at his nakedness. "The head? Clothes?"

"We should have a few moments to spare," Helva said with a laugh. His expression was small-boy-embarrassed.

"Ever the courteous hosts."

He had managed to get himself assembled by the time the glowing luminosity that was Beta Corvi's third planet filled the viewscreen. Somewhere down in that moiling envelope of methane, ammonia, and hydrogen were the Corviki. Or were Solar Prane and Kurla Ster, Chaddress or a vengeful Ansra Colmer rising in those spectacular flares to greet the visitors? If anything remained of those personalities. Helva preferred to share Dobrinon's optimistic view that those immigrants retained something of their former personalities.

Helva felt the change in the ship before it registered on the console before Niall.

"We're in orbit? We can transfer?"

The eagerness in his voice produced a perverse reluctance in Helva. Niall couldn't know, despite all she and Davo and the others had told him, how devastating that experience could be, how insidious. Now a new fear threatened her: what could that experience do to the fragile bond they'd been contriving?

"Yes, we can transfer," she said, trying to keep the growing apprehension out of her voice. And she'd thought, Dobrinon had assured her, that she'd made a good adjustment to this return. She'd fooled only herself.

Niall swung the chair round, helmet half-raised to his head.

"Is it still that bad, Helva? I can go alone if it's that hard."

"This we have to do together."

"That's the operative phrase, m'girl, together."

"Let's go—together."

"That's my Helva." The helmet masked his eyes but not the eager confident smile.

Helva fought/released herself to the experience, knowing an instant of fleeting terror at being outside her safe shell. But as the transfer occurred, she reminded herself that she had survived a worse terror of complete sense deprivation on Borealis, survived it only because of the Corviki episode.

And Niall was with her this time!

The pressure enveloped her in a deceptive comfort. She shuddered and the streamers floated up from beneath her.

"Niall!" she exuded, anxious lest in that instant she might have transferred at a distance from him.

"I'm a bloody sea monster." Niall's reassuring dominance was just beyond the large frond. "There you are!" And he emerged, a creature like herself, already coloring the shell with his own personal intensity.

A creature like herself!

"Helva! You're . . ." And they spun toward each other.

"Do not express energy in such a sequence!" A new dominance, dark, dense, powerful, overwhelmed them with its authority. "You have imperfect control of your shells."

By a force more potent than their pent-up frustrations, they were held apart. The energies which they yearned intensely to combine were dampened by the dominance.

Deliberately, Helva now sought to bury her all-too-human reactions into the Corviki ethos. "Conserve energy. Reduce spin. Lock suborbital speeds."

Niall's shell pulsed and shook with his effort to control his emotions in an alien context and because of the totally unfamiliar, for him, subjection to a supra-authority.

"The emanations are unusually rich," the Corviki emitted, withdrawing some of the repressive authority. "No similar wastage has been observed despite the variety now available for analysis." There was approval in the comment, but also a reinforcement of the initial warning.

With dark and awful despair, Helva forced her attention to the dominance, anything to distract herself from Niall's proximity. In doing so, she recognized a familiar aura in the dominance.

"Manager?"

"Of the same thermal core. There have been recombinations within the mutual group," and the entity turned such a lavender-purple of Corvikian pleasure that Helva interpreted "smugness" in his tone.

Taking cowardly refuge in the mission, Helva immediately explained the purpose of their unsolicited return. As she got to the point, she recognized approval in the Manager's density.

"From such an extrapolation of the data for use in the parameters of your race's limitations, undesirable factors might indeed result from exposing irreconcilables to stability forms," the Manager commented, rippling with muddy blues. "The multiple interaction shows commendable concern for the proper conservation of mass energies. The hypothesis is being examined. Improper equations cause ineffectual results and perverse conclusions. Matter must be expended only in constructive quantities."

Simultaneously a host of other dominances was felt, compounding the authority about her and Niall. The newcomers were, to Helva's mind, dense with experiential energies, held in lease by immense controls.

Helva had not encountered similar energy groupings in the first Beta Corvi mission, and began to emit tiny distressful losses which she was unable to contain.

"Why are you so afraid, Helva?" Niall asked. She came close to resenting his self-control.

"These entities are so gross with power," she said. "But fear is not a component in my energy loss. On Corvi, we have nothing to fear . . ."

"But ourselves," Niall finished for her, his trailing tendrils floating gently beneath him.

She kept hers tightly entwined lest they stray without her volition . . . and touch him.

"Do not waste energy so," she was advised by one of the new power group. But the directive held no censure and Helva let the suborbitals begin to spin gently so that her tendrils drifted easily, if inevitably toward Niall's. The Corviki would protect her from herself.

She was distracted by a series of condensations and dissipations, expansions and contractions, darting, it sometimes seemed, through both her shell and Niall's, as their interrogators fused momentarily or attenuated in the discussion of the problem presented by the visitors. Apparently such a use of stabilized isotopes had never occurred to the Corviki. Helva thought that amusement dominated their discreet emissions. Dense as these ancient entities were, they had never considered the possibility of such a direction for familiar energies.

One entity reasoned that, of all the handicaps through which life forms must evolve, the adolescent vigor of this particular species was, at least, divertingly resourceful.

Helva and Niall drifted in this limbo, amused by an occasional storm of colorful discussion.

Suddenly the aura changed. With paternal forbearance, the Corviki approved the c-v drive. However, there were modifications which would reduce the *cuy* particles imprudently released by such a clumsy process. An inhibiting feedback was required. Otherwise, although the envelope was unbelievably awkward and totally unnecessary, dictated as it was by the exigencies of protecting frail protein matter, they could deduce no annihilative perversion of the applied data.

They did stipulate that any further application must be accompanied by a similar inhibitor. They would know, by virtue of *cuy* particles in the galaxy, if that restriction had been ignored. Punitive action would instantly result.

As abruptly as the dominances had assembled, they dispersed, leaving Helva, Niall, and the Manager in a welter of loose fronds and burping ochre eruptions. Distant novae of emissions drifted back like the light laughter of the godly, seen and felt, rather than heard.

"Has the drive really been approved?" asked Niall, bewilderment apparent in the action of his tendrils.

"The emissions were favorable," Helva and the Manager agreed in chorus.

"Who are you now? Helva?" he demanded, swinging from one to the other, confusion making his tendrils rigid.

"I am Helva, here," she said, fighting with the desire to remain Helva for his sake and the need to remain Corvikan enough to control precarious excitations.

"Let's find out about the others and leave."

"I have," Helva said.

"Did you not feel that thermal group near you?" asked the Manager of Niall, shading to ochre neutrality.

"He had not previously encountered their dominances, Manager."

The Manager assumed more color and then, bleeding a little blue, he disappeared.

"You did have a chance to speak to Prane and—"

"I encountered them in one of the thermal groups. I'll tell you later when we're back on the ship."

"Then the mission's completed?" The triumph in Niall's tone colored his shell a brilliant orange-red and he pressed toward her eagerly.

From behind a frond, first one, then another Corvikan appeared, but Helva was diverted from their arrival by Niall's rapidly changing color.

"We cannot combine!" she cried, and tried to keep her distance from him.

One of the Corviki brushed against her, pushing her back toward Niall.

"Don't play the professional virgin with me now, Helva!" His furiously human response was emphasized by the fiery glow of his shell as every particle became excited. The Corviki who had pushed her was now throwing power toward Niall, exciting him further. It flashed through Helva's awareness on two levels that the Corviki was familiar to her. She'd no time to identify it; she had to avoid Niall.

"You don't understand! Don't, Niall! We've got to get back to the ship!"

"Helva!"

"It's not safe for us. The energy levels are too hot . . . Integrity will be violated and—"

The outer edge of his shell touched hers. Sane thought, Corvikan or human, was impossible. Explosively they began to excite one another, each level in her seeking its equal in him, slowing, speeding, delicately adjusting, seeking the merger that would be the imposition of one pattern over the other, all levels matched, all energies mutual, all . . .

Other thermal groups were attracted by the emissions, attracted and held, transferring power so that Helva felt her Corvikan envelope engorge to incredible dimensions, giving her unlimited mass to energize at an even higher excitation level. Faster the particular forces spun, faster, to match speeds, to combine, neutronic shifts of dazzling force . . .

Fission . . . an incredible stoking of the available energy . . . the atmosphere splitting with thunder as immeasurable positive forces began to recombine . . .

Distance was where she was, some black, sense-deprived consciousness, some tiny flicker of ego, lost, lost, lost. Unwilling to resume. A slow return to awareness. Exhaustion, death-deep in an overstressed mind. A shuddering violent release to fall with an endless spinning grace into unawareness, comforting and kind.

Offensive odor, acrid, strong, staining the lungs, reviving the senses that must escape that burden.

To be aware and wish for deprivation! How strange!

Reality came into focus. And, sadly, identity.

Niall's body was sprawled by the console, the helmet upturned on the deck, his grasping hand a scant inch from it. His shipsuit was dark and damp with stain. Though he seemed motionless, she never questioned that he lived. She knew that, knew it as deeply as she knew her own vitality, low as it was.

It was comforting to look at him: the fatigue-lined face unguarded and boy-young, the dark hair tousled, the wiry body limp. Soon he would rouse and then that dear form would change, would vary and not be wholly hers.

No . . . Helva hesitated. No, an intangible difference impinged on her growing awareness. She was not wholly herself. There was a subtle alteration.

Curious, she began to explore her ship self. The critical difference was not in her systems or hull. She had full command of every area.

The steady vibration of power in her idling drive, however, resonated at a new frequency.

A long groan was wrenched from her, reverberating in the cabin and down the quiet corridors, humming through the deck plates to rouse Niall.

The c-v drive was functioning. Beta Corvi! Helva's mind reeled, fighting to deny/accept the experience that surged back over her in a tsunami of emotions, abrading stunned sensibilities.

Niall crawled on his hands and knees, staggered to his feet, swaying as he took the two steps to the pilot's chair.

But they were here. They had been . . .

She hadn't the energy to transfer back. She hadn't the strength to tell Niall, who wouldn't have been strong enough to pick up the dislodged helmet anyway.

Instinct marshaled a response. She must break this disaster orbit, flee from Beta Corvi. Strange the Corvikans were silent. Humans must interdict that system to prevent the unwary from ever encountering those devastating sentients. Some progress was too costly in terms of human emotions. Who'd suggested that? She'd remember later. Right now, instinct and conditioning prevailed. She had to escape. She began to compute a flight pattern, and stopped. The ship was not in orbit around an invidious planet. They were drifting in space, far from the light of Beta Corvi.

Startled, Helva examined and identified star magnitudes, was relieved to find familiar ones about her, comfortable light-years from Beta Corvi. Safe!

She'd already escaped. How? She couldn't remember. She scanned the recording banks and realized that three days, Galactic standard, had elapsed since they had initiated that fantastic transfer to Corviki III. And, judging by the distance they'd come, she must have used the c-v drive. What had the Corvikans said about an inhibitor? Had they left a trail of *cuy* particles? Punitive action?

Niall was stirring, groggily seeking his face with hands that trembled. He leaned forward, elbows jabbing with awkward force into his knees as he held an aching head. His wiry body shook with an uncontrollable paroxysm and an oily sweat exuded from his pores.

"Drink something, Niall. It's partly lack of food," she heard herself say in a voice she scarcely recognized. "It's three days since we made that transfer."

As he lurched to his feet and stumbled to the galley, she checked her nutrients and adjusted the acid balance hastily. Niall clutched at the counter for support and fumbled for a restorative spray, gave himself a massive dose. He pulled open the first container he could reach, gulping its contents before they'd heated. He knocked down several more cans in an attempt to close his fingers around one. He finally opened a container of soup, drank it, and the shaking subsided. Still holding the restorative spray, he half staggered to his cabin, into the shower. He fumbled to turn the water on, alternating hot and cold sprays, unconcerned that he was still dressed. The treatment and liquid began to revive him and he stripped, carefully washing away the accumulated filth of three lost days.

Freshly dressed, he returned to the galley and found coffee. As the container was warming, he carried it into the lounge, dropping to the couch that faced Helva.

"Did you check yourself?" he asked anxiously.

"Yes. Acid!"

"Not surprising. What was that about an inhibitor?

300

How did we get away from Beta Corvi? No, don't explain how. I know. Fardles! Did we leave a trail of those *cuy* particles?"

"I'm not certain I'd know a cuy particle if I met it," Helva replied drily. "But they've done something to the shielding about the drive. To the alloy itself. It's denser and light. And I feel light, if that makes sense."

"Nothing they do makes sense or no sense." Niall gave a rueful snort.

"We did use that drive. D'you realize how far we went in three days?"

"Not far enough." Niall spaced the words out. "And let us not speed home, c-v drive operative or not. I'm in no shape to face debriefing. In fact, I'm going to avoid it if at all possible." But his grin was Niall-normal as he raised the hot coffee in a toast.

"That is good!" Helva said with mild surprise at the taste.

Niall blinked. "What did you say?" He leaned forward. "You tasted that?"

Inexplicably, she had savored the coffee taste in his mouth.

"Yes, that coffee tastes good," she said again after a very long thoughtful silence.

"Well!" Niall scratched his nose. "How d'you like them apples?"

"You haven't tasted me apples yet."

Niall took a deep breath that he exhaled in a long chuckle, all the while regarding the tendril of steam writhing up from the coffee container.

"Helva, we didn't complete the recombination?"

"I think," Helva spoke slowly, trying her thought out loud, "that the time limit flipped us back right at the critical moment." She felt reluctant to examine her reaction to that interference. She *knew* with that part of her which *was* Niall, just as he *knew* with his fractions of her how perilously close they'd come.

"I wonder—would we have withdrawn at all from Beta Corvi had the fusion been complete?" Niall laughed softly, his eyes brimming with amusement. "Hey gal, into which one of us would we both go? Hell, you're pint-sized and so am I, but who'd've been us? Or would we have been stuck in the shell? Say,

301

what was going on down there with that character who kept pushing you? And pulling me? Oh, that was them? Fardles, did we damned near get stuck with that Colmer bitch?" His dismay dissolved in a weak laugh of relief, and then he sat, a long time, while the coffee cooled, just staring contentedly at her panel. She knew that he, too, was mentally probing to estimate the extent of their meshing.

"I suspect it will take all our lifetimes to figure it out."

"Quite likely."

The prospect daunted neither.

"Hell, we can't wander off like this," Niall said after a long, long period of mutual introspection. He shoved himself out of the couch, lobbed the old coffee into the disposal chute, and went for another.

"So they altered the shielding?" he asked, leaning against the counter. "Is there a separate inhibitor? Or is that the alternation in the shielding? And did you grasp what the crot are *cuy* particles? Breslaw is going to want to know something more specific than that they're dangerous."

"He suspects that . . ."

"And inconvenient if the Corviki catch us making/ exhaling them?"

"I think their warning should be deterrent enough. There is a black core within the drive-isotope that didn't previously exist. There is more of that same black stuff in a specially shielded container in the supply bay. It's radiating a purple shade."

"Hey, Helva, did you actually sort out the personalities of Kurla, Prane, and Chaddress. What'n'ell do we tell Dobrinon?"

"As little as possible. No, they were there. At least I was aware of a Kurla-Prane core, but only because it was a strong combination."

She saw Niall wince with a regret that she shared.

"We don't, do we, tell him about that in us?"

"Never! I shouldn't like to have to explain something that is so personally subjective."

"Like tasting coffee?"

"Among other things. Dobrinon would take us apart

to find out which facets of you got into me in the re-assembly."

"Gal, we are together!" He enunciated each syllable with a jab of his finger. "But no one, not any one, gets any chance to dissect our feelings. Right?"

"Right!"

Then his face dissolved into a smile, part malice, part pure self-delight, part utter triumph.

"Yeah, gal, have we got a thing going together!" He shook his head and slapped his thigh. "Hell, yes! By anything that's been left holy, Helva, there's nothing *we* can't do now. C'mon, gal, pour on that power. Cycle that crotty drive to get us back to Regulus yesterday. Scatter us *cuy* particles where we may. We're going to buy the body corporate forever free of dear Railly."

If stars had ears, they'd have heard the vast hale-lujahs ringing from the partnered ship.

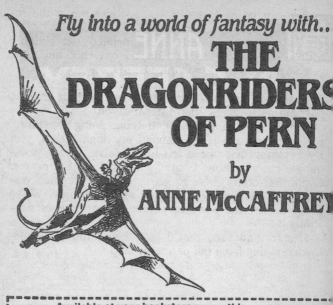

Fly into a world of fantasy with..

THE DRAGONRIDERS OF PERN

by

ANNE McCAFFREY